J. J. Connington and The Murder Room

》》》 This title is part of The Murder Room, our series dedicated to making available out-of-print or hard-to-find titles by classic crime writers.

Crime fiction has always held up a mirror to society. The Victorians were fascinated by sensational murder and the emerging science of detection; now we are obsessed with the forensic detail of violent death. And no other genre has so captivated and enthralled readers.

Vast troves of classic crime writing have for a long time been unavailable to all but the most dedicated frequenters of second-hand bookshops. The advent of digital publishing means that we are now able to bring you the backlists of a huge range of titles by classic and contemporary crime writers, some of which have been out of print for decades.

From the genteel amateur private eyes of the Golden Age and the femmes fatales of pulp fiction, to the morally ambiguous hard-boiled detectives of mid twentieth-century America and their descendants who walk our twenty-first century streets, The Murder Room has it all. **》》》**

The Murder Room
Where Criminal Minds Meet

themurderroom.com

T0352419

J. J. Connington (1880–1947)

Alfred Walter Stewart, who wrote under the pen name J. J. Connington, was born in Glasgow, the youngest of three sons of Reverend Dr Stewart. He graduated from Glasgow University and pursued an academic career as a chemistry professor, working for the Admiralty during the First World War. Known for his ingenious and carefully worked-out puzzles and in-depth character development, he was admired by a host of his better-known contemporaries, including Dorothy L. Sayers and John Dickson Carr, who both paid tribute to his influence on their work. He married Jessie Lily Courts in 1916 and they had one daughter.

By J. J. Connington

Sir Clinton Driffield Mysteries
Murder in the Maze (1927)
Tragedy at Ravensthorpe
 (1927)
The Case with Nine Solutions
 (1928)
Mystery at Lynden Sands
 (1928)
Nemesis at Raynham Parva
 (1929)
 (a.k.a. *Grim Vengenace*)
The Boathouse Riddle (1931)
The Sweepstake Murders
 (1931)
The Castleford Conundrum
 (1932)
The Ha-Ha Case (1934)
 (a.k.a. *The Brandon Case*)
In Whose Dim Shadow (1935)
 (a.k.a. *The Tau Cross Mystery*)
A Minor Operation (1937)

Murder Will Speak (1938)
Truth Comes Limping (1938)
The Twenty-One Clues (1941)
No Past is Dead (1942)
Jack-in-the-Box (1944)
Common Sense Is All You
 Need (1947)

Supt Ross Mysteries
The Eye in the Museum (1929)
The Two Tickets Puzzle (1930)

Novels
Death at Swaythling Court
 (1926)
The Dangerfield Talisman
 (1926)
Tom Tiddler's Island (1933)
 (a.k.a. *Gold Brick Island*)
The Counsellor (1939)
The Four Defences (1940)

In Whose Dim Shadow

J. J. Connington

An Orion book

Copyright © The Professor A. W. Stewart Deceased Trust 1935, 2014

The right of J. J. Connington to be identified as the author of this work has been asserted in accordance with the Copyright, Designs and Patents Act 1988.

This edition published by
The Orion Publishing Group Ltd
Orion House
5 Upper St Martin's Lane
London WC2H 9EA

An Hachette UK company
A CIP catalogue record for this book is available from the British Library

ISBN 978 1 4719 0611 4

www.orionbooks.co.uk

CONTENTS

Introduction (*Curtis Evans*)   ix

1 · The Murder in the Grove   3

2 · Constable Danbury's First Case   10

3 · The Golden T   28

4 · The People Upstairs   41

5 · The Logic of the Facts   58

6 · Mrs. Sternhall's Story   70

7 · Inspector Chesilton Reports   88

8 · The Owner of the Cross   98

9 · The Tennis Shoes   116

10 · The Reporter's View   130

11 · The Power of Attorney   141

12 · Part of the Pattern   151

13 · The Reward Bill   165

14 · The Curtain-Raiser   180

15 · "Suicide is Confession"   192

16 · Documentary Evidence   210

17 · Prelude to Arrest   221

18 · Arrest   242

Introduction
by
Curtis Evans

During the Golden Age of the detective novel, in the 1920s and 1930s, J. J. Connington stood with fellow crime writers R. Austin Freeman, Cecil John Charles Street and Freeman Wills Crofts as the foremost practitioner in British mystery fiction of the science of pure detection. I use the word 'science' advisedly, for the man behind J. J. Connington, Alfred Walter Stewart, was an esteemed Scottish-born scientist. A 'small, unassuming, moustached polymath', Stewart was 'a strikingly effective lecturer with an excellent sense of humor, fertile imagination and fantastically retentive memory', qualities that also served him well in his fiction. He held the Chair of Chemistry at Queens University, Belfast for twenty-five years, from 1919 until his retirement in 1944.

During roughly this period, the busy Professor Stewart found time to author a remarkable apocalyptic science fiction tale, *Nordenholt's Million* (1923), a mainstream novel, *Almighty Gold* (1924), a collection of essays, *Alias J. J. Connington* (1947), and, between 1926 and 1947, twenty-four mysteries (all but one tales of detection), many of them sterling examples of the Golden Age puzzle-oriented detective novel at its considerable best. 'For those who ask first of all in a detective story for exact and mathematical accuracy in the construction of the plot', avowed a contemporary *London Daily Mail* reviewer, 'there is no author to equal the distinguished scientist who writes under the name of J. J. Connington.'[1]

Alfred Stewart's background as a man of science is reflected in his fiction, not only in the impressive puzzle plot mechanics he devised for his mysteries but in his choices of themes and depictions of characters. Along with Stanley Nordenholt of *Nordenholt's Million*, a novel about a plutocrat's pitiless efforts to preserve a ruthlessly remolded remnant of human life after a global environmental calamity, Stewart's most notable character is Chief Constable Sir Clinton Driffield, the detective in seventeen of the twenty-four Connington crime novels. Driffield is one of crime fiction's most highhanded investigators, occasionally taking on the functions of judge and jury as well as chief of police.

Absent from Stewart's fiction is the hail-fellow-well-met quality found in John Street's works or the religious ethos suffusing those of Freeman Wills Crofts, not to mention the effervescent novel-of-manners style of the British Golden Age Crime Queens Dorothy L. Sayers, Margery Allingham and Ngaio Marsh. Instead we see an often disdainful cynicism about the human animal and a marked admiration for detached supermen with superior intellects. For this reason, reading a Connington novel can be a challenging experience for modern readers inculcated in gentler social beliefs. Yet Alfred Stewart produced a classic apocalyptic science fiction tale in *Nordenholt's Million* (justly dubbed 'exciting and terrifying reading' by the *Spectator*) as well as superb detective novels boasting well-wrought puzzles, bracing characterization and an occasional leavening of dry humor. Not long after Stewart's death in 1947, the Connington novels fell entirely out of print. The recent embrace of Stewart's fiction by Orion's Murder Room imprint is a welcome event indeed, correcting as it does over sixty years of underserved neglect of an accomplished genre writer.

Born in Glasgow on 5 September 1880, Alfred Stewart had significant exposure to religion in his earlier life. His father was William Stewart, longtime Professor of Divinity and Biblical Criticism at Glasgow University, and he married Lily Coats, a daughter of the Reverend Jervis Coats and member of one of

Scotland's preeminent Baptist families. Religious sensibility is entirely absent from the Connington corpus, however. A confirmed secularist, Stewart once referred to one of his wife's brothers, the Reverend William Holms Coats (1881–1954), principal of the Scottish Baptist College, as his 'mental and spiritual antithesis', bemusedly adding: 'It's quite an education to see what one would look like if one were turned into one's mirror-image.'

Stewart's J. J. Connington pseudonym was derived from a nineteenth-century Oxford Professor of Latin and translator of Horace, indicating that Stewart's literary interests lay not in pietistic writing but rather in the pre-Christian classics ('I prefer the *Odyssey* to *Paradise Lost*,' the author once avowed). Possessing an inquisitive and expansive mind, Stewart was in fact an uncommonly well-read individual, freely ranging over a variety of literary genres. His deep immersion in French literature and supernatural horror fiction, for example, is documented in his lively correspondence with the noted horologist Rupert Thomas Gould.[2]

It thus is not surprising that in the 1920s the intellectually restless Stewart, having achieved a distinguished middle age as a highly regarded man of science, decided to apply his creative energy to a new endeavor, the writing of fiction. After several years he settled, like other gifted men and women of his generation, on the wildly popular mystery genre. Stewart was modest about his accomplishments in this particular field of light fiction, telling Rupert Gould later in life that 'I write these things [what Stewart called tec yarns] because they amuse me in parts when I am putting them together and because they are the only writings of mine that the public will look at. Also, in a minor degree, because I like to think some people get pleasure out of them.' No doubt Stewart's single most impressive literary accomplishment is *Nordenholt's Million*, yet in their time the two dozen J. J. Connington mysteries did indeed give readers in Great Britain, the United States and other countries much diversionary reading pleasure. Today these works constitute an estimable addition to British crime fiction.

After his 'prentice pastiche mystery, *Death at Swaythling Court* (1926), a rural English country-house tale set in the highly traditional village of Fernhurst Parva, Stewart published another, superior country-house affair, *The Dangerfield Talisman* (1926), a novel about the baffling theft of a precious family heirloom, an ancient, jewel-encrusted armlet. This clever, murderless tale, which likely is the one that the author told Rupert Gould he wrote in under six weeks, was praised in *The Bookman* as 'continuously exciting and interesting' and in the *New York Times Book Review* as 'ingeniously fitted together and, what is more, written with a deal of real literary charm'. Despite its virtues, however, *The Dangerfield Talisman* is not fully characteristic of mature Connington detective fiction. The author needed a memorable series sleuth, more representative of his own forceful personality.

It was the next year, 1927, that saw J. J. Connington make his break to the front of the murdermongerer's pack with a third country-house mystery, *Murder in the Maze*, wherein debuted as the author's great series detective the assertive and acerbic Sir Clinton Driffield, along with Sir Clinton's neighbor and 'Watson', the more genial (if much less astute) Squire Wendover. In this much-praised novel, Stewart's detective duo confronts some truly diabolical doings, including slayings by means of curare-tipped darts in the double-centered hedge maze at a country estate, Whistlefield. No less a fan of the genre than T. S. Eliot praised *Murder in the Maze* for its construction ('we are provided early in the story with all the clues which guide the detective') and its liveliness ('The very idea of murder in a box-hedge labyrinth does the author great credit, and he makes full use of its possibilities'). The delighted Eliot concluded that

Murder in the Maze was 'a really first-rate detective story'. For his part, the critic H. C. Harwood declared in *The Outlook* that with the publication of *Murder in the Maze* Connington demanded and deserved 'comparison with the masters'. 'Buy, borrow, or – anyhow – get hold of it', he amusingly advised. Two decades later, in his 1946 critical essay 'The Grandest Game in the World', the great locked-room detective novelist John Dickson Carr echoed Eliot's assessment of the novel's virtuoso setting, writing: 'These 1920s [. . .] thronged with sheer brains. What would be one of the best possible settings for violent death? J. J. Connington found the answer, with *Murder in the Maze*.' Certainly in retrospect *Murder in the Maze* stands as one of the finest English country-house mysteries of the 1920s, cleverly yet fairly clued, imaginatively detailed and often grimly suspenseful. As the great American true-crime writer Edmund Lester Pearson noted in his review of *Murder in the Maze* in *The Outlook*, this Connington novel had everything that one could desire in a detective story: 'A shrubbery maze, a hot day, and somebody potting at you with an air gun loaded with darts covered with a deadly South-American arrow-poison – *there* is a situation to wheedle two dollars out of anybody's pocket.'[3]

Staying with what had worked so well for him to date, Stewart the same year produced yet another country-house mystery, *Tragedy at Ravensthorpe*, an ingenious tale of murders and thefts at the ancestral home of the Chacewaters, old family friends of Sir Clinton Driffield. There is much clever matter in *Ravensthorpe*. Especially fascinating is the author's inspired integration of faerie folklore into his plot. Stewart, who had a lifelong – though skeptical – interest in paranormal phenomena, probably was inspired in this instance by the recent hubbub over the Cottingly Faeries photographs that in the early 1920s had famously duped, among other individuals, Arthur Conan Doyle.[4] As with *Murder in the Maze*, critics raved about this new Connington mystery. In the *Spectator*, for example, a reviewer hailed *Tragedy at Ravensthorpe* in the strongest terms, declaring of the novel: 'This is more than a good detective tale. Alike in plot, characterization, and literary style, it is a work of art.'

In 1928 there appeared two additional Sir Clinton Driffield detective novels, *Mystery at Lynden Sands* and *The Case with Nine Solutions*. Once again there was great praise for the latest Conningtons. H. C. Harwood, the critic who had so much admired *Murder in the Maze*, opined of *Mystery at Lynden Sands* that it 'may just fail of being the detective story of the century', while in the United States author and book reviewer Frederic F. Van de Water expressed nearly as high an opinion of *The Case with Nine Solutions*. 'This book is a thoroughbred of a distinguished lineage that runs back to "The Gold Bug" of [Edgar Allan] Poe,' he avowed. 'It represents the highest type of detective fiction.' In both of these Connington novels, Stewart moved away from his customary country-house milieu, setting *Lynden Sands* at a fashionable beach resort and *Nine Solutions* at a scientific research institute. *Nine Solutions* is of particular interest today, I think, for its relatively frank sexual subject matter and its modern urban setting among science professionals, which rather resembles the locales found in P. D. James' classic detective novels *A Mind to Murder* (1963) and *Shroud for a Nightingale* (1971).

By the end of the 1920s, J. J. Connington's critical reputation had achieved enviable heights indeed. At this time Stewart became one of the charter members of the Detection Club, an assemblage of the finest writers of British detective fiction that included, among other distinguished individuals, Agatha Christie, Dorothy L. Sayers and G. K. Chesterton. Certainly Victor Gollancz, the British publisher of the J. J. Connington mysteries, did not stint praise for the author, informing readers that 'J. J. Connington is now established as, in the opinion of many, the greatest living master of the story of pure detection. He is one of those who, discarding all the superfluities, has made of deductive fiction a genuine minor art, with its own laws and its own conventions.'

Such warm praise for J. J. Connington makes it all the more surprising that at this juncture the esteemed author tinkered with his successful formula by dispensing with his original series detective. In the fifth Clinton Driffield detective novel, *Nemesis at Raynham Parva* (1929), Alfred Walter Stewart, rather like Arthur Conan Doyle before him, seemed with a dramatic dénouement to have devised his popular series detective's permanent exit from the fictional stage (read it and see for yourself). The next two Connington detective novels, *The Eye in the Museum* (1929) and *The Two Tickets Puzzle* (1930), have a different series detective, Superintendent Ross, a rather dull dog of a policeman. While both these mysteries are competently done – the railway material in *The Two Tickets Puzzle* is particularly effective and should have appeal today – the presence of Sir Clinton Driffield (no superfluity he!) is missed.

Probably Stewart detected that the public minded the absence of the brilliant and biting Sir Clinton, for the Chief Constable – accompanied, naturally, by his friend Squire Wendover – triumphantly returned in 1931 in *The Boathouse Riddle*, another well-constructed criminous country-house affair. Later in the year came *The Sweepstake Murders*, which boasts the perennially popular tontine multiple-murder plot, in this case a rapid succession of puzzling suspicious deaths afflicting the members of a sweepstake syndicate that has just won nearly £250,000.[5] Adding piquancy to this plot is the fact that Wendover is one of the imperiled syndicate members. Altogether the novel is, as the late Jacques Barzun and his colleague Wendell Hertig Taylor put it in *A Catalogue of Crime* (1971, 1989), their magisterial survey of detective fiction, 'one of Connington's best conceptions'.

Stewart's productivity as a fiction writer slowed in the 1930s, so that, barring the year 1938, at most only one new Connington appeared annually. However, in 1932 Stewart produced one of the best Connington mysteries, *The Castleford Conundrum*. A classic country-house detective novel, Castleford introduces to readers Stewart's most delightfully unpleasant set of greedy relations and one of his most deserving murderees, Winifred Castleford. Stewart also fashions a wonderfully rich puzzle plot, full of meaty material clues for the reader's delectation. *Castleford* presented critics with no conundrum over its quality. 'In *The Castleford Conundrum* Mr Connington goes to work like an accomplished chess player. The moves in the games his detectives are called on to play are a delight to watch,' raved the reviewer for the *Sunday Times*, adding that 'the clues would have rejoiced Mr. Holmes' heart.' For its part, the *Spectator* concurred in the *Sunday Times*' assessment of the novel's masterfully constructed plot: 'Few detective stories show such sound reasoning as that by which the Chief Constable brings the crime home to the culprit.' Additionally, E. C. Bentley, much admired himself as the author of the landmark detective novel *Trent's Last Case*, took time to praise Connington's purely literary virtues, noting: 'Mr Connington has never written better, or drawn characters more full of life.'

With *Tom Tiddler's Island* in 1933 Stewart produced a different sort of Connington, a criminal-gang mystery in the rather more breathless style of such hugely popular English thriller writers as Sapper, Sax Rohmer, John Buchan and Edgar Wallace (in violation of the strict detective fiction rules of Ronald Knox, there is even a secret passage in the novel). Detailing the startling discoveries made by a newlywed couple honeymooning on a remote Scottish island, *Tom Tiddler's Island* is an atmospheric and entertaining tale, though it is not as mentally stimulating for armchair sleuths as Stewart's true detective novels. The title, incidentally, refers to an ancient British children's game, 'Tom Tiddler's Ground', in which one child tries to hold a height against other children.

After his fictional Scottish excursion into thrillerdom, Stewart returned the next year to his English country-house roots with *The Ha-Ha Case* (1934), his last masterwork in this classic mystery setting (for elucidation of non-British readers, a ha-ha is a sunken wall, placed so as to delineate property boundaries while not obstructing views). Although *The Ha-Ha Case* is not set in Scotland, Stewart drew inspiration for the novel from a notorious Scottish true crime, the 1893 Ardlamont murder case. From the facts of the Ardlamont affair Stewart drew several of the key characters in *The Ha-Ha Case*, as well as the circumstances of the novel's murder (a shooting 'accident' while hunting), though he added complications that take the tale in a new direction.[6]

In newspaper reviews both Dorothy L. Sayers and 'Francis Iles' (crime novelist Anthony Berkeley Cox) highly praised this latest mystery by 'The Clever Mr Connington', as he was now dubbed on book jackets by his new English publisher, Hodder & Stoughton. Sayers particularly noted the effective characterisation in *The Ha-Ha Case*: 'There is no need to say that Mr Connington has given us a sound and interesting plot, very carefully and ingeniously worked out. In addition, there are the three portraits of the three brothers, cleverly and rather subtly characterised, of the [governess], and of Inspector Hinton, whose admirable qualities are counteracted by that besetting sin of the man who has made his own way: a jealousy of delegating responsibility.' The reviewer for the *Times Literary Supplement* detected signs that the sardonic Sir Clinton Driffield had begun mellowing with age: 'Those who have never really liked Sir Clinton's perhaps excessively soldierly manner will be surprised to find that he makes his discovery not only by the pure light of intelligence, but partly as a reward for amiability and tact, qualities in which the Inspector [Hinton] was strikingly deficient.' This is true enough, although the classic Sir Clinton emerges a number of times in the novel, as in his subtly sarcastic recurrent backhanded praise of Inspector Hinton: 'He writes a first class report.'

Clinton Driffield returned the next year in the detective novel *In Whose Dim Shadow* (1935), a tale set in a recently erected English suburb, the denizens of which seem to have committed an impressive number of indiscretions, including sexual ones. The intriguing title of the British edition of the novel is drawn from a poem by the British historian Thomas Babington Macaulay: 'Those trees in whose dim shadow/The ghastly priest doth reign/The priest who slew the slayer/And shall himself be slain.' Stewart's puzzle plot in *In Whose Dim Shadow* is well clued and compelling, the kicker of a closing paragraph is a classic of its kind and, additionally, the author paints some excellent character portraits. I fully concur with the *Sunday Times*' assessment of the tale: 'Quiet domestic murder, full of the neatest detective points [. . .] These are not the detective's stock figures, but fully realised human beings.'[7]

Uncharacteristically for Stewart, nearly twenty months elapsed between the publication of *In Whose Dim Shadow* and his next book, *A Minor Operation* (1937). The reason for the author's delay in production was the onset in 1935–36 of the afflictions of cataracts and heart disease (Stewart ultimately succumbed to heart disease in 1947). Despite these grave health complications, Stewart in late 1936 was able to complete *A Minor Operation*, a first-rate Clinton Driffield story of murder and a most baffling disappearance. A *Times Literary Supplement* reviewer found that *A Minor Operation* treated the reader 'to exactly the right mixture of mystification and clue' and that, in addition to its impressive construction, the novel boasted 'character-drawing above the average' for a detective novel.

Alfred Stewart's final eight mysteries, which appeared between 1938 and 1947, the year of the author's death, are, on the whole, a somewhat weaker group of tales than the sixteen that appeared between 1926 and 1937, yet they are not without interest. In 1938 Stewart for the last time managed to publish two detective novels, *Truth Comes Limping* and *For Murder Will Speak* (also published as *Murder Will Speak*). The latter tale is much the superior of the two, having an interesting suburban setting and a bevy of female characters found to have motives when a contemptible philandering businessman meets with foul play. Sexual neurosis plays a major role in *For Murder Will Speak*, the ever-thorough Stewart obviously having made a study of the subject when writing the novel. The somewhat squeamish reviewer for *Scribner's Magazine* considered the subject matter of *For Murder Will Speak* 'rather unsavory at times', yet this individual conceded that the novel nevertheless made 'first-class reading for those who enjoy a good puzzle intricately worked out'. 'Judge Lynch' in the *Saturday Review* apparently had no such moral reservations about the latest Clinton Driffield murder case, avowing simply of the novel: 'They don't come any better'.

Over the next couple of years Stewart again sent Sir Clinton Driffield temporarily packing, replacing him with a new series detective, a brash radio personality named Mark Brand, in *The Counsellor* (1939) and *The Four Defences* (1940). The better of these two novels is *The Four Defences*, which Stewart based on another notorious British true-crime case, the Alfred Rouse blazing-car murder. (Rouse is believed to have fabricated his death by murdering an unknown man, placing the dead man's body in his car and setting the car on fire, in the hope that the murdered man's body would be taken for his.) Though admittedly a thinly characterised academic exercise in ratiocination, Stewart's *Four Defences* surely is also one of the most complexly plotted Golden Age detective novels and should delight devotees of classical detection. Taking the Rouse blazing-car affair as his theme, Stewart composes from it a stunning set of diabolically ingenious criminal variations. 'This is in the cold-blooded category which [. . .] excites a crossword puzzle kind of interest,' the reviewer for the *Times Literary Supplement* acutely noted of the novel. 'Nothing in the Rouse case would prepare you for these complications upon complications [. . .] What they prove is that Mr Connington has the power of penetrating into the puzzle-corner of the brain. He leaves it dazedly wondering whether in the records of actual crime there can be any dark deed to equal this in its planned convolutions.'

Sir Clinton Driffield returned to action in the remaining four detective novels in the Connington oeuvre, *The Twenty-One Clues* (1941), *No Past is Dead* (1942), *Jack-in-the-Box* (1944) and *Commonsense is All You Need* (1947), all of which were written as Stewart's heart disease steadily worsened and reflect to some extent his diminishing physical and mental energy. Although *The Twenty-One Clues* was inspired by the notorious Hall-Mills double murder case – probably the most publicised murder case in the United States in the 1920s – and the American critic and novelist Anthony Boucher commended *Jack-in-the-Box*, I believe the best of these later mysteries is *No Past Is Dead*, which Stewart partly based on a bizarre French true-crime affair, the 1891 Achet-Lepine murder case.[8] Besides providing an interesting background for the tale, the ailing author managed some virtuoso plot twists, of the sort most associated today with that ingenious Golden Age Queen of Crime, Agatha Christie.

What Stewart with characteristic bluntness referred to as 'my complete crack-up' forced his retirement from Queen's University in 1944. 'I am afraid,' Stewart wrote a friend, the chemist and forensic scientist F. Gerald Tryhorn, in August 1946, eleven months before his death, 'that I shall never be much use again. Very stupidly, I tried for a session to combine a full course of lecturing with angina pectoris; and ended up by establishing that the two are immiscible.' He added that since retiring in 1944, he had been physically 'limited to my house, since even a fifty-yard crawl brings on the usual cramps'. Stewart completed his essay collection and a final novel before he died at his study desk in his Belfast home on 1 July 1947, at the age of sixty-six. When death came to the author he was busy at work, writing.

More than six decades after Alfred Walter Stewart's death, his J. J. Connington fiction is again available to a wider audience of classic-mystery fans, rather than strictly limited to a select company of rare-book collectors with deep pockets. This is fitting for an individual who was one of the finest writers of British genre fiction between the two world wars. 'Heaven forfend that you should imagine I take myself for anything out of the common in the tec yarn stuff,' Stewart once self-deprecatingly declared in a letter to Rupert Gould. Yet, as contemporary critics recognised, as a writer of detective and science fiction Stewart indeed was something out of the common. Now more modern readers can find this out for themselves. They have much good sleuthing in store.

1. For more on Street, Crofts and particularly Stewart, see Curtis Evans, *Masters of the 'Humdrum' Mystery: Cecil John Charles Street, Freeman Wills Crofts, Alfred Walter Stewart and the British Detective Novel, 1920–1961* (Jefferson, NC: McFarland, 2012). On the academic career of Alfred Walter Stewart, see his entry in *Oxford Dictionary of National Biography* (London and New York: Oxford University Press, 2004), vol. 52, 627–628.

2. The Gould-Stewart correspondence is discussed in considerable detail in *Masters of the 'Humdrum' Mystery*. For more on the life of the fascinating Rupert Thomas Gould, see Jonathan Betts, *Time Restored: The Harrison Timekeepers and R. T. Gould, the*

Man Who Knew (Almost) Everything (London and New York: Oxford University Press, 2006) and *Longitude,* the 2000 British film adaptation of Dava Sobel's book *Longitude:The True Story of a Lone Genius Who Solved the Greatest Scientific Problem of His Time* (London: Harper Collins, 1995), which details Gould's restoration of the marine chronometers built by in the eighteenth century by the clockmaker John Harrison.

3. Potential purchasers of *Murder in the Maze* should keep in mind that $2 in 1927 is worth over $26 today.

4. In a 1920 article in *The Strand Magazine,* Arthur Conan Doyle endorsed as real prank photographs of purported fairies taken by two English girls in the garden of a house in the village of Cottingley. In the aftermath of the Great War Doyle had become a fervent believer in Spiritualism and other paranormal phenomena. Especially embarrassing to Doyle's admirers today, he also published *The Coming of the Faeries* (1922), wherein he argued that these mystical creatures genuinely existed. 'When the spirits came in, the common sense oozed out,' Stewart once wrote bluntly to his friend Rupert Gould of the creator of Sherlock Holmes. Like Gould, however, Stewart had an intense interest in the subject of the Loch Ness Monster, believing that he, his wife and daughter had sighted a large marine creature of some sort in Loch Ness in 1935. A year earlier Gould had authored *The Loch Ness Monster and Others*, and it was this book that led Stewart, after he made his 'Nessie' sighting, to initiate correspondence with Gould.

5. A tontine is a financial arrangement wherein shareowners in a common fund receive annuities that increase in value with the death of each participant, with the entire amount of the fund going to the last survivor. The impetus that the tontine provided to the deadly creative imaginations of Golden Age mystery writers should be sufficiently obvious.

6. At Ardlamont, a large country estate in Argyll, Cecil Hambrough died from a gunshot wound while hunting. Cecil's tutor, Alfred John Monson, and another man, both of whom were out hunting with Cecil, claimed that Cecil had accidentally shot himself, but Monson was arrested and tried for Cecil's murder. The verdict delivered was 'not proven', but Monson was then – and is today – considered almost certain to have been guilty of the murder. On the Ardlamont case, see William Roughead, *Classic Crimes* (1951; repr., New York: New York Review Books Classics, 2000), 378–464.

7. For the genesis of the title, see Macaulay's 'The Battle of the Lake

Regillus', from his narrative poem collection *Lays of Ancient Rome*. In this poem Macaulay alludes to the ancient cult of Diana Nemorensis, which elevated its priests through trial by combat. Study of the practices of the Diana Nemorensis cult influenced Sir James George Frazer's cultural interpretation of religion in his most renowned work, *The Golden Bough: A Study in Magic and Religion*. As with *Tom Tiddler's Island* and *The Ha-Ha Case* the title *In Whose Dim Shadow* proved too esoteric for Connington's American publishers, Little, Brown and Co., who altered it to the more prosaic *The Tau Cross Mystery*.

8. Stewart analysed the Achet-Lepine case in detail in 'The Mystery of Chantelle', one of the best essays in his 1947 collection *Alias J. J. Connington*.

THE TAU CROSS
MYSTERY

HERNSHAW PARK

BELLA VISTA AVENUE

Tennis Courts

RINGWOOD HILL

Gardens

THE GROVE

No. 17

The Laurels

No. 5

Footpath

Church

LANE

GARAGES

RAVENSWOOD MANSIONS

Avondale

No. 1

SANS SOUCI AVENUE

HILL RISE

1
THE MURDER IN THE GROVE

Outside the windows of the Chief Constable's study, with their undrawn curtains, the summer twilight had faded into warm indistinctness; and the exterior dusk seemed all the darker by contrast with the electric light which fell upon the papers and town plan outspread upon the roll-top desk. For a few minutes longer, Sir Clinton checked schedule against map; then he swung round his office chair and addressed his guest, Wendover, who was ensconced with a book and a pipe in a big arm-chair.

"If I may interrupt your study of Bataille for a moment, Squire, I'd like you to give me a hand here."

Wendover obediently laid down the volume of *Causes Criminelles et Mondaines* in which he had been engrossed, came across the room, and bent over the Chief Constable's shoulder.

"Just put your pencil down anywhere on this section of the map," Sir Clinton directed, "and mention the first hour and minute that come into your head while you're doing it."

"Is this the latest method of spotting a winner?" Wendover inquired ironically.

"No, I pick 'em out with a pin," the Chief Constable retorted, with equal gravity. "Nothing like the old, old method—as used by most racing tipsters. And, by the way, Squire, talking of the success of old methods, we had to arrest a staunch conservative the other day. He was playing 'O for October'."

"'O for October'?" echoed Wendover, in a puzzled tone. "I never heard of it. What is it, anyway?"

Sir Clinton glanced up at him quizzically.

"Never heard of it? Well, it's sad to see how these good old wheezes fall out of memory. That's the justification of the old, tried methods. They're always new to somebody."

"'O for October'?" repeated Wendover stolidly.

"Ah, quite right. I was led away a trifle. Eloquence is the gift of the gods, but a curse to one's neighbours. I expect I've fallen into the habit through seeing too many strong talkative men in the films. 'O for October,' of course. You have twenty-six cards with one capital letter of the alphabet printed on each. You stuff each card into a separate envelope. The size of the envelope makes the top half of the card stick out, so that you can see the upper part of the capital letter. Then you pitch the envelopes down in a heap and offer to bet even money that no one picks out the capital O. Whence the slogan 'O for October'."

"Well, but . . ."

"Yes, there is a 'but' in it, in capital letters, too. When our man went through the young gentleman's cards he found two capital Q's. In the bright alphabet of that youth there was no such letter as O at all. Your colleague on the bench seemed to think the game almost unfair. Three months."

"A bit obvious," commented Wendover.

"Maybe," said the Chief Constable. "But my young friend had £3-7-8 in his pocket when he was arrested, and I doubt if he's ever done a hand's turn of honest work in his life. So you see it does pay to be conservative and stick to the good, old, tried methods. Which brings me to business, Squire. Down with your pencil and name an hour and minute."

Wendover obeyed, and Sir Clinton consulted his schedules.

"H'm!" he said reflectively. "This is what's what, Squire. We've been troubled by one or two smash-and-grab raids in this district lately. In the last affair, a fellow picked up a car that someone had left unwatched. He drove it to a jeweller's shop and left the engine running while he went inside. He asked to see some diamond rings, and the jeweller produced a tray of them, worth two

4

or three hundred quid. Whereupon the man knocked him out and drove off in the car with the rings. We picked up the car—abandoned—some miles away; but that wasn't much good to us, still less to the jeweller. There have been one or two other cases, minor affairs. It's making me rather unpopular."

"Looks almost as if you'd have to begin working for your living, eh?" Wendover commented sardonically. "Dreadful prospect."

"That's about the size of it," Sir Clinton answered lightly. Then, in a more sober tone, he added, "What disturbs the citizenry is that these fellows are armed, and one never knows what may happen. They've done no shooting so far, but you never can tell."

"And what's this map game? Are you trying to get me to forecast the time and place of the next raid? I never claimed to be psychic, it's only fair to say."

Sir Clinton shook his head.

"No, it's not that. One of my young lions, Squire, has been bitten by the notion that we might give better protection if we rearranged the working of our beats in a drastic way. I encouraged him to work it out on paper, and this is the result." He indicated the pile of schedules on his desk. "His scheme depends upon synchronising the movements of constables on adjacent beats."

"Not much good," Wendover said, in a critical tone. "If you have the whole thing working to a time schedule like that, it'll make it easier for criminals. If your system's rigid, then a burglar will learn in advance when a certain street is bound to be free of police and how long it will be before a constable turns up. House-breaking made easy, in fact."

"My young lion proposes to alter the timing night by night, to avoid that."

"A bit cumbrous, if you have to do that," Wendover objected.

"Yes," Sir Clinton agreed. "But that isn't my real objection to his scheme. The real objection is that if you make the thing as rigid as this, a constable will be saying to himself, 'At 10.45 p.m. the toe of my left boot has got to be exactly in line with the front doorstep of Number 65 Castor Avenue, and at 10.47 p.m. I've got to make a right turn into Ipecacuanha Park. If a man's oppressed by rules of this sort, what sort of lookout is he likely to keep? He'll be so busy repeating his timetable that he'll have no wits left for his proper work."

"Obviously."

"So we come back to my text: that the good old methods are the best, after all. The basic fault of this scheme is that it robs a man of any initiative on his beat; and initiative is what I want from my fellows. This scheme's an example of it. I sha'n't adopt it. But I'll see that my young lion gets a good mark for it. He's put in any amount of overtime, working it out; and he's evidently a person with ideas. Still, the thing's no good."

He picked up the schedules from his desk, slipped them back into their envelope, and put them away in a drawer. As he was about to fold up the town plan, Wendover stopped him with a gesture.

"Let's have a look at that, Clinton. I once stayed at Hernshaw House when I was a youngster. The district's changed a bit since then, I suppose?"

"It has. The builders have fairly cut it up. We managed to rescue a bit of the estate and turn it into a public park. Here it is on the plan: Hernshaw Park. But the rest of it's covered with flats and villas. There's been a biggish development in that district in the last five years. Of course, it was spoiled before that."

"How?" asked Wendover.

"Oh, they cut down most of the timber during the War. Nothing left but unsightly stumps. A forlorn-looking bit of countryside."

"Pity," was Wendover's regretful comment, for he had a liking for old things.

"Some of the trees are still left. This avenue they call The Grove is part of the old wood; and there are spinneys here and there in Hernshaw Park."

Wendover scrutinised the plan, evidently trying to get his bearings amid the streets and avenues of the new suburb.

"I remember now," he said. "That pool in the Park there used to be a heronry. The herons and some rooks used to nest in the trees, roughly about where my finger is."

He pondered over the old days for a moment.

"Nasty customers, herons," he continued musingly. "I remember shooting one, down by that pool. I didn't know much in those days. Shot it in the body, and down it came. I was hugely delighted, of course, big bird like that as a trophy; and I rushed up at once and stooped down over it. It nearly cost me an eye; for the brute was shamming dead, in that way they have, and as I bent down over it, the damned thing lunged at me with its spear of a beak and landed me on the forehead. I had the scar for long enough."

"So you shoot 'em in the head, now?"

"No, I don't shoot 'em at all," Wendover declared. "In fact, I'm trying to encourage them to breed, up on my little lake at the Grange."

The anecdote seemed to have revived other memories, for he leaned forward and scanned the plan with a certain regretful curiosity.

"There used to be quite a thick bit of wood here," he went on, "just where this place, The Grove, runs now. Funny what vivid impressions one gets when one's young. I went through it at night, now and again. An eerie place for a youngster, full of queer noises at times, and rum shadows, and uprooted stumps that looked like weird cuttlefish in the twilight. I was at the Macaulay stage in literature, in those days. You know how it ran in one's head, Clinton?"

Sir Clinton nodded comprehendingly.

> "But he saw on Palatinus
>   The white porch of his home;
> And he spake to the noble river
>   That rolls by the towers of Rome."

he quoted. "Yes, it did run in one's head in those days; and some of it sticks, even yet."

"Well, whenever I had to go through that wood at night," Wendover continued, "there was one bit of Macaulay that ran most uncomfortably in my head:

"Those trees in whose dim shadow
  The ghastly priest doth reign,
The priest who slew the slayer,
  And who shall himself be slain."

"I always had that feeling of creepy expectation, as if suddenly from behind one of these uprooted stumps the 'ghastly priest' *might* emerge: tangled hair, fierce eyes, only a wolfskin over him, and something glittering in his hand. One knew it *wouldn't* happen—and yet one got goose flesh all over, for all that. Ancestral memory, or something, I suppose. I could visualise that figure perfectly, and yet it was unlike any picture I ever saw."

"Interesting essay in the penal code," Sir Clinton said, speculatively. "Runaway slave makes for Aricia to pluck the Golden Bough, and finds a predecessor in charge, whom he's got to kill to gain sanctuary. And then, in his turn, he becomes guardian of the tree and has to tackle the next criminal or runaway who wants to take sanctuary. Immobilises both of them, for the good of the public, and settles one of them permanently. Also, the risk of being caught asleep must have weighed a bit on the ghastly priest's mind, one would suppose. It can hardly have been a gay life while it lasted. Now if one of my young lions would devise something of the same sort in a modern vein, it might be amusing. Make a good film, eh, Squire."

"You're a gruesome devil at times, Clinton," Wendover protested. "Though now I come to think of it, the original business would make a good scene in a classical film. Young hero *versus* the ghastly priest . . ."

"T-r-r-r-ring," rang the telephone on Sir Clinton's desk.

He picked up the instrument and gave his name.

"Yes? . . ." Wendover heard him say. "Yes? . . . Indeed! . . . Very rum. . . . He had, had he? . . . Curious. . . . No sign of the other man? . . . H'm! I think I'll come over and have a look round. . . . No, no, it's your show entirely. . . . No. . . . Well, I'll be round with you very shortly. Good-bye."

He swung round to Wendover with a grave, official face.

"Nasty business, this, Squire. Some fellow's been done in by a person or persons unknown. Curiously enough, it's in a block of flats at that very place we were talking about: The Grove. And from what they tell me, it's rather a rum affair. One might think your 'ghastly priest' had turned up, after all, to judge from some of the evidence. I'm going over there now. Care to come with me? I can't promise that it'll be a pleasant sight. But on the face of it, it's something fresh in the way of a mystery. I only remember one case like it, and in that case they didn't get the murderer. *Absit omen!*"

2
CONSTABLE DANBURY'S FIRST CASE

Police Constable William Danbury was a new recruit who meant to get on. Promotion in the police force was bound to be slow, he knew, but he had the comforting belief that efficiency is sure to tell, in the long run; and from the day of his joining, he had thrown himself with a certain joyous tenacity into the task of fitting himself for any emergency which might arise whilst he was wearing his armlet.

During his preliminary training, he bought a copy of Sir Howard Vincent's *Police Code* and set himself to master it in detail, from "Abandoning Children" down to "Youthful Offenders" at the other end of the alphabet. He had taken to heart the section upon "Education"; and in his lodgings a small stack of Woolworth exercise books testified to his zeal in composing written answers to questions which crossed his mind during his study of the "Code." In this way he had acquired a slightly Johnsonian vocabulary which he used for official purposes but discarded in private life.

He had been put through his preliminary training in the normal way; and then, owing to a fellow-constable's appendicitis, he was posted to night duty on a beat in the Hernshaw Division. Many a young man would have found this a weary business; but Constable Danbury was never bored. While pacing his beat at the regulation two-and-a-half miles per hour on the side of the pavement next the houses (as directed on page 25 of the *Police Code*), keeping his eyes open and his mouth shut (as recommended by Sir Howard Vincent), he had plenty of time to think. And Danbury being young, ambitious, optimistic, and in love, got a good deal of pleasure out of his thinking.

He reached the street corner where he was accustomed at this time of night to "touch up" with his colleague on the adjacent beat. After a minute or two, the burly form of Constable Towton appeared, accompanied by a small object which, on nearer inspection, turned out to be a piteous-looking little dog, trembling with hunger and nervousness, which Towton was leading by a string round its neck.

"There's been some talk about police dogs in the papers," Constable Danbury remarked ironically, "but I didn't know the Chief had started already. Are you takin' it for its evenin' run?"

"No. Found strayin'. No collar. Takin' it along to the station," Constable Towton replied concisely, for he was a man of few words.

"Looks a bit empty, poor little devil."

"Full o' fleas," muttered Constable Towton dispassionately. Then, in a kindly tone, he admonished the animal. "Keep off my trousers, blast you!"

He pulled out his official notebook.

"Know anythin' about dogs? What breed is it?" he inquired. "Got to put it in my report."

"Assorted, by the look of it. A dog-fancier's encyclopædia on four legs, I'd call it. Put it down 'mongrel' and you won't be far out."

Constable Towton wetted his pencil and began a laborious entry in his notebook by the light of the street lamp above him. After a moment or two he paused and looked up.

"By the way, Bill, do you spell it M-U-N-G-E-R-L-L or M-U-N-G-R-E-L-L? I never can remember these damned out-o'-the-way words."

Danbury gave him the correct version, which he accepted without demur; but as he began to write in his notebook again, Towton hesitated.

"Better call it just 'dog'," he decided. "Saves bother."

"Anythin' doin' on your beat?" Danbury inquired, when the laborious entry had been made.

11

"Number 3, Laburnum Villas. Away for the week-end, they are. Left scullery window open. Put my marks on it. That's all. Anything on your beat?"

Constable Danbury shook his head, almost regretfully.

"Nothin'."

"And a damned good thing, too," was Towton's comment.

Constable Danbury nodded an apparent agreement, but inwardly he differed from his colleague. If nothing happened on one's beat, how could one, in the words of the *Police Code*, succeed in "attracting the notice of his superior by some action, evidencing zeal, ability, and judgment" and so qualify for promotion? No one had the public interest more at heart than Danbury, but he would have welcomed arson, robbery with violence, a drunken man or even somebody "loitering with intent."

Constable Towton returned his notebook to his pocket, nodded a farewell, and sailed off into the twilight, dragging his reluctant prize stationwards behind him. Danbury glanced after the retreating figure, which looked like a battleship proceeding majestically with a picket boat in tow. Poor old Towton. Years and years of service, and still only a constable. Never likely to be anything else, for the education test floored him every time he went up for promotion.

By contrast, Danbury saw his own career unrolled into the future. A year on probation. Three more years of service. An examination. Qualified for Sergeant. Another examination. Qualified for an Inspectorship. No more exams. Zeal, efficiency, the luck of a vacancy, and then: Superintendent. And possibly he might be allowed to take his first examination before the normal date, for there was always that royal road of "Special Qualifications." Hence that pile of Woolworth notebooks at his lodgings.

The speculation on his future career brought another factor into Danbury's mind. His thoughts turned naturally, as they so often did, to the little housemaid in one of the villas of The Grove. Jenny Hayle was just the sort of girl a man could marry without fear of her letting him down when he rose to a superintendentship. He had taken her to a dance or two, and to the pictures now and again.

12

She could wear evening dress as if she'd been born in it. Better manners than his own, too, and a far nicer accent. Nothing to be ashamed of, no matter how high up one rose. A nice girl, Constable Danbury reflected. In fact, a *very* nice girl.

Passers-by might think that Constable Danbury had a lonely life of it, walking the empty streets on night duty; but their unseeing eyes never glimpsed that graceful little ghost that tripped along beside him, nor could they catch the fascinating click of high-heeled shoes which went with him along the pavements under the street lamps. Constable Danbury was never lonely in that bodiless company.

Turning into Bella Vista Avenue, he paced slowly down it to the gate which gave entrance into Hernshaw Public Park. The clearing-out bell had been rung not long before this, and when he reached the gates, they were closed for the night. On the tennis courts belonging to Ringwood Church, a belated mixed double was striving to finish a match in the dusk, but the rest of the courts were empty. The other players had given up long before and were sitting in chattering groups on the raised terrace, overlooking the courts from the clubhouse end. Their white figures showed through the dusk, and here and there was the glow of a cigarette. Behind, the clubhouse windows were lit up, and Constable Danbury could catch a glimpse of lightly clad girls and men in blazers sitting down to bridge. In the warm dusk, the whole picture appealed to Constable Danbury's sociable nature. He was young enough to envy them just a little, in that brightly lit room.

"Not much use raidin' *that* club," he reflected, with a grin. "Church mice and strictly T.T. Not even a bottle of beer amongst them."

Constable Danbury never touched whisky, but he liked his glass of beer as well as the next man; and he rather pitied cranky people who voluntarily cut themselves off from such a harmless pleasure.

Passing on from the tennis ground, he glanced up the steep slope of Ringwood Hill. How it had been thus christened, Danbury could not imagine, for it was little better than a lane serving the back gates of the gardens of the flats on the south side of The Grove. The dusk was deepening, and he could see nothing of any official

13

interest in the alley. Later in the evening it might be the haunt of courting couples—some of the tennis players lingered in it on their way home, at times. But since his association with Jenny Hayle, the constable had looked on courting couples with more enlightened and less suspicious eyes.

He turned the corner into The Grove, keeping to the south side of the road; but as he went, he could not prevent his eyes straying up the slope towards The Laurels, on the opposite side of the street. In strict confidence, he had given Jenny the approximate time when he would be passing the house; and she might have found an opportunity to be at one of the front windows to see him go by. The villa was in darkness. Evidently the family had gone out for the evening. In one of the bow windows he could see the little figure and make out its gesture of greeting as he came nearer.

"Not to loiter or gossip, but to work the beat regularly and continuously." In Constable Danbury's mind there was a brief but fierce struggle between the *Police Code* and his own natural inclination. The Mayfields were out for the night. A wave of his hand would bring Jenny down to the gate. What harm would there be in a minute's chat, and perhaps a kiss or two? He could always ask for a drink of water, as an excuse. The temptation was acute for a moment. But Danbury, though no prig, had a high sense of duty, and he put the temptation aside. His answering gesture had no beckoning quality in it, and he passed on up the hill at the regulation pace.

Suddenly he heard a muffled explosion which seemed to come from one of the back gardens of the row of flats.

"Some kid settin' off fireworks in one of the back yards," Danbury surmised. "No affair of mine, unless they start lettin' off rockets or fire balloons that might set somethin' ablaze. I'll hang about for a minute or two, just in case."

A rocket or a fire balloon would rise above the housetops, so there was no need for him to walk round the block to the supposed scene of the fireworks display. He glanced back at The Laurels and saw that Jenny was still at the window. They exchanged another wave of the hand, and then Constable Danbury moved slowly on.

Suddenly, from the entrance to one of the flats, a figure emerged. It halted on the step for a moment, as though in doubt, glanced up the street and then in the constable's direction. At the sight of him, it seemed galvanised into fresh activity and came along the pavement towards him at a scrambling trot. A closer view under a street lamp showed Danbury a stout old gentleman in a dinner jacket and black tie, hatless, out of breath with his exertions, and evidently in a state of some excitement.

"Constable! Constable!!" the old gentleman gasped, as he came up to Danbury. "Did you hear that? Did you hear that shot? Did you hear it, eh? We heard it. Startling. Gave the ladies a shock, I can tell you. Awkward affair, with ladies in the house, very annoying. It must be looked into at once. Come along and look into it. Come along!"

He was obviously a peppery and easily flustered old gentleman, the sort which needs careful handling. Danbury sought to tranquilise him by suggesting the thought which had crossed his own mind when he heard the noise.

"It may be some children playin' with fireworks in the curtilage of one of the flats, sir," he hazarded in his "official" vocabulary.

"Curtilage" sounded more impressive than the "back yard" of his ordinary language.

"Nonsense! Rubbish! Don't be a fool, Constable," the old gentleman advised, with a certain lack of courtesy. "It went off—bang!—in the flat downstairs. I know the sound of a squib when I hear one. It wasn't a squib. No, no! More like a maroon. But nobody explodes maroons in a respectable flat. I'll tell you what it was. A pistol shot, Constable, a pistol shot. Startled the ladies badly. Very plucky of them not to scream. Sudden shock, you know. But come along, Constable, come along! What are you loitering about for? This must be looked into. There's something going on, pistol-firing and Lord knows what else, and there you stand as if nothing mattered. It's your business, isn't it? Then come along and see what's happened."

Evidently this red-faced old gentleman needed careful handling. Equally evidently, he was quite right. People in a neighbourhood like The Grove don't set off maroons in their drawing-rooms. Danbury hurried along the pavement with the old gentleman panting in his wake.

"Number Five," the old gentleman gasped, with what little breath was left to him, as he saw that Danbury hesitated. "My flat's on the second floor. The shot must have come from the first floor or the ground-floor flat."

At the door of Number 5, a board lashed to the railings informed the public that Messrs. Lewes and Flockton, Painters and Decorators, were engaged upon some renovations of the premises. The door of the flats had been left open by the old gentleman, and Danbury walked into the entrance hall. On his left rose the staircase leading to the upper flats. Straight in front of him, flanking the stair, the hall extended to the back of the premises and was closed by a heavy door which obviously gave access to the back garden. But these facts hardly struck Danbury at the moment. The signboard of the painters and decorators was duplicated at the door of the ground-floor flat, on his right, and the door of this flat was ajar, though no lights showed on the premises.

"Just wait a moment, sir," said the constable in his official voice, as the old gentleman pushed past him and seemed inclined to lead the way upstairs. "The time's 9.47 p.m., isn't it?" he added, with a glance at his wrist watch.

"That's right, that's right," the old gentleman responded, after verifying the information from his own watch. "I set my watch by the wireless a few minutes ago. That's right. Come along!"

"Just wait a moment, sir," Danbury repeated patiently.

This old boy seemed to think he was in charge of the proceedings, with his "Come along!" and his general bossiness, but Police Constable Danbury wasn't the sort of man to be rushed by any excitable old turkey cock. Things would be done in proper form so long as he was responsible.

"What about this open door, sir, before we go farther?" he inquired.

The old gentleman retraced his steps down the few stairs he had mounted and stared at the entrance to the ground-floor flat.

16

"Open door?" he ejaculated. "What open door? Why, so it is! I never noticed that, Constable. Such a hurry, coming down. That's strange; that's very strange. It wasn't open when I came home to-night before dinner. I remember that perfectly, for I looked at that decorators' board as I passed. That's very strange, indeed."

Constable Danbury thought swiftly. If there had been any "funny business" going on—and it began to look as if something was out of the common here—the first thing to do was to see that no one left the premises until things had cleared up a little. He turned to the old gentleman, who was still breathing rather stertorously after his unwonted exertions.

"Now, Mr. . . . ?"

"Geddington," the old gentleman supplied.

"Thank you, sir. Now, Mr. Geddington, I've got to rely on you for some assistance for a moment or two. Will you be so good as to stand here and prevent anyone making an egress from the premises while I investigate this flat? Stop anyone who comes downstairs, and if they won't halt, you've only got to raise your voice and I'll be with you immediately. If anyone comes into the front door, just hold them in conversation till I come."

The old gentleman nodded importantly.

"Thank you, sir. I knew I could rely on you."

At the change of expression on Mr. Geddington's face, Danbury congratulated himself on his diplomacy. Give one of these old fussers a job of work to do, and it kept him from sticking his oar in where it wasn't wanted. Put him in a better temper, too, having a hand in the affair. Thus relieved in his mind, the constable strode along the hall to the door opening into the garden. It was closed, but not locked; and as a precaution against intrusion, he turned the key by thrusting his pencil through the ring and using it as a lever, so as to avoid smudging any fingerprints that might have been left on the metal. Then, under the inquisitive eyes of Geddington, he pushed open the door of the ground-floor flat, listened without result, and entered.

He found himself in a gloomy little hall, hardly better than a passage, with three doors on his right and two on his left hand.

The end of the passage was blocked by a sixth door, facing him as he entered. He listened again for a moment or two, but there was no sound from anywhere in the flat.

Danbury had a rough idea of the plan on which these flats were built. The doors immediately to the right and left of the entrance would be those of a kitchenette and a bathroom-lavatory. He verified this, flashing his lamp into each but finding them empty and stripped bare to the fittings. The two rooms on his right, overlooking The Grove, would be bedrooms. He pushed open the first of the doors and found himself in a newly papered room, clean, bare, and comfortless-looking, as all such rooms are. Not enough cover in it to hide a cockroach.

The next room was half papered and encumbered with a paperhanger's trestle, house steps, paste brushes, rolls of wallpaper, and all the normal paraphernalia. The most cursory examination showed that here also there was nothing suspicious. Yet about this stage Constable Danbury began to feel the lack of company. The report alone was nothing—fireworks, as he had assumed at first. The unlocked door of the flat by itself meant nothing—carelessness on the part of the painters, possibly. The silence in the flat was normal. But put all three of them together, he reflected, with almost a twinge of uneasiness, and you might come on something very abnormal at the back of them.

He shrugged his shoulders in impatience at himself and opened the door at the end of the passage. Nothing there but a little cubbyhole, evidently a box room or store cupboard, by the look of it. Nothing suspicious there. Only one room now, evidently the sitting-room of the flat.

"Have you found anything yet, Constable? Have you found anything? You're very slow about it, very slow. I can't wait about here all night, you know, just for your convenience," came Geddington's testy tones from the entrance hall. "The ladies upstairs will be wondering what's become of me."

"Just a moment, sir."

Now for it! thought Danbury. If there was any evil-doer on the premises, he must be in this ultimate room, and he might well be prepared to give an intruder a warm welcome. Might be hiding behind the door to give one a bash on the head as one went in. Give him a bit of a surprise, then. Constable Danbury smiled grimly. He turned the door handle with infinite caution, gripped it firmly, and then, with a swift thrust, flung the door open so violently that its crash against the jamb echoed through the darkness of the flat. Danbury flashed his light into the room.

"'Strewth!" he ejaculated, in his wholly unofficial language.

The beam of his lantern cut across the dying dusk in the room and revealed something lying on the floor by the French window. A human figure, lying in an attitude strange to Danbury but quite explanatory of one matter, at any rate.

"Dead as a doornail," was the constable's trite comment to himself.

He went forward into the room, flashed his lamp on the man's head and swiftly diverted the beam elsewhere. Very little of that would be a feast for most people. He'd had enough, anyhow, in that one glance. As he switched his light away, it caught the French window and he noted, only half-consciously, that the catch was undone and the leaves slightly ajar. Danbury drew a reel of fine silk from his pocket and wound some of the thread around the two handles.

"Constable! Constable!! What's up? What's up, eh? Have you found anything? Were you talking to some one?"

Without thinking, Constable Danbury blurted out the truth:

"There's a dead man in here, sir. Shot dead."

Old Mr. Geddington's reaction to this news might have been foreseen, and the constable could have bitten his tongue when he realised what he had done by his incautious admission. There was a scuttle of feet over the paving of the entrance hall as Geddington dashed to the outer door of the flats. Then, before Danbury could intervene, came the portentous cry:

"Murder! Murder! Police! Help! Police! *Murder!!*"

"That's torn it!" snarled the constable, as the sinister appeal went ringing through the dusk. "Roused the whole damned district, he has, with his squallin'. Damn and blast the red-faced old geezer!"

19

His own plan had been to keep the matter quiet, ring up the station on the telephone, and ensure that a posse of police was on the premises before the affair became public. Then the detectives could get to work behind a cordon, sure that nothing had been disturbed.

Since the damage had been done, Danbury made the best of a bad business. Assistance would have to be summoned as swiftly as possible. He ran to the door where Geddington was shouting himself out of breath, drew his whistle from his tunic, and blew a distress call, clear and shrill, to summon Towton from the next beat.

At the first note, Geddington ceased his clamour and leaned, panting and exhausted, against the door. He had done his work only too well. Already under the street lamp at the lower end of The Grove appeared running figures in white, tennis players from the club, racing up the slope. Constable Danbury eyed them with a scowl, knowing them to be the harbingers of a crowd. It took little enough to gather a mob, and with murder as a bait. . . . He turned to Geddington and, pushing his whistle back into its place, he spoke with a well-feigned pretence of good humour.

"Well, sir, you've invited a party, and here they come."

A swift patter of feet sounded close at hand as the swiftest-footed of the runners dashed up and halted before the door, at the sight of the police uniform. A babble of questions broke out, as the group grew in numbers:

"Who's been murdered?"—"I say, what's happened?"—"Have you got the fellow who did it?"—"Has he got away?"—"Where's the body?"—"Shut up, you fellows. Let the bobby have a chance!"

Constable Danbury stood in the doorway and shook his head stolidly in response to the cries. His duty, as laid down in the *Police Code*, was to prevent anyone reaching the body, and to give no information to anyone. The rapidly increasing group before him was showing signs of restlessness.

"Skirts among 'em, too," he reflected, in disgust. "Rushin' up to gape, like as if it was a free movie show. I'd like to take some of 'em inside and let 'em see what I saw. That'd send 'em home to happy dreams, that would!"

Would Towton never turn up? To Danbury it seemed ages since he had blown his whistle; and all this while there was the open French window unguarded. Some fools like these in front of him might climb the garden wall in the rear and mess up everything out of sheer ignorance. And if he left his post, this crowd here would surge into the house as soon as his back was turned, by the look of them. He glanced at Geddington, but already he had tasted Geddington's quality and he had no wish to trust him with any further responsibility. If only Towton would hurry up!

Suddenly a god appeared from the machine, in the guise of a tall, heavily built figure hurrying down The Grove towards the outskirts of the crowd. Constable Danbury's failure to recognise any godlike quality was perhaps pardonable, for the newcomer wore a shabby brown Norfolk jacket, unbelted, a tennis shirt open at the neck, no waistcoat, and a pair of old grey flannel trousers which, if they had seen better days, had certainly not seen a trouser press that season. Tennis shoes completed the divinity's visible outfit.

Joining the crowd, the new arrival insinuated himself into it; and by the use of his elbows and a persuasive tongue, he succeeded in worming his way into the front rank in a surprisingly short time. But instead of halting there, he shook himself free, marched boldly up to Constable Danbury, and, with the air of one pronouncing a spell, he uttered one syllable:

"Press!"

Then, seeing that the constable's features did not relax, he amplified his statement:

"Have you anything for me? I'm a reporter."

Constable Danbury read his newspaper every day; but, like most of us, he had never troubled to speculate on how news got into print, beyond a vague notion that it was collected by a class of people called "journalists." So this was one of them? Danbury's glance took in the unruly mop of russet hair, the eager brown eyes, the friendly, expectant smile which showed a glimpse of big white teeth. If there was a trace of unscrupulousness in the eyes and mouth, Danbury failed to detect it. A hearty fellow, this, a good mixer, by the look of him. The constable had always visualised reporters as weedy little beggars, somehow; and this chap was as big as he was himself, both ways.

The journalist seemed to detect a trace of fellow-feeling in the constable's physiognomy, for he made another appeal:

"Have a heart, man. This is a scoop for me. It means a lot."

The brown eyes scrutinised Danbury's face shrewdly and they noted the half-apprehensive turn of Danbury's head towards the back premises.

"Who found the body; you can tell me that, at any rate?"

Danbury's half-involuntary glance towards Geddington seemed to suggest something further to the journalist.

"I know what's worrying you. I know these flats. It's that French window at the back that you're bothered about? You can't watch both sides at once, eh? Well, I tell you what. You stand at that door at the end of the hall—open it, I mean, and stand outside. That covers the back door and the French window alongside it. You can see right up the hall to this entrance too, and cover everything. I'll stay here and keep this mob back. Interview 'em, if they try to push in," he added, with mock ferocity.

Constable Danbury was quick to see the advantage of this arrangement. He reopened the back door with the same precautions as he had used before and took his stand on the threshold. To his relief, he found that no one had as yet ventured into the garden. The gate was evidently locked.

"And now," said the journalist, "what about locking this front door and staving off the rubbernecks?"

Adroitly he steered Geddington into the hall and slammed the outer door. Constable Danbury uttered some wholly unofficial language under his breath. Why hadn't he thought of that for himself? He had been so anxious to catch the first glimpse of Towton—like a beleaguered commander watching for a relief force—that the idea of shutting the door had slipped out of his mind completely. What a fool!

"Your mate can't mistake the house, with all this mass meeting on the pavement. And when he knocks, we'll let him in."

And having thus established himself within the citadel, the journalist turned to Geddington and subjected him to a dazing hail of questions. He was evidently working against time; and he had need to, for suddenly the note of the crowd outside seemed to change. The journalist set the door ajar and glanced out. Towton's deep voice penetrated to the hall.

"Now then!"

The resonant tones lent authority to even that meaningless concatenation of words.

"You must pass along, please. No loitering! There's nothing to see, here. Pass along, please! Murder, eh? You'll be able to read all about it in the paper tomorrow. Pass along, please!"

"He's actually getting them to shift," the journalist reported. "Wonderful thing, force of personality. Here he comes."

He opened the door wider to allow Towton to enter. In a few sentences, Danbury put his colleague abreast of events. Then he called to Geddington.

"Have you a telephone in your flat, sir?"

"Yes, yes, of course. You want to use it, eh? Want to telephone to the police station? Certainly, certainly. It's upstairs. My flat's on the second floor. Come along with me and I'll show you where it is. And don't alarm the ladies. Very awkward, this sort of thing. Very shocking. Upset them and all that. More easily upset than men like ourselves, of course. That's quite natural."

"You ring 'em up," said Danbury to his colleague. "If you lock the front door, I'll see to this end."

Towton nodded, secured the door, and then followed Geddington up the stair. The journalist unobtrusively attached himself to them, and all three vanished from Danbury's range of vision. He heard fresh voices, as though they had encountered someone on the landing above. Then Towton's gruff tones with more than a touch of impatience in them:

"Come along, sir. No time to talk. Where's that telephone?"

A few minutes elapsed, then Towton tramped solidly down the stairs again, alone.

23

"Rang 'em up," he reported laconically. "He's coming. Sawbones too. And the bulb squeezer. And Wootton. A ga-*lack*-say of talent, as they say. How'd you spell 'ga-*laxy*,' Bill? one L or two? I'm all for this simplified spellin' they talk about. G-A-L-A-K-S-Y, and no more's needed."

Danbury had little interest in phonetics at the moment. He gathered that Inspector Chesilton was to be in charge of the case, and that he would be accompanied by the Police Surgeon, the official photographer, and the fingerprint expert. He sought in his memory for the advice of the *Police Code*.

"We ought to note the position of the body and see that nobody leaves the house," he pointed out. "The French window in there's open, and I'm a bit worried about takin' my eye off it."

"Dead bodies don't move," Constable Towton declared sensibly. "Still, may as well have a look round. Lock the two doors, take away the keys. Nobody gets out or in, then, except through this here flat. Barrin' they've a fire-escape upstairs."

After taking these precautions, they betook themselves to the sitting-room of the flat. At the moment of discovering the body, Danbury had no time to make a careful examination; and now, while Constable Towton cautiously tiptoed over to inspect the corpse, he made a more detailed survey of the premises.

The place had that dismal aspect of all rooms dismantled after long use. From the dingy ceiling, seamed with cracks like rivers and their tributaries, a forlorn strand of electric cord swung languidly in the faint draught from the French window. A dingy paper covered the walls, except at one point where some inquisitive person had torn away a square foot or so to see what lay below. One or two paler oblong patches showed where pictures had long hung undisturbed.

Suddenly Constable Danbury gave a sharp ejaculation which made his colleague look up. As he had cast his light hither and thither around the walls, its beam had caught the mantelpiece, and there, placed neatly side by side, stood a man's walking shoes. Danbury stepped cautiously over and examined them without lifting them. They seemed to be practically new, so far as he could see.

24

"Here! Towton!" he said eagerly. "Look at this."

Constable Towton left his post by the body and joined him.

"What about it?" he demanded, in a discouraging tone. "Belong to the painters, likely. Never noticed painters changin' into slippers to work? Don't ask why. Save their corns, maybe."

"What has *that* got on its feet?" Danbury demanded, with a nod towards the body asprawl by the window.

He did not wait for Towton to answer, but stepped across and shone his lamp upon the feet which projected from the rucked-up trousers. Tennis shoes! And split-new, by the look of them. Danbury made a rough measure of the size from the upturned sole of one; then he returned to the mantelpiece and estimated the size of the walking shoes. Identical, so far as he could tell. A vague idea began to take shape in Danbury's mind, but it was too dim for him to put into words. In fact, when he tried to clarify it to himself, he found that it merely amounted to the feeling that he had "hit on something."

Greatly spurred even by this, he now turned his attention to the rest of the room. The painters had evidently been using it as a temporary store, for painting planks lay along the skirting on one side and rolls of wallpaper were propped in a corner. The grate was full of ashes. Probably the painters had kindled a fire to boil their kettle for tea. A newspaper of that day's date had been crumpled up and thrown down beside the tiles of the hearth, possibly as a provision for fire-lighting next day.

Danbury swung his light over the floor: a rectangle of bare, time-stained boards, with a much-scraped border of brown paint ringing it round the walls. Between the French window and the hearth stood a collection of tin paintpots with brushes sticking out from the pigments.

One of them had been upset—violently, since the brush had been thrown out—and a viscid stream of paint had flowed from its rim on to the bare boards. Some obscure marks near by puzzled Danbury for a moment or two. Then he guessed what they were. Someone had trodden in the paint and had then scrubbed the sole of his shoe on the floor to clean off the paint from the leather.

Danbury stooped over the marks with his lamp, hoping to find a clear footprint. To his chagrin, only shapeless smudges revealed themselves, so that not even the size of the foot which had made them could be guessed.

Danbury stood up again and pondered for a moment. Then he examined the dead man's tennis shoes, finding them clean. He looked at the walking shoes on the mantelpiece and was strongly tempted to lift them, but caution made him refrain. He sniffed long at the welts, but could detect no odour of paint. On the face of that evidence, neither the dead man nor the owner of the walking shoes had trodden in the paint.

But now new vistas of investigation were opening up before Danbury. He pondered for some moments and then went back to the overturned paintpot. He knelt beside it and made a sketch of the pool of paint on the floor, entering measurements in his note-book as a record. Then with his finger, he explored the inner side of the paintpot and jotted down some measurements. Constable Towton observed all this activity with the sympathetic air of one seeing a friend wasting his time.

"Sherlock Holmes, eh?" he inquired, not unkindly. "Don't copy him, Bill. Silly ass! Spelled his name with an L in the middle. To make it more difficult, likely. Nobody bothers. Call him plain HOMES. So what good did it do?"

Danbury, consulting his watch and making a jotting in his notes, made no response to his colleague. Towton threw his light round the apartment before continuing.

"Dismal den, this, Bill. Gives me the willies just to look at it."

Danbury was enough of a psychologist to know that this laborious jesting rose from no mere callousness. The bleak dilapidation of the room, the body with its clothes in that horrible disarray which seems inseparable from violent death, the ominous pool of blood, and the sinister twilight of the fallen dusk: each was a factor making for eerieness in the atmosphere. Danbury felt it, despite the distraction of his clue-hunting. Towton, with no such interest, was also affected, despite his outward stolidity; and his joking was the reaction of his dull mind against the gruesomeness of his environment.

But at the moment, Danbury had little interest in Towton's mental processes. The hunting instinct was awake, and he threw the beam of his lamp eagerly, hither and thither over the floor, in search of anything which had been overlooked. A step or two brought something fresh within his range of vision, something which hitherto had been screened by the huddle of paintpots. He turned the beam of his lamp upon it and stooped down to examine the object without touching it.

"Look here!" he said, pointing it out to Towton. "Here's a man's handkerchief. It's soaked in blood—sopping. Looks as if it had been crumpled up and pitched down there."

"Better leave it alone," Towton counselled unnecessarily. "Wootton'll want to go over it for fingerprints, likely."

Constable Towton had a profound contempt for the more scientific methods in criminal-hunting.

But now their vigil was over and their responsibility at an end. There came a knocking on the front door of the flats, the sharp authoritative knock of one who knows that he will not be stayed.

"That's them," Towton ejaculated, as he set off for the front entrance.

27

3
THE GOLDEN T

Constable Towton threw open the door of Number 5, The Grove, and saluted smartly as he found himself face to face with his inspector. In the group congregated on the step, he recognised the police surgeon, Doctor Fyefield Smith, Wootton, the fingerprint expert, Sergeant Vorley, and Jelf, the official photographer. The inspector's car had nosed its way through the crowd to Number 5, and behind it stood a big police lorry from which uniformed constables had descended. Two of them were bringing cases of apparatus up to the door, whilst the remainder had already set about dispersing the crowd of sight-seers in front of the house.

"Pass along there, please! Pass along! No loitering! Pass along quietly, please!"

Inspector Chesilton, followed by his companions, stepped into the hall as Towton stood aside. He had deep set, rather sympathetic eyes, a well-cut nose, and a firm mouth which could, on occasion, relax into a friendly, if somewhat tight-lipped smile. In the street, had one looked at him twice, he might have been mistaken for a professional man: a barrister, possibly, from the deep creases which ran down to the mouth corners, and from the neatness of his dress. He "played fair" in his work; and he could have boasted truly, if his modesty had allowed him to boast, that none of the criminals whom he had brought to book ever owed him a personal grudge for the part he had played in the conviction.

As he came into the hall, Constable Towton noticed that the two vertical lines between the inspector's brows were a shade deeper than usual, a sure sign that he was tired. And, in fact, Chesilton had had a tiring day. Nine o'clock in the morning had found him at his desk, going through the reports of crimes committed in his division during the night. Then came more reports, dealing with inquiries in progress. Then the arrangements of the day's work among his staff. Telephone calls, interviews, visits to the police court, one or two unexpected emergencies, had occupied the rest of the day. Then more reports, interviews with officers and the issuing of orders. And finally, just as he was shutting up his desk, that crazy old woman who believed from time to time that she was a member of the Royal Family and called to complain that his constables did not salute her when they met her in the street. And before he had soothed her down completely by tactful handling, he had been interrupted and summoned away to this affair in The Grove. The chance of sleep that night seemed rather remote, and he would have to be at his office again by nine o'clock as usual.

"In here, is it?" he demanded from Towton, as he moved on to the door of the ground-floor flat.

"Yes, sir. Constable Danbury's in there."

Inspector Chesilton's efficiency was founded purely on a zeal for public service. By ill luck, the superintendents over him were all men much about his own age, so that any further promotion would be a matter of "chance, or an Act of God", as he put it, without repining. He liked his inspectorship. The work suited him. If he waited for dead men's shoes or the superannuation of his superiors, he never grumbled.

Inspector Chesilton, flash lamp in hand, entered the sitting-room and punctiliously returned Danbury's salute. An upward flick of his light revealed the electric cord dangling from the ceiling.

"We need more light here. Sergeant, get that Aladdin lamp in, and then splice a 300 c.p. bulb to that cord. The current's off, I expect, but you can switch it on at the house meter. Now, Danbury, what about it?"

Constable Danbury had been careful to keep the sequence of events clear in his memory. He gave a chronological account of his

29

doings, concise, accurate, and strictly confined to facts. At the end of it, the inspector nodded.

"Good!"

Inspector Chesilton had only two laudatory phrases: "Good" and "Very good!" but subtle variations in accentuation and intonation could endow them with infinite gradations of praise. In the present instance, "Good" implied "Satisfactory. Not bad for a beginner." Danbury interpreted it in this sense and was pleased, for Inspector Chesilton demanded a high standard from his subordinates when promotions were considered.

When the sergeant brought the Aladdin lamp, the inspector turned to the police surgeon.

"Perhaps you'd have a look at him"—he nodded towards the body—"before we take the photographs. You won't move him, of course. The sergeant will hold the lamp for you."

The doctor made a cursory examination.

"He's quite dead," he reported. "He must have been killed instantly. It looks as though the shot had been fired at close range. But what was he wearing rubber gloves for?"

Constable Danbury started as though stung, and an uncomfortable flush stole over him. Of all the damned idiots! To miss a thing like that! In this moment of chagrin, he forgot the mitigating factors: the uncertain light of his flash lamp and the effect which that ghastly face had made upon him when he examined the body.

"Rubber gloves?" echoed the inspector, in a musing tone. "No fingerprints, then. That clears one source of confusion out of your way, Wootton," he added, turning to the fingerprint expert. "And now, I think we'll get through with the photographing. There don't seem to be any footprints, so we can move about as we like."

The *Police Code* had instructed Danbury in the routine of a preliminary investigation, but he had never seen one carried out in practice. He watched alertly, storing up in his memory a number of what he called "useful tips." The photographer's flashlights flared up and died away. The fingerprint expert examined any smooth surfaces likely to show marks, and apparently concentrated on the French window and the pair of shoes on the mantelpiece.

The inspector and the police surgeon examined the body, taking copious notes of its attitude, and marking its position by chalk lines on the floor. Even its clothes and their disturbance were noted. Then the doctor took the body temperature and inspected the shattered head once again.

As he was finishing his task, steps sounded on the bare boards outside and Sir Clinton entered, followed by Wendover, both bareheaded. At the sight of the Chief Constable, Danbury stiffened a little. Here was the man, above all others, who could open or close the gate of promotion, the man too who was the final assessor of those "special qualifications" which the constable hoped that he possessed. And then he recalled that oversight of his in the matter of the rubber gloves. Not much "special qualification" about *that*, he reflected bitterly.

Sir Clinton greeted the inspector and the police surgeon. Chesilton knew Wendover, as it chanced, so no introduction was needed.

"We had to change a wheel on the way down," Sir Clinton explained, as though apologising for a delay. "If you don't mind, though, I'd like to have things at first-hand. Who discovered the body?"

Constable Danbury stepped forward and clicked his heels as he came to attention.

"Ah! You found it? Well, tell me about it."

For the second time, Danbury told his tale in his official language.

"I missed the fact that he has rubber gloves on his hands, sir," he acknowledged, at the end of his recital. "Doctor Fyefield Smith observed that."

Sir Clinton nodded.

"This electric light wasn't here when you came in? I noticed as I passed through the hall that the fittings aren't in place."

"No, sir. All the light I had was my own lamp."

"So you just had to poke about as best you could? Not much wonder you missed the gloves. In that light, they must have looked more or less like reddish skin. Now what about this sketch you made of the pool of paint?"

Danbury produced his notebook and handed it to the Chief Constable.

"I thought, sir, since it was overturned in the scuffle—or so I supposed—it might supply confirmatory evidence as to the time when the murder was committed. By upsetting another paintpot filled to the same original level, sir, and noting something about the rate at which the pigment spread out, I mean. You can see it's changed its contour, even since I made that sketch."

"It has," agreed the Chief Constable, with a glance at the floor. "A good idea, Danbury. But as you heard the shot yourself, did you not think that it was evidence enough as to the time of the murder?"

"I thought it was just as well to have all the evidence I could get, sir," said Danbury, not quite sure if his superior was laughing at him or not.

Sir Clinton nodded in a noncommittal fashion.

"Somebody had trodden in the paint pool, and you satisfied yourself that it wasn't done by a man wearing these shoes on the mantelpiece?"

"So far as I could, without disturbing them, sir."

"Just have a look, Inspector," Sir Clinton suggested. Chesilton drew on a pair of rubber gloves and lifted each shoe in turn to examine the sole.

"No paint here, sir," he reported, much to Danbury's relief.

"And none on the dead man's soles, either," said the Chief Constable. "So a third pair of shoes must have been in the room this evening. Did you find a handbag or anything of that sort?" he demanded, turning to Danbury.

"No, sir."

"Or a piece of brown paper and some string?"

"I didn't notice any, sir."

"Well, chevy around and see if you can find any. It may have been pitched on the floor behind some of these planks, or out into the garden. Get hold of it if you can. It may have a label on it."

Sir Clinton turned to Doctor Fyefield Smith, who had now finished his operations.

"Not much in it, I suppose, Doctor?"

The police surgeon shook his head.

"He's not been dead long, an hour at the outside, I should say. The body temperature hasn't dropped to any great extent. But you know that's not a reliable test."

"You don't want to do anything else?"

"Not here," said Doctor Fyefield Smith. "If you've nothing you want me to do, I'll get off home. Your message broke up a bridge table, and I told the others to wait for me for a while. They'll still be there, if I hurry."

"I'd like you to take a sample of his blood," Sir Clinton suggested.

"I'll make a note of it and do so when the body comes down to the mortuary," the surgeon assured him. "That's all? Then, good night."

"And now, Inspector," Sir Clinton said, as the doctor clattered away along the hall, "I'm abreast of the facts. Go ahead with your investigation."

Inspector Chesilton walked over and picked up the blood-stained handkerchief, bringing it back and exhibiting it to Sir Clinton.

"Fairly soaked in gore, sir," he commented, holding it gingerly. "There ought to be some drippings from it." He shook it out and examined the fabric. "No name or initials, so far as I can see. May be a laundry mark, though. But what possessed the fellow to dip a handkerchief in the blood and then throw it away. . . ."

"There are some spots over there," Wendover pointed to the floor not far from the painted margin between the door and the hearth. "Liquid of some sort, anyhow. I happened to catch a glint reflected from it. It may be paint, of course."

"Don't touch it, Inspector!" ordered Sir Clinton sharply, as Chesilton moved forward. "You've got that blood on the handkerchief in your hand. Sergeant, put some protection over these patches. Mr. Wendover will show you exactly where they are. When you get daylight to work by, Inspector, you might try if you can get a sample of these drops. Wash the place with normal saline—don't use water, whatever you do—and absorb some of the liquid in cotton wool. Keep it separate from everything else when you've got it. That handkerchief puzzles me a bit, and we'll need to go cautiously."

"Very good, sir. I'll just put this handkerchief into an envelope and seal it up. Then I guess I'd better wash my gloves, if I can get the water turned on here. It'll be off at present. In the meanwhile, perhaps you'd like the sergeant to search the body."

Sergeant Vorley had no nerves, and he set about his task with no reluctance. Instructing Constable Danbury to note down each article as it was found, he dived into the dead man's pockets and laid out his captures methodically on the floor.

"Left breast pocket: no handkerchief. Just a moment . . . no, he hasn't one in his sleeve, either. Right breast pocket: a notecase, containing . . . fourteen one-pound notes and six ten-shilling notes. Left side pocket: empty. Top left waistcoat pocket: self-filling fountain pen. Lower left-hand waistcoat pocket: empty. Both right-hand waist-coat pockets: empty. Right-hand jacket pocket outside . . ."

He paused, struggling with some object which resisted extraction.

"Here, come out, you," he remarked in an undertone. Then, with a wrench, he produced the thing and held it up.

"I don't know rightly how you'd describe this, sir. Seems to be a club of some sort, homemade."

Wendover saw a piece of dark wood about seven inches long, which seemed to have been sawed off a heavy office ruler. Round one end, a massive lead bandage had been wrapped and secured in place by twisted copper wire. The thing was obviously a "cosh," a murderous little bludgeon.

"Not an altogether harmless gentleman," Sir Clinton commented, "if that turns out to be his own property. The fingerprints may tell us, if there are any on it."

Sergeant Vorley laid the deadly little thing on the floor and stolidly continued his search:

"Right trouser pocket: nine-and-sixpence in silver. Left-hand trouser pocket: sevenpence ha'penny in coppers. Hip pocket: buttoned up and empty. That's the lot, so far as contents go."

He made some further investigation and then reported:

"The coat hanger at the neck of the jacket's just a plain tape. No name on it. . . . The tailor's label inside the breast pocket's been cut away."

"So every ordinary clue to his identity's been removed, either by himself or by the man who did him in," commented the inspector. "That's a nuisance, unless we can get him identified by someone who knew him."

Constable Danbury entered the room with a crumpled-up sheet of brown paper in his hands.

"I found it out in the garden, sir," he reported. "It was concealed behind some lupins. Somebody might have chucked . . . thrown it there from this window. I marked the place, sir."

Chesilton put out his hand, but Sir Clinton adroitly interposed and took the paper from the constable. "You've got rubber gloves on, Inspector. Just a moment."

He unfolded the paper carefully, sniffed it once or twice, and then held it out to Chesilton.

"Mind keeping your hands behind you?"

Chesilton bent forward and sniffed in his turn at the inner surface of the paper.

"Rubbery smell, undoubtedly, sir. I suppose that means he had his rubber gloves in this?"

"Or his tennis shoes. Or both," amplified the Chief Constable. "Let's see what the creases look like. It's fairly stiff paper and it's kept them well."

He laid the paper on the floor, handling it gingerly to avoid leaving his own fingerprints upon it.

"Looks as if it had been wrapped round a pair of shoes, certainly," he said, eyeing it. "Not many things would leave folds just like these. Question is: which shoes? Once it's been through Wootton's hands, you might try folding it round that pair on the mantelpiece and also the tennis shoes he's got on his feet. If it fits neither, then possibly the third, missing pair, may have come here in the parcel."

"When it gets light, I'll put someone on to look for the twine it was tied up with," the inspector decided. "If it was any fancy stuff, it might save some trouble. So far, the most characteristic point

I've noted about him was that he seems to have been a non-smoker. He'd no smoking materials about him, not even a matchbox."

He seemed to strike a fresh idea, for he took a magnifying glass from his pocket, borrowed Danbury's flash lamp, went down on his knees and studied the floor boards carefully at the point where the missing pair of shoes had been scrubbed on the floor to free them from paint. Soon he rose again, with a shrug.

"Nothing in it. I thought if the fellow had slightly worn shoes, the nails would project above the leather and leave scratches on the wood, when he rubbed hard on it. Nothing of the sort there, though."

Sir Clinton moved across the room and examined the body.

"Not much to be made out of that in its present state," he admitted, with a faint, expressive gesture. "He might be in the late thirties or early forties, at a guess." He turned to Danbury and pointed to the unbroken thread on the French window handles. "Your mark? Nobody got in, then, after you came on the scene. By the way, just go and see if the gate of the garden's locked or not."

Danbury returned in a few seconds.

"Locked, sir, but the key's there, inside."

Chesilton was fidgeting slightly.

"Is there anything else, sir, before we begin to shift things, and make a thorough search of the premises? Wootton has been over it all already."

The Chief Constable shook his head.

"I've seen all I want to see, thanks. Go ahead as soon as you please."

Chesilton drew his chalk from his pocket and marked the outlines of the various objects on the floor: the paint-pots, the planks, the newspaper, the blood drops, and the handkerchief which he had removed. Then, under his direction, the sergeant and Danbury made a most minute search of the apartment. They lifted the planks, raked the ashes in the grate, went over the floor, a square foot at a time, but discovered nothing which seemed of the slightest importance.

"No pistol here," the inspector reported finally. "We may find it in the garden, sir, when we get light to search by. But I expect he carried it off with him."

"I'd like to see the bottom of these paintpots," Sir Clinton suggested. "Not that I expect to find a pistol in them."

If Inspector Chesilton had overlooked the paintpots, he did not give himself away.

"Of course, sir. The pistol was what I really wanted just now. It might have had fingerprints. And, as you say, it couldn't well be hidden in a paintpot only half full, like these. It must have been a fairly heavy-calibred one, by the look of him."

He stepped over to the group of paintpots and then hesitated.

"I'd rather strain the paint through a sieve, sir," he said tentatively. "I don't like mixing things up by pouring from one pot into another, and I don't want to pour the paint away."

"Oh, feel around with a pencil in the meantime," the Chief Constable suggested. "You'll get anything of a reasonable size that way. You can use a sieve later on."

The inspector took a long pencil from his pocket and began groping with it in each pot in turn, cleaning his probe after each attempt so as to avoid contaminating one paint with the other. Two pots yielded nothing, but in the third he made a find.

"There's something here, sir," he exclaimed. "Some little thing. I'll get it out in a jiffy."

Probing and scraping with his pencil, he wedged the object against the side of the pot, and then, after several failures, brought it to the surface of the paint and seized it.

"Not much need to bother about fingerprints after that treatment," he said, pulling out his handkerchief and cleaning the adhering paint away. "It's a letter in gold—or something like it," he corrected himself cautiously. "Got a little ring at the top of it and two or three links of fine gold chain broken short. It looks like some sort of ornament, sir."

He held it out for inspection on his palm, and Wendover saw a little golden object about an inch long.

At the sight of it, some vague recollection swam up in his mind, but try as he would, it eluded him and he could not connect it with anything that seemed relevant. Sir Clinton examined the letter reflectively.

"That little ring at the top of it isn't broken?" he asked. "Just turn it round and see if it's made out of gold wire."

"It's solid, sir. No break in it. Made by twisting a heavy wire into a circle, threading it through a hole in the T and then welding the ends together. Quite a solid bit of workmanship."

Just at that moment, Geddington's voice was heard raised in tones of angry expostulation in the entrance hall of the flats.

"And you say my guests can't go home?"

Wendover heard the low level tones of the constable on guard but he could not catch the words. They seemed to excite Geddington to a higher pitch of indignation.

"It's monstrous; monstrous, I tell you, Constable! Do you mean to tell me that my two guests have to remain here imprisoned— yes, imprisoned, I say—at the pleasure of some jackanapes in of- fice? You can't prevent peaceable citizens going home when they want to. This is England, isn't it? Not Russia?"

"Very sorry, sir," said the constable courteously, "but my or- ders are not to let anyone leave the premises."

"And who gave you these orders? He'll hear more of this, I promise him! Who gave these outrageous orders? I ask people in to play bridge, and this sort of thing happens! Mrs. Karslake's a very nervous lady. She nearly fainted. Mrs. Geddington had to give her brandy. A nice experience for two ladies, just because some jack-in-the-box pops up and behaves as if he was a Continental dictator. Who gave you these orders?"

"Inspector Chesilton, sir. You'll have to get his permission before anyone leaves the premises."

"His permission!" cried Geddington, and proceeded to give a further exposition of his views.

Sir Clinton gave the inspector a quizzical glance.

"You seem a shade unpopular," he said. "Shall we go out and try a dose of soothing syrup? The sooner we interview these people, the sooner they can get off home."

The inspector nodded and, thrusting the little gold ornament into his vest pocket, he followed Sir Clinton out into the entrance hall.

"This is Inspector Chesilton, sir," the constable explained.

Geddington turned on the inspector.

"Oh, so you are the fellow who's causing all this bother? A nice affair this! These ladies upstairs, scared by your bungling methods! You'll hear more of this, I can guarantee that."

"I'm very sorry, Mr. Geddington," Sir Clinton intervened. "I quite appreciate your feelings about your guests. But a man's been killed, in there, and we have to find who did it. I'm sure that you will cooperate with us in getting the information we need."

Geddington was unpacified.

"And who are you?" he demanded. "Another of these inspectors, running about giving absurd orders?"

"This is the Chief Constable, Sir Clinton Driffield," Chesilton explained, in a crushing tone.

Geddington was at heart a little snob. Sir Clinton's title had its effect. So had his local reputation. Geddington was delighted to find that circumstances had forced him into distinguished company. Already he could see himself telling his friends, "As I explained to Sir Clinton . . ."—"As Sir Clinton said to me . . ." His change of front was shamelessly abrupt.

"Pleased indeed to meet you, Sir Clinton," he said, holding out a hand. "I'm afraid, perhaps, that I let my feelings run away with me, just a little. The duty of a host to his guests, you understand, I'm sure. And naturally, the ladies have been very much disturbed by all this; very upset, as I'm sure you guess. But of course I'd no intention of interfering with your taking all possible steps to capture this . . . this dastardly criminal. Quite the contrary. You can count on me to do everything I can to help in any way I can. Only too delighted to be of any service to you."

"You can't do much, obviously," Sir Clinton said, rather coldly, for the abuse of the constable rankled in his mind. "We must get statements from you all about the beginning of the affair: the firing of the shot. After that, your guests will be free to leave at their own convenience. Shall we go upstairs now?"

Even this douche did not damp Geddington's newfound ardour.

"Oh, certainly, certainly," he exclaimed. "We shall do all we can, you can be sure. Will you follow me, Sir Clinton? We shall be delighted to show you over our flat and to give any possible information you may need, if you'll only tell us what you want."

And with the backward glance of a dog trotting in front of its master, he began, rather puffingly, to ascend the stairs leading to the upper flats. Sir Clinton, Wendover, and the inspector followed him up.

4
THE PEOPLE UPSTAIRS

"This is Sir Clinton Driffield, my dear," announced Geddington importantly, as he ushered his unlooked-for guests into the drawing-room of the second-floor flat. "This is my wife, Sir Clinton. This is Mrs. Karslake, and her son, Mr. Karslake. And Mr. . . . . er . . . What's your name? . . . er . . . Mr. Barbican."

His introduction entirely ignored Wendover and the inspector.

Mrs. Geddington was a feminine counterpart of her husband: stout, high-coloured, with the air of one who thinks a good deal of herself. She gave the impression of being a woman who would quarrel with her maids and lose her temper with waiters. Mrs. Karslake was a frail-looking person, rather older than her hostess; and at that moment she was evidently suffering severely from nerves. Young Karslake was a man about thirty, of a stolid unimaginative type. Physically he was of much the same build as Barbican, the reporter, who stood on the hearth-rug, taking in the scene with the utmost coolness and detachment. A bridge table, with scattered cards and markers, stood under the light, in the centre of the room.

Sir Clinton rather distantly acknowledged the greeting of his involuntary hostess; then, after exchanging a glance with his subordinate, he came to business at once.

"Inspector Chesilton has some questions he would like to ask."

The inspector took his cue immediately.

"Perhaps Mr. Geddington wouldn't mind giving his version of this affair. Then I could ask any questions that occur to me."

By this time Geddington had become quite tractable.

41

"Certainly, certainly," he said, "if it's a matter of public duty, Sir Clinton, I've no objection, none whatever. Shall I begin at the beginning?"

"Say at dinnertime," Sir Clinton suggested.

"At dinnertime? Very good, Sir Clinton. We had dinner as usual, Mrs. Geddington and I; and after that we came in here, leaving the maid to clear up the dining-room. She waited until Mrs. Karslake and her son arrived. That would be about nine o'clock?" He glanced at young Karslake for confirmation and received a nod of agreement. "The maid went away, after that, didn't she, my dear?"

"Yes," Mrs. Geddington corroborated. "She's a daily maid, Sir Clinton. I don't like servants in the flat at night."

"We settled down to play bridge. We had invited Mrs. Karslake and her son to come round for a game. I don't remember anything much for a time after that, except that my partner and I got a little slam in hearts. We were playing for threepence a hundred, I should say. Not gambling, by any means, just a quiet rubber or two. Then, all of a sudden, as I was dealing—I remember that distinctly—we heard a loud report from down below us."

"Your windows are open," interjected the inspector. "Were they open at that time?"

"Yes, yes, on a warm night like this, of course they were open," Geddington answered testily. "In fact, now I come to think of it, I seem to remember that the sound came both from below and through the open window. Isn't that so?" He appealed to the company and young Karslake nodded again.

"Exactly!" Geddington continued. "As soon as we heard the noise, I said, 'Isn't that a pistol shot? Somebody must be shooting.' And Mrs. Karslake, who is rather nervous, was a little upset. She got out of her chair and turned pale; and Mrs. Geddington also rose— didn't you, my dear?—and went to the window and looked out."

"Did you see anything, ma'am?" inquired the inspector, interrupting Geddington's flow of narrative.

Mrs. Geddington shook her head.

"No, I'm just a little short-sighted, and I saw nothing that seemed out of the common. But I said to Mr. Geddington, 'You must go and see what's the matter. We can't have this sort of thing, firing off pistols and what not, in a flat of this kind. A pretty state of things to happen when one invites guests to one's house.' Mrs. Karslake was very startled, you understand, and as her hostess I felt responsible, to some extent."

"Yes," the inspector admitted. "Very awkward, ma'am. And so, Mr. Geddington . . . ?"

"And so I hurried off down the stairs to see about it," Geddington continued, "to make a complaint, if I could find a constable, and to make sure, you understand, that a stop was put to this sort of thing. Very natural, in the circumstances."

"As you ran downstairs, did you notice whether the door of the flat below you was open or closed?"

Geddington took out his handkerchief and wiped his brow as if to stimulate thought.

"Did I notice that? Well, to tell you the truth, no, I didn't notice it. It may have been, or again, it may not. I can't say, I really can't say definitely. I certainly don't remember noticing that. But there was nobody about, nobody on the stairs as I passed. That I do remember, quite clearly."

"And did you notice that the door of the ground-floor flat was ajar?" demanded the inspector.

"No, I didn't notice anything of that sort. I was very angry about this noise, you can understand, quite naturally, I think, and I didn't trouble about anything else. I thought it was a silly prank on somebody's part; of course, I'd no idea that it was—well, what it turned out to be."

"Suppose a man had been concealed in the downstairs flat— the ground-floor one, I mean—would he have had time to escape from it during your absence outside?"

"Not by the front entrance," Geddington asserted. "I would have seen him, if he'd come out."

"I wasn't thinking of the front entrance," the inspector explained. "What I meant was: Could he have made his way upstairs while your back was turned? There's a flat above this, isn't there?"

At this dim suggestion that the murderer might be still concealed on the premises, Mrs. Karslake had another nervous attack and was revived with brandy.

"I think we had better adjourn to another room," Sir Clinton suggested to Geddington. "This isn't very good for Mrs. Karslake."

When they reached the dining-room, the inspector made his suggestion plainer.

"I put it to you, sir, that the murderer might have escaped upstairs while you were out in the street with the constable. Who occupies the top flat?"

"A newly married couple, I believe," Geddington answered. "Broseley's their name, I think. They've only come here lately. Mrs. Geddington left cards on them, as a matter of politeness, but we don't know them. They've gone away—for the week-end, I believe, from something Mrs. Geddington said."

"There's no communication between their flat and the ones next door?" demanded the inspector. "No balconies or anything of that kind?"

Geddington shook his head.

"Now about the flat below," the inspector went on. "Who occupies it?"

"A Mr. and Mrs. Sternhall," Geddington answered, with a curious expression on his face. "We don't know them. They're not quite . . . well, to tell you the truth, they're not quite the sort of people we want to know. I'm not a snob, of course, but . . . well, they aren't quite in our class, you see. The man's away a good deal—a kind of commercial traveller, or something of that sort, I imagine. And his wife's French. She teaches French, and . . . well, you can understand that one doesn't like a whole lot of people tramping up to her flat at all times of the day. It's not quite nice. Nothing *wrong* about it, of course. Don't mistake my meaning, because I don't mean *that*, of course. But still . . ."

Wendover chanced at this moment to glance at the face of the journalist and was surprised to see on it a smile as if Barbican was enjoying some obscure joke. It seemed as though the reporter also was amused by the rank snobbery of Geddington.

". . . still," Geddington continued, "one doesn't like that kind of thing. It isn't quite in keeping . . ." ("with our high tone" Wendover supplied contemptuously to himself). "We complained about it after we took this flat, but we got no satisfaction from the lawyers who manage the place. They said we should have made fuller inquiries before we signed the lease. As if that was the sort of thing one expected to find."

"Hm!" said the inspector rather unsympathetically. "Very awkward, I suppose. But they conduct themselves quietly? No rows on the stair, or anything of that sort? No? Quite orderly people? I'm afraid we can do nothing for you, Mr. Geddington. And now, just another question. Can you say exactly what time the shot was fired?"

Geddington shook his head.

"No," he admitted. "I didn't look at my watch. It didn't strike me at the time. Did you happen to look, Karslake?"

Karslake shook his head. He seemed to be a taciturn person.

"And you?" asked Sir Clinton, turning to Barbican.

"Me? Lord, no! I wasn't on in this scene at all. I'm a journalist." Then, with a friendly and rather attractive smile, he asked, "Have you anything for me, Sir Clinton? An interview? Or an official statement? It means a good deal to me. You see, I've got a scoop over this affair."

Sir Clinton shook his head with an answering smile.

"If you've brought your salt-cellar, you'll have to take it away again, Mr. Barbican. But possibly Inspector Chesilton may be inclined to do something for you later on."

Barbican took his rebuff in good part.

"Well, I hope you'll bear in mind that I was first in the field," he said. "I heard somebody shouting 'Murder!' and simply flew round here as fast as I could sprint."

"Didn't even stop to tie your shoelaces, I notice," said Sir Clinton, surveying the mixture of clothing in the journalist's attire. "I think I'd do it now, if I were you, or you might trip over them."

Barbican cast a comical glance at his feet.

"Proof of my zeal," he commented. "You and your colleagues have got your shoes tied neatly, I notice. But I was on the spot before you, alert if untidy."

He stooped down and fastened the laces of his tennis shoes. The inspector turned to Karslake.

"Anything you could add to Mr. Geddington's story, sir?"

Karslake shook his head.

"No. My mother turned faint, and I had to look after her, with Mrs. Geddington's help. I haven't left this flat since I came into it after dinner."

Chesilton glanced at Sir Clinton.

"I don't think we need trouble these ladies," he suggested. "If Mr. Karslake can tell us nothing, they'll have nothing to say, either."

Barbican finished tying his laces and stood up.

"You won't address the meeting, Sir Clinton? Say a few words?" He grew serious of a sudden. "It means a good deal to me, you see."

"What paper do you represent?" Sir Clinton asked.

"None, at present, worse luck," Barbican answered ruefully. "I'm a free lance. If I could work this scoop properly, I might get on to one of the staffs. Couldn't you give me something—just a line or two?" he ended, with a serious note of pleading in his tone.

Sir Clinton glanced at the inspector.

"The most I can do for you, Mr. Barbican," Chesilton said, "is to promise you the first news of an arrest—if you happen to be available at the time," he added hastily. "In the meantime, I can't prevent your interviewing Mr. Geddington."

"Oh, that's done already," Barbican assured him, with a broad grin which showed his white teeth. "I was first in the field there, too. Zeal, again."

The inspector ignored the gibe and turned to Geddington.

"You'll have to look at the body downstairs, Mr. Geddington, to see if you recognise the man. We haven't got him identified yet."

Geddington turned slightly green at this suggestion. He had seen Danbury's face just after the discovery of the body, and he knew that he had an unpleasant experience ahead of him. However, he consented, though with obvious reluctance.

"Thanks," said Chesilton in reply. "Now I think, sir, we'd better go downstairs. If you'll wait for us on the landing below this, Sir Clinton, I'll come up again after these gentlemen have inspected the body."

Wendover had half expected Chesilton to exhibit the golden T and ask if anyone could identify it; but he said nothing, reflecting that the inspector probably had sound reason for not producing it.

A few minutes later, Chesilton rejoined his companions on the first-floor landing.

"No luck, sir, I'm afraid," he reported. "Neither of them recognised the fellow. No great wonder, perhaps, considering the state he's in at present. I've got rid of that reporter fellow, and I've told Geddington to go down to the mortuary and have another look, after the body's been made more presentable."

"Just as well," Sir Clinton agreed. "What about that gold ornament? I saw you kept it up your sleeve while the reporter was in the offing."

"I showed it to all of them upstairs, once I turned Barbican out," Chesilton reported, with a faint smile. "They're not to say anything about it, sir. I don't think they will, after I talked to them. We've drawn a complete blank there, though. None of them recognised it. I could see that from their faces."

Sir Clinton nodded his agreement with the inspector's policy.

"And now, what about the top flat? It's unlikely; but still the man we're after may have secreted himself there."

"Danbury tells me, sir, that the Broseleys left their keys at the station. The Superintendent allowed it. Mrs. Broseley's nervous about burglars, it seems. I'm going to get their present address and ring up for permission to enter their premises. In the meantime, I've taken precautions so that nobody can get out of the flat without being spotted."

"That's sound," Sir Clinton approved. "And now, suppose we see what Mrs. Sternhall has to say."

Nothing loath, the inspector pressed the bell button. For a few moments there was silence, then light steps approached, and the door was cautiously opened.

Wendover, from Geddington's description, expected to see a middle-aged, rather slovenly vulgarian; and the woman who appeared on the threshold took him a little by surprise. She was apparently in her early thirties. Dark-haired, dark-eyed, slim in her black dinner gown relieved only by the paste buckles on her shoes and a flash of brilliants when she moved her hand, she presented a complete contrast to the chromatic conflict favoured by Mrs. Geddington in evening dress. Wendover inwardly paid a rather grudging tribute to her looks, for the squareness of her jaw and chin was not altogether to his taste.

"I know that type," he persuaded himself. "As soft as a kitten in some ways, and as hard as nails in other directions." He liked a pretty girl, but this dark slim woman seemed in no need of protection. Her red lips set into a harder cast as she saw the three men on the landing before her.

"What is it that you wish?" she demanded, glancing from face to face with suspicious eyes. "It is very late to come ringing at my door. My maid has gone to bed long ago."

Her precise English, with its underlying suggestion of an alien idiom, the fluctuations in the pitch of her voice, and the faint trilling of her "r" sounds all betrayed the foreigner.

"You are Mrs. Sternhall, I believe? I'm Inspector Chesilton."

"You are of the police?"

Wendover saw a fleeting expression of alarm on her face and put his own interpretation on it. These Continentals didn't look on the police as an Englishman does. They were afraid of their *gendarmerie*. Naturally a Frenchwoman would feel nervous at a sudden visit at this time of night.

"There's nothing to be scared about," the inspector explained soothingly. "I merely want to ask if you've noticed anything out of the common in the last hour or two."

She reflected for a moment or two before answering.

"No, nothing extraordinary." Then she seemed to remember one thing. "Some time ago I heard a firework set off which made a report. Some child amusing itself, quite close,—next door, perhaps."

"No one has entered your flat in the last hour or two?"

She shook her head very decidedly.

"And you heard nothing out of the common?" reiterated Chesilton, rather incredulously. "This crowd at the door . . . ?"

"Perhaps Mrs. Sternhall was sitting at the back of the house," Sir Clinton suggested.

"Yes, of course," she agreed. "I was with my brother-in-law in my sitting-room. Ah! There was one thing I remember. My brother-in-law saw someone running across the gardens and spoke to me about it."

"I must see your brother-in-law, then, Mrs. Sternhall," the inspector explained. "He's still with you, I think. May we come in?"

Mrs. Sternhall looked at the trio doubtfully for a moment or two, as though considering her course. Then, with rather an ill grace, she stood back and allowed them to enter the flat. Chesilton, bringing up the rear, took the precaution to leave the front door ajar, so that he could call up reinforcements in case of emergency. Mrs. Sternhall led them into the sitting-room, where a man in a dark lounge suit of rather foreign cut was sitting in an armchair.

"These gentlemen are of the police," she explained, and turning to Chesilton she added, "This is my brother-in-law, Monsieur Raymond Dujardin. He understands English and speaks it well enough."

Dujardin heaved himself up from his chair as they entered the room. Though not much above middle height, he gave the impression of massiveness, which was reinforced by the deliberateness of all his movements. Wendover put him down as a man who had probably begun life in the lower middle class—a small shopkeeper or something of the sort—but who had got on in the world and risen financially, without losing the stamp of his origin. His small, close-set eyes and low brow under the stiff close-cropped hair did not impress Wendover very favourably.

Chesilton wasted no time in preliminaries.

"Mrs. Sternhall tells me that you heard a sound which caught your attention this evening," he said, with deliberate vagueness. "Would you mind giving us a description of what took place?"

Dujardin exchanged a glance with his sister-in-law, but she merely nodded noncommittally in answer. When he spoke, it was manifest that he had a liking for the "historical present" tense in his narratives.

"I do not quite know what you wish me to say," he began very reasonably. "I begin with dinner. We sit at table, my sister-in-law and I. The maid is in the kitchen. I hear a noise, something being overturned, in the kitchen, no doubt. I say to Madame Sternhall, 'Your *bonne* has spilt something, our next course, perhaps?' Madame says, 'She is always breaking dishes and chipping cups. And she denies it each time. Just watch.' So when the *bonne* comes clattering in with more dishes—and she is noisy, indeed—Madame asks her what she has been spilling, and she denies. She denies it violently. Madame looks at me and shrugs her shoulders. And we stop talking while the *bonne* clatters the dishes in setting them on her tray. Clumsiness! Incredible, I assure you."

Nothing in Chesilton's expression betrayed that all this was beside the point.

"That was at dinnertime?" he inquired, as if the matter was important.

"At dinnertime. About half-past seven. But I cannot see . . ."

"Did you hear any other sounds that struck you?" the inspector demanded, cutting him short.

"Yes, indeed," Dujardin replied, with a shrug of his shoulders. "I heard her washing up dishes after dinner. I heard little else till she was finished. She is a noisy one!"

"But in the end, I suppose, she finished her work and went to bed," the inspector said. "Did you hear anything notable after things had quieted down in the kitchen?"

"Yes," Dujardin explained. "After dinner, I sit over there, by the open window. I talk with Madame about business, engrossing matters. We hear the tennis players beyond the garden. It grows darker. All of a sudden—pan!—I hear a noise which makes me start. Then I recognise it and I say, '*Tiens! Un pétard?*' I am an amateur of pyrotechnics myself. I sit, waiting to hear more. None comes. Then I think perhaps they set off a *feu d'artifice*. I go to the window and look out. Nothing! Some small boy has been amusing himself. I look about and in the next garden, over there"—he waved his hand towards Sans Souci Avenue—"I see a figure climbing the wall into the next garden."

"Would you recognise him if you saw him again?"

"Oh, no, no," Dujardin replied. "The light was too feeble for that."

"You thought nothing of it?"

"I supposed that he had by mischance dropped something over the wall into the next garden and that he was climbing over to recover it. Why else should he make the escalade?"

Chesilton changed the subject.

"When did you come here tonight?"

"About seven o'clock. Was it not then?" he turned to Mrs. Sternhall, who nodded in confirmation.

"And you haven't left the flat since then, either of you? Not to post a letter, or anything of that sort?"

"No," said Mrs. Sternhall, intervening; "we sat and talked, just as M. Dujardin has told you."

"Did you hear anything further?" the inspector demanded, returning to the charge.

"Yes, I did," Dujardin explained. "About half-past ten or later, it may be, I heard people moving about in the flat below here, and sounds of things being dragged here and there. I say to Madame, 'This is a noisy place indeed! What are they doing now?' She explains to me that decorators are busy in the flat below. They are working beyond hours—overtime, you call it? By and by, we hear no more of it."

"When did your maid go to bed?" Chesilton asked, turning to Mrs. Sternhall.

"I do not know exactly. Half-past nine, perhaps. She was not well. She had a migraine, she told me. I gave her some aspirin and told her to take a hot drink and get into bed as quick as possible so as to get to sleep."

"I see. So you and Mr. Dujardin were here together. Where is Mr. Sternhall?"

"My husband is away from home at present," Mrs. Sternhall explained. Then she took the initiative in her turn. "We have answered all your questions. Now will you have the kindness to explain why you come to the door at this late hour of the night and ask us about this and that? I make no complaint, you understand. But one cannot help one's curiosity. It is surprising."

Chesilton had got all that he wanted for the present and there seemed to be no reason for suppressing facts any longer. The thing was already public property.

"I'm sorry to say, Mrs. Sternhall, that someone has been shot on these premises—in the flat downstairs. What you heard was the report of the pistol."

"*Vous entendez*, Raymond?" Mrs. Sternhall gasped, turning to her brother-in-law. "*Un crime a été commis, ci-dessous! On a assassiné quelqu'un!*"

Then, turning back in excitement to Chesilton, she poured out a stream of questions:

"Who is it? One of our neighbours? And have you caught the murderer? No? Have you searched everywhere, thoroughly? Not yet? But then he may be still lurking on the premises, hidden in some corner? It is not safe! He may be at the door now! I shall not be able to sleep tonight!"

Chesilton did his best to soothe her.

"If he's still on the premises, ma'am, we shall have him before he can do any more harm. You needn't be afraid; there'll be a guard over the place tonight and if you're disturbed in any way, you'll have help at hand. You can sleep quietly in your bed. As a matter of fact, he's not on the premises. Unless I'm much mistaken, Mr. Dujardin here saw him running away just after the shot was fired."

Dujardin looked up.

"The man I see escalading the wall?"

"Yes, most likely. By the way, Mr. Dujardin, what's your address? We may need you as a witness at the inquest."

"I am residing at Canterbury and Cochrane's Hotel," Dujardin explained. "My room is booked there for a week."

Chesilton jotted down the address.

"Another thing," he added, as he finished his scribbling; "do either of you recognise this?"

He held out the golden T, but so far as Wendover could see, there was no gleam of recognition on the faces of Mrs. Sternhall and M. Dujardin.

"No, I have never seen it before," Mrs. Sternhall assured him, and Dujardin gave a confirmatory nod.

Chesilton showed no disappointment. He contented himself with stringently cautioning them not to disclose the existence of the trinket to anyone—"least of all to any press man." From their faces, it was dear that he could count on this last injunction being obeyed.

"We haven't identified the man who was shot," the inspector went on. "I'm afraid I'll have to trouble you, Mr. Dujardin, to have a look at him, just in case he happens to be known to you. We can't afford to overlook even an off-chance, in a case of this sort."

"No, I have no objection," said Dujardin, with a shrug. "It is a precaution, *hein*? And if I do not recognise him? You detain me, perhaps? I do not mind, if you will let me telephone to my hotel. It will be all the better if I stay here and keep Madame Sternhall company. She will be less nervous, then. Meanwhile, I am quite at your disposition."

"A good idea," Chesilton said approvingly. "I see there's a 'phone there. Will you ring up now and say you won't be back to-night?"

Very helpfully he hunted up the number in the directory and gave it to the exchange, surrendering the transmitter to Dujardin as soon as he was through to the hotel. Wendover smiled covertly at Chesilton's astuteness in verifying Dujardin's statements without offence.

Mrs. Sternhall seemed to be reflecting over the situation, but her conclusion was a surprising one when she uttered it.

"This will make it very difficult to let that flat, will it not?"

Before any reply was necessary, Dujardin finished his message and turned to the inspector.

"At your disposition, monsieur."

Chesilton took leave of Mrs. Sternhall, again assuring her that she need not be nervous during the night, and the men turned to leave the room. As the door opened, Barbican appeared on the threshold, and the sight of him caused Mrs. Sternhall to utter a faint cry.

"What are you doing here?" Sir Clinton demanded sharply.

"Zeal, pure zeal," the journalist retorted, unabashed. "Have you anything for me now, Sir Clinton?"

"Our dictionaries seem to differ," Sir Clinton said bluntly. "What yours calls zeal, mine calls impudence."

"The door was open, so I came in," Barbican explained, with less assurance.

"And listened at this door? H'm! Well, Mr. Barbican, the front door is still open. Suppose you go out. Mrs. Sternhall, I'm sure, has no desire for your company. By the way, what's your address?"

"Number 1, Ravenswood Mansions," Barbican answered, in a sulky tone, like a child detected in a fault. "I'm sorry if I've been a nuisance. But this means a lot to me, you know."

"Well, in future you'd better bear in mind that loitering in enclosed premises is a risky trick."

Barbican slunk away, evidently regretting that he had annoyed the Chief Constable and thus lessened his chance of getting any further help from the police.

"We'll go downstairs now," Sir Clinton said to the others. "By the way, Inspector, have you any objection to using Danbury in some of your inquiries? He seems a smart lad. Send him round to question the decorators about access to the flat; and find out who gave them their orders. He can get some paint from them to try out his notions about its rate of flow. Nothing much in it, possibly, but he may as well follow it up. You've got somebody else on his beat, I suppose? Then you'd better send him home to get some sleep. He'll have his hands full tomorrow, if he's working for you."

"Very good, sir," Chesilton acquiesced. "He seems to have kept his eyes open and he might be useful."

When Dujardin had viewed the body, the inspector dismissed him to keep Mrs. Sternhall company, and returned to where Wendover and Sir Clinton were waiting in the hall.

"No good?" the Chief Constable inquired, reading ill success on Chesilton's features.

"No good, sir. You can't wonder at it. The man's own mother would be hard put to it to recognise him in that state. I've told Dujardin to see the body again at the mortuary when we've got it a bit tidier."

Sir Clinton gave a nod of agreement.

"No use looking for footmarks in the gardens till daylight," he commented. "That sort of hunting, in the dark, is worse than useless. Ring me up at once if anything fresh occurs. I'm sorry you'll lose your night's sleep, Inspector. Hard lines! Good hunting!"

Chesilton smiled rather wearily, but made a gesture as much as to say that it was all in the day's work.

"There's just one thing. You might send these blood samples to Doctor Livermere at St. Anne's Hospital and ask him to report on them as soon as he can. He does their blood-transfusion work, doesn't he? Ask him to report on whether the samples are the same type or not. He'll know what I mean."

"Very good, sir."

Wendover and Sir Clinton bade him good night and went off to their waiting car. The inspector returned to the ground-floor flat and gave his instructions to Danbury, who was delighted to find himself picked out for further employment on the case.

"And now, cut along and get some sleep," Chesilton concluded. "I'm letting you off your beat so that you'll be fresh in the morning, so no sitting up and thinking over this affair, mind!"

"Very well, sir."

Constable Danbury strode out of the front entrance to the flats, even more optimistic about his future than he had been three hours earlier. His faith in the *Police Code* was stronger than ever. He knew the section about promotion by heart, and he turned it over in his mind. "Any officer who wishes for early advancement has frequent opportunities of attracting the notice of his superior by some action, evidencing zeal, ability, and judgment, by strict attention to duty, and constant cheerful readiness for any extra work. . . ." And now he was to be entrusted with a bit of work which would show, if he succeeded, that he had those "special qualifications" which would allow him to take the qualifying examination even before the completion of the normal term of service. Jenny would be pleased when she heard that.

His pleasant reverie was interrupted almost before it had well begun. Barbican had been loitering on the pavement a little way down the street, and he now joined the constable.

"Got anything for me?" he demanded.

Danbury shut his lips and shook his head. He had no intention of giving away information.

But the journalist was irrepressible.

"Have they identified the beggar?" he demanded suddenly, as they came under a street lamp; and he scanned Danbury's features keenly, as he put the question.

"Can't say," was the constable's noncommittal reply.

Barbican's shrewd eyes had drawn their own inferences from Danbury's face, however; and he laughed gleefully.

"They haven't. Well, all the better from my point of view. 'VICTIM STILL UNIDENTIFIED.' Keeps the interest alive. Another thrilling instalment tomorrow. The public'll go on reading to see what turns up. Fine! And now I'd better be hopping down to the office, in case anyone gets ahead of me, and see what I can get out of this scoop before anyone else butts in. S'long!"

He waved his hand to Danbury and turned down a side street, walking with long, rapid strides. The constable gazed after him for a moment before continuing his way borne. Callous devil! Here was a man done to death, flung headlong out of the living world. He must have some ties, a wife, a family, a friendly circle which would suffer pain at his tragic exit into the Unknown. What did Barbican care for all that? Nothing! To him, the whole affair was simply "the chance of a scoop."

But they were all like that, Danbury reflected, in some disillusionment. There was Geddington. He had been more bothered about his "ladies" and their feelings than about the fact that a man had been killed: fussing away about those women's nerves so that he hadn't enough breath left to say, "Poor beggar!" Towton? Well, Lord knew what Towton thought about it, but he hadn't overflowed with regrets, anyhow. Then the inspector: he was simply like the photographer and the fingerprint expert, doing a bit of work that was part of his duty. The dead man was just a bit of evidence to him, like the handkerchief and the piece of jewellery. As for the doctor, once he'd done his trick, all he wanted was to get back to his bridge table and his pals. No waste emotion about him! And the Chief Constable: one could see from his face what his interest was: the hunt after the criminal, that was all. And Wendover, his pal: interested, shocked by the brutal details, perhaps, but looking at the thing as a problem which his host would have to get solved somehow. To the whole shoot of them it was just a crossword puzzle of sorts, with a splash of blood across the paper.

And then, from his pinnacle, Constable Danbury came down very suddenly. In the midst of his righteous indignation at other people's callousness, he suddenly recalled his own reactions to the tragedy. "Here's a chance of promotion!" He was no better than the rest of them, after all.

5

THE LOGIC OF THE FACTS

Sir Clinton placed a glass beside Wendover and lifted the whisky decanter from the tray on his study table. "Say when."

"A shade more than usual, thanks, after that experience. . . . When! And not too much soda."

The Chief Constable charged his own glass and went back to his usual seat, where he seemed to fall into a brown study for a few moments.

"Rum business, this," he said at last, in a reflective tone. "What do you make of it, Squire?"

Wendover leaned across, took a cigar from the box on the table, and lit it before replying.

"I'm trying to work out the sequence of events," he said, as he extinguished the match and laid it down.

"Well, let's hear you working. It sounds more convincing, that way."

Wendover appeared to assemble his ideas before speaking again.

"Let's take it logically," he said, rather weightily. "Look at the facts; group them into some order; then see what they suggest as we go along. We'll probably find some gaps. . . ."

"We shall," Sir Clinton interjected drily.

"Well, start at bedrock. Here's a man been murdered in an empty flat."

"How do you know he was murdered in that flat?" the Chief Constable inquired.

"Because I saw his dead body there, of course. I can believe my eyes."

Sir Clinton shook his head.

"So if ever I hear that your dead body, Squire, has been found neatly packed in a trunk, and the trunk is in the left luggage office at Ambledown Station, you expect me to jump to the conclusion that you were murdered on the premises and I'm to arrest the porter in charge? Don't count on it."

"Oh, that's all rot," Wendover declared good-humouredly. "The two cases are quite different."

"Admitted, without ado. All I want is to point out that we must stick to the facts. The facts are that a dead body, male, was discovered in an untenanted flat. . . ."

"By Police Constable Danbury," continued Wendover, mimicking the preciseness, "who arrived at the flats at 9.47 p.m., having been summoned by one Geddington, who had heard a report which was also heard by the constable. My memory for detail isn't so bad," he added, with a certain naïve satisfaction.

"Yes, that seems a fair statement," Sir Clinton admitted.

"On the feet of the body," Wendover continued, "were tennis shoes with rubber soles. On the body's hands were rubber gloves of the sort you can buy in any of these chain stores. In the garden was a piece of brown paper, smelling of rubber. On the mantelpiece of the room was a second pair of shoes, outdoor ones. In the pockets of the body's clothes were some odds and ends, including money and notes, and a homemade life preserver."

"Correct," Sir Clinton admitted.

"The body was rather disfigured, since it had been shot in the face at close range. No pistol was found in the flat—not in the room, at all events."

"Agreed."

"The body had no handkerchief in its pocket. On the floor was a handkerchief, soaked with blood. Further, there were some blood drops on the floor, away from the body and the blood oozing from the wound."

Sir Clinton nodded, as Wendover paused, but he did not interrupt.

"A bucket of paint had been overturned and the paint had flowed over the floor. Someone had stepped in the pool and scrubbed his foot on the planks to clear off the paint. Neither the shoes on the body nor those on the mantelpiece showed any trace of paint on the soles. And in one of the paintpots there was a little gold ornament in the form of a capital T."

Wendover's voice changed ever so slightly as he brought out this last item, and he glanced sharply at the Chief Constable. But Sir Clinton showed no curiosity on the point.

"Finally," he pointed out, "the gate of the back garden was locked, and the key was on the inner side of the door. My congratulations, Squire. You took no notes, and you seem to have remembered everything, so far. Now suppose we stop there for the moment, and you can give me your inferences from the facts, so far as you've stated them. Then we can go on to the next thrilling instalment."

Wendover was not to be drawn into a hurried exposition. He puffed at his cigar for one or two minutes, evidently arranging his ideas into a proper sequence.

"This is how I see the thing, Clinton," he said at last. "There were obviously two men—or two people, anyhow—in that flat just before Danbury arrived. The second person's presence is established by the absence of the pistol that did the business and by the fact that somebody wiped paint from his shoes, while no paint-soiled shoes were found."

"It might have been one of the painters who upset the paint and wiped his shoes clean," the Chief Constable objected, but his tone showed clearly enough that he did not take his own suggestion seriously.

"That's a gap in the evidence. It's your job to fill it, not mine," Wendover retorted, with a smile. "But if a painter upset one of his paintpots, I think he'd have jumped at once to put it straight again, instead of letting his paint go on oozing over the floor."

"Chesilton will clear up that point for us. He's a very thorough fellow. Proceed, Squire."

"We've established that there were two men in the flat," Wendover continued. "Did they come in together, or separately? And how did they get in at all? After their day's work, the painters must have locked up the flat. They wouldn't leave it open to any passerby, seeing that they were leaving their brushes and so forth there all night. I assume that the flat was locked when they went away."

"Chesilton will find that out also," Sir Clinton said. "But assume, if you like, that the flat was locked."

"Then one or other of the two men must have had duplicate keys to the premises."

"Keys?" queried Sir Clinton.

"The garden gate was locked and the key was on the inside. The house agents, whoever they are, would hardly leave that key about for anyone to pick up."

"Very sound, Squire. Chesilton will find out about it."

"Did the two men come in together or separately? I've no doubts on that point, and I don't suppose you have, either. The dead man changed his outdoor shoes for the rubber-soled ones after he got to the flat. He also put on rubber gloves. Couple that with the homemade life preserver in his pocket, and I think it's plain that he came there prepared to attack the other man, and to attack him unexpectedly. The rubber soles would let him creep about noiselessly. The rubber gloves would prevent him from leaving telltale finger marks. Obviously he came to do the other fellow in, if necessary. He arrives first, changes his shoes, puts on his gloves, and waits for the other fellow. I think this means that he must have been the one who had the keys of the premises. Further, he must have made an appointment with the other fellow. It's too big a coincidence that the second man should drop in by accident, just when Number One was ready for him."

"The logic seems all right," Sir Clinton admitted, after a moment's thought. "Now what happened next?"

"The second man arrived by appointment. There was some sort of struggle, in which the paintpot got upset. The newcomer had a pistol with him and shot his antagonist. Then he bolted out of the French window and was seen by Dujardin as he was running away."

"A bloody-minded pair, evidently," Sir Clinton commented. "And now, Squire, to quote your old friend, Macaulay: 'Who slew the slayer?' So far, unfortunately, we don't even know who the would-be slayer was when he was alive."

"Another gap for you to fill," Wendover pointed out, with a smile. "Busy time ahead, for you and your men."

"There's one detail you've omitted from your masterly survey, Squire. Intentionally, I suppose," he added, with a quizzical glance at his companion.

"You mean the gold ornament?" Wendover retorted, with something in his tone that showed he thought he had a surprise in store.

"Yes, the little gold letter in the pot of paint."

"Oh, one of the men was wearing it—on a chain—and it got wrenched off in the scuffle and fell into the paintpot. The murderer didn't notice its fall, so he made no attempt to recover it."

Sir Clinton nodded.

"A golden T," he said enticingly.

Wendover was not to be drawn immediately.

"A golden T?" he said, as though in doubt. "What do you make of it, Clinton?"

Sir Clinton laughed.

"The same as you do, I expect, mystery-monger. It isn't a letter exactly, it's a symbol. It's a Tau cross. How did you happen to spot it?"

"From heraldry," Wendover explained. "As soon as I saw that gold affair, it reminded me of the way the Tau cross is blazoned."

"I struck it first in Sir Thomas Browne's *Garden of Cyrus*," Sir Clinton volunteered. "'*Nor shall we take in the mystical Tau* or the Crosse of our Saviour . . .' and so on. That made me curious, and I hunted it up. It's pretty old. That vigorous gentleman Tertullian wrote about it seventeen centuries ago. *Haec est littera Graecorum* τ, *nostra autem T, species crucis*. I believe it's called St. Anthony's cross too, because it's embroidered on his cope in religious pictures."

"I didn't know you were a student of ecclesiastical history," Wendover commented ironically.

"I'm not," Sir Clinton confessed. "Only, I hate to be puzzled, and that reference in *The Garden of Cyrus* piqued my curiosity."

Wendover took a sip of his whisky and soda and stared across the room for a moment or two.

"Then you think some priest or clergyman may be mixed up in this business?" he demanded at last, with obvious reluctance to accept the idea himself.

Sir Clinton shook his head.

"You're running a bit ahead of the facts, Squire. Lots of people besides priests might carry a cross on a chain—lay brothers, nuns, even laymen of a religious turn of mind or girls with a bent in the same direction. Or the thing may have a merely sentimental value for the wearer—a legacy from an old friend, or something of that sort. Calm yourself! I don't propose to start raiding the neighbouring vicarages on the strength of that little ornament."

"Of course, it might have belonged to the dead man," Wendover suggested.

"Or to the murderer. Or to some unknown party who came on the scene and left it as the only trace of his visit. Or it may even have dropped out of the pocket of some pious house painter, during his work; for there's no real proof that it got torn off in a struggle, you know."

"True, perhaps, but not very helpful," Wendover grumbled.

"No? Perhaps not," the Chief Constable admitted. "Still, unless we can find someone to identify it, I'm afraid that Tau cross doesn't help us much. However, this is a digression, Squire. Go on with your story. What impression did the rest of the *dramatis personæ* make on you?"

Again Wendover paused in reflection before voicing his views.

"I'll take them as we met them," he said at last. "Geddington was the first. I put him down as a fussy little brute, a bit under his wife's thumb, by the look of him, and a rank snob. No real harm in him, probably; but not the sort of man I'd want to have living next door to me."

"It *is* useful to have a handle to one's name at times," Sir Clinton mused, rather irrelevantly.

"Yes. He was rude to the inspector, and then he fairly crawled to you," Wendover said, with a contemptuous smile. "His wife seemed to me much the same. As to the other two, the old lady's faint turn looked to me genuine enough. She'd obviously suffered a shock of some sort."

"And her son? What did you make of him?"

"Not very brisk in the brain. The sort of silent man who keeps quiet simply because he can't think of anything to say. I didn't talk to him, but he was better than that damned journalist."

"Barbican?"

"Yes, that's his name. I've no liking for that brand of ghoul. I hate all this modern business of intruding on people, shoving your way into their houses, and making yourself a nuisance. 'I'm a reporter!' It makes me mad, sometimes, to hear about the way these fellows go bothering the relatives of people who've been killed in some accident. 'I say! Have you heard your husband was killed in a railway accident this morning? No? Well, he was. And now give me a few notes about him for my paper.' Men like that ought to be fried alive in oil."

Sir Clinton knocked the ash from his cigar. He seemed in a captious mood, for he queried Wendover's indictment.

"Put the blame on the right shoulders, Squire. Now, just suppose you're a reporter with a wife and family depending on you. Your editor sends you out to get the information. You get it for him, or you get the sack. The fault's with the man who gives the orders, it seems to me."

"Then that editor ought to be fried."

"Yes, but behind the editor, you've got the proprietor, who insists on the circulation being kept up. The editor's in the same position as the reporter. Get on or get out."

"Well," Wendover sneered, "I'm not going to get sentimental about the wives and families of newspaper proprietors."

"No. But you haven't reached the real culprit yet. If that sort of stuff helps the circulation of a newspaper, it's because the public wants to read just that sort of stuff and will pay money for it. So the ultimate blame for it all lies with the readers."

"Yes," Wendover agreed, "that holds all the way for a reporter on the staff. But this fellow Barbican isn't on the staff. He's a free lance. He could take on this job or leave it alone, to suit himself. He's not doing it under orders. Nobody forced him to come barging in, listening at doors—ugh!—and all that sort of thing. That's over the score, Clinton, and you needn't try to fake up a case to defend it. The man's a complete outsider by all decent standards."

"He's a pushing young fellow, certainly," the Chief Constable admitted, and his tone did not suggest that he altogether admired this particular specimen of the type. "If he gets much out of my men, though, he'll be cleverer than I think he is."

"Then he'll invent something instead," Wendover declared. "That sort wouldn't stick at faking up anything that will sell."

"A stranger might almost think you were getting heated over it," Sir Clinton said ironically. "Let's stick to the facts just now. What did you make of the people on the first floor?"

Wendover seemed this time to have his material ready.

"Mrs. Sternhall's French, of course. I can't say, but she looked to me more like a Parisian than a provincial type. She's a good Catholic, I suspect."

"Oh, you saw that rosary lying on the chair, did you?" Sir Clinton said, with a slight cock of his eyebrows. "I doubt if Chesilton spotted that."

"I can't quite place her," Wendover admitted. "But she seemed to me a shade better class than that brother-in-law of hers. When they speak French—I heard them talking as we left the flat—his accent's different from hers."

"We can check that, later on," the Chief Constable promised. "Did you make anything of Dujardin himself?"

"He's a Norman, by his accent. A 'careful' fellow, I'd guess. He seemed very much struck by things like chipped cups and so forth. A man who'd count his change carefully. Most Normans of that type are pretty keen on money, and can make a sou do a full five centimes' worth of work before they let it out of their hands. Notice his eyes? Rather mean. I'd put him down as a fellow who has got on in the world more by skimping and saving than by any real capacity or big ideas."

"Yes? Now, suppose we leave the thought-reading business and get back to hard facts. Dull, but necessary. What did you make of their evidence?"

"They seemed a bit startled by our intrusion."

"So would you be, if a *sergent de ville* dropped in on you after dinner at a Paris hotel. I'd have thought more of it, if they hadn't been surprised."

"I thought it a bit strange that Dujardin paid no attention to the man climbing over the wall—that is, if there *was* a man."

"A stranger in a strange land's rather apt to turn a blind eye to that sort of thing. Besides, it might have been somebody who was there on quite legitimate business. Dujardin himself gave you his view of it, in that sense."

"It'll be easy enough to tell whether he was lying or not," Wendover conceded. "After the rain this morning, there ought to be footprints on the flower beds, if any man was trying to get over the wall."

"Chesilton will check that as soon as it's light. Until he draws blank, we'll have to assume that the murderer got away via the French window and over the garden wall.

"I don't see why? The key was in the garden gate. Why didn't he go through that, and get off the premises as quick as he could?"

"A sound objection on the face of it," Sir Clinton admitted. "But you only saw the place in the dark. I happen to know what it looks like in the daytime. That back garden gate is in full view of the tennis courts; and even in the dusk those tennis players might have spotted a man escaping that way, and he might have had a hue-and-cry after him, if any of them had recognized that the bang was a pistol shot."

"How do you know that there was anyone at the tennis courts at that time of night?" Wendover demanded.

"Because I saw some people in flannels hanging about the street as we drove up. I know there's a tennis ground behind the house."

"That sounds as if Dujardin's evidence might be accurate, then," Wendover admitted.

"By the way," Sir Clinton demanded, "when Chesilton showed that Tau cross to these people, did you see anything to suggest that it was recognised?"

"No. My impression was that neither of them had ever seen it before. I watched their features, and so far as I could make out, there wasn't a glimmer of recognition anywhere. They just stared at it, as if you'd shown them a lump of coal."

"I thought so, too," Sir Clinton concurred. "Curiosity was all they showed."

He seemed to ponder for a moment or two before continuing.

"Suppose you were in charge of this case, Squire, what would you set about finding out?"

Wendover took another sip from his glass.

"First of all, I'd want to know how the murdered man got access to that empty flat."

"He had a key," Sir Clinton explained. "At least, there was a key on the inner side of the front door of the flat. You missed that, Squire."

Wendover concealed his chagrin at this by putting his demand in a fresh form:

"I'd want to know how he came by the key that he used to get into the flat."

"I expect Chesilton will worry that out before this time tomorrow. Go ahead."

"The next thing I'd want to know was what sort of pistol was used, and what became of it."

"I expect the post mortem will answer the first part. The bullet may be in his head. As to the second part, somebody as yet unknown took the pistol away with him. Beyond that, I don't see how we can go, till we find the second man."

"The third thing I'd want to know would be the whereabouts of a pair of boots or shoes with paint on their soles."

"Call again later. The information bureau's closed at the moment."

"Then I'd want to know who owns or owned that Tau cross."

"So would I, Squire. But I don't see where we are going to get the news. By advertisement, perhaps."

"Very funny," said Wendover, sardonically. "And I'd want to know who the dead man was when he walked the streets."

"I was wondering when you'd take some interest in him." Sir Clinton said, with a twinkle of amusement. "I'm not altogether without hope that we may solve that problem."

"Neither Geddington nor Dujardin recognised him."

"I don't blame them for that, even if they knew him. You didn't see him at close quarters, Squire. He was rather disfigured and . . . well, untidy. We needn't give up hope until they've had a look at him after he's been made more presentable. And, apart from that, he was quite a decently dressed person. People of that class don't vanish from their usual haunts without exciting remark. Somebody will miss him and put us on the track."

"He certainly didn't make it easier by cutting the label out of his breast pocket," Wendover mused. "And there wasn't a paper or anything identifiable in his other pockets. He must have taken special care to have nothing of that sort about him."

"Obviously he had his wits about him if he set out to kill somebody," the Chief Constable commented. "He didn't mean to run any risk of leaving compromising articles behind him."

The phrase gave Wendover a fresh idea.

"Then the Tau cross didn't belong to the dead man," he inferred. "It's a fairly striking object. He'd have left it behind with the rest of his identifiable property."

"Yes," Sir Clinton admitted. "On the face of it, that sounds like a winner of a deduction, unless," he added, with a return to captiousness, "the gold cross was essential at the interview, so that he couldn't leave it behind."

"The next thing I'd want to know about," Wendover continued, ignoring this, "is who left his handkerchief on the floor, soaked in blood."

"There do seem to be a lot of extra fittings in this case," the Chief Constable admitted. "Three pairs of shoes where two would be enough. Two separate blood-stains on the floor. . . ."

"Yes, I'd want to know how they came there, too," Wendover interjected.

"Perhaps somebody's nose bled in the excitement of the moment," Sir Clinton suggested. "That would account for the key, too. They'd need it to put down the fellow's neck to stop the bleeding."

Wendover looked rather annoyed at this levity.

"Very amusing," he commented, acidly.

"Interesting, too," the Chief Constable rejoined with perfect good humour. "That's why I gave those directions about the blood-stains."

Wendover changed his mental attitude.

"The blood-transfusion expert?" he asked. "You think you've got something there?"

"The chances are against it," Sir Clinton admitted frankly, "but we'll know when we get Livermere's report. By this time tomorrow night, we ought to have a lot of extra information. Chesilton ought to have got going and picked up a bit. And I'm rather interested to see how young Danbury gets on. He seems to have glimmerings of ideas, that young man. He kept his eyes open to some purpose in the short time he had, before we came on the scene. If he can only make good in this business, he might get on."

He glanced at his watch as he spoke.

"Later than I thought. What about bed, Squire? The next thrilling instalment will be broadcast tomorrow night. I'll tell Chesilton to come here to report. I don't want to worry him during the day, for I expect he'll have his hands full."

6
MRS. STERNHALL'S STORY

When Wendover appeared in the breakfast-room next morning his host was already there, going through his letters. After Wendover had helped himself from the side table and taken his seat, the Chief Constable passed him a note from among his papers. Wendover glanced first at the signature, "J. F. CHESILTON, Inspector, 2d. Division," and realised that it was a brief official report. He read it with raised eyebrows.

"So Dujardin identified the dead man as his brother-in-law, when he saw him at the mortuary?" he commented. "And Geddington confirms this more or less, though he had only a nodding acquaintance with Sternhall. That seems to narrow things down a bit, Clinton. But why didn't they spot who he was when they saw him at the flat?"

"He wasn't pretty, then," Sir Clinton pointed out, briefly. "He'd be easier to identify after they'd made him presentable at the mortuary."

"This note didn't come by post?"

"No. No time for that. Chesilton sent it over by hand early this morning."

"Well, things look more hopeful now," Wendover declared, as he helped himself to toast. "Now you know who he is, it should be easy enough to find out all about him. It's not like groping in the dark."

"Oh, quite simple," Sir Clinton retorted ironically. "By the way, Squire, who murdered him? You seem to have it all cut and dried for us."

"That would be snatching credit away from humble people like chief constables, inspectors, and other small fry," Wendover pointed out, with equal irony. "It wouldn't quite be playing the game. But seriously, Clinton, it does clear up the business a bit, doesn't it, when you know who the fellow was? You can get on to his relations, friends, business associates, and what not. Something's bound to turn up that will suggest the motive. It's mere routine work for Chesilton."

"Yes, the kind of routine that's never heard of in court except when it's summarised in the phrase: 'From information received.' And about ninety per cent. of it represents nothing but the waste of a good man's time."

The Chief Constable seemed disinclined for further discussion, so Wendover devoted himself to his own correspondence. When they had breakfasted, Sir Clinton led the way into his study. Wendover followed, carrying the *Times* in his hand. It was his daily practice to glance through all the news columns of that journal, from start to finish; and he even included the Agony Column advertisements in his survey. The cipher messages which appeared therein from time to time were a hobby of his, and he enjoyed pitting his brains against those of the advertisers.

As they entered the study, the desk telephone rang sharply and the Chief Constable stepped across the room and lifted the receiver. Wendover, unfolding his *Times*, heard the one-sided talk.

"Yes, he's speaking. . . . Good morning. . . . Oh? I'm afraid that's Inspector Chesilton's business. . . . I'm afraid there are no 'private affairs' in a murder case. . . . She won't?" The Chief Constable seemed to reflect for a moment or two. "Very well, if she insists. . . . I shall bring a magistrate with me. . . . Oh, of course, any information will be kept strictly for official use and not given out to the public. . . . That reporter has been bothering you again? Then don't give him any information unless you want to see it in the newspapers. . . . Yes—Mr. Wendover. He's a Justice of the Peace. . . . Very good. We'll come over shortly. Good-bye."

He put down the receiver and turned to his guest.

"I've got you a front seat in the stalls for the next act, Squire. Some of this routine you were talking about. That was Dujardin ringing up."

"The brother-in-law?"

"Yes, the man without a past, so far as his tenses go. It's a bit of a nuisance. Mrs. Sternhall wants to see me—possibly to tell me the sad story of her life or something of the sort. I suggested Chesilton, but she won't hear of that. She insists on dealing with a gentleman, it seems; and she's unsophisticated enough to suppose that a handle to one's name puts one in that class. The bother is that we've no power to screw information out of her. If Chesilton goes, she'll refuse to speak at all—and then, where are we? So I had to agree to her terms, since we must get what we can out of her and Dujardin. I thought you might like to hear what it's all about, so I made a stipulation of my own. They'll imagine you're a *juge d'instruction*, or something of the sort, no doubt; so you can look as wise as you please and take any notes you choose. I've a sort of feeling that Mr. Dujardin's rather a slippery fellow, and an independent witness will do no harm in dealing with him."

Wendover threw the *Times* on to a chair.

"When do they expect us?"

"As soon as we can get round. We'd better go now."

It did not take them very long to reach the door of Number 5, The Grove. A constable, on guard on the ground floor, saluted Sir Clinton; but apart from him, there was no one visible. Leaving him behind, they climbed to Mrs. Sternhall's flat, where they were admitted by a scared-looking little maid and ushered into the room they had seen on the previous night.

Dujardin heaved his bulk out of his chair as they entered, but Wendover gave him hardly more than a passing glance. All his sympathy was for the woman who had suffered so tragic and unexpected a loss within the last twelve hours. Her face was whiter even than on the night before. She looked worn out, and there were dark lines under her eyes, which seemed born of a sleepless night. But, to his surprise, there were few signs of tears. Her expression puzzled him. She seemed strung up, nervous, desperately worried by some problem or other, but not grief-stricken, as he had expected. At the sight of her features, he felt some of his commiseration ebb away, though he could hardly have explained why his feelings were altering.

Sir Clinton bridged over the initial awkwardness of the situation with a few tactful phrases; but it was evident that he had no desire to waste time. He turned to Dujardin.

"You've no doubt, M. Dujardin, that it was actually Mr. Sternhall whom you saw at the mortuary?"

"Ah, no," Dujardin asserted positively. "When I see him downstairs, I take a very hurried glance, you understand? It seems to me improbable that I should know him. And naturally I had never seen him like *that*. But later, at the morgue, he was different"—he made a gesture as though he were sponging his face—"and I recognised him almost at once. It is beyond discussion."

Sir Clinton seemed to reflect for a moment or two. He turned to the woman.

"You asked me to come to see you. There were some things you wished to explain? But Inspector Chesilton would have served your purpose just as well, surely?"

Mrs. Sternhall made a gesture, inviting them to take chairs, and seated herself on a big settee near the window. Wendover unobtrusively examined her face again. That elusive expression was still there. Apprehension, anxiety, worry in an extreme form: it might have arisen from any of them. He noticed her slim fingers picking unconsciously at the fabric of the settee.

"Perhaps M. Dujardin did not make himself quite clear on the telephone," she said at last. "Perhaps I can put it better, so that you may comprehend. The police will want to know all about us. That is natural; and I have no objection. But for reasons of my own, which I will make clear later, I do not desire that this information about my affairs, my private affairs, should be discussed by everyone and printed in the newspapers. That would not suit me. Therefore I first ask a promise that what I shall tell is to be used only officially and not divulged to journalists and persons of that type."

Her English, Wendover noted, was correct enough. Only her over-precision, her Latinised vocabulary, and a faint accent, betrayed the foreigner.

"Inspector Chesilton would have given you that promise, I've no doubt, if you'd asked for it," Sir Clinton pointed out.

Mrs. Sternhall made a slight gesture, accompanied by a faint shrug.

"Yes. But that is different. If I deal with a gentleman—like yourself—I can have reliance on his word. But this inspector, I know nothing about him or about his promises."

"But I shall have to give him the information, in any case," Sir Clinton explained. "He is in charge of the matter."

"Yes, yes. But if you tell him and say to him, 'This is confidential,' then he will not talk, for fear of offending you, who are the master. But if he made me a promise . . . I am nobody. It is not the same thing."

"Very well," said Sir Clinton, with a touch of impatience; "your information will not be used except officially. Is that sufficient, or shall I put it in writing?"

Mrs. Sternhall bent her head slightly in acknowledgment of the promise. When she spoke again, Wendover had the impression that she was telling a story which she had carefully thought out in detail beforehand. It sounded too well put together to be an extempore narrative.

"It will be clearer, I believe," she began, "if I go back to the beginning, when I first met my husband. Then, when you have heard me, you can put questions, if I have not been quite plain. Or you can ask questions, as I tell my story. Whichever you please."

The Chief Constable glanced at his wrist watch, as a plain hint to her to condense her narrative.

"Do not fear," she said, with an odd little smile, "I shall say no more than is necessary."

Sir Clinton drew a notebook from his pocket, opened it, and waited for her to begin.

"My name—that is the first thing, isn't it? My name was Lucienne Barsac," she began, speaking slowly, so that he could take

74

it down. "There were three of us: my father, my elder sister Liane, and I. We were what you would call an upper middle-class family. My father speculated heavily and after the War he was unfortunate, so we lost all our money. Then he died, and my sister and I found ourselves almost without a halfpenny. She married M. Dujardin here. But in those days M. Dujardin had not yet 'made good,' as you say. They had very little money, and although my sister offered me a home with them, it would have been mere charity. I was too proud to accept their offer, though I was grateful for it."

She threw Dujardin a glance which he acknowledged with a perfunctory gesture.

"I looked about for a living," she went on, "but I had no training of any sort. I had no certificates which might have helped me to become a governess. I had no voice which might have helped me on the stage; and, besides, in Paris, the entrance fee into that life was one which I did not care to pay. All that I had was my looks and some fine dresses, left to me from our prosperity.

"Then I saw by chance an advertisement. A famous illusionist—a conjurer—wanted a good-looking girl as an assistant. His name is beside the mark; I need not give it. I presented myself to him and his wife, a hard woman, difficult to please. I was engaged, perhaps because I was a little different from the usual applicant.

"You can surmise my part in the performance. I was the pretty girl who comes on to the stage at the critical moment, with a glass of water or a bouquet, and distracts the attention of the audience from the conjurer. His wife trained me. How to look interested; how to look bored; how to sit down and cross my legs—so!—to draw the audience's eyes away from the conjurer. All these little tricks that must be timed to an instant, if they are to do their work.

"And I had other parts to play, also. My employer was not clever at sleight-of-hand; he specialised in big mechanical illusions that demand brains and machinery rather than manual dexterity. You have seen these things, of course. 'The Bride' was one. An empty tent on the stage turned into a sleeping-room, with a girl lying in a big double bed. 'The Electric Chair' was another. I sat in a big chair;

men from the audience were allowed to tie me to it; and then I vanished and a skeleton appeared in the chair. It is an advantage to have a pretty girl for the part. The men from the audience do not like to tie a cord too tightly round neat ankles or slender wrists. And I was taught to flinch a little, as if they were hurting me, if they were too businesslike in their work."

"Yes, yes," Sir Clinton interjected, in a slightly impatient tone.

"At first," Mrs. Sternhall continued, "things were quite satisfactory. We had engagements in Paris, and his wife watched him, very sharply indeed. But then he was booked for an English tour; and she remained behind in France. She spoke no English and she hated your climate here. When we got to England, things became difficult for me. He grew . . . well, enterprising, you understand?

"I was miserable. At any moment, he might discharge me, chase me into the street. I spoke English, but that would have been little help if I had been sent away with a week's salary in my pocket. And my salary was reckoned in French money, which meant less in English money in those days, with the exchange against the franc. He had counted on that, you see, and had taken advantage of my ignorance when I signed his contract. The money I earned would hardly pay for the most miserable lodgings, and I had to half starve myself to make ends meet. When I asked for more money, he laughed and said he would think about it when I changed my ideas. I was desperate, alone, underfed, helpless in a strange country; and I was lonely, terribly lonely. It was so different from the life I had lived when my father was alive."

Wendover, always soft-hearted where a pretty woman was concerned, found that his sentiments were changing with regard to Mrs. Sternhall. Evidently she had gone through a difficult time, and if it had left some hardness in her character, she was not to blame.

"At last," she continued, "we went to Helmstone, where we were booked for two successive weeks. You know Helmstone, perhaps: a big, bleak, rainy city, with muddy streets, drab shops, and a hard-faced people thronging the wet pavements. Its gloom and dullness ate into what little courage I had left, and I had not much courage left by then. And my landlady was rude and dirty, and the fire smoked, and the rain beat upon the windowpanes. It is easy now to smile and say: 'Why remember such trifles?' But when one is alone, friendless, dispirited, even trifles loom very large. 'The last straw,' as you say.

"After the performance on the first night at Helmstone, Mr. Sternhall waited for me at the stage door. I was used to that sort of thing. I hated these men with their avid eyes. I had never gone with any of them. Even a bedroom with a smoky fire had been better than their company. But that night I was miserable, at the end of my tether, as you say; and I needed even the pretence of friendliness. He offered me supper and there is no harm in that. I let him take me to a restaurant. When we sat down, he saw how hungry I was. He was very quick in seeing some things. He pressed me to eat, tactfully: 'Now you must really try this other thing. They make a specialty of it here, and you mustn't miss it.' That was the first satisfying meal I'd had for weeks. Oh, not very romantic, I confess; but the food put fresh courage into me, and that was better for me than any romance, I think, just then.

"While I supped, he talked to hide that he himself was not eating. He talked about myself, asking careless questions without seeming inquisitive. It was what I most needed: someone I could speak to freely and get my troubles 'off my chest,' as you say. He made me like him; he seemed kind, in a way; and he was the only man who had been sympathetic to me since I had come to England.

"Of course, after supper, he suggested what I had been expecting all along. But now I had got back some of my courage, at his expense; and I left him at the door of the little restaurant. He was quite nice about it; and that made me like him better. The next night he took me to supper again, and every night after that, during the week. I looked forward to those suppers—not altogether be cause of the food.

"I must try to give you some idea of what sort of man he was, or you will not understand. He was not handsome, but he had a curious magnetism, and a wonderful voice—very sympathetic when he wished it to sound so. And he had something that makes a man attractive to women. He could 'put the come-hither on a woman.' That is your phrase, isn't it? But not on me. And because he failed with me, it stirred up his pride, I think. If I had wished to entrap him, I could not have played my cards better, as I found when I came to know him well. He was one of those men who see a thing; then they want it; then, if they are balked, they must have it; and finally, they must have it *now*. Up to a point, no one could calculate more coolly than he could; but once that point was passed, he threw calculation to the winds. He would take any risk or pay any price that would get him what he desired, without delay, instantly.

"It seems he fell in love with me, so far as a man of that type can fall in love. I had balked him, and that seems to have raised his desire and hurt his pride. He made love swiftly, impetuously. It seemed as if I were the only thing that counted. I could see things in those cold blue eyes of his. At last, he offered me marriage. I had won the game without meaning to do it. I put him off, and that made him even more eager.

"Then the crash came. My employer had learned of these little suppers and he imagined things—the sort of things a man like that *would* imagine. It made him furious, as was natural enough, in a man of his type. I had resisted him and now I had given in to another man: that was the sting, to him. He picked up a girl from the rest of the company to take my part, and he gave me a week's notice. That meant that when I had worked out my week, I should be stranded in Helmstone, where there was no employment for me; and if I paid my fare to London, I should land there with less than would keep me for a week, and with no better chance of employment there. And I had found a ladder in my stocking the day before and had spent most of my little reserve in buying a new pair—fine ones, for the stage.

"These are the moments when one must think quickly. I was still too stubborn to ask my brother-in-law here for aid, for he had little enough for himself and my sister, in those days. I was not in love with Mr. Sternhall; but I liked him. At that moment, he would pay the price I asked: marriage. But in another week I might have to take less. I was not silly enough to think that it was a *grande passion* on his side, either. But he would be kind to me; and just then I needed kindness so very much. I met him for supper that night, and we arranged it all.

"There were some little difficulties, because I am, of course, a Catholic, whilst he—I have really no idea what he was, if he was anything. The first priest we went to made some difficulties because it was a mixed marriage. Things were smoothed over in some way with another priest. Mr. Sternhall was not likely to make too many difficulties when he was on the verge of getting what he desired. So we were married."

"Where?" asked Sir Clinton, looking up at her.

"In a chapel at Mardengray. It is a suburb of Helmstone. The date was the 3d of November, 1924. It is engraved inside my wedding ring."

She slipped off the circlet and handed it to Sir Clinton for him to verify the figures.

"We went to an hotel for our honeymoon, and then I began to see something else in my husband. He was jealous. If a man spoke to me in the lounge, Mr. Sternhall would stand by, not frowning, but ready at the end of a sentence to thrust himself into the conversation and exclude me from it. If I looked twice at a man, even out of curiosity—well, he was not pleased with me. *He* might do as he pleased with other women; but if I so much as looked sideways at a man, I could feel that jealousy mounting up and up behind my husband's mask of indifference. It was a compliment, I suppose; but to a girl who had been free to do as she chose, it was . . . rather trying.

"We came here, after our honeymoon, to this flat. I was not at all unhappy, you must understand. You see, I was not in love with him madly, not by any means; so I was not jealous of him as I might have had cause to be if he had meant more to me than he did. I knew he was interested in other women from time to time. But he had given me security, and for that I was grateful. It may not seem much to you, who have never been insecure, but I have learned a horror of insecurity. I would do almost anything, I think, to keep myself where I am. I have no homesickness for the gutter, I assure you.

"We were not rich, by any means, but we had enough to go on with. He was always grumbling because he had no capital. If he had capital, he said often, he saw a good opening. It was a continual cry of his, that."

"What was his business?" Sir Clinton interjected.

Mrs. Sternhall shook her head.

"I never knew. He was very silent on some things. It took him away a good deal, for weeks at a time, sometimes for months. After the first year or two, I was not sorry for that. It relieved me of his continual jealousy, among other things. For although he soon tired of me, he remained always jealous. There was something of the East in him, if you understand me; I was like the woman in the harem; no one must so much as look at me with out offending his jealousy, but he need not confine himself to one woman. He had one law for me and another for his own conduct.

"But when his absences grew longer, I began to feel bored. I wanted something to do, left all alone. I took up the teaching of French. He did not like it, but I insisted. At first he demanded that I should have only women as pupils—that jealousy again, you see? But one cannot lay down a rule of that kind and hope to keep to it. By-and-by, he gave in, though most unwillingly, and allowed me to take male pupils as well, but he was always suspicious and used to ask questions about them and try to trap me into making admissions about them."

She smiled rather scornfully, as though her words had called up memories.

"And now," she went on, after a moment or two, "you can guess why I do not want my private affairs to be discussed in public. Suppose the newspapers say: 'Mrs. Sternhall is a young Frenchwoman. She was on the music-hall stage, not long ago, but now she gives French lessons.' What will be the result of that? I know the people here. They will nudge each other, and wink, and say: 'French lessons! Pretty young Frenchwoman? Used to be on the stage, you know. Oh, yes! Quite so!' And I shall have men coming here, pretending they desire to learn the French language, but who desire something quite different. 'French actress, eh? Good for a bit of sport, what?' That is what they will say to themselves, and I shall be put to the trouble of disenchanting them. No, no! That would not suit me. And they would give me a bad name, simply by coming here; and I should lose some of my genuine pupils, most probably, on that account."

Wendover could understand this point of view, but Sir Clinton seemed to pay little attention to Mrs. Sternhall's explanation.

"You propose to go on teaching?" he demanded. "That reminds me of a question which I must ask. How will Mr. Sternhall's death affect you—financially?"

"I shall not have much to live on," Mrs. Sternhall said vaguely, after a moment's consideration.

"What about Mr. Sternhall's business? Will it still be carried on and bring you in some income?"

Instead of replying, Mrs. Sternhall threw a glance at Dujardin, as though leaving the matter to him. He seemed nothing loath, though his expression betrayed some astonishment at his own story.

"Figure to yourself, Monsieur," he said, "our surprise. Last night, we go through his papers, Mrs. Sternhall and I. We search his desk, we look everywhere, we examine everything. We find no information whatever, not a scrap that bears upon his business. A cheque book, we find, and a passbook of the local bank. Bundles of receipts and accounts too, but for household expenses only. There are no business papers, no office correspondence, not even an address book of his clients. It is unusual. Very disconcerting. Not so much as the address of his business premises. One hardly knows what to make of it, does one? But truly he was always a very secretive person, this Sternhall."

"Evidently," Sir Clinton admitted, drily. "Did you find a copy of his will—his testament?"

Dujardin shook his head.

"No, it is not among his papers."

"At the bank, probably," Sir Clinton suggested. "I may want to see it."

Mrs. Sternhall seemed on the verge of saying something, but checked herself at the last moment.

"Do you know if he has made any will?" the Chief Constable demanded, turning towards her.

"I could not say," she answered, after a moment's hesitation. "That would be a matter for his solicitor, would it not? He could inform you, no doubt." She hesitated again. "But I do not know the name of his solicitor. That was business, you understand? And all matters of business he kept to himself. I did not come into that side of his life."

"Ah, indeed!" Sir Clinton said, in a noncommittal tone. "Now there's another point. Was he insured?"

Mrs. Sternhall gave a curt nod of assent.

"There was an insurance policy, in my favour, I think. It also should be in the charge of the bank. It is not among his papers."

"I shall want to see it also," Sir Clinton pointed out. He seemed to reflect for a moment or two before putting his next question.

"Can you throw any light, of any sort, on his death? You told us that he was very jealous. Does that suggest anything to you?"

Mrs. Sternhall shook her head composedly.

"I gave him no cause to be jealous," she returned quietly. "It is possible, it is even probable, that he may have imagined things. He was that sort of man. But he had no cause for jealousy."

"You had a number of pupils for your lessons?" the Chief Constable pursued. "Gentlemen as well as ladies? Would you be so good as to write me out a list—with the addresses—of those who have taken tuition from you in the last twelve months."

"The gentlemen only, I presume?" Mrs. Sternhall questioned, with a touch of scorn in her tone.

"Oh, no. Your pupils of both sexes."

Mrs. Sternhall went over to a small escritoire, took out a sheet of paper, and set to work. Evidently the compilation of the list gave her some trouble, as she paused from time to time and tapped her lips with her pencil, as though striving to recall some elusive information. At last she rose and handed Sir Clinton the list.

"Thank you," he said. "Now another question, Mrs. Sternhall. Last night I learned that your husband was not staying in this house recently. He was away from home. When did you last see him?"

Mrs. Sternhall considered for a short time, as though trying to fix a definite date.

"It was about six months ago, I believe—after Christmas."

"Were you expecting him home again soon?"

Mrs. Sternhall made a slight graceful gesture.

"Oh, no," she explained. "He never gave me any warning of his returns. I see you have not comprehended me altogether. He was so jealous that he preferred to arrive à l'improviste—quite unexpectedly. Perhaps he imagined that he would discover something by that method, catch me out, as you say. Certainly I never knew when he might walk into this flat."

"Did he ever meet your pupils?"

"Oh, no. That was no affair of his, you see. I made that very plain to him. I would stand no nonsense. He would have made it impossible for me, if I had allowed that. No, he may have known their names, or he may have met them on the stair, but that was by accident. I was not under his thumb, you understand," she ended, with a swiftly suppressed flash of temper.

"I understand," Sir Clinton assured her, rather indifferently. "By the way, what was the amount of that insurance policy, do you remember?"

"It was for nine thousand pounds," Mrs. Sternhall explained.

"Then you will not be left quite penniless," the Chief Constable commented, with a rather bleak smile. "That's very fortunate."

He rose from his chair, and Wendover followed his example.

"One question more. Had he any relations?"

"I believe he had a brother in America, but I never saw him. He never mentioned any others."

"Thanks, Mrs. Sternhall," said Sir Clinton. "Now we need not trouble you further for the present. You may feel assured that this statement of yours will be used only officially and will not be communicated to any newspaper. Inspector Chesilton will bring you a copy of my notes, and you might sign them as a matter of form. There is just one thing I'd like to say, though. It's just possible that somebody else might ferret out part of your story quite independently of ourselves, and for that we have, of course, no responsibility. But nothing from us will find its way into the newspapers. That I can promise definitely.—Good morning, M. Dujardin."

When they were back in their car, Wendover turned to the Chief Constable.

"Let me have a look at that list of names she gave you, Clinton."

Sir Clinton had already glanced through it, and he passed the paper over without comment. Wendover cast his eyes down the list.

"The Reverend Ambrose Y. Bracknell," he read out, in a meaning tone. "That's the first name on the list."

"Well, what of it?" Sir Clinton inquired, with a faint smile.

"It's the first name on the list," Wendover repeated. "It was the first that came into her mind when she started to write. That suggests that it's more important to her than the others."

"Ah, psycho-analysis, eh?" the Chief Constable inquired. "An interesting speculation, Squire. But not the only possible one. To me it suggests something quite different."

"Indeed!" said Wendover, slightly put out. "And what does it suggest to you?"

"Merely that he is a recent, or even a present pupil, so that his name was easy to remember. She had difficulty in recalling one or two, you observed."

Wendover pondered for a moment or two, evidently disliking the thing he was going to say.

"The Reverend Ambrose Y. Bracknell," he repeated. "And there's that Tau cross as a factor in the case."

"Damning, eh? Gentlemen of the jury, here is a clergyman, here is a cross, and there is a murdered man. Consider your verdict. I hate to seem cold-waterish, Squire, but the evidence appears to have more gaps than links in it. You may be right, but you're far from proving it."

"Just a guess," Wendover admitted amiably. "What did you make of Mrs. Sternhall?"

"Neither she nor Dujardin had much sleep last night."

"She did look washed out," Wendover agreed. "Naturally, this affair must have been a bad shock to her."

"Yes, of course," the Chief Constable said, with more irony than agreement in his tone.

"What do you mean?" Wendover demanded.

"I think she and Dujardin spent most of the night in hunting through Sternhall's papers and in putting together that yarn she told us," said Sir Clinton bluntly. "She didn't spend any of it in weeping for the dead, by the look of her eyes."

"Suspicious devil, you are. You think it was all lies?"

"Oh, no," the Chief Constable assured him. "It was like your guess, a minute or two ago. Everything of importance was left out. They'd edited the real story a good deal; that's how it struck me. What she did tell us is probably true enough. They know we can check most of it, if we want to. But it isn't the whole story, by a long chalk, unless I'm much mistaken."

"What makes you say that?" Wendover demanded.

"Look at her anxiety to keep her yarn out of the newspapers. The reason she gave was pretty thin, I thought. But suppose it had got into the newspapers, what then? Somebody who knows more than I do might read it, begin to think, and drop me a note with some further information—which might not suit Mrs. Sternhall. That's always a possibility."

"We both seem eager guessers this morning," Wendover commented, sardonically. "Let it go at that. One thing she did do. She gave a fairly clear picture of Sternhall, I thought. Not very attractive, her portrait of him: jealous, ambitious, evidently a woman-hunter, with a sort of cold calculation."

"Yes, until his passions got the better of his judgment," Sir Clinton interjected. "If he'd waited a week longer, he'd have been able to buy her at a cheaper price. She practically admitted that."

". . . Leaving her for weeks and months at a time," Wendover continued, without noticing the interjection, "and secretive to an abnormal degree. That reminds me, Clinton, can you conjecture why he should have been so careful to keep no documents which might have given a clue to his business?"

"I could suggest a dozen, if you like. But before that, I'd like to be sure that no documents of the sort were left."

"But they've been through all his papers. They explained that."

"Try another guess, Squire. Suppose it didn't suit them to have any such documents found. Here's a man murdered. And the first thing his sorrowing widow thinks about is to go through his private papers. That strikes even my dull mind as peculiar. In fact, it almost looks as if they'd destroyed anything that could throw light on something. There were no ashes lying about, I grant you. But I think Dujardin might have risen to the height of burning papers on a wet newspaper on the hearth and washing the ashes down the sink when he'd finished. Pure hypothesis, of course. Still, on the face of things, they're hiding something."

"He must have had some sort of income," Wendover admitted. "The premium on a nine thousand pound insurance policy amounts to some hundreds a year, I expect."

"Some people would cut your throat for much less than nine thousand pounds," Sir Clinton pointed out, grimly.

"It's these long and irregular absences from home that puzzle me," Wendover mused. "If they were genuine, then he must have been abroad, or he could have dropped in at week-ends from time to time. All the more likely, in view of his jealousy. It looks as if he went abroad. Or else . . . by Jove! he may have been leading a double life. Just the sort of man who might be carrying on an intrigue elsewhere. That's not impossible."

"Nothing's impossible except a four-sided triangle, and a few other things like that," Sir Clinton admitted. "I see you're determined that this is a *crime d'amour*, as Mrs. Sternhall would say in her native language. It's your romantic temperament, Squire. I've no doubt Chesilton is looking for something rather more sordid. And on the basis of probabilities, he's more likely to be right, I fear. It's only a very bedraggled kind of romance that gets into the police courts, so far as my experience goes."

Wendover pondered for a moment or two before speaking again.

"Tired of her, but still insanely jealous: that was the impression she gave of him. She says she gave him no cause for jealousy. But suppose he was jealous without any cause. It sounds quite in character with what we heard. That reminds me, Clinton, why did you get the names of all her pupils? Wouldn't a list of the male pupils have been enough?"

"Because, with his amorous proclivities, he may have made someone else jealous."

Wendover digested this in silence before asking a fresh question.

"What makes you think she's hiding something?"

"Various things. Two phrases that she let slip, among other points. One was: 'I would stand no nonsense' and the other was 'I was not under his thumb.' Her tone when she said that suggested that he was under her thumb, to some extent. Here's an insanely jealous man who acquiesces in her taking male pupils after having protested violently against her doing anything of the kind. Obviously, she had some hold over him. It wasn't her personal attractions. He'd grown more or less tired of her, she said frankly. It's not going too far to suggest that she had some hold over him. But she took care not to tell us how that came about."

"And you didn't ask, for fear of putting her on her guard?"

Sir Clinton confirmed this with a nod.

"That's the sort of question one can ask later on, if necessary," he pointed out. "We may be able to check it then with evidence from other quarters."

7
INSPECTOR CHESILTON REPORTS

It was late that evening when Inspector Chesilton, tired, unsuccessful, but still cheerful, was ushered into the Chief Constable's study. Sir Clinton, after a glance at his face, indicated a decanter and syphon.

"Thank you, sir," Chesilton said gratefully. "I wouldn't feel the worse for a pick-me-up."

He helped himself generously and took the seat which the Chief Constable indicated.

"No great luck?" Sir Clinton inquired sympathetically.

"No great luck, as you say, sir. I'll just run over the main heads of the business as they come, not in chronological order."

He took a long drink from his glass, dabbed his lips with his handkerchief, and began without preamble.

"Constable Danbury, Sir, went to the firm of painters and decorators as soon as they opened this morning. He questioned the men employed at Number 5, The Grove. They asserted that they had locked up the premises carefully when they left work at 5 p.m. yesterday afternoon. The paintpots were all right then. None of them spilt. He saw the keys of the premises which they had. All present and correct. He retained them and tried them on the doors He learned that the decorators, Messrs. Lewes and Flockton, were taking their orders in the matter from a firm of solicitors, Messrs. Abery, Pepler, and Abery. . . ."

"I know them," Sir Clinton interjected. "Quite a reputable firm."

"Oh, quite, sir," the inspector concurred. "I rang them up and inquired who gave them instructions in the matter. It was Mrs. Sternhall."

Chesilton paused, without any intention of dramatic effect, but merely to take a second drink from his glass.

"So she owns that flat?" Wendover exclaimed, in some surprise.

"She owns the whole of Number 5, sir," Chesilton explained. "So the solicitors told me. The title deeds are in her name. They had no dealings with Mr. Sternhall, they told me; knew nothing about him, in fact, I gathered."

"She didn't tell us that," said Sir Clinton drily, with a glance at Wendover. "She seems to have kept a good many things in reserve, just as I thought. H'm! Of course, if, she owns the whole of Number 5, she may have duplicate keys for the ground-floor flat. And her husband might have had a set also, either with or without her knowledge. Suggestive point, perhaps. Go on, Inspector."

"The next bit's rather a wash-out, sir, I'm afraid," Chesilton admitted. "Danbury, when he'd got that part of the business off his hands, got the painters to mix him some paint as near as possible to the stuff that was upset on the floor. He made a lot of experiments with it—his notes are really not bad, sir—trying to work out how long the paint had been oozing over the floor before he came into the flat. He'd some idea that it might give a hint as to how long the murderer and Sternhall had been talking together before the murder, if the pot was spilt at the start of the interview."

Chesilton leaned back in his chair and shook his head. "I'm afraid he got nowhere near it, sir. All my eye and Betty Martin, unfortunately. Two hours between the upsetting of the bucket and his own entry into the flat, that's what it worked out at. But the bucket must have been upset in the struggle between the two men at the moment that Sternhall was shot, obviously. That leaves no two-hour gap possible. Too many factors in the business, I suppose, like the rate of flow, and the spread, and so on. We know the murderer cleared off the premises just as Danbury turned up, and that leaves no room for a two-hour gap."

Sir Clinton proffered a box of cigars to the inspector, who helped himself unfastidiously.

"Thank you, sir. The next thing is, I rang up Mrs. Sternhall and asked her about that nine thousand pound insurance policy you told me about. What company issued it? She made no bones about that. It was issued by the Humber and Hereford Insurance Company. I asked her to whom she paid the rent of her flat. She was very indignant—but I think it was play-acting, sir—about prying into her private affairs. However, she seemed to think better of it. She admitted that she owned the flat she occupied. She didn't volunteer anything about the rest of the place, and I didn't let her guess I knew all about it. That was right, sir?"

"Oh, yes," Sir Clinton agreed.

"Seeing she's keeping things up her sleeve, I thought a bit of a jar might do no harm," Chesilton explained. "Now she sees how easy we get on to things, she'll perhaps think better of hiding other affairs that might be useful to us. That's how I looked at it, sir. Then I rang up the Humber and Hereford people. I didn't go to the bank and ask for the policy itself, because banks are sticky sometimes about their depositors' affairs. The H. and H. people told me all I wanted. The policy was taken out five years ago. Premiums all promptly paid. The policy's in her name, insurance on Sternhall's life. Insurable interest quite O.K., of course, seeing she's been dependent on him all this time."

He broke off and rubbed his chin rather thoughtfully.

"It's a tidy sum of money," he said, after a moment or two. "I'd say, sir, that she's had a double stroke of luck: getting rid of a husband she wasn't too keen on, and getting nine thousand pounds all in the same day, so to speak. Very lucky!"

"I agree with you, there," Wendover threw in.

"Meanwhile, sir," the inspector continued, "Sergeant Vorley was detached to see what he could make of the people whose names were on the list you got from Mrs. Sternhall. The first thing he did was to go to Mrs. Sternhall's flat. I'd warned him about Mrs. Sternhall's objection to publicity and so forth. He got hold of the maid. Information got that way doesn't come under your agreement, sir, of course. The maid was able to tell him what pupils had been there on the afternoon of the murder. There was Miss Muriella Upham from 2.30 to 3.30 p.m., and there was Mr. Ambrose Y. Bracknell from 4.30 to 5.30 p.m."

"Ah!"

The inspector disregarded Wendover's ejaculation.

"Vorley, sir, went round to interview these two, first of all. He had to start somewhere on the list, and these seemed the most likely. He's drawn blank, so far as useful information goes. Miss Upham's a little woman about forty, rather bright and noticing, Vorley thought. She'd seen nothing. Mrs. Sternhall gave her an hour's lesson, elementary French about the du-dela-des stage, I gather. She didn't notice anything unusual in Mrs. Sternhall's manner. No signs of any upset or anything of that sort. Just like she generally was, apparently."

He paused again and took a sip from his glass.

"Vorley then went to see Mr. Bracknell. He lives just round the corner from The Grove, sir, in Bella Vista Avenue, Number 17. He's not a native here. It seems he's one of these young fellows who've come here lately in connection with that 'Christians, Awake!' movement. You know the thing, sir. He calls himself a Centurion and he's supposed to rake in a hundred followers. Very popular, he's made himself, so Vorley reports, especially with the young women. He's a big, good-looking fellow. He's living in rooms, with attendance. Vorley asked him why he was taking French lessons. It turns out he means to go to France, later on, with this 'Christians, Awake!' business, and he was brushing up his French as a preliminary. He'd been at Mrs. Sternhall's flat from 4.30 to 5.30 p.m., just as the maid said. He goes to her to practice French conversation, discuss books, and so forth. He'd noticed nothing out of the common, either. Vorley's working through the rest of the list, of course; but these were the only two pupils that afternoon. In fact, as Vorley heard from the maid, they were the only people—bar message boys—who rang the bell at all between lunch and 7 p.m., when Mr. Dujardin came in."

91

"I suppose Vorley didn't confine himself to interviewing these people?" Sir Clinton inquired. "He found out more about them?"

"Yes, sir. I was coming to that. Miss Upham's quite well known hereabout. She's got enough to live on and keeps one maid, about as old as herself, who's been with her for years. Reads, knits, goes to the pictures thrice a week, listens to wireless, gardens a bit. Just what one might expect from that. Life like an open book to all her neighbours. We can leave her out."

"And Mr. Bracknell?" Sir Clinton demanded.

"He'd never been here in his life, before he came with this 'Christians, Awake!' business. He goes about a good deal, addressing meetings, and so forth. Sometimes he helps with affairs at Ringwood church, in connection with the movement. He plays tennis, too, at the tennis courts alongside the church. Fairly popular with everyone, Vorley gathered, but specially with the young unmarried women. It seems he's been making rather strong running with a Miss Huntingdon, but nothing's come of it so far. She fairly threw herself at him, I gather from Vorley, and she gads about to all the meetings he goes to. That's common gossip."

The Chief Constable seemed to be following a different train of thought.

"I wonder what newspaper he takes in," he said thoughtfully.

"I suppose we could find out, sir, if it's essential," the inspector said, with a rather puzzled glance at his chief.

"Yes, but I particularly want no questions asked about it," Sir Clinton explained. "Suppose you instruct the constable on that beat to be on hand just when the paper boy arrives. He can hold the boy in talk for a moment at the gate, and he'll see what papers he's going to deliver at the house. That'll be sufficient."

"Very good, sir."

"Has Doctor Livermere made any report yet?"

"I was just coming to that, sir," Chesilton answered in a faintly aggrieved tone. "He hasn't made an official report yet, but I rang him up and got his preliminary results. It seems that the blood on the handkerchief and the blood spots on the floor are of the same class. I don't know what he means by that, exactly. The blood of the body's a different kind of blood, according to him. I put it to him: 'Does that mean there was one other man besides the victim?' He said: 'One, at least'."

"So evidently the murderer was injured in the struggle, and bled," Wendover suggested.

"Of course, sir," the inspector agreed. "Since it was murder, there must have been a second man there; and this clinches it, if common sense wasn't enough."

"It's just as well to get things nailed down," the Chief Constable pointed out. "Though that phrase 'at least' opens up some possibilities. There may have been two men mixed up in the business in addition to the victim, perhaps."

"Then why the struggle?" demanded Wendover. "Two men could overpower a fellow like Sternhall easily enough. He wasn't a pocket Hercules."

The Chief Constable seemed disinclined to push his speculation further. He changed the subject.

"What about that gold ornament, Inspector? By the way, it's a cross, though it doesn't look like it."

"A crucifix, do you mean, sir?"

"No. A crucifix has a figure of Christ on it," Wendover pointed out informatively. "It's just a cross—a Tau cross, it's called, because it's shaped like the Greek letter Tau."

"Religious symbol, anyhow," said Chesilton, evidently not interested in such refinements. "That's worth knowing, sir. I've been wondering how the letter T came into the business. Now it seems I've been barking up the wrong tree. If it's a cross, that'll mean looking at things from a fresh angle."

"How do you look at things from an angle, fresh or not?" Sir Clinton demanded, with a smile. "I could never manage it myself. I just look at them and let it go at that."

"Well, it's just a manner of speaking, sir. Everybody uses it. It never struck me before how silly it sounds. But this T being a cross—so to speak," he added hurriedly, "makes a bit of a difference."

"You were very wise not to show it to that reporter fellow," Sir Clinton said. "And I think you'd better continue to keep it dark.

We may find a use for it yet. Properly handled, it might serve as a bait; so we'd better keep the spotlight off it for the present. Barbican didn't know what we were talking about, if he overheard anything; for there's nothing about it in the newspapers. Now there's another thing, Inspector. Did you find any footprints in the gardens to corroborate Dujardin's tale?"

"I was just coming to that, sir," said the inspector again. "That part of Dujardin's story seems to be quite all right. We found a trail of footprints made by a man who'd climbed over the garden walls, just as Dujardin said. I've had casts of them made. It's a biggish foot with narrow toes and not much sign of a heel."

"Did you notice what sort of footgear was on the feet of the people we interviewed that night?" the Chief Constable inquired, with a peculiar expression.

"By Jove, sir!" Chesilton ejaculated. "Pumps, of course. I ought to have thought of that when I saw how shallow the heel marks were."

"That hardly answers the question," Sir Clinton pointed out. "We interviewed quite a few people, some of them ladies—and they weren't wearing pumps, so far as I noticed."

Chesilton and Wendover racked their memories for some moments, trying to recall details. The inspector was the first to break silence.

"Geddington was wearing pumps. The reporter fellow Barbican had tennis shoes on, if I'm not mistaken. Karslake . . . I'm not dead sure what he was wearing."

"Dress boots," Wendover supplied.

"Perhaps you're right, sir," Chesilton acquiesced. "He lives close by, and they wouldn't get soiled by a walk of that distance. I'd have noticed if they were soiled, at any rate, I think."

"And Dujardin?" inquired Sir Clinton.

"Dujardin was wearing pumps," Wendover supplied, not a little pleased at being able to exhibit the accuracy of his observational powers. "I suspect he came to the flat in boots and changed into pumps when he arrived. They'd be easier on his feet. He looks the sort of man to be careful of his creature comforts."

"One doubtful point is when these footprints were made," the Chief Constable pointed out. "If you accept Dujardin's evidence, they were made at the time of the murder. But they might have been made earlier."

"As a blind?" Wendover demanded.

"I'm merely taking all possibilities into account," Sir Clinton said, with a rather impish grin.

Wendover seemed struck by a fresh idea.

"What about this smash-and-grab lot that you told me about?" he asked. "They're armed. Isn't it possible we're on a wrong scent and that fellows of that sort may be mixed up in the case? They might have broken into the flat to steal whatever they could lay hands on."

Sir Clinton shook his head.

"No go, I'm afraid. First, no criminal would break into a flat at that time of night, when he could just as easily get in after dark— always assuming he's sane. Secondly, that hypothesis won't account for the ugly little weapon found in the dead man's pocket. Unless you're going to assume that the burglar put it there specially for our benefit."

"Very well, then," said Wendover, slightly damped but still fertile in resource. "What was Sternhall's mysterious business? For all we know, he may have been a crook, and this affair may be the result of a squabble with a subordinate."

"Something in that, perhaps, sir," Chesilton admitted, but his tone was anything but enthusiastic. "But on that basis, where does this gold cross come in?"

"Oh, a mascot, probably. You know how superstitious some criminals are."

"You suggested using it as a bait, sir," Chesilton reminded the Chief Constable.

Sir Clinton made a slight gesture which indicated some perplexity.

"I wish we could hold our hand for a day or two," he said. "That might lull the owner's suspicions better. But we can't afford to lose time in this affair. We'll just have to chance it and hope that we'll get a rise. Only, we'll have to make the thing look as genuine and innocent as we can."

"No placards outside the police stations, then," Wendover hazarded. "A private advertisement, I suppose you mean: 'Found, in The Grove, a gold cross . . .' or something of that sort?"

"I'm afraid that won't do," Sir Clinton pointed out. "There's less than your usual subtlety in that suggestion. You may safely bet a hundred to one that to the owner's mind 'The Grove' calls up the word 'Murder' immediately. And that's the last thing we want him to think about. We must give the impression that the thing's been lying about and has been picked up somewhere else than in The Grove."

He reflected for a moment and then turned to Chesilton.

"You might take this down. 'FOUND on' . . . better put today's date there . . . 'in Hernshaw district, gold trinket. Apply Burns, Number 35 Sandown Crescent, between 6.30 and 7.30 p.m. this week.' That seems to wrap the fleece over the wolf well enough."

"But who's Burns?" Wendover demanded.

"His other name's Wendover," Sir Clinton explained. "We need somebody solid, steady, and so forth, for the part; somebody who'll inspire confidence at first sight. I'd do it myself, but I might be spotted."

"Oh, I don't mind," Wendover agreed, not unwilling to be in the thick of the case. "But what about this address. Who lives there?"

"A specialist friend of mine has his consulting rooms there. His hours are 2.30 p.m. to 5.30 p.m. His last patient will be off the premises long before half-past six."

"But why 7.30 p.m.?"

"Because I don't want to shift our dinner hour. No one shall say I ever led a guest into irregular habits. Half-past seven gives you plenty of time to get back here and dress comfortably."

"Thanks," Wendover said ironically. "And now, I suppose that if the owner of the cross turns up, I'm to elicit all the information I can. But I'll have to give him the cross, if he proves he's the owner, won't I?"

"That would hardly suit our book," Sir Clinton disagreed. "The cross may be wanted as an exhibit at the trial. No, we can't leave you to the tender mercies of a possible murderer. The inspector and I are going to occupy the waiting room. When you're sure you have the owner in front of you, ring the bell twice on some excuse. The chorus will then appear, upstage, singing:

'When constabulary duty's to be done,
    To be done,
  A policeman's lot is not a happy one,
    Happy one.'

"That should strike terror into the miscreant's heart."

"Undoubtedly," Wendover concurred, in a rather disgusted tone. "Well, it'll be an interesting experience. Do you call on him to 'stand and deliver,' or what?"

"The inspector will run the dialogue," Sir Clinton assured him. "My part will be a thinking one."

He turned to Chesilton.

"I suppose you can get that advertisement into the papers—all the local papers—quietly, without anyone knowing it's a police affair? I think you'd better insert it thrice, say every second day. That ought to catch the eye of anyone interested."

"Very good, sir."

"Do you really think you'll get a rise?" inquired Wendover, rather doubtfully.

"One can't be sure. But I think the owner of that cross would be very glad to have it back in his own hands, and I'm banking on that. In his place, I think I'd want to get hold of it, if possible. The fewer clues left about, the better, from his point of view. And he doesn't know where it was picked up, I imagine. We really stand to lose nothing except our time, and we may get something worth while. It's a reasonable gamble."

8
THE OWNER OF THE CROSS

For two nights, Wendover sat in the doctor's consulting-room without getting so much as a nibble at the bait. On the first evening, he had been all alert, expecting every moment that the doorbell would ring, and speculating upon the possible appearance of the hypothetical inquirer after the Tau cross. Rather disillusioned by failure, he equipped himself for the second evening's vigil by laying in a stock of evening papers. He was allowed to peruse them without interruption. At the end of this spell, he made a few remarks to his host about the futility of setting traps to catch sunbeams, milking he-goats into sieves, and catching weasels asleep, all of which the Chief Constable received with perfect equanimity.

On the third night, Wendover had wholly lost confidence in the scheme, and he viewed the prospect of the remaining appointments with ill-concealed boredom. To while away the time of waiting, he took a pack of Patience cards with him.

This time, however, he was to get his nibble. Hardly had he begun his private variation of "Demon," when he heard the trill of the front doorbell; and at the sound of it, he hastily gathered up the cards from the desk and thrust them into his pocket. The consulting-room door opened and the maid announced:

"Mr. Malton, sir."

Wendover had amused himself by trying to forecast the various kinds of people who might answer the advertisement, but he was a little surprised at the appearance of his caller. Mr. Malton was a rather down-at-heel person, wearing a suit of blue serge, shiny in

98

places with wear, and carrying a greasy old felt hat in his hand. He sidled into the room, bringing a faint aroma of alcohol with him, and, coming to a halt, he regarded Wendover with an air which mingled boldness and furtiveness in almost equal proportions.

Wendover knew the value of silence at the opening of an interview, so he held his tongue and waited until Mr. Malton was forced to begin.

"You advertised about a gold trinket you'd found, sir?" he inquired, in rather wheedling tones which affected Wendover disagreeably. "I've a copy of the ad. here, sir."

He felt in his waistcoat pocket, pulled out a newspaper fragment and extended it in an unwashed hand.

Wendover had been coached by Sir Clinton in his tactics. He glanced at the torn scrap of newspaper, without taking it, and said in an inquiring tone:

"Yes?"

"Well, sir, seeing that you found it, and you've been so kind as to advertise, I've come for it. I'm a poor man, sir, as you can see, if you look at me. You wouldn't expect a reward from the likes of me, I'm sure."

"No," said Wendover, in a friendlier tone. "Where did you lose this thing, by the way?"

The answer came promptly enough.

"In the Hernshaw district, sir, of course, same as it says in the ad."

He held out his hand, palm extended, as a hint to his host to get down to business and waste no more time.

"In the Hernshaw district?" Wendover repeated doubtfully. "Whereabouts, can you tell me?"

"I could hardly tell you that, sir. If I knew where I'd dropped it, I could have gone and looked for it myself, and found it, most likely."

"That's quite true," Wendover admitted, with a pleasant smile. "And now, if you'll describe it . . ."

Mr. Malton seemed taken completely aback by this request.

"Describe it?" he repeated. "You mean, give a description of it, like? I see, sir, I see. Well, it was a little gold thing." He fixed his

furtive eyes on Wendover's features. "A little gold kind of an ornament. A trinket, you know, sir. The kind of little thing you carry
about with you."

Evidently he imagined he detected something in Wendover's
expression, for he went on hurriedly:

"Oh, I see, sir. I see what's puzzling you. Of course, it's not the
sort of thing a man would be carrying, not in the ordinary way.
The fact is, sir," he dropped his voice half a tone, "it belonged to
my poor dear wife—God rest her soul! That's why I'm so anxious
to get it back, sir. It has a sentimental value, sir. It's the only thing
I have to remember her by, sir."

"I quite understand," Wendover assured him. "A locket's sentimental value. . . ."

"Exactly, sir. I took that little gold locket from her neck when
she was lying stiff and cold, sir, in her last sleep. A little gold locket,
sir, with a ring on it to hang it round one's neck with."

Again he held out his hand, and Wendover saw in his eye an
expression of mingled triumph and contempt. Evidently Mr. Malton
regarded his host as a mug of the "easiest" sort. It had been no
trouble to pump him, Mr. Malton's eye declared, though his attitude remained slightly cringing.

"That's a pity," Wendover said regretfully. "You lost a locket, and
I found something quite different." He rose and rang the bell once.

Mr. Malton's face lost its confiding expression. He seemed un-
able to believe his ears for a moment. Then, with a snarl, he made
as if to speak.

"The maid will show you out," said Wendover, "and if you use
any bad language here, I'll come and kick you down the front steps."

Mr. Malton closed his mouth with surprising suddenness and
made a hasty exit. Wendover heard the front door close behind
him. He went into the waiting room, where Sir Clinton and the
inspector were waiting.

"Number 1 has been a disappointment," he reported. "He was
a seedy gentleman looking for a gold trinket that he hadn't lost, so
far as I could judge."

He explained what had happened, and Sir Clinton laughed.

"Some people would have given the thing up without asking questions," he said, "and then they'd have found themselves in trouble, when the real owner turned up. Pity we can't lay that fellow by the heels. But he'd swear he did lose a gold trinket and we couldn't prove he didn't. Better luck next time," he concluded, with a glance at Wendover.

"Oh, I don't mind interviewing a dozen like him," Wendover assured them. "He was amusing, with his attempts to diddle me. But he wasn't what we're looking for. He was an obvious fake."

"Oh, yes, when the right person comes, he'll be able to describe the thing straight off," the inspector agreed. "No point in his coming, if he didn't."

Suddenly the front doorbell rang again.

"You'd better get to your den before the maid answers the bell," Sir Clinton said.

Wendover wasted no time but withdrew hurriedly to the consulting-room. As he seated himself again at the doctor's desk, he wondered what the next dip into the lucky bag would bring. He had rather enjoyed his interview with Mr. Malton; but he could not help hoping that the next applicant would, at any rate, be cleaner and less alcoholic.

"Miss Huntingdon, sir," the maid announced.

She ushered in a slim, fresh, brown-haired girl in a light summer dress. In his speculations about possible applicants, Wendover had not anticipated this type. He rose and offered her a chair beside the desk, and she thanked him, accompanying her words with an engaging smile in which both her lips and eyes took part.

"Her manners are all right," he commented to himself, as he sat down again. "She's not a shopgirl, with that accent. And she can't be more than twenty, or so. What the devil is she doing, mixed up in an affair like this?"

Then it occurred to him that there might be a mistake. She might have lost a gold trinket—not the Tau cross, but some little thing of her own; and the advertisement might have misled her.

The girl wasted no time, but came straight to the point in a businesslike way.

"I saw your advertisement, Mr. Burns," she explained. "It was very good of you to advertise, and you must let me pay whatever it cost you. I'm so glad you picked the thing up. I thought it was gone for good."

Evidently she expected Wendover to produce the trinket, but he made no motion to do so.

"I suppose that really I ought to have handed it over to the police," he confessed. "That's what I'd have done finally, if the advertisement had brought nothing."

He watched her covertly as he mentioned the police, but the word seemed to have no effect upon her. She merely looked at him as though she wondered why he did not hand the thing over at once.

"You won't mind answering a formal question or two?" he went on. "The fact is, not ten minutes ago, I had another applicant who put in a claim."

"Another applicant?" Miss Huntingdon was obviously both surprised and puzzled. "I don't understand how that can be."

"Well, I'm afraid he wasn't quite genuine," said Wendover, with a pleasant smile, as though taking her into his confidence. "He was rather a wrong 'un, I'm afraid. But if I hadn't asked him a question or two first, I might have handed your trinket over to him—and that would have left me in an awkward position now that you've turned up, wouldn't it?"

"It would—rather," the girl agreed, with a flash of her white teeth.

"And, of course, the trinket I found may not be what you lost at all," Wendover pointed out. "It may be somebody else's lost property."

"That's soon settled," said Miss Huntingdon. "What I lost was a little gold thing, like the letter T. I'll sketch it for you," she volunteered, picking up a sheet of notepaper and a pencil from the desk. "This is what it's like. I've drawn it roughly about the actual size."

She handed the paper across to Wendover and he found she had drawn a very fair representation of the Tau cross; accurate even to the curving lines of the arms.

"It isn't really an initial T," she explained. "You won't recognise it, but it's really a cross. It's got some special Greek name, but I forget that; so you see, I don't want to lose it. Is that the sort of thing you found? I hope so."

Wendover stared at the paper in his hand. There was no mistaking the thing. And she even knew that it was a Tau cross. This was the genuine owner, beyond a doubt. And yet, how could this pretty, eager girl, hardly out of her teens, be mixed up in that grim business at The Grove? She hadn't shown the slightest sign of discomposure when he mentioned the police. There was no trace of nervousness in her manner, nothing to indicate that she feared a trap. In fact, in other circumstances, he would have been convinced that she was simply a girl come to claim a lost trinket in the most natural way in the world. And yet . . . what could one think?

"Just a moment," he said, rising and ringing the bell twice. "I think I have your trinket safe; I've just sent for it."

He took a step or two and sat down in a different chair, leaving the desk chair vacant.

"I'll be so glad to . . ."

Miss Huntingdon broke off in what seemed genuine surprise as Sir Clinton and the inspector entered the room.

Wendover, man of the world though he was, felt acutely uncomfortable. When he had lent himself as a decoy, he had not foreseen a situation of this kind; and the knowledge that he had led this girl into a trap and was now handing her over to Chesilton's hands was anything but pleasant. If she had been furtive, or nervous, or had shown the slightest sign of a guilty conscience, he would have found some justification for the part he had played. But she had been so obviously unsuspicious, so natural, and . . . "well, damn it, such a nice little thing," that he had pangs of conscience.

However, he had his part still to play.

"This is Inspector Chesilton," he explained to the girl. "He has your trinket."

A look of surprise crossed the girl's face, but she seemed in no way daunted by the inspector. She made an almost imperceptible bow as an acknowledgment of Wendover's introduction. Chesilton seated himself at the desk in the chair vacated by Wendover, which brought him within arm's reach of the girl. Sir Clinton, after bowing to Miss Huntingdon, had moved over and was looking out of the window, as though the affair had no interest for him.

"You have my little ornament, it seems?" Miss Huntingdon asked, looking the inspector in the face. "You might give me it, please. I think I've proved that it's my property."

She half rose from her chair, but the inspector made a detaining gesture.

"One moment, Miss . . ."

"Huntingdon is my name, Marjorie Huntingdon."

"And the address, Miss?"

"Avondale, Hill Rise."

Chesilton had drawn some sheets of paper from a drawer in the desk. He laid them out before him, took out his fountain pen, and jotted down the information she had given him. When he had finished, he glanced up and asked another question:

"When did you lose this trinket?"

Miss Huntingdon hesitated for a moment before replying.

"I can't remember the day of the month," she explained. "But it was last Friday that it was lost."

Wendover could scarcely repress an involuntary movement as he heard the words. "Last Friday" was the day of the tragedy in The Grove. The evidence was too plain to admit coincidence. What were the chances that two Tau crosses had been lost on the same day in the same district? And yet this girl seemed more puzzled than perturbed by the question of the inspector. So far, Wendover had detected nothing which suggested conscious guilt.

Chesilton had not moved a muscle of his face when the girl mentioned the ominous date. He put his hand into his vest pocket and, producing the Tau cross, laid it on the desk in front of him. Wendover, examining it sharply, observed that the links of gold chain had been removed. The inspector made no movement to hand the trinket to the girl. When he spoke, it was in the casual tone of one offering careless advice.

104

"Now that you've recovered it, Miss Huntingdon, I'd advise you to use something stronger than silk cord to hang it round your neck. That was how you wore it, wasn't it? Very unsafe, as you've found. You might not be so lucky another time."

"Yes, that was how it was worn," she confirmed, with just the slightest hesitation in her voice. "I'll take your advice, I think, and get something safer."

Chesilton picked up the trinket and showed it to her more closely, but still he did not hand it over.

"You are the owner, of course?" he inquired, as though rather bored by a formality.

"Yes, it belongs to me."

This time there was no hesitation, but almost a faint note of challenge in her tone.

"Had it long, Miss?" Chesilton asked, as he turned it over in his fingers and made a show of examining it.

"Some time."

Wendover had no difficulty in detecting the hesitation in this reply.

"You can't tell me where you bought it, Miss? I've a friend who's interested in things of that sort—by way of being something of a collector. He might be able to get another for himself at the same place."

Miss Huntingdon was now evidently more than a little suspicious under these questions, but the turn of the inspector's inquiry left her nothing which she could resent openly.

"I didn't buy it, I'm afraid, so I can't help."

"Ah, I see. A present, was it?"

"Yes, a friend gave it to me."

She rose from her chair, evidently intending to show that the interview had lasted long enough. Chesilton paid no attention, nor did he relax his hold on the cross. He jotted down some notes on the paper in front of him before looking up again. When he spoke next, it was in a sharper tone.

"Sit down, Miss Huntingdon, please. I'm afraid I'll have to ask you a few more questions before we finish. You *are* the owner of this cross?"

"Yes, of course. But what does this mean? You've no right to speak to me in that tone. If you're a policeman, surely your business is to give me back my property at once, since I've proved it *is* mine."

"Now this is serious, Miss Huntingdon," Chesilton said, not unkindly. "You say you lost this trinket on last Friday. Can you prove that? I mean, did you tell anyone about your loss?"

For some reason, this question seemed to flurry the girl. She looked away from the inspector, obviously avoiding his eye, and her face showed that she was trying to concoct some answer to his question.

"I . . . I'm not . . . No, I didn't mention it to anyone at the time."

"Sit down, please."

She reseated herself automatically, crossed her legs, and clasped her knee with her hands. Something tense in her attitude struck Wendover in contrast to her easy poses during the earlier stages of the interview. Now she was all alert, braced to meet the cross-examination, and plainly hostile. And yet, behind all this, Wendover thought he saw something puzzled in her expression.

"Can you produce anyone who's seen you wearing this thing?" the inspector pursued, with just the faintest suggestion of a rasp in his voice. "Your family? Anyone?"

Miss Huntingdon's face showed that, in some way, this question was a home thrust; but she replied, without perceptible hesitation:

"No, I don't think I could."

Wendover had grown more uncomfortable with the new turn to the interview. An ugly business, badgering a girl under the eyes of two male strangers. His protective instinct was roused. Someone ought to take her part. And, as a possible explanation flashed into his mind, he put it into words.

"If you wore that cross round your neck, Miss Huntingdon, it would be hidden by your dress, wouldn't it? No one would know you were wearing it, unless you told them? Isn't that so?"

"No one knew that I ever wore anything of the kind," the girl admitted immediately.

She did not seem especially grateful to Wendover for his intervention. Despite her apparent frankness, there was something in the watchful expression of her eyes which suggested that she was fencing with the inspector and that every effort of her intelligence was being brought to bear in her parries to his questions. She shifted her clasp on her knee, and two tiny vertical furrows appeared between her brows.

Chesilton seemed a shade perplexed by Wendover's intervention and its result. He tried again, in a fresh direction.

"You got this as a present," he pointed out. "Surely the person who gave it to you would know that you wore it?"

"Nobody knew that I wore it," was the reply, delivered with a firmness which surprised Wendover. "But I don't see what right you have to pry into my affairs like this. You're not accusing me of stealing it, are you?"

"Oh, no, nothing of the sort," Chesilton assured her, in a more kindly tone. "I haven't the slightest idea of that sort, Miss Huntingdon. But we've had some trouble over a cross of this kind, and I'm trying to clear the matter up, so far as your cross is concerned. Now, you lost this on last Friday, didn't you? Have you any idea at all about where you may have dropped it?"

Apparently Miss Huntingdon was reassured by the inspector's hint that his inquiries were a mere side issue of some other affair which did not directly concern herself. She relaxed her attitude, leaned back in her chair, and lost the tenseness of expression which she had shown before.

"Oh, so that's it?" she said. "Why didn't you tell me that before, instead of bullying me the way you did? How was I to know what you were driving at? No, of course, I can't remember where I . . . where the thing came loose. A thing isn't lost if you know where to look for it, is it?"

"No, I suppose not," Chesilton admitted, letting a smile play across his face. "You have me there, I admit, Miss Huntingdon. But this is important," he went on, as though taking her into his confidence. "Would you make an effort to recall what you did during that day? Start with the morning and see if you can carry your memory on."

Miss Huntingdon seemed more at her ease now, though her eyes were still wary.

"In the morning?" she repeated ruminatively. "Let's see. . . . In the morning I had nothing special to do and I stayed in the house. I didn't go out before lunch, that day. I can remember that quite well. . . . Now, let's see. . . . Oh, yes, after lunch I went out to play tennis. I play at the courts on the edge of Hernshaw Park."

The inspector held up his hand.

"One moment. I'm just testing your memory. How did you go from your house to the tennis club?"

Miss Huntingdon had no difficulty here.

"The way I always go: down Hill Rise, then along The Grove, and then down Bella Vista Avenue. It's the way I always take."

"Not down Sans Souci Avenue and round by Ringwood Hill?"

"No, I never go that way."

"So you played tennis," the inspector went on. "And after that?"

"Let's see. . . . Oh, yes, I had tea at the clubhouse and then I went to do some shopping at the foot of Sans Souci. I went along Ringwood Hill that time. . . . And then I came home. I didn't go out in the evening."

"I see," said Chesilton.

He seemed to have come to a blank end, and for a moment or two, he apparently racked his brain for a fresh line of inquiry.

"You got this cross as a present, you said," he continued, after a pause. "Who gave it to you?"

"Is that of any importance?" Miss Huntingdon demanded, with a trace of asperity. "It was given me by a friend. We're both in the 'Christians, Awake!' movement. I don't see that his name's of any importance."

Suddenly Sir Clinton turned round from the window and addressed the girl for the first time.

"May I ask one question, Miss Huntingdon. You're the owner of this cross. But did you actually lose it yourself? I mean, were you wearing it, when it . . . came adrift?"

To Wendover's amazement, this question seemed to disturb Miss Huntingdon more than all the inspector's probing had done.

She flushed like a person caught in a lie, and all the tenseness came back into her attitude, as she drew herself up in her chair to face her interrogator on as much of a level as possible. For a moment Wendover was perplexed. Then he hit on an explanation which seemed to clear up the matter. Suppose she had lent the cross to someone; and the borrower was the man they were seeking. She might be trying to shield this friend. He waited eagerly for her answer.

"No," she stammered, "I wasn't wearing it myself when it was lost."

Sir Clinton's expression betrayed something like admiration, but no sympathy.

"You are really a very clever young woman, Miss Huntingdon," he said, without a trace of irony in his tone. "I've listened to all you've said, and you haven't diverged a hair's-breadth from the literal truth all the way through. And yet, if you don't mind my saying so, you've contrived to give a wholly false impression of the facts, haven't you? You are, of course, the owner of this Tau cross. It was given to you as a present. I don't doubt either of these statements. But . . . was it given to you before or after it was lost?"

"What do you mean?" she demanded shakily.

"I think you understand me well enough. Because a man loses an article, it doesn't cease to be his property. And if it's his property, he can make a gift of it to a friend, even if he can't produce it at the moment. You told us no lies; that I admit at once. But you made a little slip in your reply to one of Inspector Chesilton's questions; and that gave me an inkling of how we stood. Now, who is this friend of yours?"

A hint of unwonted sullenness came into the girl's expression.

"I'm not going to say," she said curtly.

Sir Clinton addressed the inspector, but Wendover could see that he was keeping a sharp eye on the girl as he spoke.

"What's the name of Mr. Bracknell's landlady?" he asked.

"Mrs. Shobden, sir."

Wendover paid no attention to the reply. He, too, had been watching the girl keenly when Bracknell's name was mentioned, and he had seen the start of surprise which she had vainly attempted to conceal by shifting her attitude. Bracknell was the man. That was plain enough. And in Wendover's mind, several pieces of evidence suddenly fitted themselves together to show a common connection. Bracknell was in the "Christians, Awake!" movement, like the girl herself. That was probably how they had got acquainted. Bracknell was a pupil of Mrs. Sternhall; and that connected him with Number 5, The Grove. And now he was directly connected with the Tau cross, since he had sent this girl to reclaim it, and had obviously primed her with the yarn she had spun to them. And behind that manoeuvre lurked the obvious fact that he had not dared to apply for it himself. Wendover reflected, rather sourly, that a girl would hardly have lent herself to an affair of this kind unless she was pretty keen on the man who asked her to carry it through. So that was that.

Sir Clinton picked up the directory which lay beside the doctor's desk telephone and turned over the leaves rapidly in search of a number. Apparently he was unsuccessful in his search, for he did not use the instrument. He put down the directory and turned back to the girl.

"Now, Miss Huntingdon," he said, in a kindlier tone, "I'm not going to preach to you. We'll say no more about the way you've been trying to mislead us. I'm quite sure you don't realise what a serious business you've got mixed up in."

He paused deliberately, and then added:

"What we're working on is that murder in The Grove."

If the girl was acting, she did it well enough to deceive Wendover. This time, there was no effort to hide the start that she gave; and the swift look of mingled amazement and horror on her face seemed far beyond any feigning. For a moment or two she sat rigid, as though Sir Clinton's words had been an incantation which deprived her of the power of movement. Then, with an effort, she pulled herself together.

"The murder case?" she repeated, in a dazed tone. "But I don't know anything about that. I don't know anything at all. Why, I never heard the name of Mr. Sternhall till people began talking about the thing. I don't know anyone in these flats, even. I don't see how you think I've anything to do with it. I can't tell you anything about it; I can't, really."

To Wendover's ears, her protestations had the ring of truth in them. He had been disgusted when she set herself to mislead the inspector. It wasn't what he had expected, from her face and manner when she first entered the room. Too clever by half, he judged, and not a very nice kind of cleverness at the best. But this was a different matter altogether. She seemed genuine enough, now. The shock had obviously been a bolt from the blue, and she had reacted under it just as he would expect a normal girl to do. If she was really mixed up in the case, her connection with it could hardly be more than a remote one, or she would have seen what lay behind all the inspector's questionings.

"Sometimes we have to investigate things which turn out in the end to have little bearing on a case, Miss Huntingdon," Sir Clinton explained. "But they have to be looked into, even if they turn out to be mares' nests. Now I think you told us that on the evening of Friday, you went home and you did not go out again that night. Can you prove that? Your family would be able to say, I suppose, or your maid?"

Some seconds passed without any reply to his question. The girl's pose betrayed concentrated thought, a tenseness of mental effort quite unnecessary for the mere answer to the question. It was plain that she was revolving in her mind some larger problem which taxed all her resources. Wendover was both puzzled and chilled by this evidence of calculation. What could she be devising now?

At last she looked up again, seeming to have taken her decision.

"I'm afraid you'd get no help from them," she explained, as though measuring her words as she spoke them. "Father and Mother dined in town that night and went to the theatre. They didn't get home till late. It was our maid's afternoon out. We only keep one maid. So she couldn't say anything, either. I came home and found the house empty. I didn't bother about dinner. I just

111

got myself a scratch meal of some sort. I wasn't very hungry, as it happened."

"Nobody called that night?" asked Sir Clinton.

Again came that pause for reflection, and this time it was even longer. Evidently some fateful decision hung in the balance, and Marjorie Huntingdon could not make her choice without the greatest difficulty. At last she apparently settled the question in her mind.

"Mr. Bracknell came to the door," she admitted, rather huskily, as if it cost her an effort even to get the words out.

"Mr. Bracknell? So he would at least be able to say that he saw you. Did he come in?" Sir Clinton's tone was almost uninterested.

Again there was a faint hesitation before the answer. "Yes, he did come in. I asked him."

Wendover's sympathy veered away from the girl again. These pauses when a straight answer was required, this evident calculation before admitting anything, hardened his feelings and made him suspicious once more.

"What time did Mr. Bracknell arrive?" Sir Clinton asked.

Marjorie reflected again before answering, though this time the pause was a shorter one.

"It must have been some time between seven and half past seven. I got home about a quarter past six, I remember, took a bath, changed my dress, and was just finishing my picnic supper when the bell rang. That would make it about a quarter past seven, I think. Not as late as half past. I'm quite sure of that."

She had ceased to protest against being questioned. Now she sat upright in her chair, her hands gripping its arms, her feet pressed together, and with every muscle tense as though by physical rigidity she could keep her mind under closer control. She seemed to wait warily for the next question, watchful, like an animal which suspects a trap. But she had not lost her courage. The tilt of her little chin suggested that clearly enough. She was fighting for something, evidently: something which meant very much to her. Wendover had little difficulty in guessing what it was. "She must be very keen on that fellow," he reflected, "for she knows how serious the business is, and yet she's prepared to lie deliberately and risk the chance of detection."

"Your maid washes up the dishes when she comes in?" Sir Clinton inquired casually.

"Of course. Oh, I see what you mean. You can check what I'm saying by asking her? Is that it?"

"We have to check everything," Sir Clinton admitted. "Now, Mr. Bracknell arrived at a quarter past seven, we'll say. Did you invite him to come in?"

"Yes, I did."

There was something just a shade defiant in her tone.

"And he stayed until, say, nine or nine-thirty?"

"He stayed until after ten o'clock. I looked at my watch at a quarter to ten."

Again there was a note in her voice which made her seem to be overemphasising her certainty.

"And during all that time, did you not think of offering him anything—a cup of tea or something like that? He can't have had any dinner."

The wary look in the girl's eyes deepened and this time she did not answer immediately.

"You're thinking of the maid and the dishes, I suppose," she said, with a touch of scorn in her tone. "No, I offered him nothing, so there were no dishes to wash."

"We have to check everything," said Sir Clinton, patiently. "So Mr. Bracknell went away after ten o'clock? Before your parents came back from the theatre, then? And when did your maid come in?"

"About half-past eleven, I think. She usually catches the last tram from town."

"You and Mr. Bracknell didn't go into the garden, by any chance?"

Miss Huntingdon shook her head.

"So there is no one to confirm your story?" the Chief Constable said, in a tone of faint regret. "Except Mr. Bracknell, of course," he added.

"Nobody," Miss Huntingdon admitted at once.

"Forgive me but . . . are you and Mr. Bracknell engaged?"

A swift flush swept over the girl's cheeks.

"Not exactly," she said.

"I understand," Sir Clinton said, with a touch of cynicism. "So it would be no use my asking what you and he talked about?"

"No, I'm afraid it wouldn't."

"Did you mention this visit of Mr. Bracknell to anyone?"

"No. Why should I?"

"One more question. Can you tell me how Mr. Bracknell was dressed that evening?"

This manifestly caught the girl unawares. For a few moments she made no reply, and Sir Clinton waited, not attempting to hurry her.

"I think he had a grey suit on," she declared at last.

"What kind of shoes, can you recall?"

"Brown—or at least, I think so."

"And a clerical collar?"

"No, he doesn't wear clerical collars. A soft collar."

"Hat?"

"He never wears a hat—at least, not on weekdays."

Sir Clinton seemed to have finished his inquiries. He turned to Chesilton.

"Anything more, Inspector?"

Chesilton looked up from the notes he was taking.

"I'd just like to ask, sir, when Mr. Bracknell presented this cross to Miss Huntingdon."

Evidently Marjorie had lost track of her evidence in the early part of the interview or had resolved to abandon some of her bluff.

"On Saturday," she admitted.

"H'm! Probably discovered the loss of it on Friday night," the inspector commented, jotting down her answer.

"Perhaps you'll read over your notes to Miss Huntingdon and get her to initial them," the Chief Constable suggested. Then he turned to the girl. "I've a car at the door. Would you let me take you home in it? You've had rather a trying experience, I'm afraid."

Marjorie rose rather stiffly to her feet.

"No, thank you," she said icily. "I'd much rather find my way home by myself."

Wendover, noting the slim figure, the droop of the mouth corners, the anxious and perplexed eyes, felt pity for the girl. But though evidently daunted, she seemed to refuse to admit defeat. She had done her best for Bracknell, and she would stick to her tale, even with all its flaws, unless it could be demolished by counter-evidence.

"I doubt very much if that fellow's worth it, even at the best," Wendover commented to himself. "He can't be much of an angel if he primed her with all those lies."

9
THE TENNIS SHOES

Sir Clinton took the wheel and the other two climbed into the car. But instead of starting his engine, the Chief Constable drew out his case and lit a cigarette, keeping his eyes all the time on the slim figure in the light summer frock which went hurrying along the pavement, away from them into the twilight. Only when it was almost out of sight did he start his motor and drive slowly after the girl at a pace just sufficient to keep her in view.

"What's your game now, Clinton?" Wendover demanded, in a rather sulky tone. "You don't suppose she's given a false address, do you?"

"No," the Chief Constable assured him. "But there's just a chance that friend Bracknell may be hanging about, waiting for her. And in that case, we might save ourselves some trouble. But I rather think a telephone call office is her first port. There's one at the end of this road, just round the corner."

At the end of the road, they saw Marjorie stop a passerby, apparently to ask a question, for the man pointed up the crossroad.

"Bull's-eye," said Sir Clinton, with a chuckle. "Well, she won't do much harm there. Bracknell's landlady isn't on the 'phone. I looked in the directory to see. So she can't get ahead of us and warn him. But now she'll probably take a taxi, so we'll have to show some speed. We must pick up a man at the station, Inspector. We may need him to keep Master Bracknell amused."

He pressed the accelerator and the car swept past the telephone booth just as Marjorie entered the little box. Stimulated by the whir

116

of the engine, perhaps, the Chief Constable hummed below his breath an air to which Wendover fitted the words:

> "When constabulary duty's to be done,
>   To be done,
> A policeman's lot is not a happy one,
>   Happy one."

"No, I should think you'd feel that, after bullying that unfortunate girl into contradicting herself again and again," he said acidly. "You won't use me as a decoy again, in a hurry. I've seldom felt more uncomfortable and less like a gentleman."

"Little girls shouldn't tell lies. Then they wouldn't be made uncomfortable, either," was Sir Clinton's retort. "And by the way, my dictionary defines 'bullying' as 'Overbearing with blustering menaces.' I ask you, candidly, did you observe either the inspector or me blustering or menacing? Moderate your language. You might hurt the inspector's feelings."

"Not yours, though, I imagine," was Wendover's reply.

"No, so long as a grateful county pays me my salary, I propose to earn it, and I keep my finer feelings for private life."

"Well, I didn't like the business," Wendover admitted frankly. "And being an unpaid magistrate, I can't salve my feelings with the thought that I'm earning my salary."

"I think your quarrel ought to be with the fellow who dragged her into the dirty business—and not with us."

"I'm not forgetting him," Wendover declared, with some show of bitterness in his tone.

At the police station, Chesilton got out of the car to give some orders. He returned almost immediately, accompanied by a constable who joined them in the motor.

"I've sent out an all-stations message, sir," Chesilton reported, "telling them to keep a lookout for Bracknell. His photo has been in the press over this 'Christians, Awake!' business and I expect he's well enough known to most of our men. I've taken one or two other steps as well. We'll have him very soon, in any case."

117

"I'm in hopes that we may find him at home," Sir Clinton said, with a glance at his wrist watch.

Number 17, Bella Vista Avenue, turned out to be one of a terrace of houses, with tiny gardens in front. As the car stopped, Sir Clinton turned to the uniformed constable in the back seat.

"You'll stay at the gate, here," he ordered. "If a taxi drives up, with a young lady inside, you'll detain her in talk as well as you can. I don't want her to come inside. If a taxi drives up and doesn't stop, take its number but don't interfere with it. Watch where it goes."

Followed by Chesilton and Wendover, he went up the little flight of steps which led to the front door. The bell was answered by a middle-aged, rather gloomy-looking maid. Yes, Mr. Bracknell was at home. She'd inquire if he was free.

"Don't trouble. Just show us in," Sir Clinton said.

The maid gave a curious glance at the uniformed man at the gate and made no demur. She opened the door of a sitting-room on their right and ushered them in.

Bracknell looked up sharply as they entered. He was sitting in an armchair with his back to the light. An open book was on his knee, but he seemed to have broken off his reading to ponder over something, for he held the volume slightly askew. Apparently he had recently come back from tennis, for he was in flannels and his feet were encased in immaculate tennis shoes. As his visitors came in, he rose to his feet with a movement of surprise. His flannels set off his athletic figure. Wendover, despite his prejudice, could not deny his good looks.

"The perfect young Adonis of the suburbs," he commented inwardly. "Just the kind of fellow a silly girl would fall in love with at first sight. She wouldn't notice that his eyes are a bit too close together."

Bracknell surveyed the rather incongruous trio before him: Sir Clinton, neat, inconspicuous, and rather detached; Wendover, a typical country squire of the finer type; and the inspector, burly, tired, and with something in his eyes and lips that suggested a man who suffered from few illusions. Bracknell made no attempt to hide

118

his surprise, and with a gesture he invited explanation of the intrusion.

At an almost imperceptible sign from Sir Clinton, the inspector took charge of the proceedings.

"Mr. Bracknell? I'm Inspector Chesilton. I'm in charge of the murder case in The Grove. I'd like to ask you some questions."

In the circumstances, Chesilton believed that rushing tactics would gain him an advantage.

"Won't you sit down?" Bracknell asked, with a gesture toward the chairs scattered about the sitting-room.

"No, I'll stand, thanks."

Wendover noted that Bracknell had made no show of surprise when the inspector mentioned the murder. That contrasted sharply with Marjorie Huntingdon's reaction to the test.

"Now, sir," Chesilton went on, "we've got some information, and I think you can help us."

Wendover noticed a flicker of an expression passing through Bracknell's eyes. It might have been relief at the inspector's words.

"Certainly I'm willing to help," he said at once. "Horrible affair, that."

The inspector ignored the comment.

"It is a question of covering the movements of somebody on Friday night," he explained. "I'm asking you no leading questions, sir, you'll notice. I don't want to mention a particular name. Just tell us, if you can remember, what people you spoke to on Friday night from, say, six o'clock onwards to midnight."

Bracknell stood with his eyes downcast for some seconds, and his whole pose suggested a man racking his memory for elusive details.

"At six o'clock," he said at last, with the hesitation of a man anxious to recapture details even to the last moment, "I was at the Tennis Club at the foot of the Avenue—along there, you know," he pointed towards Hernshaw Park. "The last set I played in was a mixed double. Let's see. Miss Staple, Miss Whitgift, and Mr. Cale."

". . . Mr. Cale," repeated Chesilton, who was jotting down the names in his notebook. "What time did you finish, can you remember, sir?"

"I really can't say. Somewhere about half-past six, or a shade later. I didn't look at my watch."

"And then?"

"We chatted for a while, sitting in front of the clubhouse. Then Miss Staple and Miss Whitgift went away."

"Together or separately?" demanded the inspector suddenly.

"Together, I think. Cale turned to talk to someone else, a man I didn't recognise, and I went into the clubhouse to look at the illustrated weeklies. I sat there for a while . . ." he paused, as if racking his memory. "I think Mr. Woodford was there at that time. That's my recollection, at any rate."

He paused again, but Chesilton refused to help him out. After a moment or two, Bracknell continued.

"The clubhouse was nearly empty by that time. Now I think of it, I must have been the last to leave. Most of them had gone home to dinner, I expect."

He halted again, glancing at Chesilton as if he expected him to put a question. But the inspector held his tongue.

"I don't know exactly when I left the clubhouse. It must have been seven o'clock or after it a little, most probably. I remembered then that I had forgotten a message I should have given, something about a meeting. I went to Avondale, in Hill Rise."

"Just a moment, sir. Who was the last person you remember seeing before that?"

"Mr. Woodford. I passed him a copy of *Punch*, I remember."

"Which way did you take, going to Avondale? I'm simply trying to test your memory," Chesilton explained, with a faint smile.

"Oh, I went up that kind of lane . . . what do they call it? . . . the thing that borders the tennis courts. . . . Ringwood Hill, that's it."

"You got to Avondale at . . ."

"Shortly after seven, I imagine. But that's a guess. Somewhere before half-past seven, at any rate."

"The maid opened the door," Chesilton went on, as if anxious to cut short the details. "Does she know you? I mean, has she seen you often?"

"She knows me. At least, I've been there once or twice. But you're wrong. She didn't open the door. Miss Huntingdon opened the door. Her maid was out. So were her parents. She asked me to come in. I went in."

"Just a moment," interrupted the inspector. "What was she dressed in? Be exact, if you can."

"Some dark stuff . . . an evening frock of some sort. I've seen her in it before."

"And then?" prompted Chesilton.

"I stayed there for the rest of the evening."

"Did Miss Huntingdon offer you a meal of any sort?"

Bracknell's eyes narrowed a trifle and he paused before answering:

"No, she didn't."

"But . . . You mean you missed your dinner?" demanded the inspector, in the tone of one who has never missed a meal in his life.

"It was a sweltering night. I wasn't very keen on dinner."

"But I suppose you got a snack when you came home again? It's a long time to go without food," Chesilton suggested sympathetically.

"You seem very worried about my meals," Bracknell said ironically. "No, I didn't take a snack, as you call it."

Chesilton ignored the irony completely.

"You stayed at Avondale until . . . when?" he demanded.

Wendover saw a gleam of something like amusement in Bracknell's eyes. Evidently here he felt himself on safe ground.

"Until after ten. I looked at my watch as I got up to go, and it was after ten o'clock then. I'm quite certain of that point."

The inspector seemed to take special care in entering this in his notes. He looked up again as he put a fresh question.

"Three hours you spent there, then. Can you remember any of the things you talked about?"

For a moment, Bracknell seemed to give this some consideration. Then, with a smile which Wendover disliked, he replied:

"The usual sort of thing one talks about when one's alone with a girl. Herself and myself. Nothing of public interest."

"You came home along The Grove, I suppose? It's the shortest way. Did you recognise anyone in the crowd that was outside Number 5 at that time?"

"No, because I came home by the other way—up Hill Rise, and away from The Grove. I knew nothing about the murder until I saw it in the papers next day, if that's what you mean."

Chesilton refused to take up this point at the moment. He glanced over his notes, as though he had finished his inquiry and then, apparently remembering something, he asked:

"You're the Reverend Ambrose Bracknell, aren't you?"

Bracknell shook his head with a smile.

"Just plain Mr. and no Reverend. I'm a helper in the 'Christians, Awake!' movement, but no more reverend than you are."

"A lay preacher? I see. Salaried, I suppose?"

"No. My expenses are paid by a nice old lady who's interested in the movement. A Mrs. Canham. She lives in another part of the country altogether."

"I see," said the inspector thoughtfully. "Very nice of her, I'm sure." He fumbled in his waistcoat pocket and produced the Tau cross. "I think this is yours, Mr. Bracknell?"

Wendover saw the momentary glimmer of fear in Bracknell's eyes, as the inspector held out the trinket in the palm of his hand.

"No, it doesn't belong to me," came the emphatic denial.

"Quite correct, sir, I believe. My mistake. What I should have said was, 'This was in your possession on Friday night.' I think that hits the mark?"

Bracknell seemed completely taken aback. He glanced at the cross, and then gave a furtive look at the faces in front of him. Some seconds passed before he found his voice.

"I've nothing to say about it."

"I'm afraid I'll have to press you, sir. Found where it was, it seems to need a bit of explaining."

Wendover admired the manner in which the inspector turned his phrase, giving nothing away, but striking a note of acute suspicion.

"Where did you find it?" Bracknell demanded, with a touch of hoarseness in his voice.

"Where did you lose it?" retorted Chesilton. "That's the point we want to get at."

"I don't know," Bracknell declared, in a strained tone. "If I knew where I'd dropped it, wouldn't I have gone back to pick it up?"

"Not in some circumstances," said the inspector crisply. "Did you know Mr. Sternhall?"

"Not even by sight," Bracknell declared, with a curious ring of assurance in his tone. "If I'd met him, I wouldn't even have known who he was."

"You knew Mrs. Sternhall, though?"

"I took lessons from her, if that's what you're after. That was purely a business affair. I mean, I didn't know her as an acquaintance."

"And you never met Mr. Sternhall in your life; that's what you say?"

"If I met him, I certainly didn't know he was Mr. Sternhall. I may have met him in the street, for all I know."

This time Wendover detected something that rang false in Bracknell's tone. There was all the assurance of a man who makes a statement which will stand the test of inquiry; and yet . . . somehow there was something in the background, something in the man's manner, or in his eyes, which just failed to carry complete conviction.

Wendover suddenly caught the glimmer of a possible explanation. This was the fellow who had primed Marjorie Huntingdon in her tactics when he sent her to recover the Tau cross. And what was her method? To stick to the truth unswervingly—up to a point—and yet to leave an entirely false impression on her hearers. Well, if the pupil used that trick, was it not probable that her teacher was able to play the same game? Was this assertion of Bracknell's another of these deceptive "truths"? He tried hard to recapture the exact words which Bracknell had used, but the precise phrases had slipped from his memory while he was pondering on the problem.

"This sort of thing's no use, Mr. Bracknell," the inspector exclaimed, with a rasp in his tone. "What you've told us doesn't concur with other evidence that we have. I'm giving you a chance to clear things up, and I advise you to take it."

Bracknell's rather heavy underlip set stubbornly.

"Have you any legal right to extract any more from me?"

The inspector shied away from this question.

"I'll ask you once again, sir, where did you lose this gold cross? If you can clear that up, why don't you do so? It'll make a lot of difference, perhaps," he added meaningly.

"Find out for yourself, if you're so clever," Bracknell snapped savagely.

Chesilton sighed obviously, like a man put to unnecessary trouble.

"If you can't be more straightforward with us, sir . . ." The unfinished sentence was a threat in itself.

Bracknell seemed to recover his temper by an immense effort.

"I'll tell you this," he said. "I was never introduced to Mr. Stern-hall. I had no acquaintance with him of any sort. You can't bring a single witness who can say we had the slightest connection with each other. I didn't so much as know him by sight or reputation. That's the plain truth and nothing but the truth. Why should you be dragging me into this business . . ."

He broke off abruptly.

"You won't clear things up, then?" Chesilton asked coolly. "Very well, sir. I've done my best with you."

He went to the window and summoned the constable from the gate.

"I'm giving you a minute or two to think over things," he said to Bracknell, when the man appeared. Then he turned to Sir Clinton. "I'd like a word with you outside, sir."

As they filed out into the little hall, Chesilton left them and rang the front doorbell to summon the maid. She arrived almost at once, obviously very inquisitive and slightly perturbed.

"Mr. Bracknell has a pair of tennis shoes in his room, hasn't he?" Chesilton demanded. "Let me see where they are."

The maid shook her head, however, instead of showing the way.

"Tennis shoes?" she echoed. "The only tennis shoes he's got are the ones he's wearing now."

"Oh, is that so?" Chesilton said, with no disappointment in his tone. "That simplifies things. You're quite sure he's no others? We'd better take a look."

"No, he hasn't," declared the maid, in the tone of one who knows what she is talking about. "He's got but the one pair. These are new ones. He destroyed the other ones he had."

Something in her tone suggested that this was for some reason a grievance with her.

"Destroyed them, did he? How?" demanded Chesilton. "When was that?"

"It was Saturday afternoon. He asked me to lay a fire for him in his sitting-room—just fancy a fire in this weather. And the trouble of setting it and cleaning it out afterwards. Full of stinking burnt rubber, the ashes were. And the smell in the house while he was cutting them up and burning them. . . . Ph! Enough to choke anybody. And all the sticky stuff left in the grate. I had a pair of good cleaning gloves fair ruined with it; enough to make anyone vexed! And not so much as 'I'm sorry,' from him, over it, though he saw quite well what a mess he'd made."

Something in her tone suggested to Wendover that Bracknell had not been very generous in his tipping.

Chesilton produced his notebook, and at the sight of it, the woman seemed to feel suddenly important.

"Just you take it down," she said. "Last Saturday afternoon. Fire asked for in the middle of summer and a lot of burnt rubber and sticky mess left in the grate. That took me quite a while to clean up, you can put down. And don't forget about the gloves. I could swear to all that on my Bible oath."

"Don't you forget the date," Chesilton advised her. "Now another thing. On Friday, did he order his dinner as usual?"

"Yes, he did." From her tone, this was another grievance. "A bit of roast lamb. And that one a broiling day. And I had to stay in and cook it, because the missus turned poorly that afternoon. And it was my early evening off, too. And when half-past seven came, he never looked near. I had to wait on. For an hour I waited, expecting him to come back. But not he. And so, when I did get out at last, it was late. And I'd meant to go to the pictures and I couldn't get in, after all. Some people have no consideration for girls."

"Well, you can remember that too," Chesilton advised her.

"What's he been doing?" the woman demanded inquisitively.

"I don't know, yet," Chesilton said, with a quickly suppressed grin. "But I want to see his room. Where is it?"

She led the inspector upstairs, chattering volubly about her grievances and making efforts to coax the inspector to divulge his secret. Sir Clinton did not trouble to follow them. He could trust the inspector to miss very little. In a short time Chesilton returned and dismissed the maid.

"Nothing there, sir," he reported. "Two or three pairs of shoes but not a trace of paint on their soles. I went over them with a magnifying glass. A pair of pumps, though. I've got them in my pockets. No paint on them, either, so far as I can see; but I want to make sure. The tennis shoes were the dangerous things, or why did he destroy them?"

"Any pistol to be seen?" Sir Clinton asked.

"No, sir. But I only made a very rough search. I'll go into things more carefully later."

Obviously Sir Clinton read more into this last statement than its actual words, for he nodded.

"What do you think of his yarn?" he asked.

"Like the curate's egg, eh? Some parts of it are excellent—but the rest can't be swallowed at any price. I don't much care for this young man. What do you propose to do, Inspector?"

"Well, sir, we can't afford to lose sight of him now."

"No doubt about that," the Chief Constable concurred.

"I don't quite like to go the length of arresting him just yet, or even charging him, till I've more up my sleeve. What about detaining him on suspicion, sir?"

"I think so," Sir Clinton agreed, and then he added, a little to Wendover's surprise, "That kills two birds with one stone."

"Two birds? Which birds?" Wendover demanded.

"Well, it makes sure that he doesn't get hold of Miss Huntingdon and prime her with more lies. And besides, it avoids all chance of trouble about the competence of a witness."

"I don't follow that," Wendover admitted. "Try to be a bit less like the Oracle of Delphi, if it isn't too much of a strain."

"Well, wasn't it fairly clear that he's got a strong influence over Miss Huntingdon? A girl of her sort wouldn't lie like that for the first comer, would she? And if one brisks things up a bit, it's always possible to get married within a couple of days, isn't it?"

"I see! You mean a wife can't give evidence against her husband?"

"I had it in mind. But if we detain him, there'll be no question of any prank of that sort. I'd detain him, Inspector"

"Very good, sir. You don't want to ask him any more questions?"

"No, I leave him to you. There's no need for Mr. Wendover and me to stay any longer. Good night."

"Good night, sir."

When they had taken their seats in the car again, Wendover turned to his companion.

"I hadn't thought of his persuading that girl into a quick marriage," he admitted. "You think it was likely?"

"From what I saw of the girl, it's possible; and there's no use in risking a thing of that sort. They're both liars, Squire, to put it bluntly. But she was lying to save him, whereas he was lying to save himself. There's a difference. Candidly, I think she might find somebody better than Master Bracknell, without having to go very far to find the article."

"His eyes are too close together," said Wendover, with apparent irrelevance.

"His blood interests me more than his eyes, at present. But you can't punch a suspect on the nose without cause given. Now if you had only let your manly indignation rise a bit, Squire, you might have done us a service. And it wouldn't have cost you more than, say, ten bob for a common assault."

"I've lost a good deal more than ten bob's worth of self-respect over your doings with that girl," Wendover said acidly, as his earlier grievance recurred to his mind.

"Clever little thing," Sir Clinton commented indifferently. "Good stuff used in a bad cause."

Almost as soon as they reached Sir Clinton's house, the telephone rang. The Chief Constable took up the receiver, listened to the message with one or two comments which conveyed nothing to Wendover, then put the receiver down again.

"This fellow Danbury seems a sharp lad," he said, turning to Wendover. "Chesilton was 'phoning. It seems that when he got to the station with our awakening young friend, he found a report from Danbury, left by him when he went on duty. Here's the gist of it. Danbury, it seems, has got a girl, a maid at one of the villas in The Grove, a little farther along the street from Number 5 and on the opposite side. Naturally, seeing that Danbury played a part in the discovery at Number 5, the two of them have discussed the whole affair, up and down. And in the course of talk, it turns out that the girl had seen our young friend Bracknell in The Grove at about 7.30. She had been putting the last touches to the dinner table and went to close an open window. She happened to glance out, and she saw Bracknell go along on the opposite pavement and turn into Number 5. That was not earlier than 7.25 p.m., she declares, since she gauges the time from the dinner hour. They dine at half-past seven in that house, it seems. Danbury didn't attach much importance to it, I gather, but put in a report merely in the way of business—'information received,' which might possibly have some use."

"That knocks the bottom out of his attempt at an alibi," Wendover commented, "for this girl of Danbury's has no axe to grind in the affair, obviously. Also, neither she nor Danbury could know anything about Bracknell's connection with the affair at all. It seems unbiased evidence of the best sort."

"Yes," Sir Clinton agreed, but he added in a thoughtful tone, "I would rather like to know what took our awakening friend to Number 5 at 7.25 p.m., when his dinner was waiting him at home, round the corner, at half-past seven. You remember the maid's grievance was that he didn't come back at 7.30?"

"So it was, now I think of it. He must have been going to see Mrs. Sternhall."

"But in that case, he would have run into Dujardin, who was with Mrs. Sternhall from seven o'clock onwards. But neither Dujardin nor Mrs. Sternhall mentioned his calling at the flat. Nor did he himself. In fact, his whole yarn started from the basis that he saw nobody he knew from the time he left the clubhouse to the time he rang the Avondale front doorbell. If Mrs. Sternhall's maid answered the bell of the flat—assuming he went upstairs—why did he not mention her? She's bound to know him, since he's a pupil of Mrs. Sternhall."

"Well, I shouldn't take his word for much, I'll admit that."

"Another thing," Sir Clinton continued ruminatively, "Since he didn't see Mrs. Sternhall just then, why didn't he go home for the dinner that was waiting for him round the corner?"

He reflected for some moments, then some thought seemed to occur to him.

"You know, Squire, I really think I'll have to do something for young Danbury. He seems to have some special qualifications for detective work. I must keep an eye on him."

10
THE REPORTER'S VIEW

"Care for a game of chess?" Sir Clinton inquired.

They were old opponents and each knew the other's methods to a nicety.

"If you care to play," Wendover acquiesced, though without his usual enthusiasm. "I'm not quite in the mood for it, tonight, though, and you'd beat me rather too easily."

The Chief Constable did not press the matter.

"Another time," he said, offering Wendover a cigar. "Sorry I'm seeing so little of you this visit, Squire. I've been kept at it, today."

"On the case?" queried Wendover.

"The case? Oh, you mean the Sternhall business. No, it was mostly routine work and another affair altogether. We're trying hard to get on the track of these smash-and-grab artists. No success, so far, unfortunately."

Wendover's interest in the smash-and-grab gang was tepid at the best. It was the Sternhall murder which fascinated him.

"Has Chesilton got any farther forward?" he demanded.

"Not very far, as yet, I'm afraid," the Chief Constable confessed. "He interviewed that Huntingdon girl again, but she stuck to that yarn of hers like a limpet to a rock."

"And what about Bracknell? Has he said anything more?"

"Not a word. But Chesilton has more hopes of breaking him down. We've found another witness—an old fellow Mitford, who lives in Number 1, Ravenswood Mansions, just round the corner from The Grove, and he recollects seeing somebody who answers

130

to Bracknell's description in the street at 7.45 p.m. Mitford described him as looking 'not quite ordinary'—a little excited-looking, apparently. But that may be merely imagination working on Mitford's recollections. The point is that he's quite sure that it was as late as a quarter to eight. He was out posting a letter, in a hurry to catch the post at the pillar near by, and he'd looked at his watch because it was a close thing."

"That seems pretty conclusive," Wendover commented. "Two independent witnesses—the maid and this Mitford man—with no axes to grind. It's pretty plain that Bracknell wasn't at Avondale till close on eight o'clock, instead of shortly after seven, as he and the girl asserted. Has Chesilton put this to Bracknell yet?"

"No, we might get something more. No use springing a mine till you've got it fully charged."

Wendover heard a car come up the drive and stop at the front door. The bell rang, and in a few moments a maid brought Sir Clinton a card. He glanced at it, seemed to hesitate momentarily, then told her to show the visitor in.

"A friend of yours, Squire," he said, putting the card down on a table at his elbow.

Wendover had been looking forward to an undisturbed evening in his old friend's company, and this interruption was not much to his taste. He swallowed his disappointment, however, reflecting that Sir Clinton's friends were usually interesting people, who could contribute their share of talk without becoming boring. But when the visitor was ushered in, he felt a spasm of vexation. It was the reporter who had invaded the flats on the night of the murder in The Grove. Barbican was less negligently dressed now, but he had lost none of his assurance. He came jauntily into the room with the air of one who takes his welcome for granted. "Good evening, Sir Clinton. I'm a reporter. Name's Barbican, you remember. Have you anything for me? Anything fresh about the Sternhall murder?"

He sat down without waiting for the formality of an invitation and fixed his bright, eager eyes on the Chief Constable. Wendover, his temper on edge, owing to his dislike of the journalist, wondered why Sir Clinton had allowed such a creature to get beyond his door-step. He consoled himself with the reflection that this visit, at any rate, would not last long.

"No, I've nothing for you at present, Mr. Barbican," Sir Clinton replied, with a smile of frank amusement.

"But I've come all the way down here," protested Barbican.

"Then it'll be a nice change of scenery when you go all the way back again," Sir Clinton pointed out sardonically. "A road looks quite different, according to whether you're coming or going."

"A bright thought, that, though I've heard something like it before," the journalist retorted, with a tinge of impertinence in his tone. "But come, now. Won't you spill a drop or two of information? It's a hard life, a free lance's. Have a heart. Why are you detaining Bracknell?"

"You know that, do you?" said Sir Clinton, without surprise. "Have you asked Inspector Chesilton about it?"

"Have I? I asked him seven times over, and I was just putting on the record for the eighth shot when he kicked me out."

"Only metaphorically, I suppose," said the Chief Constable, with a shade of regret in his tone. "If he'd done it physically, it might have suggested to you that he minds his own business and expects you to mind yours."

"But everybody's business is my business," Barbican protested good-humouredly.

> "'Let observation with extensive view
> Survey mankind from China to Peru.'

What's the harm in my wanting to observe Bracknell, Chesilton, and Company?"

"You're quoting from Johnson—*The Vanity of Human Wishes*," Sir Clinton pointed out drily. "The title's rather a bad omen. But survey till you're blue in the face, in vulgar parlance, if you wish to do so. Only don't expect any assistance from me at present."

"You don't sound very helpful and that's a fact," said Barbican flippantly. "One might almost take it as a hint that I ought to go. Well, if you've nothing for me, I can't afford to waste my time."

He rose from his chair; but, to Wendover's surprise and annoyance, Sir Clinton made a restraining gesture.

"Not so much hurry," he said. "Sit down again. You've put me to the trouble of receiving you, so I may as well make use of you."

"Always eager to oblige, so long as there's anything in it for me," Barbican assured him. "What follows is not confidential and won't be treated as such. That's understood?"

"Oh, quite," Sir Clinton assured him. "I only want a word about one of your neighbours, a Mr. Mitford. He lives in the same set of flats as you do?"

"Number 1, Ravenswood Mansions. Quite correct. How you sleuths find out these things . . ." he broke off in mock wonder.

"From the Post-office Directory. Now enough of this foolery, please. What do you know about Mr. Mitford?"

Barbican's eyes narrowed when he heard the question, and he dropped some of his pertness. He paused for a moment before answering, evidently to search his memory.

"Old Mitford?" he answered. "He's a rum bird, if you like. He lives in the top flat—there's an architect's office on the floor between us. I'm going to make an article out of him, some day. Say a guinea's worth. He's an old clerk. Got too stupid for his job, or something. Got the push too. He told me all his sad story once. So he lives up under the slates on tuppence-ha'penny and a fund of optimism. Funny old devil! He's quite mad about Japan, for some reason. Owns a priceless collection of works by the Old Masters—British Museum coloured postcards, you know. He's got one or two real Japanese things, though. Butterfly crawling on a leaf with Fujiyama in the background. Bird flying over lake, with Fujiyama in the background. Man crossing a bridge, with Fujiyama all present and correct, as before. Each one worth its price as waste paper. Also about half-a-dozen modern fake netsukes and sword guards. He asked me what they were worth, once. I said I couldn't put a price on them. Nor could I. You can't price rubbish. He hasn't a thing in the lot that I'd give five bob for, and then half-a-crown of that would be charity."

"You're evidently an authority," Sir Clinton commented. "What would you say this was worth?"

133

He picked up a Japanese sword guard from the mantelpiece and held it out to Barbican. To Wendover's surprise, the journalist scrutinised it carefully and then mentioned a figure which Wendover did not catch, but which was obviously not far off the mark, as Sir Clinton's face betrayed.

"H'm! You do seem to know something about it," the Chief Constable admitted, with more respect than he had hitherto shown. "I took it you were bluffing, as usual. Where did you pick up your information?"

"Behind the counter of a curiosity shop," Barbican boasted. "'One man in his time plays many parts.' Shakespeare was thinking of me when he wrote that. We're kindred souls, you know. I've been all sorts of things. I began in the Church. 'Ah me! I was a pale young curate then.' But it didn't last. I used to stroll home in the dusk after service with some fair young thing, discussing my sermon and what not. You know what it's like: smell of honeysuckle from the hedges, bats fluttering overhead, and Venus in the ascendant in the blue. I turned aside into Lover's Lane with one or two of the damsels—and the Church didn't like it. In fact, I cast them off and looked for another job. I've been a writing master, too. Do you an engrossed testimonial in any style you like to pay for and write anything from copperplate to cuneiform. I can make a pen do anything except say, 'Pretty Polly!' Garage mechanic, I've been. The best of that job is teaching a pretty girl to drive. You lose your head and clasp her round the waist when she makes a muddle of her steering. One thing leads to another, I've found. Cheapjack, I've been that, too. That's when I lost my shyness and got my present heartiness. Palmist—I've given that up, long ago. You read faces, not hands, on that lay. Guess what they're thinking about, and then tell 'em. Fine training in psychological physiognomy. You should try that phrase on your drunks. Beats 'British Constitution' hollow. Pedigree hunter, bagman, guide to the Great Metropolis, solicitor's clerk: I've tried 'em all. I've been on the stage, too, like Shakespeare. Never played big parts, though; which makes another resemblance between us. My highest flight was a one-man quick-change show on the Halls. I was a literary agent once upon a time. At least, my advertisement said I was. I took fees from confiding young authors, but the publishers wouldn't take their books, so the bottom fell out of that spec. I'm like Panurge," he confessed, in mock ruefulness. "I've suffered badly from the disease called cramp in the kick."

"Panurge?" said the Chief Constable musingly. "He had three-score and three ways of getting a living, of which the most honest was petty larceny. Another kindred spirit of yours, Mr. Barbican? But I gather that you've put aside the indiscretions of your youth?"

"Oh, Lord, yes," said Barbican airily. "I had a bit of luck in the Sweep, and now I'm a gentleman."

"Wasn't there somebody in the Steinie Morrison case who called himself a gentleman on the strength of a gold watch and an income of a pound a week?" Wendover inquired.

"Well, you've got a chromium-plated wrist watch and ten thousand pounds a year, I suppose," retorted Barbican. "The principle's the same. You don't work for your living. That's all it amounts to."

"You couldn't make gentlemen out of some people, even if you gave them one hundred thousand pounds a year and a grandfather clock to carry about with them," objected Wendover, with intention.

"Meaning me?" returned Barbican, with complete indifference. "It's a mere matter of definition. Don't let's argue about it."

"We seem to have wandered away from Mr. Mitford," Sir Clinton pointed out. "You can write out the story of your life, some-time, and let me read it. But in the meanwhile . . ."

"Oh, Mitford? He comes down and talks to me about Japan and Japanesy stuff now and again. I think he gets his news out of the Public Library books. He's never seen a decent bit of lacquer in his life, I should think; but he can reel off chat about it as long as you'll stand it. No harm in the old bird, so far as I know."

His eyes grew suddenly alert.

"What d' you want to know about *him* for?"

"Oh, curiosity. He comes in between China and Peru, you know."

"Well, I've given you a run over his points already. He's got the worst collection of cheap Japanese and pseudo-Japanese stuff that ever was gathered together. He reads Japanese fairy tales, all about the Forty-seven Ronins—or is it forty-nine, whatever they were. He'd live on rice if his digestion could stand it, and smoke opium if he could lay hands on it, just to get the atmosphere of the thing, I expect. He's quite uninteresting, except that he's a bit off his chump."

An idea seemed to strike him; possibly he imagined he had found a way to turn Sir Clinton's flank.

"By the way, that little Huntingdon piece will be a bit put out by your arresting Bracknell."

"'Detaining' is the word," Sir Clinton corrected him. "Why do you think that?"

"Oh, young blood. Holding hands in the dusk and making life one grand sweet song, and all that. At least, that's her trouble. I'm not so sure about him, myself. But naturally, with things in that state—I've watched 'em coming up Ringwood Hill together from the courts in the twilight—she'll be a bit put out by your brutal methods."

"You take an interest in them?" Sir Clinton asked, without troubling to mask his irony.

"Oh, one can see a lot from my windows with an opera glass," Barbican confessed shamelessly. "And that reminds me, young Bracknell used to hang round Mrs. Sternhall a bit."

"I believe he took French lessons from her."

"Oh, yes, very French, they were."

"Is this more of the results of your opera-glass work?" Wendover asked, exasperated by the man's expression.

"Well, you can see part of her sitting-room from my window," Barbican explained, without hesitation. "Those Frenchwomen! Well, well! Still, I think that young hero might be content with one romance at a time. And now, on top of it all, he gets suspected of outing poor old Sternhall! Tut! Tut!"

"Any other titbits of local information?" Sir Clinton asked, with a smile, refusing to rise to the offered bait.

"Oh, I'm full of 'em," Barbican declared, taking his defeat with a grin. "Take your choice. The cat at Number 3 The Grove will be raising another family soon, or I'm no judge of form. The maid at

Number 10 goes out of the back gate every night before closing time, swinging a jug in a devil-may-care way and comes back again, carrying it as if it were full of molten gold. Your P.C. on the beat at night is sparking a maid in The Grove, a pretty bit of goods, too. The bell in Ringwood Church keeps me awake on Sunday mornings and I'm thinking of lodging a complaint."

"And yet, with all this observation, you missed the one thing worth seeing, lately," Sir Clinton pointed out.

"What's that?"

"The murderer leaving Number 5 after doing his work."

"Yes," Barbican admitted, in a tone of regret, "I did miss that. 'Twould have been a bit of a scoop, wouldn't it? But I was busy tinkering up the connections of my wireless set, just then, worse luck. You can't keep an eye on the world when you've got a hot soldering-iron in your fist. Besides, I expect he went out by the front door, and even my opera glass won't see through a row of houses."

"A handy man, are you?" Sir Clinton asked.

"Oh, yes," Barbican declared, rather boastfully. "I've got a little workshop of sorts. I used to make something out of it. 'Jigsaw Puzzles, 200 pieces, 276, post free; 500 pieces, five bob.' Cut 'em four at a time or so, with a treadle machine. That's another of my accomplishments. But this free-lance journalism's more to my taste. Now, what about an interview with the Chief Constable? Have a heart. No? I'll bring some rock-softener with me next time. It's badly needed in this district." He swung round to Wendover. "What about a chatty little article: 'Country Life. Moles, Voles, and Foals, by a Landed Proprietor'? No? Nothing doing? Ah, well. I must chase after the Huntingdon girl and see if she'll weep out her troubles on my collar stud or thereabouts. Good night, everybody. Good night."

As Barbican left the house, Wendover picked up the evening newspaper.

"I don't admire your choice in callers," he commented, as he unfolded the sheet. "It's your house, of course, Clinton. But you might draw the line at a survivor of the Gadarene herd."

"Oh, he doesn't look old enough to be that," said Sir Clinton, soothingly. "You must be mistaken, Squire. And he's really a very observant fellow. You can't deny that."

"He's a damned nosing, ill-bred, impudent . . ."

"You'll find Roget's *Thesaurus* in the bookcase, left-hand end of the third shelf," the Chief Constable pointed out. "You can sit down tomorrow and copy out all the words you need. In the meanwhile, I rather agree with you about him. Let's leave it at that."

Wendover shrugged his shoulders and returned to his newspaper. But after a few minutes, he uttered a sharp ejaculation of surprise.

"I say, Clinton, here's a weird coincidence—if it is a coincidence. Just listen to this."

After hunting for his place in the newspaper columns, he read out slowly:

> "ATLANTIC LINER MYSTERY
> PASSENGER MISSING
>
> "A wireless message to a passenger on the liner *Martaban* has revealed a mystery which is not yet cleared up. Mr. Sternhall, the passenger in question, boarded the liner at Liverpool. He was seen by the purser and his cabin steward. Later, it was found that he was not on board, though his luggage was in his cabin. It was assumed that he had gone ashore at the last moment and failed to return before the ship sailed.
>
> "Two days later, a Marconigram for him reached the *Martaban*, which contained the news that his wife had died after an operation for acute appendicitis. This indicated that his family believed him to be on board the liner.
>
> "When the *Martaban* reached New York, Mr. Sternhall's luggage was claimed by some person who produced a proper authorisation. The affair is further complicated by the receipt of a letter from Mr.

Sternhall, addressed to his wife, with a postmark showing that it was mailed in New York on the day the *Martaban* reached port.

"Mr. Sternhall is a well-known business man, resident in Charponden. He is connected with the firm of Domuten, Ltd., and it is known that his business took him to America once or twice a year."

Wendover completed his reading, put the paper on his knee, and glanced across at Sir Clinton with slightly raised eyebrows.

"Sternhall's not a common name," he pointed out. "If this is a coincidence, Clinton, then coincidence has got a longer reach on its arm than usual."

The Chief Constable came over, picked up the paper, and studied the news item without comment. Wendover, completely puzzled, fell to speculating aloud.

"It may be another Sternhall, of course," he admitted, "and even if it is, it's a rum enough business. But two Sternhalls, both getting into trouble in a week, is too much to swallow. To me, at any rate. Suppose it's the same Sternhall, what then? His wife isn't dead of appendicitis. Was somebody playing a practical joke over the wireless? It would take your late visitor to think of a thing like that. No decent man would do it."

"Then, obviously, there are two Mrs. Sternhalls," said Sir Clinton, looking up from the paper, "and it's the other one that's dead."

"He was leading a double life, you mean? By Jove, that would account for his secretiveness, and all that sort of thing," Wendover ejaculated. "And his trips to America, too. I expect he spent half the time at The Grove instead of in the States."

Sir Clinton threw down the paper and took a pace or two up and down the room, thinking deeply. Then he turned to Wendover.

"There was a case rather like this one in London, a good many years back," he said. "Sir Melville Macnaghten was Chief of the C.I.D. at Scotland Yard in those days. It beat them. And in his reminiscences Macnaghten quotes a parody of a popular song of those days:

'I've searched from Dan even to Beer
   Sheba, to make this mystery clear;
But I only end where I did begin,
   Who did him in?'

An hour ago, I was in much the same state as regards The Grove case. But now I think I see a glimmer of sense in it."

"Only a glimmer?" echoed Wendover.

"Only a glimmer. But luckily, Charponden happens to be in my county, though it's at the other end of it. Care to come over there tomorrow, Squire, and have a look round? We'll take Chesilton with us. It may be interesting. And if it turns out to be a different Sternhall, it'll still be interesting. I haven't got a herald with trumpet and tabar to announce our coming; but we'll make shift with the trunk wire."

He picked up the telephone from his desk and asked to be put through to Charponden.

11
THE POWER OF ATTORNEY

"Local Headquarters first, I suppose?" Wendover inquired, as the car ran through the streets of Charponden next morning. "You'll want some pointers, I take it?"

The Chief Constable shook his head.

"No, I got all I wanted on the 'phone last night. We're going to pay a call on a respectable citizen, so you needn't unleash your suspicions for the present."

"Who is he?" Wendover demanded, rather nettled at having been kept in the dark.

"A worthy burgess answering to the name of Henry Scawen, when civilly addressed. . . . We go round here, I think. . . . He's by way of being a financial associate, so to speak, of the missing passenger. . . . Next turn on the right, I believe. . . . You'd better let me manage the interview, Inspector. We'll try to be only semi-official, so far as our manners go. . . . We're nearly there, now. It's on the left hand, if I'm not mistaken. . . . Ah! Here we are."

The car swung in at the gate of a big, half-timbered, cream-tinted villa, standing back from the road in a garden of shady lawns, box-edged paths, and flower beds all aglow with colour. Wendover scanned it with critical approval.

"Roomy quarters for an old bachelor," Sir Clinton commented. "Next door—if it interests you—is the abode of Mr. Sternhall Number Two."

They were evidently expected and were ushered without delay into a pleasant, sunny morning-room. Its windows opened on a long pergola leading to a pool in a rock garden. As the visitors were shown in, a tall, slight, white-moustached man rose from his chair, removing as he did so a pair of heavy-rimmed reading spectacles. Sir Clinton briefly introduced his companions.

"I don't like to intrude on you in this way, Mr. Scawen," he began, after they had settled down, "but we are rather perplexed by this disappearance of Mr. Sternhall. I understand that you know something about his affairs?"

Scawen nodded courteously. When he spoke, Wendover had approved of his voice and his accent; and his rather old-fashioned manners suggested a likeable personality.

"Yes, I hold a power of attorney," he volunteered. "When he gave me it, I never dreamed that it would be used in a state of affairs like this, though."

"A full power of attorney?" queried the Chief Constable. "Not the kind with the five-shilling stamp?"

"A full power of attorney," Scawen explained. "It is quite in order, since it was drawn up by his solicitor; and it empowers me to deal with all his financial affairs without limit."

"By the way, Mr. Scawen, I never met Mr. Sternhall. Could you give me a description of him?"

Scawen hesitated for a moment, then he went over and searched in the drawers of an escritoire beside the window. After a moment or two, he came back with a little leather photograph case which opened out to reveal the portraits of a man and a woman. Sir Clinton glanced at it and then passed it to his companions. Wendover, at the first glance, recognised the man as the victim of the Grove tragedy. So obvious was the resemblance that he paid no further attention to it, but gave the woman's face a closer inspection.

"H'm!" he reflected to himself, as he passed the photographs to the inspector. "She's not my type, though she may be good-looking. Discontented eyes, she has; and that droop of dissatisfaction at the corners of the mouth; and yet there's something that suggests she thought a good deal of herself, too. Not a shrew, by the look of her; but she might prove more wearing even, in the long run. Sternhall must have been a fascinating fellow to net these two women, all the same."

The inspector received the photographs, scanned them closely, and returned them to Sir Clinton with the faintest confirmatory gesture, so slight that it escaped Scawen's attention.

"This power of attorney," the Chief Constable continued, ignoring the photographs in his hand; "evidently Mr. Sternhall trusted you implicitly, Mr. Scawen?"

"I suppose he did," Scawen admitted deprecatingly. "To tell you the truth, I had trusted him in some matters to a great extent—in sundry financial affairs. In fact, I lent him a good deal of the capital with which he started Domuten, Ltd. He got the rest from his wife, I believe. And since then, I've come to his aid from time to time when he needed further capital to extend his operations. He was always wanting more money to open up fresh lines, always. To tell you the truth, I had more money in Domuten, Ltd., than he had himself, I believe; so it was not unnatural that if a power of attorney became necessary, I should be the person selected to exercise it."

"Domuten, Ltd.," mused the Chief Constable. "I can't quite place it, though it's a curious enough name. What sort of business is it?"

"A kind of olla podrida, I'm afraid," Scawen explained with a whimsical smile. "A sort of fish-flesh-and-fowl of a business. He meant to call it 'Domestic Utensils, Ltd.' when he started it; but I thought that was too much of a mouthful and I suggested contracting it and using the contraction 'Domuten' as a trademark. It was built up largely on the basis that the public will buy a new form of an old utensil, partly because it's new, partly out of curiosity, partly because they hope it may work better than the old pattern. A new brand of egg-slicer, a modified apple-parer, a fresh line in tin-openers, or a novel design for an ashtray: these were the things he did business in. He wasn't inventive himself; all he did was to buy somebody's idea for a fiver or so. He'd no turn for factory management, so he got the things made on contract by other firms, and I believe they were shipped straight from the factories to the distributors. So far as he was concerned, his business was mainly contracting and bookkeeping, and it didn't matter where the offices were. He made it pay; I've nothing to complain about, as an investor in it. But he was insatiable for more and more capital, as I told you. An ambitious fellow, determined to get on, I believe. And, of course, his wife, poor girl, was much the same. He wanted to get on in business; she wanted to get on in society."

"When were they married?" interjected Sir Clinton, checking the old man's flow of information for a moment.

Scawen thought for a moment or two, then evidently managed to recall the year, by some obscure process of association.

"In 1926," he said, with the smile of a man who has accomplished a difficult feat. "Yes, 1926. It was in September that they came back from their honeymoon, if I'm not mistaken. A very short engagement, I believe; she met him at some hotel or other in the summer. They came back to the house next door to this. Her father and mother left it to her, with about a thousand a year as well. I remember her, poor girl, when she was a little thing in short frocks, with something plaintive in the droop of her mouth, even in those days. Ju, they called her. Ju Degray. I'm almost sure it was short for Judy; but when she grew up, she insisted on being called Juliet. She had rather a bee in her bonnet after she got married. Social ambitions and that kind of thing; wanted Sternhall to work himself up to a knighthood, and so forth. And she became rather a bore, poor girl, about her family; the ancient lineage notion, don't you know. Ridiculous, of course, but it always seemed to me rather pathetic. She didn't tell Sternhall about it, I know; I think she was keeping it as a surprise for him, when he got his knighthood. She was a little sentimental in some ways; she gave me that case with the portraits as a birthday present last year, poor girl, though it was no use to me. To tell you the truth, I've reached the stage where I'd rather people would let me forget about my birthdays. But, about this craze of hers; a bit of pure moonshine, to my mind. She'd got it into her head that her name Degray was really de Gray—which might be true—and that this was a corruption of de Grey—which I doubt—and that she was related to a lot of the big families—which . . . well, she's dead, poor girl, so what's the use of saying hard things? She'd certainly persuaded herself there was something in it, for I know she spent some money in getting her family tree traced out by one of those firms that specialise in that kind of business. She talked to me about it, often. Very boring."

"Did you know any of Sternhall's relations?" Sir Clinton inquired, damming the flood of rambling information again.

Scawen shook his head slowly. He was not quick in shifting his mind from one topic to a fresh one.

"No," he admitted, "I didn't. In fact, I don't think he had any in this country. He had a brother in America, but I never came across him. He used to run the American side of Domuten, Ltd., though Sternhall used to go over to the States from time to time to look into things personally."

"Did you ever see a portrait of this brother? Was he like Sternhall—noticeably like him, I mean."

"I did see a photograph of him once," Scawen admitted. "Mrs. Sternhall had a copy she'd got from America; I told you she had a sentimental side. But it wasn't in the least like Sternhall. You'd never have guessed they were brothers."

Sir Clinton weighed the photograph case in his hand for a moment as though coming to some decision. Then he took out his pocketbook, extracted an official photograph, and handed it across to the old man.

"Can you recognise that?" he demanded.

Scawen took the print, searched for his spectacles, adjusted them astride his nose, and inspected the print. The first glance startled him out of his normal placidity.

"Good God! It's Sternhall. But he's terribly disfigured."

"You recognise him? Beyond any doubt?" demanded Sir Clinton.

"Oh, yes. It's he, there's no mistake about that. I knew him intimately, you know; and I haven't the slightest doubt. But I don't understand . . ."

"Haven't you seen the newspaper accounts of his death?" the Chief Constable asked. "The papers have been full of it. Didn't the name strike you? It's not a common one."

"I seldom look at the local papers," Scawen explained. "To tell you the truth, my eyes are rather weak, and I find reading a strain, so I take my news from the *Times*, because the print's clear. There was nothing about it in the *Times*—or else I missed the paragraph."

"But you knew that Sternhall had disappeared? That he was missing from the *Martaban*?" Sir Clinton pointed out swiftly. "How did that news reach you?"

"As a matter of fact," Scawen explained, "the first I heard of it was from a reporter, who came to the door to make inquiries. When Mrs. Sternhall, poor girl, went into the nursing home for that wretched operation, the house next door was closed and the servants were given a holiday. This reporter—his name was—let me see . . . Jordan . . . yes, that was it, Jordan. . . . He could get nothing next door, of course, so he came here to see if I could tell him anything about Sternhall."

"You didn't give him much, to judge by the reports in the papers."

"I referred him to the local directory," Scawen explained, with quiet satisfaction. "I dislike this publicity and poking a nose into people's private affairs. But you haven't told me anything about his death. I can't imagine why anyone should want to murder him. He may have had commercial enemies, but I never guessed that anyone could have a private score against him—a big enough score to end in murder, at any rate," he corrected himself.

Sir Clinton gave him an abbreviated account of the tragedy at The Grove; but Wendover noticed that be omitted all reference to the second Sternhall establishment.

"You haven't come across a man Bracknell, in connection with Sternhall?" he asked casually, as he finished his account.

Evidently the name conveyed nothing to Scawen. He shook his head in his usual deliberate fashion.

"No, I never even heard the name before," he admitted. "But this is a dreadful affair; really, it's a terrible business. Poor fellow."

Sir Clinton cut short his pitying exclamations.

"You can see, Mr. Scawen, that any information may turn out useful to us in this business. One never knows what a hint may lead on to. Would you mind giving us an account of your dealings with Sternhall? You got to know him after his marriage, in 1926?"

"Yes, in 1926," Scawen agreed. "After the marriage. I'd known her all her life, poor girl, and we were next-door neighbours. So naturally, I saw something of them both. Almost at once, he dragged me into his financial schemes. But perhaps dragged isn't the right word. I was willing enough to join him. He'd worked out the whole of this Domuten business on paper; he'd got estimates of costs; he knew everything about the project from start to finish, and could produce every fact and figure that was needed to make it a convincing scheme. He was really a very able man, Sternhall, poor chap. Rather like Nelson in some ways: for he'd plan and plan beforehand, and then act with decision and swiftness. In fact, that was the only thing I didn't like about him and his methods. He'd dash into a thing so recklessly, once he'd finished his planning."

He made a faint deprecating gesture, as though to show he had hardly agreed with Sternhall at times.

"He was very convincing. To tell you the truth, he had very little difficulty in getting me to supply him with capital; and his wife, poor girl, let him have a good deal of her money. He hadn't a penny of his own, so far as I knew. Brains were what he put into the business, brains and energy. He meant to get on. One could see that, the first time one met him. Nothing was going to stand in his way. And, of course, she wanted to get on too, poor girl, in another field. They suited each other admirably to that extent."

"Not in other ways?" demanded Sir Clinton.

Scawen shrugged his shoulders slightly.

"There was some trouble over one of his typists," he admitted. "But it blew over. The girl was dismissed, finally, and that put an end to the affair, I believe."

"Obviously he had no financial troubles, or he would not have given you that power of attorney," Sir Clinton observed.

"Defalcations, you mean?" Scawen answered. "Oh, no, nothing of that sort. The business is doing better than ever."

147

"I shall want to see his cheque-books, counterfoils, and so forth," Sir Clinton explained. "I suppose you have access to them?"

"As a matter of fact," Scawen admitted, "I've looked through them since this disappearance, to see if I could find anything. They are in a safe place next door, and I have the keys. She gave them to me when she went into the nursing home, poor girl. And I took it that my power of attorney covered the case."

"You noticed something?" Sir Clinton queried, after a sharp glance at Scawen's face.

"Nothing amiss," Scawen protested at once. "Nothing of that kind. Oh, no. But my attention was certainly roused by some of the figures on the counterfoils I saw. Cheques to "Self or bearer" endorsed by himself only, and for quite large figures—hundreds of pounds. To tell you the truth, it puzzled me more than a little to know why he could have wanted so much in fluid cash, for he must have cashed the cheques over the counter himself. One of them was for seven hundred fifty pounds, remember; and they were all for round figures—no odd units on the cheque."

"With your permission, we'll examine these by-and-by," Sir Clinton suggested. "Now, another question. You knew both him and his wife. Were they jealous of each other?"

Scawen obviously disliked discussing the point, but he made an effort.

"Well, I suppose they were," he said reluctantly. "She was very angry at the time of the affair with that typist, I know. And he certainly struck me as being jealous of her, too. I've seen her talking to another man after a bridge drive, and Sternhall seeing it and shouldering his way through the crowd to break into the tête-à-tête. It was rather marked. People looked round, I mean."

"There was never any question of her divorcing him over the typist trouble, was there?" Sir Clinton inquired.

"Oh, no, none whatever. She believed in Sternhall's future, and she meant to go up side by side with him in the social scale. A divorce would have finished her, socially. Or so she imagined, I gathered. In some ways she was extraordinarily limited, poor girl."

"And Sternhall could hardly have carried on without her capital behind him?"

"No, I don't think he could. I'd supplied all the money I cared to sink in a single business; and although he might have raised capital to pay her off, it would have meant hampering himself with less easy-going partners than myself. No, he'd never have risked that, I'm sure."

"You've no objection to . . . but, by the way, who are his executors, do you know?"

"He appointed his wife and myself in his will. Since she's dead, poor girl, I suppose I'm the sole executor."

"Then there'll be no trouble. We shall need to see his private correspondence. It may throw light on some side of this affair. And I shall want the address of his brother in America. It's bound to be somewhere, either among his private letters or in the office correspondence."

"I see no objection to that," Scawen decided, after a moment's thought. "Now I've done my best for you; and it's my turn, if you don't mind, Sir Clinton. This is the point. Before Sternhall went away this time, poor chap, he gave me a sealed letter and some instructions about opening it. If I had certain news of his death, I was to break the seal and act upon the contents. That contingency seems to have occurred; and I think I ought to open the envelope. But I'd rather do it in the presence of witnesses, since I don't know what may be inside."

He went over to the escritoire and, opening a drawer, took out a heavily sealed letter. Putting on his reading spectacles, he broke the seal and drew out a single sheet of notepaper covered with writing which he read through twice with exasperating deliberation before handing the paper to the Chief Constable. Sir Clinton perused it much more swiftly and then handed it back to Scawen.

"I see no reason why you shouldn't," he said. "But we, officially, do not undertake to circulate anything of the sort. You must make your own arrangements about it. A thousand pounds is a lot of money," he added musingly. "You'll find your postbag swelling considerably—full of wildcats, most likely."

Scawen replaced the document in its envelope.

"He must have had some premonition of trouble," he said thoughtfully. "He was always planning the step after next; and he seems to have carried his plans even beyond the grave, poor chap. And now, if it suits you, I can take you round next door and show you any documents that you wish to examine."

12
PART OF THE PATTERN

The investigation of Sternhall's papers took less time than Wendover had anticipated. The deceased man had been methodical, filing every document which he kept; but it was plain that he had destroyed a considerable proportion of his correspondence, since the surviving papers seemed a meagre allowance for the seven years he had spent in accumulating them. Sternhall apparently had the habit of preserving all cancelled cheques returned to him through his bank; and Wendover gathered that from Sir Clinton's point of view, this was an unexpected piece of good fortune.

It was rather a dull business for Wendover. The Chief Constable and the inspector sat on opposite sides of a table, going systematically through the correspondence, exchanging curt remarks, and making jottings. When a document was disposed of, Chesilton returned it to its appropriate file. Wendover could make little out of the routine; whilst Scawen, obviously bored, hovered uncertainly in the background, as though he could not make up his mind to leave the officials unsupervised.

He insisted on taking them round to his own house for lunch, which made a break in the monotony of the search; but neither Sir Clinton nor the inspector seemed in a communicative mood during the meal, and Wendover was left very much in the dark as to their results.

Even when they had finished with the Sternhall papers they had further work to do. First, a call at the local police headquarters, where Sir Clinton cross-questioned the Superintendent in charge on numerous points which seemed to Wendover of rather secondary importance. Then, on the road home, the Chief Constable broke his journey to visit Mrs. Sternhall in The Grove and ask some more questions. He left Wendover in the car at the door, taking the inspector upstairs with him.

"No use invading the flat in force," he explained, in semi-apology for leaving his guest outside. "We can talk it over tonight and you'll get the stop press news."

During dinner, the Chief Constable seemed preoccupied, and Wendover kept away from the subject of Sternhall's affairs. Sir Clinton disliked discussing professional affairs at meals, with servants present. But when, after dinner, they went into the Chief Constable's study, Wendover's impatience could no longer be held in check.

"Well, did your visit throw any light on things?" he demanded, as he settled down in his favourite armchair.

Sir Clinton watched the blue spiral curling up from his cigar for a moment or two without replying. Wendover assumed that he was reviewing the events of the day; but when he spoke, he attacked the subject from a different standpoint.

"This is a troublesome business, Squire. In most affairs, one has some concrete stuff to go on. The murderer leaves something that one can take hold of. But unfortunately, this case isn't like that. We've got precious little to go upon, so far as exhibits are concerned. No fingerprints, no documents, no special weapon, no peculiar poison. In fact, as a friend of mine would put it, We've got 'sweet damn all' except some blood samples, some footprints that we can't identify, a paintpot, a bullet taken out of a dead man's head, a pair of rubber gloves, a bloody handkerchief, and a gold trinket."

"It seems an imposing enough collection," Wendover said, with mock encouragement.

"The trouble is," the Chief Constable retorted, "that I don't see them as parts of a whole, though they may perhaps fit neatly together in the long run. No, Squire, we'll have to tackle this case from another side. Ask ourselves what personalities were mixed up in it and how they reacted on one another. And the difficulty is that one portrait's missing from the gallery, or it's wrongly labelled at present."

"You mean the murderer's?"

"I do," Sir Clinton agreed gravely. Then he added, with ironic gravity, "Obviously."

He drew thoughtfully at his cigar once or twice, then turned to Wendover.

"You've seen the people we've come across, Squire. I'd rather like to have your impressions of them. Sternhall's the pivot of the business. Neither of us has seen him—alive, I mean; but we've heard something about him. How does he strike you?"

Wendover was ready for this question. He had spent not a little time speculating upon the dead man's personality as it was gradually revealed by various witnesses.

"In essence, I'd say, he was a calculating devil, none too scrupulous in his methods, ambitious along his own line, and impulsive in some things, in spite of all his calculation. Obviously he had a way with women, since we know of three of them who fell under his influence: his wife, his bigamous partner, and that unfortunate typist."

"A nice assortment," Sir Clinton commented sardonically. "Marriage, bigamy, and seduction. A versatile fellow, Sternhall. And there's one point you omitted from his character, Squire; he wanted more capital always. Therefore I take it that he did not part with largish sums without some pressure."

"Those cheques, you mean?" demanded Wendover. "You haven't told me about them yet."

"Money talks, they say," Sir Clinton said reflectively. "And certainly these cheques seemed to tell a story or two. I'm speaking of the ones drawn to 'Self or Bearer' and endorsed only with his own name. They fell easily into four groups: one set was for small sums, just pocket money drawn at odd times; then there was one for two hundred pounds, which I'll explain in a minute; then there was a regularly recurring series for one hundred twenty-five pounds which turned up each year in January, April, July and October;

and finally, there was a series of cheques for steadily increasing sums—the last one was for a cool thousand—which were dated at irregular intervals through the last four years. Now the two hundred pound one is accounted for easily enough, since it coincided with the flare-up over that wretched typist, as I learned from the Superintendent at Charponden. Not official knowledge, of course; but the thing wasn't exactly private, it seems."

"H'm!" said Wendover. "So that leaves the recurring quarterly cheque for one hundred twenty-five pounds to be explained, and the other lot—the ones with increasing figures. Well, I suppose the one hundred twenty-five pound ones represent his allowance to his real wife, Mrs. Sternhall of The Grove. That seems the obvious solution. Did you ask her?"

"Yes. She admitted it at once, though she seemed a bit taken aback when I mentioned the exact figure. It's a not ungenerous allowance to a woman living alone most of the time, considering that at The Grove Sternhall was not supposed to be more than a commercial traveller. I didn't press the matter; no need to make her incriminate herself. Though, as a matter of fact, she's a married woman and could hardly be hauled up for screening her husband *post facto*. Anyhow, I let sleeping dogs lie. The point was that, as I suspected, she had a hold on Sternhall, and that hold could only have been her knowledge of his bigamy."

"*Post facto?*" queried Wendover. "You think she didn't know about it beforehand and fall in with his scheme of marrying the other woman?"

"I don't think so. I asked her where she was during August and September, 1926, and she answered quite frankly that she was in France, staying with her sister. She was quite positive about it; and when I politely distrusted her memory, she was very indignant and went off and fetched some old letters with the envelopes addressed to her in France. The postmarks were quite all right."

"So while she was away, Sternhall met this Miss Degray at some hotel or other, learned that she had money, and made a conquest of her?"

"So it seems. He was very impulsive in these affairs. Remember what we heard about his courtship of the first wife. But with the second one, I suspect the real bait was her capital. He had all this Domuten business planned to the last dot, at that time. All he needed was the cash to set it going. And look how quickly he roped in old Scawen who, for all his rambling, isn't a fool when it comes to money, they tell me."

"That leaves the last lot of cheques unexplained," Wendover mused. "It doesn't seem difficult. Sternhall's position was about as insecure as it could well be. A whisper, and he'd have gone to gaol for a year or two. No jury has much sympathy with a bigamist. I take it that these cheques—the increasing amounts are significant—were used to stop that whisper. Somebody knew about the bigamy; and he wanted his price for keeping his mouth shut."

"He or she," Sir Clinton corrected. "Let's give each sex a chance. Now who was 'he or she'?"

"Well," said Wendover reluctantly, "Mrs. Sternhall knew, if what you say's correct. I mean Mrs. Sternhall of The Grove. But she was drawing an allowance already that amounted to hush money, by your way of it."

"That didn't necessarily preclude her from opening her mouth a bit wider from time to time," Sir Clinton pointed out. "Who else?"

"If she knew, then that brother-in-law of hers might have picked up a hint and gone into business on his own account," Wendover suggested. "Or he may have been put up to the dodge by her and they may have shared the profits."

"Admitted at once. And a French subject blackmailing an Englishman from France is in rather a happy position, since the French don't surrender their subjects to be tried in our courts."

"But in that case," Wendover objected, "he was a fool ever to come over to this country, where he might be arrested and tried, if Sternhall happened to face the music."

"Sternhall wasn't going to face that kind of music," Sir Clinton commented. "Did I tell you that he was a respected Town Councillor and had his eye on the mayoralty very soon? And that, with a little management—say the opening of new waterworks by Some-body Eminent—might have got him his knighthood. No, Sternhall couldn't let his friend talk. But go on with your catalogue, Squire."

"It's just possible that somebody may have seen Sternhall in each of his personalities and put two and two together, on the strength of it. And that reminds me, he must have been rather a clumsy devil, Sternhall, or he wouldn't have used his own name in courting his second 'wife'."

"No difficulty in explaining that," Sir Clinton retorted. "He had to, whether he liked or not. According to the tale, he met her quite casually as a fellow-guest at a hotel. Obviously, he'd given his own name when he went to the hotel. After that, he couldn't change it for another. You can hardly imagine him explaining to his fiancée, 'I'm sorry, darling, but I've just remembered that my real name is Jones.' Sensation! Eh? What surprises me is that he wasn't clever enough to see a simple way out, after the marriage."

"What way?" Wendover asked, after puzzling for a moment.

"Change his name to Degray by deed poll, of course. That would have flattered his wife's fancies nicely, and got one risk removed at the same time."

"Yes, he might have done that," Wendover conceded. "As it was, he must have been running risks all the time. Charponden's no vast distance away from here. But, of course, here he was a very ob-scure person. Probably he banked on that."

"Probably he did. But get on with your catalogue, Squire."

"I don't see anyone else who could have tumbled to his game," Wendover protested. "Mrs. Sternhall of The Grove; her brother-in-law; somebody spotting the facial identity of the two Sternhalls; that seems to fill the bill."

"You can't think of anything else? What about someone who'd never seen Sternhall in the flesh and wouldn't have known him by sight, even if he'd come across him?" demanded the Chief Con-stable in a significant tone.

"It doesn't sound likely," Wendover decided. Then, as a fresh idea occurred to him, he added, "What age would you say young Bracknell was?"

"Twenty-two or twenty-three, possibly."

Wendover's face betrayed that some inference had gone wrong.

"And this blackmailing has been going on for four years, according to the evidence of the cheques. H'm! If Bracknell was the blackmailer, he must have begun fairly young. That doesn't seem to fit."

"I once knew a fellow who blackmailed his brother before he was sixteen," Sir Clinton said, in a tone of reminiscence. "Quite clever at it, too. When you're professing to take *everything* into account, Squire, you can't neglect the possibility of a juvenile criminal. They do exist."

"One thing does puzzle me," Wendover admitted frankly. "When you questioned Bracknell, he was very positive that he'd never seen Sternhall and wouldn't have known him if he'd met him. That was what you were hinting at a minute ago, wasn't it? Well, I don't mind admitting that he sounded then as if he were speaking the truth. In some of the other things he said, I wasn't convinced that he was straight; but that particular point sounded genuine to my ears. The tone, and thát sort of thing, I mean. You didn't find any trace of blackmail amongst Sternhall's correspondence, did you?"

"No," the Chief Constable admitted. "But Sternhall was too clever a man to keep anything of that sort amongst his papers, even if letters had passed between him and his blackmailer."

"I daresay. But isn't blackmail usually carried on by word of mouth, so that there's no documentary evidence left about? And in that case the blackmailer must meet his victim face to face. This is getting a bit tangled up," Wendover admitted ruefully.

"It can be straightened out, if you'll drop your prepossessions, Squire. You're thinking of the ordinary blackmail case where some old gentleman has been trapped in compromising circumstances by a professional gang. Then in comes the bully, storming and pretending to be the injured husband or the horrified big brother or what not, and in a good many cases he jars the old gentleman off the rails by sheer shouting and personality. In these cases, the blackmailer and victim do meet face to face. But this Sternhall affair is quite different. Suppose anyone discovered the facts of Sternhall's bigamy. It can be proved up to the hilt from official documentary evidence. There's no bullying needed: Just a statement of the facts and a demand for cash. That can be made through the post without the blackmailer putting in an appearance at all. His case is unbreakable. And if he keeps under cover, he can always send information to the police and finish Sternhall without it being possible to connect him with blackmail at all. Obviously, secrecy is his best weapon. He's got nothing to gain by a personal interview."

"He'd have to give some address, or how would he get his money for his trouble?" Wendover demanded.

"He could use an accommodation address: One of these shops where they take a fee for receiving letters for their clients. We're going to work that line, Squire, though I'm not optimistic about results."

"No more am I," said Wendover, rather contemptuously. "How are you going to trace a dozen letters in four years, sent to an unknown man at an unknown accommodation address?"

"Not easily," admitted the Chief Constable. "But there's a bit of legislation called the Official Secrets Act, 1920, which may help. Every keeper of an accommodation address has to register with the police and keep a book, which the police can inspect at any time. In that book he must enter the names and addresses of persons for whom the letters are received, any instructions they may give as to delivery, particulars of *the date and place of posting shown on the postmark of every letter received by them*, and the name and address of the person to whom it is delivered. The recipient must give a receipt for the letter. So every one of these books in the county is being inspected to see if it contains a record of any letter bearing the Charponden postmark and a date shortly before the cashing of any of these cheques. What I hope to get is a specimen of the recipient's handwriting on the receipt for the letter. But it's a very long shot, as you can imagine."

"It is," said Wendover drily. "First, the accommodation address may not be in your county at all; second, the blackmailer may have sent someone to collect his letters, instead of going himself; third, Sternhall may not have posted his letters in his home town; and fourth, the money may not have been sent to an accommodation address at all. You've less chance than you'd have in backing a number at roulette, it seems to me."

"Agreed, *nem. con.*," Sir Clinton conceded. "Still, we can't overlook even the faintest chance."

Wendover nodded absently, as though his mind were busy with some other problem. At length he looked up.

"Let's try to fit the whole affair together," he suggested, "just to see how it looks and what loose ends there are."

Sir Clinton evidently did not take the proposal too seriously.

"Put your fingertips together and lean back in your chair, Squire," he advised. "That's how Sherlock Holmes used to manage it. Nothing like a good example to follow."

Wendover ignored the suggestion.

"Let's go right back to the beginning," he began. "We don't know who Sternhall was or where he came from originally. His first appearance is during his courtship of that French girl—if you can call that sort of thing a courtship. On the basis of what she told us, Sternhall comes out as a calculating devil who has success almost within his grasp and misses it by impulsiveness at the last moment. He never meant to marry that girl when he set out; but when it came to the pinch, he hadn't enough coolness left to carry the thing through. My reading of him is that normally he was a cool, cold, calculating devil, but that given a strong enough impulse, he could act impulsively on the spur of the moment. A fellow of that sort may do the most unpredictable things."

"Rather an awkward type," Sir Clinton said critically. "When you think he's acting by calculation, he may make an impulsive move; and when you look for impulse, he may go on calculating. Not easy to say what a man of that sort might be up to next."

"Well, on impulse, he ties himself up to this Frenchwoman," Wendover proceeded. "She wasn't fond of him; she told us as much. And he seems to have tired of her. They hadn't much in common. And he couldn't get free. If she'd been a Protestant, he might have got her to agree to divorce him; but since she was a Roman Catholic and probably a strict one, to judge by results—she wouldn't fall in with that. His only chance was to catch her tripping herself. That might account for all this 'jealousy' of his."

"It might, before he committed bigamy," Sir Clinton admitted. "But once he'd married the other woman, the risk of a divorce case with the Frenchwoman would have been too big. It would just have precipitated a smash. She'd have given him away for certain; and even if she held her hand, somebody would have put two and two together. No, I think he was like these Orientals who can contrive to be jealous of every woman in a whole harem."

"That's as it may be," Wendover returned, in an unconvinced tone. "Anyhow, the next stage is that she goes off to France for a holiday, and he meets this girl Degray at an hotel, sees the chance of getting hold of her capital, and makes up to her. He must have calculated a good bit over that business. It must have cost him a sleepless night or two, I imagine, before he decided to take the risk. He got what he wanted, anyhow. He must have had a strong attraction for women. She evidently was too pleased with him to ask any awkward questions.

"It's pretty clear that his real wife had suspicions and that he paid her five hundred pounds a year to quiet her. As she owns these flats, he may have given her cash outside the five hundred pounds a year as well. Still, I'm a bit surprised that she didn't cut up rough."

"So far as I could gather from an incautious phrase of hers," Sir Clinton explained, "she looked on his second marriage as of no importance. It was a Protestant affair entirely and simply amounted to his having taken a concubine. And she wasn't in the least in love with him, not enough to be jealous, even. In fact, this second marriage suited her book. It kept Sternhall away from The Grove for months at a time."

"There's something in that," Wendover admitted. "Bet let's go on. Once Sternhall had his two establishments running, his brother in America must have been useful. A methodical fellow like Sternhall could write out a series of letters, dated at intervals, and send then under cover to his brother. The brother could then post them on the proper dates at various places in the States, during his own business trips, when he was pushing the Domuten goods. That accounts for that posthumous letter which arrived, posted on the day the *Martaban* reached port. It also accounts for the brother claiming Sternhall's luggage at New York. Most likely the second Mrs. Sternhall used to see Sternhall off at the quay now, and again, so he daren't risk removing his luggage from the boat at the last moment. His brother would send it back in plenty of time. And if his 'wife' met him on the quay on his return, it would be easy enough to manage things in the confusion of passengers landing from a big liner."

"I suppose that if he turned up with luggage all present and correct, she'd ask no questions," Sir Clinton agreed. "Go on with the next thrilling instalment, Squire."

"The trouble with the typist amounts to nothing, so far as this case is concerned," Wendover continued. "We can leave that aside. But very soon, the blackmailer turned up. Sternhall evidently saw there was nothing for it but to pay. And he went on paying for a while. But each time, to judge by the cheques, he had to pay a bigger lump of hush money. A clever man like Sternhall wouldn't be long in seeing where that was leading to—bankruptcy and exposure, eventually. For bankruptcy would mean awkward questions about these cheques and what became of the money."

"Curtain up for the Fifth Act," Sir Clinton commented, in mock excitement.

"Well," said Wendover, unperturbed, "take a calculating fellow like Sternhall and put him in that position. What's the likely result? You can never buy off a blackmailer permanently. He's always got the goods for delivery, no matter how much you've paid him in the past. Further, when you're in Sternhall's delicate position, you can't call in the police to deal with him. And the only other way of stopping the nuisance is to silence him, once for all. I take it that Sternhall reasoned it out on these lines.

"I'll admit the possibility that Sternhall had never seen the blackmailer in the flesh. It's immaterial to the reconstruction. The point is: he decided to eliminate the fellow, whoever he was. And

161

on that basis, Sternhall set to calculating every step in advance. He was corresponding with his wife—the Frenchwoman, I mean. He could easily suggest the repainting of the empty flat. That would ensure its being untenanted for some days, when he needed it. That's where he proposes to lure the blackmailer and square accounts with him. He considers the business, point by point. There must be no more noise than necessary. Hence the tennis shoes he brought with him. The killing must be done silently: hence the homemade bludgeon. And there must be no fingerprints: hence the rubber gloves. And when he's murdered his persecutor, all he has to do is to walk upstairs and resume his well-established personality as Mr. Sternhall, the commercial traveller, home for a spell. And the body will not be discovered until next morning, when the painters come in. Who's going to suspect Mr. Sternhall? He's left nothing behind him that could identify him; for you remember that his whole outfit was new or else had no identification marks on it of any description."

He broke off, as a thought crossed his mind.

"By the way," he asked, "had Sternhall a pistol, by any chance? I mean Charponden Sternhall."

"Charponden Sternhall had a firearms permit," Sir Clinton informed him. "He took it out a good long time ago. Afraid of burglars, was his ground. He wanted a revolver. I told the Superintendent in charge at Charponden to search the house thoroughly for it; but he didn't find any trace of it. So he told me on the 'phone, tonight."

"It's possible he got rid of it," Wendover surmised. "Anyhow, that doesn't matter. My idea is that the blackmailer knew Sternhall personally—knew his character, at any rate—and that he realised on his side that trouble might blow up. So he went armed to the meeting-place in the flat. There was some sort of a struggle: the overturned paintpot shows that, and so does the wrenched-off Tau cross. The blackmailer was wounded, since there were two kinds of blood in the place, according to your expert. The blackmailer pulled out his pistol, shot Sternhall, and bolted through the French window. Within a few minutes, Danbury came on the scene, summoned by old Geddington. That's how I see it."

Sir Clinton assumed a pose caricaturing a favourite one of Sherlock Holmes.

"Excellent, Watson," he murmured. "You know my methods. Now this case of yours turns upon our finding a wounded blackmailer. There was quite a lot of blood on that handkerchief, you may remember. Our friend Bracknell doesn't walk with a limp, or any sign of one. When seized by the arm in a friendly way, he doesn't wince. His more intimate garments have been examined while he slept, and there's no trace of blood on any of them. And yet the Tau cross belongs to Bracknell. And Bracknell not only lied himself, but he persuaded that nice little girl to lie on his behalf. We shall have to go a bit further into this business, Squire. I'm not completely convinced by your masterly exposition, so far as it deals with what happened at The Grove. The rest of it looks sound enough to me. The trouble is that it doesn't give the slightest clue as to the identity of the murderer. And that's what really interests me."

"You think there may have been two blackmailers?" asked Wendover, with a flash of imagination. "One was hurt and got away completely; the other may have been Bracknell?"

Sir Clinton avoided a direct reply by changing the subject.

"There's one further bit of information I picked up at Charponden," he said slyly. "You know what sort of person Sternhall was: ambitious, unscrupulous, and ruthless. Well, it seems he was rather meanly vindictive as well. He had a clerk in his office, getting a bit old and not over-efficient, I gather. He shot this poor little devil out into the street without the slightest pity, though he knew how hard it would be for the man to find another post. Not only so, but he went out of his way to pursue the poor wretch, advising possible employers against him and making it virtually impossible for him to get a job. In fact, he left him as near as possible a down-and-out. That kind of treatment is apt to make bad enemies."

"What was the clerk's name?" Wendover asked, rather idly.

"George Mitford," Sir Clinton replied, with a twinkle in his eye. "And he lives at Number 1, Ravenswood Mansions, as you heard, a flat or two above our bustling friend Barbican, the free lance."

"Ravenswood Mansions? That's just round the corner from The Grove, isn't it?"

"Yes, it's in Sans Souci Avenue."

"By Jove!" Wendover suddenly saw light. "He knew Sternhall in Charponden; he may have met him round about The Grove; he wouldn't be long in putting two and two together, if he'd any sense. How long has he been living in Ravenswood Mansions?"

"Oh, four years or so, I'm told."

Wendover digested this fresh information in silence.

13
THE REWARD BILL

With his letter in his hand, Mr. George Mitford paused before the pillar box and examined the dial to ascertain the hour of the next collection. Physically, Mr. Mitford was not at all impressive. Undersized, round-shouldered, slightly bandy-legged, he suggested some furtive little animal whose timidity is its chief protection in the struggle for existence. His shabby suit of blue serge was shiny at the shoulders and elbows; his black knitted tie had reached fraying point and was shiny also; whilst his shirt cuffs, when they showed themselves, betrayed that they, too, had seen better days. The yachting cap which surmounted his wizened, nutcracker face seemed out of character, as though he had borrowed it temporarily from some seafaring acquaintance. A passer-by, glancing at the insignificant little figure, would have summed up his general impression in a phrase: "A born underdog."

As Mr. Mitford thrust his letter into the slot, his eye was caught by a hoarding across the street, and he scanned it in search of a placard which he had seen elsewhere, earlier in the day. Yes, there it was. He lingered by the pillar box and reread the wording attentively.

£1,000 REWARD!
Whereas, at 9.45 p.m. on Friday, the 20th of July, a man was fatally shot with a pistol by some person unknown who effected an entrance into the ground-floor flat of No. 5, The Grove

£1,000 REWARD

will be paid by me, Henry Scawen, of Carronlea,
Minard Road, Charponden, to any person who shall
give such information as may lead to the discovery
and conviction of the said delinquent.

INFORMATION to be given to me, at the above address,
or to any Police Station.

(Signed) HENRY SCAWEN

Mr. Mitford finished his perusal of the placard and turned
homeward, going slowly, as though in a brown study. It seemed as
if the advertisement had set him an intricate problem which he
was doing his best to solve. Should one make assurance doubly
sure, or was it better to leave things as they were?

He seemed to come to a decision, but he did not quicken his
pace. He strolled on, abstracted, with unseeing eyes, wrapped in a
reverie.

When Constable Danbury paced the lamp-lit streets on night
duty, one little girl-phantom tripping by his side was company
enough; but Mr. Mitford's dreams required a vaster scope. Nothing less than a whole new world sufficed for him as he wandered, a
shabby little figure, through the drab suburban streets. He was
hardly conscious of his surroundings. The baking July pavements,
the parched greenery of the little gardens, the dull familiar house
fronts: all these vanished from his ken. Deep in a daydream, he
trod the roads of far-away Japan, with petals of cherry-blossoms—
pink and white—scattered about his path. For it was always "cherry
blossom time" in Mr. Mitford's dream-Japan, a season of blue skies
crossed by high-sailing clouds like cotton wool, of warm zephyrs
which stirred the trees and brought the petals drifting to the ground
like weary butterflies; of a spring freshness in the air, eternal and
unchanging as the white cone of Fujiyama in the background.

Mr. Mitford's real footsteps might shuffle over the level pavements of an English town; but in his fancy he rambled through
quaint uneven byways, climbed the terraces of templed hills,
crossed over queer, canted bridges of strange design, lost himself

among odd fragile dwellings built of paper and bamboo, or explored the Yoshiwara where brightly clad geishas danced to the music of the koto, and mousmees waited upon his every desire. This was his land of refuge into which he could pass at will to escape from the dullness and dreariness of real life.

In the days when Mr. Mitford had just learned to spell his way through simple sentences, an enterprising firm published a series of little square booklets on crinkled Eastern paper, with coloured woodcuts by Japanese artists. Each tiny volume contained one of the fairy tales of old Japan. Mr. Mitford's uncle, in a burst of un-wonted generosity, presented him with the set; and thenceforward Mr. Mitford's life-history had borne the stamp of that gift. At a receptive age, he had pored over the stories of the Tongue-cut Sparrow, the Accomplished and Lucky Teakettle, the Crackling Mountain, and the Badger's Money. They became to him what Grimm's Fairy Tales were to most children of his day. And in the Story of the Old Man Who Made Withered Trees to Blossom, he encountered for the first time that blossom which became an essential feature in the Japan of his visions.

The quaint, un-European woodcuts, too, stamped themselves on his childish memory, to furnish, later on, the groundwork of his dream-landscapes.

He grew older, became an office boy, a drudge, the butt of the other clerks, and the old fairy tales faded from his conscious memory. Then, one day in his receptive adolescence, he chanced to examine the box of books at the door of a second-hand dealer. On the back of a dingy volume his own surname caught his eye, and out of curiosity he picked up Mitford's "Tales of Old Japan." And, suddenly, as he turned the pages, his care-free childhood seemed to sweep back and blot out the dingy present. Here once more were the old woodcuts he had pored over so often: the kimono-clad Tongue-cut Sparrow entertaining its old master; the Accomplished and Lucky Teakettle dancing with absurd furry legs upon its tightrope; the Hare and the Badger in their boats, fighting to the death amid those impossible waves. He bought the book at the cost of his lunch that day.

And now a new Japan opened out before him, a Japan which enchanted him and satisfied his stunted little aspirations towards romance. He read the tale of the Forty-seven Ronins, and entered a new world: a world of stately courtesy, quaint ceremonial, undying fidelity, and ruthless vengeance. He read it again and again, until each episode seemed to be more real than his daily drudgery.

To young Mitford, the baldly told tale was the very essence of romance. Here was something far removed from the drabness of daily life, something to dream over while one went mechanically about the dull routine of a clerk's existence—a country of Mikados, shoguns clans, daimios and ronins, like a fairy tale born into reality. And slowly there grew up in Mr. Mitford's mind a single ambition: to visit Japan in cherry-blossom time and see these wonders with his own eyes.

But a man who lives much of his time in dreamland is not well fitted for success in business. Mr. Mitford had no real interest in his daily work, and hence no initiative could be expected from him. So he grew into his thirties, reached middle age, and passed on into his fifties, and still the little man had not seen "Japan in cherry-blossom time."

And, meanwhile, disquieting things were happening on the other side of the globe. Factory chimneys were springing up; great clanging shipyards were opening; instead of little men in coats of woven grass and exotic headgear, there were now little men in European dress and bowler hats; instead of rickshas there were Ford cars. Dimly Mr. Mitford realised that his dream-Japan was passing away and that, unless he made haste, there would be none of it left for him to see at the end of his voyage.

Then came disaster. He was growing older, and the firm which had employed him for many years saw the prospect of having to pay him some sort of pension when he got past his work. Domuten, Ltd., advertised for a head clerk, and Mr. Mitford's firm gladly gave him flourishing testimonials which secured him the new post at a higher salary. But head clerks who live half their lives in a dream-Japan do not last long in modern offices. Sternhall soon found what sort of man had been foisted on him and he dismissed Mr. Mitford with a month's salary. Mr. Mitford never forgave him for the things he said at their last interview.

Mr. Mitford was too old to hope for another post, especially as Sternhall pursued him with a personal vindictiveness when he attempted to find a fresh clerkship. He gave up the effort at last, bought his yachting cap as a symbol of independence, and settled down to live upon his small savings and a tiny annuity inherited from his mother, till something turned up, for he was an optimist by nature.

As he approached The Grove, still pondering over the placard he had seen, his reverie was broken by a voice addressing him. He pulled up with a start and lifted his cap awkwardly, as he found himself face to face with Mrs. Sternhall.

"Ah, good afternoon, Mr. Mitford! Isn't it hot? I've been down into town, shopping"—she held up one or two packets—"and I am almost exhausted."

Mr. Mitford, with a clumsy movement, secured the parcels and fell into step by her side. He was shy with women. Once, in his young days, he had proposed to a girl who had more good looks than kindliness. She had rejected him in terms that left Mr. Mitford's sensitive soul wounded to its core. She had, in fact, regarded his proposal as "a bit of dashed cheek from a fellow like him," and she had made him realise, more than ever before, how poor an appearance and how little capacity he had. That had daunted him permanently. Besides, what had he to offer any girl? He did not even become a misogynist. He simply avoided women, and grew more angular and awkward when he was thrown by chance into their company.

Then had come a wonderful day. At the door of his flat, he found a stray kitten, a pathetic little furry thing with a ribbon about its neck, mewing piteously to an unheeding world. It ran up to him confidently when he appeared, back arched, tail erect, and began to rub itself against his legs, while its mewing took on a different note. Mr. Mitford was not fond of cats; but he had a soft heart, and this helpless little beast called for help and sympathy and kind treatment. He took it in, gave it milk, and as he watched its little pink tongue busily lapping, and heard its shrill purr of happiness, he was almost tempted to keep it. But then there was his canary to consider. The risk was too great. He regarded the kitten with perplexity. It was well cared for, by the look of its fur; and the ribbon about its neck proved that somebody was fond of it. He would have to discover its owner; some child would probably be grieving now and wondering where her lost pet had gone. The tiny creature could not have wandered far. Its home must be somewhere near by.

So, when the kitten had lapped its fill, he put on his yachting cap, and sallied out, carrying the little beast securely tucked in a fold of his jacket, from which its inquisitive eyes and big ears poked forth to examine a world which was no longer unfriendly. He visited house after house with the inquiry, "Have you lost a kitten?" and the replies he got were angry, sympathetic, or would-be helpful, according to the temperament of the person who answered his ring. Some people were openly suspicious, only too obviously mistaking him for a burglar's accomplice. It was a disheartening search, and the kitten grew restless, but at last somebody directed him to Number 5, The Grove.

"Oh, you've brought back our kitten!" the maid exclaimed, as her eye fell on the little head peering out from under Mr. Mitford's jacket. "She'll want to thank you. She's been that worried about the little thing since it strayed."

She did not say "Sir." To her eyes, Mr. Mitford was so obviously not the kind of person who gets that title. Nor did she ask him to enter. "You wait there, a minute. She'll be that delighted."

Mr. Mitford, uneasily resentful of this suggestion of a forthcoming reward for his trouble, shifted from one foot to the other. He was about to move away, after depositing the kitten on the mat, when "She" came out of her sitting-room into the cramped little hall. Mr. Mitford gazed, slightly aghast at the situation. He had expected a child—not this dark-haired beauty. He fumbled with his coat, extracted the kitten, and held it out in both hands.

"Oh, you've brought back my Mimi?" she cried, taking it from him with gentle, eager hands. "Thank you ever so much! You've no idea how worried I've been about the poor little thing."

She held it up against her face, fondling it and murmuring French endearments to it. Mr. Mitford never forgot that picture: the striped, contented little face of the kitten against the pale cheek and raven hair.

"But you must come in," Mrs. Sternhall insisted. "I must thank you properly. I have so worried over the poor little thing. She's so tiny and so helpless, you see. When I thought a dog might have caught her . . . Dreadful!"

Almost before he knew what was happening, Mr. Mitford found himself sitting on the edge of a chair, dangling his yachting cap from both hands, while opposite him sat this young graceful figure, with the kitten on her lap, her fingers idly caressing it as she talked. And little by little, as she talked to him in her low soft voice, with its faintly exotic accent, Mr. Mitford began to realise that he had missed something in his life, missed it just as he had missed "Japan in cherry-blossom time." His mother had died when he was only a boy, and since then no woman had spoken to him like this: sympathetically, "as if he was a human being after all," as Mr. Mitford expressed it to himself. Mrs. Sternhall, grateful at first to the saviour of Mimi, drew him out tactfully, allowed him to talk about himself. No one had listened to Mr. Mitford before without a covert contempt; and in his case Mrs. Sternhall metaphorically repeated the miracle of the Old Man Who Caused Withered Trees to Blossom. He was something new to her, and under her sympathetic prompting, he grew fluent and his naïve enthusiasm came to light.

"But it is extraordinary that you should be so interested in the East," she said at last. "Extraordinary in this way, I mean. I have a cousin-german out in Annam; and he writes to me almost every mail: most beautiful letters, describing the places and people he has seen. They would interest you. He has a vivid way of writing, and he makes one see the things he describes. When the next mail arrives, you must come to tea and see his letter; or no, perhaps you don't read French? Ah, then I shall have to translate it to you, though that will be less vivid, I fear. Then that is agreed? Good! I shall write you a note when the mail comes in. But I forgot. I have not your address."

171

Mr. Mitford gave it to her.

"Oh, that is it? Just at the corner of the street? So we are neighbours?"

She rose to her feet as she spoke; and Mr. Mitford, with a guilty glance at the clock on the mantelshelf, stumbled up from his own chair.

"Now I must thank you once again for being kind to my poor kitten. Say 'Thank you!' Mimi."

She held the kitten up to her cheek again, and with that picture in his mind, Mr. Mitford said farewell and made his way out of the flat.

Mr. Mitford trod on air as he turned his steps homeward. He had not fallen in love with Mrs. Sternhall at first sight. But she was something new, wonderful, sympathetic. His feelings for her were like those of the hobbledehoy in the gallery, when he sees the star actress on the stage: marvellous, desirable . . . but far out of all possible reach.

Still more wonderful, she did not forget her promise. A week or two later, he received a letter in an unfamiliar hand. Letters were rarities to Mr. Mitford, who had no relations and hardly a friend. He glanced at the signature: "Lucienne Sternhall," and the surname made him start with surprise. A coincidence, merely, he concluded, turning eagerly to the message itself. A letter from her cousin-german had arrived, she wrote. Would Mr. Mitford come to tea and hear its contents?

Mr. Mitford went, shyly but rejoiced. He sat before her, his feet tucked under him, embarrassed by his yachting cap. The kitten jumped up on his knee and served to break the ice, and the intimacy of the tea table further encouraged him. By the time the letter was produced, he was almost natural.

The cousin-german, it appeared, rather fancied himself as a prose poet and had not the slightest scruple in practicing his art in his letters. It was tawdry stuff, but to Mr. Mitford's stunted mind it was the authentic magic, it carried the glamour of the silken East. Not "his" Japan, certainly, but a poor relation of that wonderland.

For some months Mr. Mitford lived only for these intermittent visits to The Grove. Mrs. Sternhall took a certain liking for the lonely little man; he reminded her, in some indefinable way, of a stray puppy, with its wistful longing for kindness and protection from the world's harshness. And, without quite knowing it, Mr. Mitford adored his hostess. Used to so little, he exaggerated the tiny favours she did him, until in his eyes she seemed little less than the angels.

Then, abruptly, the invitations ceased; and Mr. Mitford learned that Mr. Sternhall had returned. It never occurred to him to feel aggrieved. Everything Mrs. Sternhall did was right in his eyes; and it was natural enough that she should give all her time to her husband while she had him with her. The idea of jealousy found no foothold in him; his feelings for Mrs. Sternhall were not on that plane at all.

And then, one day, himself unobserved, he caught sight of Sternhall in The Grove, and recognised the man who had thrown him into the street without a thought. So *that* was the husband of this girl who had been so kind!

Mr. Mitford was a slow thinker, but he had not walked twenty paces before the implications of the whole affair had forced themselves into his mind. He had Sternhall at his mercy. He, alone, knew that Sternhall of Domuten, Ltd., and Sternhall of Number 5, The Grove, were identical. One sentence scribbled on a postcard, and that game would be up. There was revenge, ready-made, for the way that Sternhall had served him.

Slowly it dawned upon him, however, that such an exposure would have repercussions in quarters other than the premises of Domuten, Ltd. Sternhall had been married twice. The existence of two Mrs. Sternhalls settled that; for it never crossed his simple mind that one of them might be "Mrs. Sternhall" by courtesy only. One of them was Sternhall's legal wife. But which? His kind lady of The Grove might be Sternhall's victim, not his wife. And if she were, then the explosion of his mine would carry disaster into the very last place that he desired.

Then a brilliant solution flashed across his brain, a solution which had every desirable ingredient except common honesty. Why not blackmail Sternhall? And as he balked at the word, there rose in his mind that vision of Japan ablaze with cherry-blossoms, his life's ambition within his grasp. And more than he had ever dreamed. For Sternhall could pay, not in mere hundreds, but in thousands, given time; and with that capital at his back, Mr. Mitford could leave for good this drab Western World and settle down, secure, wealthy by Eastern standards, in the land of his dreams. Not a mere flying trip, leaving behind it the aching desire for return, but ten, twenty years perhaps, "out yonder."

Ideal solution! But full of prickly points, as Mr. Mitford discovered as he ruminated upon it, day after day. How does one open a campaign of blackmail? The Sunday papers supplied him with hints, but none of the methods appealed to him. And behind this problem loomed another which touched him more closely. "Could you, George Mitford, blackmail Sternhall and still meet his wife on the old terms without giving yourself away?"

In the meanwhile, Mr. Mitford found, the thought of revenge is one which can be brooded over with no little satisfaction when you cannot be cheated of it. He staged a new dream-world for himself: scene after scene in which he bearded Sternhall in his office, or accosted him in the street, or visited him in his home. "Can you spare me a few minutes, Mr. Sternhall? Or shall I call on you at Number 5, The Grove?" Just like that: noncommittal, but devastating.

So Mr. Mitford brooded for days and weeks, with a certain bitter joyousness, until at last he reached a decision. In the meanwhile, he continued his visits to Mrs. Sternhall. They had become to him what opium is to the addict, something which could not be relinquished.

And now, with the Sternhall tragedy over and done with, here he was, walking by her side in the sunshine, carrying her little parcels for her, listening to her voice. They reached the door of her flat and she held out her hand for the parcels he was carrying.

"You must come to tea again, soon, after my brother-in-law has gone back to France," she said, with a smile that enchanted him. "I have several letters from Annam to show you. I kept them specially. And you must see Mimi with her kitten, such a darling little ball of fur, and so funny."

She acknowledged his confused acceptance with a graceful movement of her head and turned into the entrance to the flats, leaving Mr. Mitford, dazed with happiness, on the pavement. It was a second or two before he collected himself and moved off towards his own abode.

In its first youth, Number 1, Ravenswood Mansions, had been the residence of a prosperous solicitor who flowered in the Later Victoria Age: a great giver of interminable dinner parties and musical evenings, a noted player of whist, and a sound judge of port. Every morning, rain or shine, his brougham came round from the mews at the back of the terrace and conveyed him, at a sedate trot, either to his office or to church on Sundays. Things were different now. Houses like Number 1 were unsuited to a less prolific generation. They became unsalable, unlettable, and were finally broken up into flats with the least possible expenditure on alterations

No brougham came to the door of Number 1, nowadays. Barbican's third-hand car occupied one of the garages which had replaced the mews. And Mr. Mitford reigned in solitude over the top flat of Number 1, which had originally been the servants' quarters. Mid-Victorian servants were not coddled in the matter of accommodation; and Mr. Mitford's abode under the slates was by no means spacious or convenient, since odd angularities in its ceilings were apt to strike the unwary visitor in more senses than one. But it was cheap, which appealed to Mr. Mitford.

As he entered his sitting-room, his canary burst out into a song of welcome. It was the one creature in the world that seemed always glad to see him; and he crossed over to its cage and whistled in reply—a little breathlessly, for the stairs had tried him. Then he cast an approving glance round the miserable attic. The Japanese, he knew, furnished with simplicity; and he prided himself that he had caught the spirit. A cupboard, a rickety bamboo table, two chairs, and a fender occupied carefully chosen positions. The only other article was a desk which had grown old in service without gaining value as an antique. Mr. Mitford had picked it up at an auction, and to his surprise there had been no competitive bidders.

Another Japanese idea which Mr. Mitford had adopted was the concentration of beauty in a single object. "They only put out one ornament at a time, and they change it before they get tired of looking at it, so it never gets stale," he would explain. The article of beauty for the current week was a chipped and battered vase which stood upon the mantelpiece. To any dealer, it would have been useless; but Mr. Mitford handled it with the most minute care and pored over its design as a lover scans the face of his mistress. "Real cloisonné," he murmured, picking it up to gaze on it once more.

With the vase in his hand, Mr. Mitford stood, evidently deep in the consideration of some problem. The glaring lettering of the placard: "£1,000 REWARD!" danced before his mental vision, alluring and ominous. At last he came to a decision. After all, he reflected, he had already put his shoulder to the wheel. There was no drawing back for him now; and he might as well make assurance doubly sure.

He replaced the vase tenderly on the mantelpiece, sat down at his battered desk, and began to write. The letter gave him trouble, for despite a life spent in quill-driving, Mr. Mitford found it difficult to express his own thoughts with a pen. When at last he had finished, he addressed the envelope to "The Chief Constable, Police Headquarters," and stamped it, ready for the post.

Then he prepared his simple evening meal. It was a hot night, and food did not tempt him. He washed up afterwards, resentfully, for he was not an expert dishwasher; there seemed always to be a film of grease over his utensils after he had done his best for them. Then he put on his yachting cap, picked up his letter, gave a valedictory chirrup to his canary, and quitted the flat.

Leaving Mr. Mitford's flat was a simple process: you opened the sitting-room door, and there you were, on the little landing outside. In the reconstruction of the old house, the landlord had not thought it worth while to provide an entrance hall to Mr. Mitford's part of the premises.

Mr. Mitford, still clutching his envelope, descended the stairs. His fingers still felt greasy from the washing-up, and this tiny annoyance irritated him. As he reached the flat below, Barnard the architect emerged from his office.

"'llo, Mitford!" the architect greeted him, as they met on the landing.

Mr. Mitford was always gratified, but slightly confused, when Barnard took notice of him. The architect was a busy man. He liked to appear even busier than he actually was, because he thought it good business to seem busy. He appeared to be so busy that he seldom could find time to insert a subject in his sentences, preferring to leave that to the imagination of his hearers. Sometimes even the verb got left out in the haste of the moment.

"Good evening, Mr. Barnard," Mr. Mitford responded respectfully.

"Saw you passing up the street a while ago, with Mrs. Sternhall," Barnard informed him, in the loud, carrying voice he affected because he believed it inspired confidence in clients. "Fine-looking woman, that. Moves gracefully, too. Bearing up well under it all?"

"Under what all?" asked Mr. Mitford, whose slow mind had not quite followed the machine-gun rattle of Barnard's clipped phrases.

"All this chatter," the architect explained. "The murder, you know, and what young Bracknell was to her, and whether she'd a hand in things, and so forth. All chatter, of course. Irritating, though, for her, I expect. And this bigamy, too. . . ."

"What bigamy?" demanded Mr. Mitford, startled.

"Not seen the papers? It's all come out in the wash. Our friend downstairs is full of it. Complicates the case a bit."

Mr. Mitford had not seen the papers. He economised on newspapers by reading them at the local Free Library; and he had not visited that for a couple of days. The Sternhall case was a subject which he preferred to avoid in print. And now the story of Sternhall's bigamy was public property for any office boy to gloat over!

He made no reply to Barnard, and the two descended the stairs side by side. The front door of the flats opened and they heard footsteps racing up the lower flight towards them.

"See they're offering a reward for the murderer," Barnard boomed. "Thousand, no less. Must be somebody with money to

177

burn. Wonder what interest he had in the deceased. Nice plum for somebody."

Mr. Mitford glanced guiltily at the letter in his hand. Barnard, who had sharp eyes, followed his look and read the inscription in Mr. Mitford's large clerkly hand.

"'The Chief Constable'," he exclaimed in tones that resounded down the well of the stair. "Having a dash at it, eh? Well, good luck! Stand me a dinner when you get your thousand." Then, with a change of tone, he demanded seriously, "Know anything about it, really?"

"I think I can give the police some information of value," Mr. Mitford declared modestly. "I had not at first connected it with the tragedy. It only occurred to me when thinking things over."

He broke off abruptly as Barbican appeared at the head of the lower flight of stairs and came forward towards the door of his flat before which they were standing. The reporter was obviously in the highest spirits.

"How-de-do, Barnard? How-de-do, Mitford? How-de-do both—making three in all. I say, I've got another scoop! Did you see my stuff? The Sternhall bigamy affair? Keep your eye on the Chief Constable: that's the tip in this race. I got wind he'd been over to Charponden, so I followed up his trail and unearthed a solemn old ass, one Scawen. The bloke who's offering the reward so open-handedly. He gave me enough to put two and two together and make 4.001 out of them, which is as near the truth as need be. The Star Reporter, eh? And that reminds me, Mitford, your Frenchee friend's an honest woman, it seems: the genuine, copper-bottomed, pukka Mrs. Sternhall, with government stamp on the packet. It was the other wench he led up the garden, according to the dates. A bad lad, the late lamented."

He shook his head in mock deprecation, while Mr. Mitford fidgeted under the crudity of the phrases.

"Better look out, Barbican," Barnard warned the journalist. "Mitford's entering for the Sherlock Holmes Stakes. Got a clue already: footprint, cigarette ash, or what not. Hot on the trail. Have to look slippy or you'll only get a place." He glanced at his watch.

"By Gad! That time already? Must scratch up some dinner and get back here by half-past eight. Took on a fresh contract today, and all the rest have to move up one. Damn this builders' strike. Coming with me, Mitford?"

As Mr. Mitford turned to follow the architect, Barbican put out a detaining hand.

"You're not doing anything, are you? You can post that by and by. I've read these notes you left for me. There might be something to be made out of them—middles for the *Monitor*, perhaps. The Vampire Cat yarn. Some people are interested in cats, God knows why. But I need a point or two more, before I can write it up. Come inside for a jiffy and put me wise. Ten per cent. to you, if I get it accepted."

He opened his door with his latchkey and ushered the reluctant Mr. Mitford inside.

"'Night!" Barnard's stentorian voice rumbled up the well, as he clattered down the stairs to the front door. Barbican leaned over the rail and hailed him as he descended.

"Sleep well! 'Let no ill dreams disturb your rest . . .' as the hymn says. I know who the murderer is. Read the next thrilling instalment when it appears."

14
THE CURTAIN-RAISER

Wendover's glance ranged round the little room at the police station, idly examining the neat rows of files on the shelves, the official notices pinned on the walls, and the scanty furnishings. Chesilton, pen in hand, sat at his desk, ready to take notes. Sir Clinton stood with his back to the empty fireplace, looking down on Bracknell, who had been brought up for a further examination.

Detention had altered the young man, both physically and morally. His clothes looked as if they had been slept in. His hair had been carelessly brushed. Without being actually slovenly, he gave the impression that he had lost interest in his appearance. There was a corresponding change in his manner, too. His eyes looked as if he had spent sleepless nights, and he seemed to have lost the confidence he had displayed when Wendover first saw him. When questioned, he had repeated his lies in a toneless voice, as though he himself did not believe what he said but merely repeated something learned by heart. The Chief Constable had listened with an air which suggested boredom closely verging upon irritation. Now he broke silence.

"I've given you every chance, Mr. Bracknell," he said incisively. "You haven't been charged—yet. I've offered you several opportunities of telling the plain truth, and you've refused them all. Instead, you've persisted in telling us a pack of lies—well, half-truths, if you like that better. I'll tell you now that we have unimpeachable witnesses who can prove that you're lying."

Bracknell looked up, startled at the words, and Wendover could see that he was thinking hard.

"Who are they?" he demanded huskily.

"That's our business," Sir Clinton said crisply. "Now, unless you can give us something better than these fairy tales, we'll have to charge you. Your only chance is to tell the plain truth, whatever it is. If you won't, then there's no escaping the obvious deduction. If you're an innocent man, the truth won't hurt you. If you're guilty, of course . . ."

"But you don't believe me, in any case," protested Bracknell, in obvious anxiety. "You wouldn't believe me if I told you everything. Circumstances are dead against me; I know that well enough."

"I'd know truth if I heard it," Sir Clinton retorted impatiently. "The trouble is, I haven't heard it from you, as yet. But please yourself," he added, with a slight shrug which conveyed indifference to the outcome of the interview. "It's immaterial to me whether you hang or not. I get no commission."

The calculated brutality of the phrases seemed to galvanise Bracknell. He sat up in his chair, and his fingers played nervously with the cloth of his trousers, clinching it into folds and then taking a fresh pinch of fabric. The Chief Constable ignored him completely. Bracknell saw him draw a printed document from his pocket and study it, as though verifying something in it. At last the young man collapsed and surrendered without further effort.

"I'll tell you exactly how it happened," he said, in an unnatural voice which had a certain hopelessness in its tone. "You won't swallow it. I can't expect that. But it's the plain truth; the truth, the whole truth, and nothing but the truth," he quoted, with an hysterical giggle.

"I hope so," the Chief Constable rejoined curtly. "That will be a pleasant change. Get on with it. You've wasted far too much of our time already. Give him some brandy and water, Inspector," he added contemptuously, "or we'll have him in tears."

Chesilton fetched a glass and Bracknell gulped down the mixture. It seemed to revive him, and when he spoke again, it was in a less hysterical tone.

"What I told you before was perfectly true, up to the point when I left the clubhouse," he began sullenly. "You can test that as you like, for it's quite correct. When I left the clubhouse, I remembered something. I'd been taking French lessons from Mrs. Sternhall; and on my last visit to her flat, I left a book behind me, one of the books we used."

Sir Clinton glanced at the inspector, who nodded, as though to convey that he would check this detail.

"Was your name written on the title page?" Sir Clinton demanded.

"No, but I'd underscored some words in pencil here and there in the text, words I wanted to ask her about," Bracknell answered.

"Go on, then."

"I remembered about this book, and I went along to Number 5, meaning to get it back from Mrs. Sternhall."

"What time was it when you reached Number 5?"

"Just before half-past seven. I know that, because I was due at my rooms at half-past seven for dinner, and I'd just time enough to call at Number 5 on the way back."

The truth at last, Wendover reflected, as he recalled the evidence of the maidservant which bore on this point.

"I went up the steps and into the entrance hall of Number 5," Bracknell went on, with a hesitation in his voice which betrayed that he was coming to a difficult point in his tale. "As I went into the hall, I saw that the door of the ground-floor flat was half-open. Somebody was standing behind it. I caught a glimpse of him. He was lurking in the shadow and peering out, as if he were keeping an eye on people passing through the hall. That flat was being done up by some firm of painters and decorators, I knew; and I took him for one of the workmen who had stayed on to work overtime or something.

"When he caught sight of me, he opened the door wide and stood on the threshold, staring at me. I didn't know him from Adam; but he seemed to know me, or at least it seemed as if he'd been expecting me to turn up. He came a step forward and said, 'Oh, there you are!', or something of that sort. I don't remember the exact words. Then he beckoned me into the flat and led me through to the back room. I didn't know what he was after, but I thought he might be needing some help, some job or other that he couldn't manage single-handed."

"Did you notice anything about him: face, figure, clothes, or anything of that sort?" Sir Clinton interrupted.

"I didn't see him very well at the start," Bracknell explained, hesitatingly. "It was a bit dim in the entrance hall, and he was in the shadow of the flat's door. He wasn't my height; I think he came up to my chin, or thereabouts. He was clean-shaven, I think; at least, I don't remember his having a moustache. And barring that he wore a lounge suit, I can't describe his clothes. But I did notice he was wearing rubber gloves. I remember that, because I couldn't think what he had them on for, and then I guessed he might be an electrician or something of that sort."

Bracknell seemed to have regained a little confidence, now that he had taken his plunge into confession. He spoke more fluently as his tale unfolded itself.

"It was lighter in the room at the back of the flat; it has a big French window opening on the garden. The leaves of this were ajar, I remember. On the floor were some paintpots, brushes, and painters' things. That was all I had time to see, for I was hardly inside the door when the fellow turned on me with a snarl like a wild animal; and before I knew where I was, he'd gripped me by the throat. . . . It was a fight for life. . . ."

"Yes, yes," said the Chief Constable testily. "We quite understand. Very unmannerly conduct for a total stranger. But don't trouble to be melodramatic about it. The plain facts will do."

Bracknell had begun to act the scene, but at Sir Clinton's plain hint he ceased to gesticulate and went on with his story in a cooler tone. "I was half-choked by his grip on my throat, and a bit dazed, too, by the suddenness of the whole affair. He hit me in the face, and my nose began to bleed. He hit it in the scuffle. Then I saw he was feeling in his pocket with his other hand, and I gripped that arm. We wrestled about the room, staggering round; but I managed to keep my feet. Once I tripped over one of the paintpots and that nearly brought me down. I forgot to say that when he gripped my throat, he must have got hold of that gold cross I wore by a chain round my neck, under my shirt. My tennis shirt had been torn open in the struggle and I suppose the cross got torn away. It disappeared, anyhow, I know."

Wendover, listening intently and fitting each piece into its place in the jigsaw of evidence, became convinced that at last they were getting the truth.

"By and by he tired," Bracknell went on. "He was a smaller man than I am, and he wasn't in good condition. Suddenly he fell back from me, towards the window; and again I saw him fumbling in his pocket."

"You didn't think of shouting for help?" demanded the inspector sceptically.

"I was half-choked straight away, and after that I was saving my breath to tire him out. Besides," he added simply, "I just didn't think of it; I was so taken aback and busy fending him off."

"Well, go on. What happened next?"

"As soon as I could get my breath, I asked him what he thought he was playing at. That seemed to surprise him, somehow. He kept his hand in his pocket and stood there, with his back to the window, taking a good look at me, and I could see a queer expression coming into his face, like a man who realises he's made a bad mistake of some sort. Then he asked me the last question I expected: 'What's your age?' I was so taken aback, I said, 'Twenty-three' without thinking what a weird question it was in the circumstances. Then he bit his lip, like a man who's angry with himself for some blunder, and he asked, 'Do you know who I am?' I said, 'No, I never set eyes on you before and I haven't a notion what you're up to.' That seemed in some way to ease his mind, and he turned quite apologetic. I was standing there, mopping my nose with my handkerchief till it was soaked with blood and I threw it away somewhere on the floor. He pulled out his own, a perfectly new one, and insisted on lending it to me. By and by the bleeding slowed down a bit.

"Then he began a long rambling explanation to account for his doings. His wife, he said, was carrying on with another man; he'd got information about that, but he didn't know who the other man was. So he'd laid a trap for them, in this empty flat, and when I turned up, he'd naturally thought I was the other man. It didn't sound the sort of story one could easily believe; but he insisted on it and repeated it, with all sorts of new details each time, until I didn't know but that it might be true. It accounted for things, anyhow.

"But I was angry, of course, after being manhandled like that, so I said, 'Well, that's nothing to me. You've committed a common assault and I'm going to hand you over to the police.' And at that he dropped his truculence altogether; he got more apologetic even than before. He admitted that it would mean gaol for him; he could hardly expect to get off with a fine; and that would be a scandal, and so on, and so forth. Finally, he looked at me as if he was trying to size me up, and he said, 'If there's any charity you're interested in, I'd subscribe anything reasonable to its funds.' Well, by that time I had cooled down; there didn't seem to be much point in hauling him before the Beak, though he deserved it; and I'm interested in the 'Christians, Awake!' movement. In fact, I've made arrangements to go to France to help on the work, over there. So a subscription would be useful enough. So, after thinking it over for a minute or two, I said, 'All right. How much will you give?' I'd thought of ten guineas, or something like that; and he staggered me completely by saying, 'Fifty pounds. Will that do?' I said, 'All right. You can send the cheque to Ambrose Bracknell, Number 17, Bella Vista Avenue.' But to my surprise, he shook his head, pulled out a note-case, and handed me three tens and four flyers on the spot. I put them into my pocket. When I offered to give him a receipt, he waved the suggestion aside.

"After that, of course, I couldn't show ill feeling. He seemed really sorry for what he'd done. I missed my gold cross, and he and I hunted everywhere for it, but we couldn't find it. And, by that time, it was getting on in the evening; and now he seemed only anxious to see me off the premises. By the way, during the struggle, I'd set my foot in some of the spilt paint, and I scrubbed the sole of my tennis shoe on the floor, to try to clear the stuff off. That ought to have left some trace, and it'll show you I'm telling the truth."

"And you came away from the flat . . . at what time?" demanded the inspector.

"I don't know, really," Bracknell admitted, with apparent frankness. "I didn't look at my watch. I knew I was far too late for my dinner, anyhow; and besides, with the hot night and the exertion of struggling with the man, I didn't feel inclined to tackle dinner. So I tidied myself up; there was no real damage done, now that my nose had stopped bleeding: and I went off downtown to a picture house. I wanted to soothe down my nerves after all that affair, and the pictures seemed about the right treatment. I stayed there till the show closed down, and then I came straight home to bed."

"Yes," said Sir Clinton, as Bracknell paused at this point. "And now you can explain how you came to concoct all these fairy tales you told us."

Bracknell wriggled slightly in his chair, an ungraceful movement for so big a man.

"I knew nothing about the murder till next morning," he began. "Sternhall hadn't even told me his name when we met in that flat. I knew nothing about him. I certainly never connected him with Mrs. Sternhall. It wasn't till next morning, when I saw a newspaper, that I found out what had happened in The Grove after I left. And when I saw the headline in the paper, I began to see what a mess I might have got into.

"It was like a nightmare, coming all of a sudden on me like that. I lost my head, I suppose you'd say. I saw all sorts of awkward questions turning up if I admitted that I'd been on the premises at all; and then I remembered that I'd seen nobody, either going or coming. If I kept my mouth shut, I thought, nobody would ever connect me with the affair. Why should they? I didn't know the dead man; I didn't even know if the dead man was the one I'd met in the flat, for the newspaper description was very vague. On the spur of the moment, I made up my mind to keep my mouth shut. I had nothing to do with the affair, and the less I was mixed up in it the better."

"For yourself, you mean," Sir Clinton supplemented. "But if *we'd* had your evidence at the start, we'd have been saved a lot of trouble."

"Oh, I dare say," admitted Bracknell, "but that's your business, isn't it? It wasn't any affair of mine."

"Pray continue," said Sir Clinton, with exaggerated politeness. "May I suggest that the plain facts will do? Your mental reactions are not so important. What did you *do?*"

"I thought of the things that might connect me with the affair," Bracknell went on sullenly. "The worst of them was that batch of banknotes. For all I could tell, the numbers of them might have been taken; and if they were found in my hands, it was plain enough that people would say, 'Here's the motive. He killed Sternhall to get the money.' So I burned them as soon as I thought of that."

"You didn't take the numbers of them yourself?" Chesilton inquired, looking up from his desk.

"No, of course not. That would have left a clue, wouldn't it? If you'd found a note of the numbers in my pocket, I mean. No, I just burned them immediately. Then there was the paint on my tennis shoes; and if that were spotted and linked up with the overturned paintpot in the flat, I might be hauled into the business. So I burned the shoes also. Then there was the handkerchief I'd thrown down on the floor of the flat, because it was all soaked with blood and I didn't want to put it back into my pocket. It was a new one, and I hadn't got it marked, so it didn't seem likely that it could be traced to me. Anyhow, I could do nothing about it. And I burned the handkerchief he'd lent me. I found I'd stuffed it into my pocket mechanically."

He paused for a moment, evidently feeling that his next instalment was going to bring him onto less comfortable ground.

"That left the gold cross. It was missing, and it might be lying about in the flat, somewhere. I didn't think it was; for he and I had searched the floor fairly thoroughly, and it hadn't turned up. I felt pretty sure I'd lost it at the tennis courts or somewhere else, before I went to the flat at all; but I didn't care to take the risk of making inquiries about it, just in case. Then that advertisement appeared; and I felt a bit relieved, for it seemed pretty plain that I'd lost the thing in the street—outside the flat, at any rate."

"Why didn't you apply for it yourself?" demanded the inspector.

"You don't realise the state of mind I was in," complained Bracknell. "The last thing I wanted was to connect myself with the affair; but at the same time, I wanted to know if the cross had been found outside the flat. That would have relieved my mind, don't you understand? It would have meant one chance less of my being mixed up in the affair. Then it occurred to me that if somebody else applied for the cross, somebody quite different from me, then nobody would think anything about it. So I got Miss Huntingdon to apply for it instead of me."

"How did you persuade her into that?" asked Sir Clinton.

"I made up a story about a bet," Bracknell confessed, unashamedly. "I told her I'd bet that anyone could go and get lost property, and so on. She didn't like the idea at first, so I said, 'Well, I'll make you a present of the cross; so now you're the owner, but you're not the person who lost it, and that's what we had the bet about.' And then, while I was talking to her, another thing crossed my mind. If I had an alibi for the evening, then I'd be on velvet, if any casual inquiries were made about me. So I persuaded her to say I was with her from seven o'clock onwards."

"Did you tell her the whole story?" demanded Sir Clinton.

"Not much!" said Bracknell vulgarly. "I'm not a fool. No, I told her it was all part of a joke: the cross and the alibi. I made up the whole thing on the spur of the moment, and she swallowed it without any bother. She's rather keen on me, you see, and that helped a bit, I expect."

"An ingenious fellow, evidently," Sir Clinton commented. "But you must have been more plausible with her than you've been with us. And although you were so anxious to keep clear of trouble yourself, you didn't mind dragging Miss Huntingdon into an awkward position."

"Well, what could I do?" demanded Bracknell naïvely. "I had to get someone to give me an alibi, hadn't I? And she was the likeliest person to do that for me."

"So you coached her in the lies you wanted her to tell?"

"Well, I had to smooth things down, hadn't I? She thought it was just some joke or other that I was playing on somebody."

"And now, after she's committed herself up to the neck as an accessory to your doings, you turn round and let her down?"

"She won't mind," Bracknell asserted rather fatuously. "I'll make it all right with her."

"By a few more lies? Well, we'll see. From what I've seen of Miss Huntingdon, you'll find it less easy than you think," Sir Clinton said contemptuously. "Now have you told us the whole story? No little mental reservations, or anything of that sort? Very well. You can initial this copy of your statement. Give it to him, Inspector. And . . ." he added a few words in an undertone, which Wendover did not catch.

"Very good, sir," Chesilton answered, and left the room after handing over the papers for Bracknell to read through.

In a few minutes, Chesilton returned.

"Mrs. Sternhall has found the book in her flat, sir. It's marked as he described, and he did leave it behind on the day of the murder. I've arranged about the other thing also."

Sir Clinton nodded and turned to Bracknell.

"You can go, when you've signed that statement."

Bracknell, evidently on tenterhooks to be gone, scribbled his signature on the papers and then, with a backward glance which received no acknowledgment, shambled out of the room.

"I never fancied that young man," Sir Clinton commented, as the door closed.

"Miserable young cur!" Wendover said angrily. "Dragging a girl into this business and persuading her to lie, because he was afraid to tell the truth himself. And then letting her down, without a quiver. Ugh!"

"That reminds me," said the Chief Constable, glancing at the inspector. "We'd better get that evidence of hers withdrawn as soon as possible. Nothing like having things shipshape. We can relieve her mind, too. Most likely she's picturing our young friend immured in our dankest dungeon, with brutal guards putting him through the Third Degree."

He looked at his watch.

"We'll go up there now, Inspector. But there's no need to hold a mass meeting in her mother's drawing-room. You can go in alone and break the glad news. And make the position quite clear to her, please. I think she'd be rather thrown away on a person like Mr. Bracknell."

Wendover and Sir Clinton waited in the car whilst Chesilton carried out his mission. It did not take long, and he came out again, looking sardonically pleased.

"I saw her, sir," he explained. "My telephone call had jarred her up a bit, I'm afraid, since I hadn't stated why I wanted to see her. She looked a bit white and anxious. Not been sleeping well, I imagine, these last few nights. She wasn't pleased to see me, and, barring her curiosity, I don't think she'd have seen me at all if she could have helped it. I just asked her if she meant to stick to her story. She fired up at that—she's not the meek-and-mild kind, I gather—and said that she did. So then I told her that Bracknell had blown the gaff and let her down completely. No comments; just the unvarnished tale, with enough detail to convince her. She was absolutely knocked out, sir, I could see. 'But he couldn't do that,' she said. 'But he did, Miss,' I said. 'And if you don't realise how near you've been to burning your fingers badly, then I'll tell you.' And I drew a fancy picture of a perjury trial. Not that she ever was on oath; but I thought it would do good; and after all, she'd no business to lie to us. I think she's a bit shaken up by it all. But whatever comes on top at the end of the shaking, it won't be a belief in Mr. Bracknell. I'm sure of that, from one or two remarks she made."

"She's withdrawn her evidence?"

"Oh, completely, sir. I've got her signed statement to that effect in my pocket."

"She must be feeling very sick, poor girl," said Wendover sympathetically.

"Better sick than sorry," retorted Sir Clinton, with a laugh. "But unless I misjudge her, Master Bracknell will be both sick and sorry when he goes to explain his doings. Step in, Inspector, and we'll get back to Headquarters."

15
"SUICIDE IS CONFESSION"

"'Be the day short or never so long,
    At length it ringeth to evensong,'"

quoted the Chief Constable, leaning back luxuriously in his arm-chair and addressing his guest. "Why is it, Squire, that some days seem to pass like lightning and others drag like Alexandrines?"

"Quotation for quotation," returned Wendover ironically.

Kiddies and grown-ups too-oo-oo,
    If we haven't enough to do-oo-oo,
We get the hump—
    Cameelious hump. . . .

"It's an easy life, a Chief Constable's, evidently, when you get to this state. Why not take a little interest in The Grove case? You don't seem to be making the progress I expected from your talents."

"Oh, The Grove case is solved," said Sir Clinton rather apathetically. "At least, I know who the murderer is, I think. But the bother in these cases is that we've got to convince a jury. And it doesn't do to make a slip in a murder trial. You can't put a man in the dock twice for the same offence."

"Who is he?" demanded Wendover.

"Tut! Tut! Squire; remember the law against slander. A nice business: 'Chief Constable Charged with Defamation.' It would make another scoop for your reporter friend, if you took him into your confidence."

"So you're holding your hand and hunting for more evidence?"

"I'm holding my hand—and I hate having to do it," the Chief Constable confessed, with something in his tone that made Wendover look at him keenly. "I'm just the least bit afraid of his slipping through our fingers."

"It isn't Bracknell?"

Sir Clinton laughed rather curtly.

"Trying to get at it by elimination, Squire? That's too easy a way. Exercise your reason. There's enough evidence pointing one way to make a moderate certainty, and you know it all."

"It isn't Bracknell," said Wendover decidedly.

"Bracknell's story tallies with the facts," Sir Clinton admitted. "It even tallies with facts that he knew nothing about. For instance, it accounts for the blood on the handkerchief being different from Sternhall's blood; and it fits neatly into Danbury's results from his paint-spilling experiments, which made him put the overturning of the paintpot at two hours before the murder, with a fair margin for experimental error. That agrees more or less with Bracknell's tale that it was upset at about 7.40 p.m. And the fact that we found no handkerchief on Sternhall's body also fits in. Very convincing, isn't it, Squire?"

"Very," said Wendover drily, "except for the fact that even now Bracknell hasn't an alibi for the time of the murder. What was to hinder him going back to the flat for a second visit?"

"Nothing," admitted Sir Clinton blandly. "That's why we're still keeping an eye on him, though he doesn't know it. But to turn to brighter things, Squire, I'm rather pleased with young Danbury. He seems to have the right stuff in him. He and Towton had the same chance in that affair; Danbury showed initiative; poor old Towton didn't. He just did his job. . . ."

The telephone bell rang briskly.

"Damn!" ejaculated the Chief Constable heartily. "There's no peace in this house nowadays, with that thing, and it never seems to bring good news."

He picked up the receiver; and as the message came through, Wendover saw a sudden frown contract his brows. Evidently the telephone was living up to its reputation.

"I'll come over," he said curtly, putting down the instrument and turning to Wendover. "That was Chesilton. You remember that reporter-fellow telling us about his neighbour, Mitford? It seems he's committed suicide. Shot himself. And the pistol he used was the one belonging to Sternhall, the one we couldn't trace, you remember. I've said I'll go round and look into things. You needn't come, Squire, unless you like."

There was a half-invitation in the phrase, and Wendover interpreted it in that sense. As fast as a car could take them, they hurried to Ravenswood Mansions. In the entrance hall they found a small group, from which Barbican detached himself at once.

"You remember me, don't you?" he demanded. "I'm a reporter. Have you got anything for me, Sir Clinton?"

"A few questions later on, perhaps," the Chief Constable replied, brushing past the group and beginning to climb the stairs, with Wendover in his wake.

The light on the first-floor landing was lit, but beyond that the stairs were in darkness. Sir Clinton pulled out a flash lamp and they made their way up to the garret where Mitford had lived. The door of the sitting-room was ajar, the lights inside were on, and the landing was dimly lit by the illuminated doorway. Inside the room were Chesilton, Sergeant Vorley, and the police surgeon, the two detectives making notes whilst the doctor examined the body which lay on the floor close to the threshold. Sir Clinton turned to the inspector with a glance of inquiry, and Chesilton made a brief report.

"Just after nine o'clock, sir, I had a 'phone message from Mr. Barnard, an architect who uses the flat below this as an office. He was somewhat excited. It seems he was working late this evening, and while he was busy with some plans, he heard a shot go off in this flat. He ran upstairs and tried the door of this flat, found it locked, hammered and shouted, but got no reply. A moment or two later, Barbican joined him—he lives in the flat below Barnard. He'd been attracted by the noise and came up, just as Barnard had done. They both did their best to attract Mitford's attention, and listened at the door, but nothing stirred inside. Barnard then went down to his office and rang us up."

"The lights are out on the stair," Sir Clinton pointed out. "Were they out when you came?"

"Yes, sir. The fuses seem to be blown. I tried the switches but nothing happened. When I got the 'phone message," he continued, "I came up here after warning Doctor Smith. Barnard and Barbican were waiting in the hall."

"Who occupies the ground-floor flat?"

"It's shut up just now, sir. The tenants are away on holiday."

Sir Clinton nodded and the inspector went on.

"When we arrived, sir, this door was locked, but the key was on the inside, and I turned it with a pair of long-nosed pincers. When I tried to push the door open something was holding it on the inside. I pushed gently and got it ajar just enough to get inside. Mitford's body was just as you see it. He'd fallen or sat down against the door evidently, so that in opening it we displaced the body a little. He'd been shot in the head, as you can see; and the pistol was on the floor by his side. As I told you, sir, it originally belonged to Sternhall. At least, it tallies with the particulars we got from Sternhall's firearms certificate at Charponden. That seems suggestive, sir."

"I see your drift," Sir Clinton admitted. "But we can discuss that later on. In the meanwhile, let's see what we can see. What do you make of things, Doctor?"

"The body's quite warm," Doctor Fyefield Smith reported. "It hasn't had time to cool yet, of course. Death was obviously instantaneous. The bullet has lodged somewhere inside the skull."

"I want that bullet," the Chief Constable explained. "You'll get it in your P.M. examination, Doctor. Don't scratch it in taking it out, please."

Doctor Smith nodded and continued:

"The shot let out a lot of blood—you can see the pool on the floor, there. There's some coagulation round about the wound."

Sir Clinton bent down over the body, turned on his pocket torch and examined both the wound and the pool of blood on the floor. Rather to Wendover's surprise, he seemed to give the matter more consideration than it demanded. When he stepped back again, his brows were contracted, as though he were thinking hard.

"Well, we'd better not miss anything," he said at last. "Would you mind taking samples of that blood, Doctor? Take them from different parts of the pool and make a diagram showing where you take them. And when you do your P.M., would you take a sample or two from different organs not involved in the smash-up, the heart and an artery or two. Hand them over to Doctor Livermere and ask him to test if they are all the same. We got something out of the blood-stains in The Grove affair; we may as well be thorough."

Doctor Smith nodded and made a note in his pocketbook.

Sir Clinton cast his eye over the immediate surroundings of the body.

"What do you make of that little rubber band hanging loose on the shaft of the key inside the door?" he asked, turning to the inspector.

"I've made a note of it, sir. I haven't got as far as thinking about this business yet. I'm just gathering facts, at present."

"Any clue to his motive in shooting himself?" the Chief Constable inquired. "Any paper he'd left? Confession, or explanation, or anything of that sort?"

"Nothing's turned up, so far, sir. But we've hardly had time to go through the place thoroughly yet."

"Were the lights on in this place when you came in?" was the next question which Sir Clinton put.

"No, sir. We switched them on."

The Chief Constable considered this for a moment or two.

"Of course, it was twilight up here, when the shot was fired," he said, in the tone of one who is trying to convince himself of something. "The lights wouldn't be needed, unless he'd been writing."

He stared down at the body for a moment or two.

"There's no blood anywhere else, is there? This mess here is all you've noticed?"

The inspector thought he saw the drift of this.

"You mean he might have shot himself in the middle of the room and staggered against the door as he fell, sir? I don't think so. The blood's all in the one place."

Sir Clinton seemed to have lost interest in the point.

"I think we'll go downstairs now and interview these two people below," he said. "The sergeant can remain here and hunt about for anything that seems likely to be useful."

They descended the stairs and at the door found Barnard and Barbican discussing the affair with two constables who were on guard. Outside the flats an inquisitive group of spectators had gathered, but one of the constables guarded the entrance.

"I think we'll interview these people separately," Sir Clinton said in an undertone to his companions. "If we take them together, they may get confused with each other's tale. Just ask Mr. Barnard to come up to his office, Inspector. We can talk to him there."

They retraced their steps to the second floor. Barnard fumbled in the dark with his key, opened his door, and ushered them into his office, in which the lights were still burning.

"Now, Mr. Barnard, I want your assistance," Sir Clinton began pleasantly, putting the architect at his ease immediately. "When did you see Mitford alive last?"

Barnard answered this without hesitation.

"About a quarter past seven. Looked at my watch as I left him, I remember. Bolting to get some dinner. Had to be back by half-past eight, as I told him."

"How did you happen to come across him then?"

"Met him on the stairs. He was coming down to post a letter as I left my office. Egad! That reminds me! I noticed the envelope. It was addressed to you. Chief Constable, aren't you? Well, it was addressed to you."

Sir Clinton seemed interested in this point, not unnaturally.

"You saw the envelope with the address?"

"Holding it in his hand. Happened to glance at it. Big clear handwriting, you know. Couldn't help seeing it. Chaffed him about it, poor devil. Asked if he was applying for the thousand-pound reward. He said he thought he had some information that might interest the police. Didn't say what it was, though. Barbican turned up at that moment, interrupted us and Mitford evidently didn't want to give anything away."

"And what happened then?"

"We talked for a minute or so. Barbican had been getting some information from Mitford about Japanese tales, I gathered. Wanted to talk over some points. Took Mitford into his flat as I cleared out. By Jove, that reminds me. As I was going downstairs, Barbican leaned over the banisters and said something about knowing who The Grove murderer was."

"And then you went off to dinner? Now this is a purely formal question, so don't be offended. I suppose you can produce someone who saw you at the place where you had dinner—a waiter, or the commissionaire?"

"Oh, easily," Barnard assured him. "I had my usual table and the waiter knows who I am."

"And then you came back here at half-past eight? Were these lamps on the landings working when you returned, or had the fuses gone by that time?"

"Couldn't say," Barnard answered promptly. "Didn't switch on as I came upstairs. No need, you see. Gone up and down these stairs often enough to do without lights."

"You noticed nothing out of the way?"

"Nix. Went into my office. Started work. Next thing I knew, Bang! Off went a pistol upstairs. No mistaking the sound."

"And what was your reaction to that stimulus?"

"Rushed out onto landing, naturally. Looked up and down the stairs to see if anyone was about. Nobody. Not a sound. Rushed up to Mitford's door. Hammered on it and called his name. No reply. Then heard feet on stairs below and Barbican came racing up. We tried to get some answers from inside. No good. I said, 'Come on! Must telephone the police. Don't like the look of this.' So we both went down to the office here, and I got the inspector on the 'phone and told him what was up. That's all I remember about it."

"Thanks, Mr. Barnard. There's just one point I want to be clear about—this letter you saw with my address on it. You're quite sure you're making no mistake about that?"

"Not the slightest," Barnard declared positively. "No error. Dead certain of it. Tell you why, Barbican arrived, full of a scoop he'd made, following you to Charponden or something, and ferreting out the Sternhall bigamy business. Got a scoop, he said, and very pleased with himself. I remember I said he'd find Mitford had been doing a bit of Sherlocking too. Dangerous rival, and so forth. Couldn't have said that, could I, unless I'd seen the envelope? No, no mistake there."

"Mitford gave you no indication of what was in his mind?"

"None. Don't wonder at that, with a thousand quid as a prize in the competition. Didn't like my speaking of it before Barbican, even, I could see. Tactless of me, that," he admitted frankly, but obviously without blaming himself too severely.

Sir Clinton, with an unusual gesture of reassurance, took the architect by the left arm.

"I shouldn't bother about that," he said. "Now . . ."

Barnard winced at the touch and a sharp intake of breath betrayed a twinge of pain.

"Ouch!" he ejaculated. "Go easy! That arm's sore. Touch of rheumatism in it, lately. Made me jump when you caught it."

"Sorry," Sir Clinton apologised, withdrawing his hand. "I was just going to say we needn't trouble you further just now. Inspector Chesilton will show you a note of your evidence, later on, and perhaps ask another question or two that may be necessary to clear up details. But for the present, good night, Mr. Barnard."

They left the architect fidgeting about his work table, evidently anxious to get something done but too upset to settle down to anything needing concentration.

As they came out of his office, the fingerprint expert met them.

"I think I'll go upstairs with you," Sir Clinton said, leading the way up to Mitford's flat. "I want to have a look at the revolver he used; and I didn't touch it until you'd had a chance to put in your work. Begin with it, please."

The expert went through the routine of his examination.

"Only one set of fingerprints here, sir," he reported, "and so far as one can judge from rough examination, they seem to be the dead man's. I'll be more certain about it by and by."

"I don't want to touch the thing," Sir Clinton said. "Just look at the chambers, if you can get the breach open without making a mess of things. You're more accustomed to that sort of thing than I am."

The expert did as he was asked and reported:

"It's a six-chambered revolver, sir; but only four chambers have been loaded. There's an empty case under the hammer and live cartridges in the next three chambers."

"That's what I wanted to know," the Chief Constable answered; "we'll leave you to go ahead, now."

He led the way out of the flat and, stepping over to the railing, gazed down the dark well of the staircase to where, in the light of the entrance hall, they could see the heads of Barbican and a constable, evidently in conversation. The Chief Constable ran his fingers idly to and fro on the rail. Suddenly he made a movement as though he had touched something abnormal.

"Don't say anything," he cautioned Wendover and the inspector, "but look where I shine my torch."

He pulled out his flash lamp and, shielding the light with his hands so that only a fine beam escaped, he turned the light on the rail. Wendover, peering into the bright illuminated area, saw something on the flat of the rail: a dull patch perhaps an inch or more in diameter, as though the polish of the banister had been dulled by something. As the torch shifted, he saw tiny shadows spring out, showing that fragments of some material were adhering to the wood. Sir Clinton switched off his lamp and turned round to the door immediately behind him.

"H'm!" he said. "We'll need to protect this; and yet I don't want to show interest in it at present. I wonder . . . You've got an extra man down below, haven't you, Inspector? Call him up, will you?"

By the time the man had ascended the stairs, the inspector had followed Sir Clinton's directions and brought out a chair from Mitford's room, which he planted down with its back to the rail, opposite the mark.

"Oh, it's you, Cutler," Sir Clinton addressed the constable, as he reached the landing. "I want a watch kept on this flat all tonight. You'll sit on this chair and watch the door till you're relieved. You understand? You're not to move about. And another thing," he added, in a severe tone, "you'll not talk to anyone or allow them on this landing on any pretext. I heard you discussing this business with the reporter down below. No more of that, please."

The constable, rather abashed at being detected, saluted and took his seat as ordered. Sir Clinton and his two companions descended the stairs. When they had passed Barnard's flat, Sir Clinton seemed to have a fresh idea.

"No need for us to go down. I think we'll call Mr. Barbican up, for a change."

He leaned over the banisters and hailed the reporter. "You might come up here, Mr. Barbican, if you don't mind. I want your version of this affair."

The reporter seemed nothing loth. He came racing up the stairs, three steps at a time; and Wendover sardonically reflected that probably he was hoping, in the course of the interview, to pick up some odds and ends of information from the officials.

"We'd better have our talk in private," the Chief Constable suggested, with a glance down the well of the staircase. "Have you any objection to offering us the hospitality of your flat for a moment or two? I once had the privilege of entertaining you in my house, you remember. Cutlet for cutlet."

Barbican made no objection.

"You can have Scotch or Irish," he said hospitably, as he unlocked his door and ushered them in. "I don't run to champagne suppers. But I recommend my soda. Bubbles just as well as champagne and leaves no ill effects. Not a headache in the bottle."

The sitting-room in Barbican's flat was roomier than Mitford's attic, and better furnished; but it had nothing of the garret's tidiness. Everything seemed to have been thrown down anyhow. In one corner was an unsightly pile of old newspapers. An unpainted wooden table was covered with tools and gadgets which showed that Barbican fancied himself as a craftsman in wood and metal. Evidently he had been working on a wireless set, for condensers, valve-holders, and dials were scattered around a half-completed chassis, with an electric soldering-iron beside them. On another table stood a bottle of whisky, a cut lemon, and a phial of aspirin tabloids. The windows were wide open, and a draught waved the curtains as they entered.

"Phew!" exclaimed Wendover, as he crossed the threshold. "A blazing fire on a night like this? You must be a salamander."

"I've got the devil and all of a chill," Barbican explained, pointing to the kettle which stood by the hearth. "It's flu, or something. I feel a bit all-overish."

He sniffed, once or twice, then went over and shut the windows.

"I hope the odour of eucalyptus doesn't offend your nostrils?" he inquired, with insolent politeness, turning to Wendover. "I'm trying everything to get rid of this cold."

Sir Clinton saved Wendover the trouble of an answer by intervening in a businesslike tone.

"Now, Mr. Barbican, what have you to say about this affair?"

Barbican transferred his inquisitive glance to the Chief Constable. His opening sentence took Wendover by surprise.

"In that reward bill, it said, 'Such information as may lead to the discovery and conviction of the delinquent.' Suppose Sternhall's murderer's dead, and I give information proving that he was the criminal, where do I come in?"

"Nowhere," said Sir Clinton tersely. "You can't convict a dead man."

Barbican's face fell at this decision.

"That's rough on me," he complained. Then, brightening up, he added, "Well, it'll be a scoop for me, at any rate. I'm first in the field again, and that's something."

"The sooner you tell us your tale," Sir Clinton pointed out, "the sooner you'll be free to write up your stuff. When did you last see Mitford?"

"About seven o'clock, it was. I was coming upstairs when I ran into him and Barnard coming down. Met them just outside the door, here."

"What happened?"

"Barnard made some remark about Mitford going into the Sherlock line and ferreting out Sternhall's murderer. Mitford had a letter in his hand. Addressed to you, I saw. Well, I'm a free lance. Any news is good news to me, if I can get it into print. Besides, I'd been doing a bit of thinking myself. I smelt a rat—higher than venison. In fact, I felt pretty sure of my ground. So I invited him in here, meaning to apply the stomach pump and extract whatever was nearest to his heart."

"And then?"

"Oh, he didn't want to come. He seemed a bit queer in his manner, I thought. But I persuaded him."

"Like this?" Sir Clinton demanded, with a smile, catching the journalist by the left arm and leading him forward a pace or two.

"Well, not so much like a lobster's grip," Barbican declared, rubbing his arm gently. "A bit more friendly and persuasive. Anyhow, he came inside."

"And you parted from Mr. Barnard?"

"Yes, he was off downtown. Oh, I forgot. I was pretty sure of my ideas by that time, and I told Barnard I knew who'd killed Sternhall. Just a bit of brag."

"And after that?"

"Well, then I had a chat with Mitford. He'd given me some tips about Japan that I meant to work up into an article, and I wanted to ask him a question or two. So I started with that. He seemed a bit *distrait*, if you know what I mean."

"I do," Sir Clinton assured him.

"The spread of education, eh? Well, anyhow, he seemed not quite *compos mentis*. A bit off his balance, in plain English. I asked him some questions, mostly about what he called 'Harry Keary.' You know what that means?"

"Honourable suicide," Sir Clinton interpreted, for the benefit of the inspector. "To atone for some fault you've committed."

"Yes, you've got the idea," Barbican agreed. "He talked a lot about the high standard of honour in Japan and what a fine action 'Harry Keary' was. It was about that Satsuma man—ah! that sticks you?"

"Not at all," Sir Clinton assured him. "You mean the Satsuma man who misjudged Kuranosuke and committed hara-kiri to atone for it when he discovered his mistake?"

"He knows everything!" Barbican declared, in mock admiration. "But to get on. He talked about the Forty-seven Ronins and how fine it was to square off an account, knowing that at the end of it you'd got to commit 'Harry Keary' and so on and so forth. In fact, his mind seemed to be dwelling on suicide just then."

"Well, go on."

"Well, as the talk went on, I began to be more certain I was right in my judgments. So I turned the talk on to the Sternhall affair. That made him uncomfortable. One could see that, with half an eye. So I was pretty sure I'd got the right end of the stick. And at last I wormed out of him something that was next door to a confession that in some way he'd been mixed up in the Sternhall murder. He didn't admit he'd done it. Not quite that. But he tried to look wise and pretend he knew something about it. And then he went off to talk about 'Harry Keary' again. His mind seemed to run on it. And at last he got up, clutching his letter, and went off to the pillar box."

"What time was that?"

Barbican reflected.

"About half-past seven or a quarter to eight, I'd say. I can't put it nearer. Perhaps getting on for eight o'clock."

"You saw him out? Were the stair lights on, then?"

Barbican shook his head.

"No, it was light enough to see easily enough in the well of the stairs."

"And that was the last you saw of him? At that time, I mean."

"Yes, I never saw him again."

"What happened after that?"

"Well, I told you I've got a devil of a chill. I started in to doctor myself for it."

He nodded towards the various medicaments on the table.

"And after that?"

"The next thing I remember was hearing Barnard come back to his office. He rather fancies himself on his voice, does Barnard. Why, I don't know. Depraved taste, I think. Anyhow, he came upstairs, trolling some ditty or other; and I heard him bang the door upstairs. Then, by and by, I heard another bang and I thought he'd let something fall on the floor. Then I heard him rush out of his office—the floors in this place are hardly deadened at all—and I wondered what was up. I thought I'd better go and see, so I went out on to the landing. Pitch dark; couldn't see anything. So I tried the switch. No go. Then Barnard was making a devil of a fuss upstairs, so I dashed up and found him hammering on Mitford's door. No reply. So we hammered and yelled. Nothing doing. So then we came down and 'phoned the police station. I had a pretty good notion what was up—all that chitchat about 'Harry Keary,' you understand? And a bang. And a locked door. 'Two and Two make Four,' as my dame school taught me in happier days. Obvious, eh?"

"H'm!" Sir Clinton said, rather sceptically. "You leap to conclusions all right, Mr. Barbican. But we prefer some grounds to go on. Have you anything to back up all this?"

Barbican sat down on the arm of his easy chair, and his sharp eyes ranged round the company.

"No chance for that thousand?" he demanded.

"Not a hope," Sir Clinton assured him. "You'll just have to act altruistically for once."

"Altruistically?" Barbican repeated the word, syllable by syllable. "I don't like that word. A sub-editor would never pass it. Too high-brow. Well, if you want the vulgar facts, here are some of them. I ferreted them out myself."

"Go on," Sir Clinton suggested, with a glance at his watch. "You can do the trumpet solo when we've gone."

"Well, here are the facts," said Barbican, with relish. "First of all, Mitford had been employed by Sternhall at Charponden and had been fired."

"How did you learn that?"

"Followed you to Charponden the other day and nosed round a bit. You put me on the scent yourself. Well, Mitford got fired, and retired to live on twopence a week. Then he picked up Mrs. Sternhall, the one that lives round the corner. She fairly dazzled the poor little devil. I used to chaff him about her, and he'd turn geranium colour. A hopeless case. She could do anything she liked with him. He even . . . Oh, well, he's dead now. Anyhow, you can take it from me that she had him in her pocket completely. He used to go round there and spend hours with her. I've watched 'em at times through my glasses: Mrs. Sternhall leaning back in a chair with a generous amount of leg showing, and poor old Mitford sitting goggling at her, with that old yachting cap of his clutched between his hands. She simply played with him. Very exciting for an old man who's been repressed all his life. Anyhow, that's the gist of it. She had him completely under her thumb."

"Any further facts?"

"Well, these seem suggestive, anyhow," Barbican pointed out. "Suppose she wormed out of Mitford the tale of Sternhall's other establishment? He knew about it. She'd have no trouble in getting it out of him, a simple old codger like that. Once she got that bit of news, she'd communicate it to her dear brother-in-law, the black-a-vised gent you met on the night of the murder. And if Dujardin isn't the fellow to see money where money is, well, I'm much mistaken. He looks that brand to the naked eye."

"You don't usually boggle over phrases," Sir Clinton pointed out. "Do you mean blackmail?"

"That's your business," Barbican answered, with unusual caution.

"If I understand your delicate insinuations, you mean that Mrs. Sternhall used the information she got from Mitford to put the screw on her husband?"

"Seems reasonable, doesn't it?" Barbican countered. "At any rate, she owns that block of flats; and that means a good round sum."

Sir Clinton walked across the room and stared absently at the dying fire for some moments, as though weighing the value of Barbican's hypothesis. The grate was full of grey ash. Barbican had evidently been destroying papers on an extensive scale. Sir Clinton picked up a piece of burnt paper which had fallen into the hearth and put it back onto the coals.

"Some of your masterpieces?" he inquired ironically.

"Yes, I used to keep copies of all the papers with my articles in them. Meant to paste them into a book, sooner or later. Got too big a job to tackle, though, before I'd started on it. So I took the opportunity of the fire tonight and made a start of disposing of them. 'All, all my pretty ones!' But there's a lot still to go," he added, pointing to the pile of newspapers in the corner of the room. "I've seen the vanity of a press-cutting book. Besides, when I thought it over, I don't think I wanted to reread the stuff. And I've no grand-children to leave it to, in my will."

"The beginnings of modesty?" said Sir Clinton caustically.

Barbican looked up with a grin.

"Good title for an article, that. I'll write it up. Historical retro-spect: Eve and the fig leaf. Main theme: the raising and lowering of the skirt since the War, and all it implies. Grand finale: Back to the ankle again; did our fathers know best? Might be a guinea in it. Skirts and ankles always make the public prick up its ears."

"And now," Sir Clinton interrupted, "perhaps you'll explain how you came to fix on Mitford as the murderer."

"Well, suppose Sternhall cut up rough in the end, and they had to get rid of him? That's just a bright thought, of course. It's for you to find the evidence. Mitford was like wax in Mrs. Sternhall's fingers. Rotten simile that, far too old. He'd do anything for her. And he hated Sternhall; one can imagine that. What better tool could the Sternhall and her brother-in-law want? With his Japanesy notions of honour, Mitford would keep his mouth shut, no matter what happened, apart from being potty on the woman. 'Harry Keary'—that was always the way out, if the worst happened. And now I'll tell you what made me certain, once I'd put two and two together. That night of the murder, I was standing at the front door here, for a breath of fresh air. And round the corner of Ringwood Hill came old Mitford, with his yachting cap askew, and a bit out of breath. And the next thing I heard was somebody yell-ing 'Murder!' in The Grove."

"And you didn't think of Mitford as the murderer till long afterwards?"

"Never a thought. Who'd suspect a harmless little beggar like that, merely because one saw him turning the corner? No, it took me a lot of thinking before I hit on the connection. I didn't even know that he knew Sternhall, then. But when I began to ask him a few questions tonight, just hovering tactfully round the fringe of the subject, he more or less gave himself away. I don't mean he said in so many words that he'd done it. But he . . . well, I got a strong impression that my guess was right. Now he's shot himself; and that's a confession, of course. He must have had an inkling that he was being found out. Curse the luck! If he only waited another day, I'd be a thousand quid better off. Hard lines, that! When I die, you'll find 'Harry Keary' written across my shirt front."

"You'll still be able to make your scoop over the business," Sir Clinton pointed out consolingly. "When you've initialed the notes of your evidence, we'll leave you in peace, and you can go ahead with your precious writing."

When this formality had been carried out, Sir Clinton led his two companions out on to the landing, closing the door carefully behind him.

"Just go downstairs," he ordered Chesilton in a low voice, "and take out the fuse plugs in the box in the hall. There are only four of them. No, wait a bit! Take out the two plugs with blown fuses and another one with the fuse intact. You can replace them by fresh plugs later on. There may be nothing in it, but we may as well be thorough."

Chesilton did as he was told; and on his return Sir Clinton switched on his flash lamp and led the way up to the landing where the constable still sat opposite Mitford's doorway. Sir Clinton summoned the fingerprint expert, who was still at work in the flat.

"I think you'd better take some fuse plugs out of the box in Mitford's flat," he said to the inspector, as the fingerprint expert appeared, "and put them into place in the box down below. You can take those that won't shut off the light in his sitting-room. The original hall ones were the same pattern as the ones controlling the flat lights, I expect, and they'll be interchangeable."

The inspector carried out his work quickly, and the lights blazed up on the stair.

"Now," said the Chief Constable to the fingerprint expert, "try that rail and see if you can find anything."

"Some stuff adhering to the banister," the expert reported, "but no fresh prints, sir, so far as I can find."

"I want these fragments of stuff collected. There isn't much, but I think there's enough for our purposes. Keep it safe. And clean the rail after you've finished."

"Yes, sir. What is the stuff?"

"Modelling wax, I think," answered Sir Clinton.

16
DOCUMENTARY EVIDENCE

On coming down to breakfast next morning, Wendover found his host already at table, glancing through the contents of his morning's mail. Wendover helped himself and took his seat.

"Up early," he commented ironically.

"Yes," said the Chief Constable blandly; "while you've been sleeping quietly—or possibly snoring—the tireless guardians of your peace have been awake and busy. I've just been telephoning to Livermere, our chief bloodhound. He's been working a bit overtime for me, last night, and he's got out something. Pass the toast this way, if you're finished with it."

Wendover obediently handed the rack across the table, but before he could comment on Sir Clinton's remark about the blood expert, the Chief Constable turned to a fresh subject.

"Now here's something interesting, Squire."

He held up an envelope on which Wendover read: "URGENT. The Chief Constable, Police Headquarters. . . ." Sir Clinton gingerly extracted the enclosed sheet of cheap notepaper and read the letter aloud.

"It's headed 1, Ravenswood Mansions," he explained. "Here's the text:

> "August 8th, 1934
>
> "Sir,
>
> "I feel it my duty to confess that I am solely responsible for the death of Mr. Sternhall.

"I know I am under suspicion, and I shall commit hara-kiri tonight to save myself from the dishonour of execution. You will find my body in my flat. I shall die by the same weapon as Sternhall did, as Kotsuké died by the dirk of Takumi no Kami.

"George Mitford."

"Quite explicit in some ways, but rather vague in others," Sir Clinton pointed out. "No reason alleged, you notice, for having polished off Sternhall, though the point seems not without interest. But one mustn't be too critical of a man's last message, perhaps."

"No," commented Wendover, rather shocked by his host's callousness. "You'll probably die with the word, 'Police!' on your lips. But nobody will take any notice of it."

Sir Clinton thoughtfully returned the letter to its envelope and placed it beside his plate.

"Too early in the day to interpret cryptic remarks, Squire. Do you mean I shall be calling for help? Or that I shall be seeing Constable Death tapping me on the shoulder and asking me to come along quietly? Or do you suggest that my last thoughts will be for my beloved Force? Or perhaps something even more subtle. Too deep for me. Change here for the next subject. I was going to tell you something about Livermere. It seems he's identified two different brands of blood amongst the samples that were taken last night. And the cream of the jest is that they're mutually antagonistic bloods, so to speak: they couldn't co-exist in a man's veins. He'd collapse, because the serum of the one blood would attack the corpuscles of the other blood. So there we are, and where *are* we?"

Wendover pondered over this intelligence in silence for a few seconds.

"Then there must have been two people there, both losing blood?" he hazarded.

"Oh, possibly Mitford insisted on doing the thing in proper form," Sir Clinton suggested lightly. "There was always a second to assist the principal in hara-kiri, you remember."

"Yes," admitted Wendover doubtfully. "The principal eviscerated himself, and as soon as he'd done so, the second sheared off his head with a sword. But Mitford shot himself."

"No expert swordsman handy to act as second, probably; so he had to do the best he could."

"But the door was locked on the inside," Wendover objected. "I know that's not an insuperable difficulty. Still . . ."

"I'm a bit sceptical of locked rooms," Sir Clinton said drily. "I've thought out about six different ways of managing the locked-room trick. Just as an intellectual exercise, it's a suggestive theme."

"Then you don't think it was suicide at all?"

"I'm pretty sure it wasn't. And I think that, like our reporter friend, I could put my finger on the man who did it. If I'm not mistaken, the whole of this case started from Mrs. Sternhall's high-falutin' notions about her fine relations—the connection between plain Miss Degray and the big people."

Wendover had a flash of illumination at this. "I see what you're driving at, Clinton."

"It's a blessing that murderers have tongues, like the rest of us," Sir Clinton declared. "If they were born dumb, where would the police be? Now the next business on the agenda is to call in Freddie the Forgery Ferret. You don't know Freddie, Squire? Nor do I, officially, by that name; but that's what his pals call him. Officially, he's Detective-Sergeant Frederick Tottenham. He takes a special interest in documentary evidence and he's been remarkably useful in one or two cases, with his technique. Not that I expect this affair will give us much trouble."

"Let's see that letter again," Wendover requested, being rather on his mettle. "I don't want to touch it, for fear of leaving prints. Just lay it on the table."

Sir Clinton obeyed, leaving the envelope beside the sheet of notepaper. Wendover pored over them for a short time.

"The envelope and the contents seem to have been written by the same pen—a broad-pointed one," he commented. "The notepaper doesn't match the envelope. The stamp's stuck on very neatly with its edge parallel to the edge of the envelope. The ink seems the same in both. Lend me your magnifying glass a moment."

Sir Clinton took a Coddington lens from his pocket and Wendover scrutinised the writing.

"Not traced, so far as one can see," he decided. "It's freehand writing with no halts and hesitations about it."

He returned the lens to his host with a certain air of having scored not at all badly.

"You've forgotten two things," Sir Clinton pointed out, with a cheerful air. "They're rather important, Squire. For one thing, Mitford had been a clerk for years. For the other, we ought to ring up the Post Office."

Wendover scanned the papers again but failed to see the point.

"Thank heaven, it's less smudged than usual," Sir Clinton offered as a hint.

"Oh, the postmark, of course!" exclaimed Wendover, chagrined at missing so obvious a detail. "Let's see. It's marked '11.20 p.m.'"

"Yes. Delivered at Headquarters by the early post and sent on at once to me, since it was marked 'Urgent'."

"I see your point," Wendover admitted, rather crestfallen.

Sir Clinton had finished his breakfast, and he rose from the table.

"You go ahead, Squire. I'll be back in a moment. I want to do some telephoning."

Wendover went on stolidly with his meal, and in a few minutes his host returned.

"I rang up Headquarters," he reported. "They have the contents of Mitford's pockets there; and amongst them is a fountain pen with a broad nib. So that's that, whatever it amounts to. And now, Squire, I think I must tear myself away. I leave you to the delights of the *Times* crossword puzzle, and I hope it's a good stiff 'un today, to keep you busy. If that fails, you can listen to the advertisements from the Continental wireless stations. I suspect some of them are cipher messages to armies of spies. See if you can worry them out for the good of your country. I can't get back for lunch, I'm afraid. Amuse yourself meanwhile and I'll see you at dinner."

213

Wendover took his friend's advice, and luckily that day's cross-word puzzle happened to be stiffer than usual. He stuck at it doggedly, and finally had the satisfaction of filling in the ultimate letters. Sir Clinton's ample library furnished him with sufficient amusement after he had taken a long walk and had a chat with his host's gardener on fertilisers for lawns, a subject on which they held dissimilar opinions, which the gardener was prepared to argue out in detail.

When Sir Clinton arrived, he was evidently in good spirits; but during dinner he made no reference to official affairs. Wendover waited in patience until they had retired to the study.

"Well?" he demanded.

"See how thoughtful I am," Sir Clinton pointed out. "By rights, these papers ought to be in my office safe at Headquarters; but I've brought them along to show you them."

From an attaché case he extracted frames, in each of which a paper was clamped between two sheets of glass, so that both sides of the sheets were open to inspection. Sir Clinton laid two of the frames on the table in front of his guest.

"These you've seen already," he explained. "They're Mitford's letter of confession and the envelope it came in. You saw them this morning. Just glance over them to make sure there's no deception, Squire. You can handle them freely. The glass is there to keep extraneous marks off them."

"Some extraneous marks have got on, all the same," Wendover pointed out. "I see your fingerprint expert's been at work with his powder. I can spot two sets of prints at least on this envelope: one with a scar on the thumb."

"That's Mitford's sign manual," Sir Clinton explained. "We found a faint scar on the right thumb, corresponding to this print; an old cut, or something of that sort."

"These prints are very clear," Wendover commented. "The others are not up to much."

"It was a hot night, last evening," Sir Clinton reminded him. "Mitford held this envelope in his hands for a good while, according to Barnard's evidence and Barbican's; and I expect his thumb was rather moist with perspiration. Hence the clear imprints. The other prints were probably made while it passed through the post. They belong to sorters and postmen, who don't hold a letter for more than a second or so at most. Now, if you've gazed your fill, we'll pass on to the next exhibit."

He laid down a second frame containing an envelope and a larger one holding a longer letter, occupying two sheets of note-paper.

"These," he explained, "came in this afternoon, late, with a covering letter from Scawen at Charponden; you remember him. Just glance over them, Squire, and then you'll be abreast of the times."

Wendover bent over the frame containing the letter, and read as follows:

> "1, Ravenswood Mansions
> "Brandford
> "8th August, 1934.

> "Henry Scawen, Esq.
> Carronlea
> Minard Road
> Charponden.
> "Dear Sir,
> "With reference to the bills in which you offer a reward of One Thousand Pounds (£1,000) 'to any person who shall give such information as may lead to the discovery and conviction' of the man who murdered the late Mr. John Sternhall on Friday, 10th July, 1934, I think that perhaps I may be able to give such information, and I therefore desire to put in a claim for the reward offered, namely: One Thousand Pounds (£1,000).
> "On the night of 29th, July last, I was on the pavement in front of my house at the above address. It was a hot night, and I felt the need of fresh air, which accounts for my being there. I did not hear any shot. I observed a man coming out of the road

215

known as Ringwood Hill which leads down from my house to the tennis courts, and on to which the back gates of the houses in The Grove open. He wore a blue serge suit and had evening slippers on his feet, the kind which I believe are called pumps. I recognised him and could identify him without any possibility of error.

"I saw him again, later on, amongst the crowd which assembled in front of No. 5, The Grove; but by that time he had changed his clothes.

"If he should prove to be the wanted man, I wish to establish my claim now, and am prepared to give you more information if you will treat the matter as confidential, so far as my connection with it is concerned.

"I have private reasons for this request.

"I am, dear Sir,

"Your obedient servant

"George Mitford."

"Well, what do you make of it?" demanded Sir Clinton, as Wendover finished his perusal.

"The long letter was posted before the short one, wasn't it?"

"According to the postmarks, it was."

"Let's take the envelopes first," Wendover suggested, putting the two appropriate frames side by side. "What about these fingerprints? Your man says that Mitford's thumb print is on both the envelopes?"

"Yes, Freddie says so, and so does Wootton. You can take that as sound, Squire."

"The envelope paper's the same, so far as I can see. Both came from the same packet, by the look of them. The stamp's put in the corner of each with the same care. The two addresses are in almost exactly the same position on the envelope surface; they'd pretty nearly superimpose if one were put behind the other. Add the fingerprints, and I don't see how you escape the inference that Mitford wrote them both."

"So Freddie says," Sir Clinton confirmed.

Wendover pushed aside the two frames and took up those which contained the two letters.

"The literary style seems different in these epistles," he said suspiciously. "The confession's almost snappy, whereas the demand for the reward's a rambling production, full of detail."

"Would you not expect something of the sort?" the Chief Constable inquired, with an inscrutable expression on his face. "One was written at leisure, perhaps, whilst the other was scribbled in a hurry just before the pistol went off. One has to admit that the emotional situation might colour the style. But that raises a fresh point."

"What point?" Wendover demanded, irritated by this tantalising reference.

"Well, it's obvious that there's a difference in tone between those letters, posted with a very short interval between them. The interesting point is: 'What caused that change of tone?' But leave that aside for the present, Squire, and go on with your analysis."

Wendover studied the two documents for a moment.

"There are some of Mitford's fingerprints on the letter to Scawen, but I don't see that any have developed on the note to you—the confession."

"So Freddie pointed out," Sir Clinton admitted.

"And yet they were written within an hour or two of each other, on a hot night."

"So one assumes, unless Mitford wrote the Scawen letter much earlier in the day and didn't post it till evening."

"Yes, that's possible," Wendover admitted, though in no welcoming tone. "Now here's another thing, Clinton. You know that most of us have a fixed way of dating a letter. We may write '1st January, 1934', or 'January 1st, 1934', but whichever we do, we stick to it throughout. Now these two letters are dated differently. The Scawen letter '8th August,' whereas the confession is dated 'August 8th.' That's curious."

"So Freddie said," Sir Clinton confirmed blandly. "Continue, Squire. You may get ahead of Freddie yet."

"I don't care a damn what Freddie said," Wendover on retorted, in slight irritation. "What I'm sure about is that these two documents weren't both written by Mitford. The space between the lines is different, slightly, but unmistakable; the breadth of margin is different in the two cases. One man allows a margin of about an inch on the left-hand side, whereas the other fellow is content with half that amount of freeboard. And the indentation at the beginning of a paragraph's different in the two letters. These two documents were written by different people, in spite of the similarity of the writing."

"So Freddie says."

"And I suppose he noticed that though the envelopes are of the same make, the notepaper is different in the two documents?"

"Freddie pointed that out in his report."

Wendover preserved a dignified silence, scanning the various documents in turn.

"Your man Wootton doesn't seem to have developed any fingerprints on the letter of confession," he pointed out.

"No. None came up. Not a trace of them."

Wendover looked puzzled.

"I'd swear that letter was written freehand," he declared.

"So Freddie says," interjected the Chief Constable, with a smile.

"And it was a hot night," Wendover ruminated. "I don't see how the writer managed to do it, no matter who he was, without leaving traces of some sort."

"Suppose we take another side of the same problem," Sir Clinton suggested. "To put the cards on the table, there were no fingerprints on Mitford's fountain pen when we came to examine it. That seems a shade unusual, Squire, especially after two letters had been written with that pen on a warm night."

"That clinches it!" Wendover exclaimed.

"I don't doubt it clinches it; but unfortunately, it doesn't explain the absence of fingerprints on the confession. But Freddie and I seem to have solved that little problem."

"How?"

"Well, I suggested that Freddie might have a run over the paper with a microscope. He spotted it at once."

"What?" repeated Wendover.

"Particles of lycopodium," Sir Clinton answered. "Some of them were clinging to the paper surface; some were caught in the ink of the writing. They're quite easily recognisable; but Freddie got some lycopodium for comparison."

"Lycopodium?" queried Wendover. "That's the stuff they used in the old days to imitate lightning on the stage, isn't it? They blew the powder over a candle flame and got an instantaneous flare which looked quite like a flash of lightning offstage. But what's that got to do with the present affair?"

"One use of lycopodium is in surgery, as an absorbent, I believe," Sir Clinton explained. "Or so it says in the dictionary. But from my point of view, another of its properties is more interesting. If you dust lycopodium over a finger, Squire, you can dip that finger into water and draw it out again, and the water won't have wet you. Conversely, if you rub lycopodium powder over your hand, and write a letter, you'll leave no fingerprints on the paper. The perspiration won't get through the lycopodium coating from inside, any more than the water will get through from the outside to wet your skin in the first experiment. And when you've finished writing, you simply blow away any grains of powder that may have fallen on to the paper—and there you are. It looks all right, if you don't put the microscope to work. I must say I admire the fellow who thought of the scheme. It's so simple and so effective—within limits."

"Very neat," Wendover admitted.

"Unfortunately for the writer in this case," Sir Clinton went on, "it's rather damning evidence. Not many people buy lycopodium at the druggist's. Hence it won't be hard to find out who has been buying any lately in this district. As a matter of fact, we've already ascertained about all the sales in the last few weeks."

"Quick work, that," Wendover conceded.

"Just a matter of telephoning on a large scale. I had several men at work on it; and I've little doubt that we can identify the purchaser whenever we want to."

"You mean that Mitford was murdered, like Sternhall?"

"Yes, by the same man."

"How do you make that out? Oh, of course, the pistol in the Mitford case was one that originally belonged to Sternhall, and that links up the two cases?"

"Obviously. So the fellow who bought the lycopodium is the man who killed Sternhall, on the face of it. And now we've actually got a witness who can identify him: the druggist's assistant who sold him the lycopodium. Barring that, we hadn't a witness left who could go into the box and swear to his identity."

"Then you're ready to make an arrest? Pity you couldn't have done it sooner, Clinton. Then that poor little devil Mitford might be alive today."

"How could I foresee Mitford's foolishness in brandishing his letter to me in the face of everyone he met? That was outside the normal bounds altogether."

"True, I suppose," Wendover admitted. "Still, it's a pity. I'm still a bit in the dark about some points, Clinton. Suppose you give one of your expositions; tell me how it struck you as the case developed, will you?"

17
PRELUDE TO ARREST

"You want to play Devil's Advocate, eh?" Sir Clinton queried, with a shrewd glance at Wendover. "All the better. If there are any weak spots, we may as well recognise them, while there's still time to fill in the gaps. Do your worst, Squire."

"I have my eye on one or two things," Wendover admitted. "But let's see how you get on."

Sir Clinton seemed to require very little time to put his thoughts into order. He leaned back comfortably in his chair and began in a reflective tone:

"When we arrived at Number 5, The Grove, on the night of Sternhall's death, one thing stared us in the face. The victim, whoever he was, had come on the scene fully prepared for trouble. He'd seen to it that there were no clues to his identity about his person. He'd brought a neat parcel with a pair of tennis shoes in it, and he'd changed into them, so that he could move about silently. In one pocket, he had a murderous little club—homemade. In the other—as we can guess now—he had a fully loaded revolver. He came there deliberately to do somebody in."

"Hold on a moment," Wendover interrupted. "I can't pass that. He might have expected trouble from the other party and taken his precautions for self-defence."

"He was wearing rubber gloves," Sir Clinton pointed out. "If he'd been expecting a mere rough-and-tumble, with the other man left alive to identify him, there was no point in the gloves. They were to prevent his leaving fingerprints, obviously. And that implies that he meant to silence the other party for good and leave no traces. You can't explain the gloves on any other basis, Squire."

"Well, pass that, then," Wendover conceded.

"The next thing was that somebody, murderer or victim, had a key of the flat and a key to the back gate. That limited things considerably, on the face of it."

"You can pass over the handkerchief, the blood-stains, the Tau cross and all that," Wendover suggested. "We know the true explanation of them now."

"I dare say," Sir Clinton admitted, "but they puzzled me a lot at the time. However, leave them for the moment, if you wish. The next thing that struck me was that the French window was open. Quite obviously, the man who entered the flat first got into it by means of a key. He must have come either through the front hall or via the back gate and the back door. He couldn't get in through a closed French window. Ergo, the French window was opened later by someone. It might have been opened by Sternhall, when he threw out the paper and string of his parcel. That seemed most likely. In any case, it was open; and, being open, it furnished a third means of exit for the man who killed Sternhall. It yielded nothing in the way of fingerprints that was any use to us. Probably Sternhall opened it after putting on his rubber gloves."

"And if the murderer went out that way, a shove with his elbow would push it open wide enough for exit," Wendover amplified.

Sir Clinton nodded in agreement and helped himself to a fresh cigarette.

"The next thing was to comb the house," he continued. "The top flat was empty, which saved us trouble. When we tried the one below it, we found the Geddington *ménage*, the Karslakes, and your friend Barbican."

"Looking as if he'd just crawled out of bed and dressed himself in the first clothes that came to hand," said Wendover scornfully. "Even his shoelaces were undone. Untidy devil!"

"I'm afraid your charitable excuse breaks down," Sir Clinton pointed out. "He hadn't 'just got out of bed.' He was tinkering with his wireless set when the shot went off. You remember he told us so when he dropped in here one night."

"He annoyed me at the very start," Wendover growled. "Jeering at Chesilton and bragging about being first in the field."

"He wasn't that, by any means," Sir Clinton commented. "Quite a crowd had assembled at the front door before he put in an appearance. Perhaps he tripped over his shoelaces," he added, with a faint grin. "Or something else delayed him. Anyhow, I warned him about his shoelaces. 'Be always kind to animals' is one of my mottoes."

Wendover seemed to think the reporter had received enough attention.

"The Geddington crew had no hand in the business," he declared, "unless all four of them were mixed up in it; and that's too tall an order."

"So I thought myself," Sir Clinton agreed. "So we went down to the next flat and interviewed Mrs. Sternhall and her rather unprepossessing brother-in-law—the man without a past."

"You didn't get much change out of them," Wendover said, in a faintly sardonic tone.

"Only three things. Mr. Sternhall was evidently a curious person of erratic habits. But that threw no light on things just then, since we didn't know that the victim downstairs was actually Sternhall. The second thing was Dujardin's tale of seeing a man climbing the wall. That had to wait till morning for confirmation. And the third thing was the noise Dujardin said he heard during dinner, which might or might not have been the sound of a scuffle in the flat below. It was that bit of evidence that set me thinking whether there hadn't been two acts played out in the ground-floor flat and not merely a single episode."

"There wasn't much to go on, at that stage," Wendover confessed. "Victim unidentified, and not a glimmer of a motive on the horizon. I didn't know what to make of it."

"Nor did I," Sir Clinton admitted frankly. "But next day gave us plenty to think about. The identification of Sternhall cleared up one side of the affair, especially when we found out that Mrs. Sternhall owned the whole set of flats. That pointed to Sternhall having access to the keys and suggested that he was the first person to arrive in the empty flat. There was no proof of how long he'd waited there for his intended victim; so my vague idea about two episodes began to strengthen a bit, especially when Danbury showed that the paintpot had been upset early in the evening, at a time fitting in with the noise Dujardin said he heard at dinnertime. I got a dim picture of Sternhall coming to the empty flat, putting on his tennis shoes and rubber gloves, and waiting for his victim. Somebody came in, some time after seven o'clock. But was that somebody the murderer? If so, why was the shot not fired till a couple of hours later? I was still in the dark, but it seemed possible that two people had come to the flat in addition to Sternhall, and that one of them was not the man Sternhall meant to kill. If this were so, that man must have got away again and kept his mouth shut. But that was all the purest guesswork, and I didn't take it too seriously."

"Why should Sternhall come so early to the flat?" Wendover demanded.

"Probably his train got in at an awkward time and he didn't want to hang about in the open too much before hand. He wanted to leave as little trail behind him as possible, I judge, so he went to cover in the empty flat as soon as possible. But that's mere surmise."

"It's a possible explanation," Wendover admitted, "and we'll never get the truth now. Proceed. I've no fault to find so far."

"The two brands of blood in the room proved nothing at the moment," Sir Clinton went on, "for we already knew that at least two men had been in the flat: the victim and the man who carried off the revolver that did the trick. The Tau cross was of no immediate help either. But the footprints that Chesilton found in the gardens were suggestive. Pumps were about the only shoes that could have made such prints. That suggested that either the man had come in a car or else he lived in the immediate neighbourhood, for no one walks far from his own house in pumps. Further, it suggested that the man had not expected any trouble at the meeting in the flat, or else he would have worn something rather less distinctive on his feet. Ergo, he hadn't taken a revolver with him. Most likely Sternhall himself was the man who brought the revolver."

"I'll admit the last part," Wendover conceded. "Still, he might have come in a car, as you say, and in that case, he obviously did not live in the vicinity."

"No car was at the door of the flats that evening, so far as we could discover. Geddington would have seen it drive off, if the murderer escaped in it."

"It might have been parked in a side street," Wendover objected.

"I dare say it might, if it had existed. But you'll see later that we don't need to assume a car. One thing was quite clear—that the murderer knew the locality. The normal rather flustered murderer, not knowing the lay of the land, would have gone out of the back gate in his escape. But this fellow knew that the back gate was in full view of the tennis courts, and he crossed the garden walls until he was just out of sight of the courts before he emerged into Ringwood Hill. That points to sound local knowledge."

"He might have reconnoitered the place beforehand," objected Wendover.

"Admitted. We kept that in view, of course. Still, put the tracks and the pumps together, and the case for a local man is fairly strong, you must admit."

"If you like," Wendover acquiesced, though in a doubtful tone.

"Then we had Mrs. Sternhall's rather unattractive picture of her husband and his doings. And she also incautiously dropped a hint that she had some grip on him. What did that amount to? He was leading some sort of double life, evidently, and it was the second half of it that gave her the hold over him. He would do anything to raise capital. The easiest way to get money is to marry it. That was suggestive, certainly. But it went for nothing, in the way of proof. Still, if she knew something which enabled her to keep Sternhall under her thumb, then someone else might have the same information and use it for his own benefit. Blackmail crossed my mind. Very vague, no proof, of course. But it did offer the glimmering of a possible solution. And obviously there was some hush-hush business mixed up in the affair, else why did Mrs. Sternhall and that precious brother-in-law spend that night searching through Sternhall's papers? To destroy something? A will? Or some documents which might throw an awkward light on Sternhall's affairs, if we got hold of them? Anyhow, it was plain that there was something a trifle shady about the Sternhall *ménage*."

"I didn't like the look of that brother-in-law," Wendover concurred. "He's not a man of Mrs. Sternhall's class. You can see it at a glance. I wonder what the sister's like."

"No idea," said Sir Clinton, without interest. "Now the next stage in the affair was what Watson would have called The Adventure of the Tau Cross. We got wind, you remember, of Bracknell destroying his tennis shoes. Couple that with the foot-scrubbing on the floor of the flat, and his religious proclivities, and you've got something that needs looking into, obviously. I got Chesilton to find out what newspaper he read, so as to make sure he saw our advertisement. You know the rest, Squire. For your peace of mind, I may say that according to my latest information Miss Huntingdon stares through Bracknell if she meets him in the street nowadays. So we've done her one good turn in the course of our labours for the public."

"I'm glad to hear it," growled Wendover. "A cur, that fellow."

"You're almost as bad as Barbican," Sir Clinton said, in a mock-plaintive tone. "You don't seem to like any of the *dramatis personæ* in this affair. Sternhall, Bracknell, Barbican, Dujardin: you've got a grouse against each of them; and I suppose it's only your natural chivalry that keeps you from damning the fair sex as well. I've never known you so misanthropic before. Well, let's get on with it. When the Bracknell affair came out, it was plain enough that there *had* been two episodes in the empty flat that evening: Bracknell's visit at half-past seven, and then a visit about ten o'clock by somebody who shot Sternhall."

"And that somebody might, or might not, have been Bracknell, of course," Wendover put in.

"Quite so," the Chief Constable concurred. "We'd no evidence on the point, barring his own, which was wholly unreliable. But the Bracknell affair brought to light a fresh character in the Sternhall drama: this little chap Mitford, who helped us to break down Bracknell's attempt at an alibi."

"Yes, I remember you asked that reporter fellow about him, that night he came down here and displayed his bad manners."

"He talked a lot, didn't he?" said Sir Clinton drily. "A shade egotistical. Gave us his complete life-history, you remember, which was not without interest, Squire. You were perhaps too peevish to be interested, though. A very versatile cove, by his own account."

"A nasty-minded sweep!" was Wendover's verdict. "He spent most of his breath making insinuations against everybody connected with the affair. He seems to spend his life snooping with his opera glasses, prying into other people's private affairs. And then spreading tales to the first comer. Ugh!"

"Sad that he missed the one thing worth seeing," the Chief Constable commented reflectively. "At the very moment when his opera glasses might have done useful work, he was tinkering with his wireless set; so he didn't see the murderer escaping through the gardens in the dusk."

"Always assuming that these footprints were the murderer's and not a fake," Wendover interjected, in his role of Devil's Advocate.

Sir Clinton nodded, as though admitting the criticism; but instead of answering it, he turned to a fresh theme.

"The next turn of the affair was the 'missing passenger' business. Of course, that cleared the air considerably after we'd seen Scawen. Out came the whole scheme of Sternhall's bigamy and the double life he'd been leading. And that lent fair probability to the blackmail idea which had always been at the back of my mind. An undetected bigamist is the easiest mark for a blackmailer with good information. So naturally Chesilton and I went into Sternhall's financial affairs, looking for unexplained payments. We found signs of them running back, you remember, through four years."

The Chief Constable paused for a moment or two, as though reflecting on the order in which he should present the next part of his account.

"Assuming that Sternhall had been blackmailed—and I had no doubts by that time—the problem was to put one's finger on the blackmailer, who was probably also responsible for Sternhall's death. Who knew about the bigamy?"

Wendover took up the implied challenge.

"Mrs. Sternhall probably knew," he admitted grudgingly. "But she was already making something out of Sternhall, apparently. I rather doubt if she'd bleed him for extra money. But I suspect that brother-in-law of hers knew also. She may have told him. And he may have put a finger into the pie off his own bat, quite without her knowledge. Then there was that little man Mitford. He had a grudge against Sternhall, and by sheer chance he came to live just round the corner from The Grove and may have seen Sternhall. He came there just about four years ago, notice, and struck up a sort of friendship with Mrs. Sternhall of The Grove. He's a possible."

"Then why didn't he go off to Japan?" demanded Sir Clinton, playing Devil's Advocate in his turn. "That was his one ambition, you know. And by bleeding Sternhall he could have raised all the cash necessary for a trip. A screw loose there, Squire."

"Oh, well, that's as it may be," retorted Wendover. "I'm only professing to pick out the possibles, not necessarily the right man. There's just a chance that Bracknell might have been the murderer; but he's too young to be the blackmailer—unless he was merely a tool in the hands of some older fellow, as some of these young blackmailers are."

"You've missed one possibility at least," Sir Clinton pointed out. "If you remember, the blackmail started—to judge by the dates on the cheques—after the second Mrs. Sternhall employed a firm to trace out her family history. One of the people employed on that job might have run across the secret, if he happened to look into her husband's record, which he might very well do in order to round off the particulars of her marriage. And one gentleman recently boasted to us that he'd been a pedigree-hunter in his day."

"Quite so! Barbican," Wendover confirmed, with no particular surprise. "I've had my suspicions of him for a while."

"I didn't expect to astonish you, Squire," the Chief Constable admitted. "The thing's been growing more and more obvious as time went on. But, most unfortunately, investigations take time; and he used that time to kill that poor little devil Mitford."

"Can you prove it?" Wendover demanded, a shade anxiously.

"Oh, we'll prove it, all right, if I have to go into the witness box myself," Sir Clinton returned grimly. "We'll not take him on the Sternhall case, for I believe that was merely manslaughter, and he'd get off with a term of imprisonment. The Mitford case will put him on the drop."

He frowned, evidently thinking of Mitford's fate.

"Here's the outline of the business, Squire," he said, after a moment or two. "We haven't got all the ends of it yet, but we have enough to be sure. Barbican was employed by the firm who looked up the pedigree of Mrs. Sternhall the Second. We can establish that. Chesilton's been in touch with them. He got their name from Scawen. Barbican retired from that business almost immediately, and he said nothing about his discoveries, naturally. He came here and settled down at Ravenswood Mansions as an independent gentleman, using this freelancing to cover up the fact that he had another source of income. My impression is that he chose his new abode so as to be able to keep an eye on Mrs. Sternhall in The Grove. Perhaps he hoped that she had run off the rails too, and he might bring off a second coup by blackmailing her also. With both of them under his thumb, he would have been in clover.

"He never met Sternhall in his life, until the night of the tragedy. He was too wily for that. Everything was done by post, through an accommodation address. Thanks to the Official Secrets Act, we've found that accommodation address and we can prove that letters with the Charponden postmark were received there on the various crucial dates—corresponding to the dates of the Sternhall cheques. Possibly we may even be able to get him identified by the keeper of the shop; for in some ways he's been amazingly clumsy and he may have been fool enough to call personally for these letters.

"Meanwhile, Sternhall was leading his double life, half at The Grove and half at Charponden, with his brother in America keeping him covered when he was supposed to be in the States on business.

229

But eventually Sternhall cut up rough. With his insatiable craving for fresh capital, Barbican's demands were hitting him in the worst spot; and at any moment exposure might come. So he planned to rid himself of his parasite, once for all. The whole affair fits exactly with his real wife's description of him. Everything most carefully planned beforehand; and then a sudden impulse at the last moment.

"So he wrote to Barbican, inviting him into a trap. There was the empty flat at Number 5, in the hands of decorators. He invited his persecutor there, and he meant to finish him quietly with that murderous little life preserver that he'd put together. A clean knockout; no cries, or anything of that sort. Then he meant to lock up the flat, go upstairs, resume the normal life of the well-known Sternhall of The Grove. And when the body was discovered on the following morning—minus all clues to identity, which he would remove after the death—who was going to connect him with it at all? We could hardly have established the hour of death closely enough, then, to prove a coincidence in time.

"That, I'm sure, was his original scheme. But he must have thought of another point. He had never seen the blackmailer. He himself was a middle-sized fellow of no great physique. What if he muddled his stroke and failed to knock out his opponent? So he takes a fully loaded revolver with him, foreseeing the possibility that the blackmailer may be a powerful fellow capable of disarming him when he tries the bludgeon business.

"He goes to the flat and waits for the Unknown. In comes Bracknell, whom he naturally mistakes for the blackmailer. He beckons him into the flat and attacks him straight off, throttling him to prevent an outcry. Then, in a pause of the struggle, he sees that Bracknell is a mere youngster, far too junior a person to have been carrying on that long course of blackmail. In surprise, he asks what age Bracknell is. And almost at once he sees he has made a blunder."

"I see you've been corrupted by association with Dujardin," said Wendover slyly. "You're using the historical present tense very largely."

"Too late to think better of it now," Sir Clinton retorted. "I proceed. But I wish I had a packet of voice lozenges. This is taking longer than I expected."

"I'm all ears," Wendover assured him.

"Like King Midas? Well, let's go ahead. Sternhall got rid of Bracknell. Probably he sized him up and concluded that a round sum given in the guise of a subscription would stop that young man's mouth and never get farther than his pocket. That would stop Bracknell from talking, pretty efficiently. Then Sternhall awaited his real victim. Barbican was a tougher customer than he'd expected, so out came the revolver. There was a struggle for it. The thing exploded and blew Sternhall's head in. Barbican cut away across the gardens. He was dressed in a blue serge suit and he ran into Mitford at his own door. Hard luck for Mitford, that. He might have been alive now, but for that chance encounter."

"But why didn't Sternhall simply bargain with his enemy, when he found he was too big to tackle with the life preserver? The noise of the shot was bound to knock all his original plan askew," Wendover objected.

"Impulse getting the better of his calculation, I expect. It's all in character, you know. He probably trusted to a clean getaway by the back of the house. And then, who would connect him with the affair? He'd taken care to leave no traces of his identity."

"It sounds likely enough in that form," Wendover admitted.

"Now let's put ourselves in Barbican's shoes for a moment, and see how things looked to him," Sir Clinton continued. "He'd got clear away. Probably Mitford would never connect his appearance with the murder. Two things strike him at once. He needs something that will look like an alibi; and he must know as much as he can learn about the police investigations. You remember, Squire, that in his delightful autobiographical sketch he told us that he had once been on the stage as a quick-change artist? That experience served him well. He changed completely—lest anyone should have seen the blue serge suit a few minutes before and recognise him in the crowd—and he dashed off to force himself on us in his guise of free-lance reporter, and bluff himself into the flats on pretence of a scoop. Very ingenious, for if he saw the inquiry veering towards his detection he could clear out and make a getaway instanter. But he talks too much, does Mr. Barbican."

"You mean?"

"I mean that he told us he was tinkering at his wireless set when the shot went off. Obviously, if Mitford remembered having seen him on the pavement . . . h'm! . . . a bit awkward for Mr. Barbican."

"I hadn't thought of that," Wendover confessed. "So that's at the back of the Mitford murder?"

"It helped, I'm afraid," Sir Clinton said, in a tone of regret. "But to continue the yarn. Finding that we didn't seem to be on his tracks, he got a bit above himself, I think. A good many murderers do, in the first flush of apparent success. When he heard that we were detaining Bracknell on suspicion, he felt he was quite safe. So just to advertise himself in an innocent role, he came down to my house in the journalistic guise, probably hoping to pick up a tip or two, if we were incautious. I led him on, simply because he amused me; and he forgot his caution in his high spirits. He babbled out all these autobiographical details which I found very useful later on. And he also did his best to blacken the character of everyone connected with the case, you remember. Probably on the basis that the more smoke you raise, the less people will be likely to look in the right direction."

"Oh, so it wasn't just foul-mindedness?" said Wendover. "That surprises me, I must admit."

"Then came our visit to Charponden," the Chief Constable proceeded. "That must have given Master Barbican a few awkward moments. Suppose there was some reference to the blackmailing among Sternhall's papers? At any moment we might stumble upon the key to the whole affair—as we did. That shook him up, and he followed us to Charponden to see if he could find out anything about our doings.

"Two more nasty jars were waiting for our friend. The first was the release of Bracknell, which showed that we were no longer following that false trail and might get on to the real one at any time.

The second was the posting up of Scawen's £1,000 reward bill. That would obviously make the man in the street scratch his head and take a keen interest in the case. Somebody might go over his recollections more carefully and produce a fact or two which would turn a searchlight on Barbican. Money can't do everything; but it can sometimes do a good deal."

"Half a jiffy," interrupted Wendover. "There's a point there that puzzled me. Sternhall was evidently taking everything into account, his own death included. That letter Scawen had was to be opened only in case of the writer's death. Why didn't Sternhall give away the whole story of the blackmailing in it—he would have gone to his account when it was opened—and make sure of pinning down the right man?"

Sir Clinton ground the stub of his cigarette on the ashtray and opened his case before answering.

"Just think, Squire," he said quizzically. "If you'd committed bigamy, would you be inclined to put a statement about it on paper and hand it even to a trusted friend? It might go astray. Even trusted friends are careless. Or his safe might be burgled, and the document might fall into unfriendly hands. Or a lot of other things might happen before you were dead and safe from trouble. Sternhall wasn't such a fool as all that. He meant to have a posthumous revenge, if things did go wrong; but he took no risks. That Scawen document might be read by anybody, and all it would suggest was that most likely Sternhall was a bit touched and had a trace of persecution mania in his make-up. It gave nothing away."

"Something in that," Wendover agreed.

"There, again, Barbican let his tongue wag too freely," the Chief Constable resumed. "The 'missing passenger' story was in the newspapers, with Sternhall's name in full. If Barbican had been the keen news-hound he professed to be, wouldn't his first move be to race off to Charponden as soon as he saw the coincidence in the names? Did he? Not a bit of it. He knew all about that already, and the last thing he wanted was any stirring up of inquiry in that field. But when he heard that we had gone to Charponden, *then* he followed, hotfoot—as he was silly enough to blurt out—to see if he could nose out the results of our inquiries. It's only a trifling point in itself, but it helps to lengthen the chain of evidence."

"He does seem to have let his tongue wag at both ends," said Wendover. "I always thought he talked more than was good for him."

"Now we come to the issue of the reward bills," the Chief Constable resumed. "Hitherto, there had been nothing to remind Mitford of that awkward meeting on the pavement on the evening of the Grove murder. Apparently he had forgotten all about it. But the money reward might jog his memory. Barbican's safety depended on his being completely unsuspected. Once the searchlight turned on him, he must have felt, trouble wouldn't be long in coming. And then, one evening, he met Mitford on the stairs; and in Mitford's hand was an envelope plainly addressed to me. To a guilty man like Barbican, that would suggest only one thing. The game was up.

"Not quite, though. There was one desperate throw that he could still make. The letter might be intercepted and Mitford reduced to silence, if one took the final risk. After all, it meant no more punishment. You can only be hanged once. So he more or less dragged Mitford into his flat and had him at his mercy.

"I've an idea that it wasn't altogether an impromptu move. He must have regarded Mitford, all along, as his chief source of danger; and I think he probably had the whole affair cut and dried in his mind. He must have bought the packthread beforehand, at any rate, for it's not likely he had it by chance."

"The packthread?" Wendover demanded. "It's the first I've heard of packthread in the case."

"It's a figment of my imagination," Sir Clinton explained. "I can't produce it in evidence. We'll come to it in due course."

Wendover nodded, to show that he was prepared to wait.

"You remember that when the three men met on the stairs, Barnard—the architect—explained that he was going to a restaurant to get some dinner and would not be back for an hour or so. That removed Barbican's last difficulty. He had the coast clear for an hour."

"Yes, I see," Wendover said. "Everything seems to have been unlucky for poor little Mitford that night: having the fatal letter in his hand instead of in his pocket; meeting Barbican by chance on the way downstairs; and Barnard being off the premises. Hard lines indeed!"

"The next bit's pure imagination," Sir Clinton admitted frankly. "Nobody except Barbican knows what really happened. But I think this comes near it. He got Mitford into his flat and stunned him, probably from behind, so that the little man made no outcry. Then he probably covered his scullery floor—walls too, most likely—with old newspapers. Then he dragged the unconscious man in there, and most likely shot him with his head over the sink. Properly done, that would leave very little trace of blood except in the sink and on the newspapers. He used Sternhall's revolver, of course, which he'd brought away with him on the night of the Grove murder. That finished the danger from Mitford."

"But the shot would be heard all over the place," objected the Devil's Advocate.

"Not if you used a silencer on the pistol," Sir Clinton rejoined. "Turn back to the Barbican autobiography, Squire. He told us he'd been a garage mechanic in his time. He must have had a fair notion of the construction of silencers. He was a handy man with tools, too. You remember the outfit we saw in his room? It wasn't beyond his powers to make a crude silencer. But that must have been ready at the moment. Ergo, the Mitford murder had been in his mind for some time. So long as the little man wasn't dangerous, he let him alone; but he had everything ready to deal with him, if the worst came to the worst.

"Now Barbican has made blunder after blunder in this affair, Squire, but I take off my hat to him when I think of the quickness he showed in this emergency. There was that fatal letter addressed to me. Barnard had seen it in Mitford's hand. If it were sent the trouble would begin at once. And on the spur of the moment, our good friend devised a plan to use that very letter to turn suspicion away from himself. He's a cool-headed beggar, one must admit.

"To continue. First of all, I think, he lit a huge fire. Those blood-spattered newspapers had to be destroyed as quickly as possible.

Then he steamed open the envelope of the letter and read the contents. I expect they were very much the same as what Mitford had written to Scawen earlier in the day. The little man was just making doubly sure of the reward by writing to both Scawen and myself. That went into the fire straight off. Then Barbican sat down *with Mitford's own fountain pen*—observe how quickly he must have seen these little points—and he forged that mythical confession and announcement of suicide."

"That's asking one to believe a lot," the Devil's Advocate objected. "Forgery's none so easy as all that."

"See the Barbican autobiography," Sir Clinton rejoined with a smile. "Didn't he boast to us that he could make a pen do everything except say, 'Pretty Polly!' when he told us he'd been a writing-master? And poor little Mitford had been giving him notes on Japan, hadn't he? So he'd plenty of models to draw from. To avoid fingerprints, he used lycopodium, as I explained to you before. Then he cleaned the pen and put it back in Mitford's pocket, sealed up his forgery in Mitford's own envelope addressed to me, and that was that."

"You make it sound plausible," Wendover admitted rather grudgingly. "And the lycopodium grains certainly need some explanation which isn't clear if Mitford had written the confession."

"Now for a further stretch of imagination," the Chief Constable went on. "Barbican's a big powerful chap. It would be no great task for him to carry a little fellow like Mitford upstairs. He dumps the body inside the door of Mitford's flat. And now he must have an absolutely unbreakable alibi. He's had enough trouble over that in the last affair. This time, he'll make sure.

"No fingerprints! That's the first point. Rubber gloves, then. He may have picked up that tip from Sternhall; but he was smart enough to think of it himself, and you can buy these things at any chain store nowadays. He must have had them ready. He cleans all fingermarks off the revolver—Sternhall's revolver, remember—and in the chamber he puts next for firing a doctored cartridge which he had prepared beforehand. Taken out the bullet, I mean, and closed the end sufficiently to give a decent bang when the thing exploded. He takes Mitford's hand and puts a few of the dead man's fingerprints on the revolver as a guarantee of good faith.

"Then a flaw in his arrangements suddenly strikes him—an almost fatal flaw. He's seen how much blood Mitford lost when he was shot. There isn't nearly enough on the floor. A sharp doctor might spot at once that there was a screw loose. More blood has to come from somewhere. So he takes off his jacket, rolls up his left shirt sleeve, jabs his penknife into a vein, and lets it bleed till he thinks the quantity's sufficient. Then he bandages his arm with his handkerchief and puts on his coat again. He couldn't risk a leg wound; it might have made him limp and so betrayed itself."

"Ah, that's how you account for the two kinds of blood on the floor by Mitford's body?"

"Well, there were two kinds of blood. Can you find a simpler explanation, Squire? And I hope, before we're done, to establish that blood Number 2 is identical with Barbican's gore. We may have a stroke of luck in that field."

"Well, go on," Wendover urged impatiently.

"When I arrived on the scene," Sir Clinton explained, "the first thing that struck me was the fact that two fuses had been blown. One fuse blows from time to time; but it's rare that two fuses go simultaneously. It looks a bit like intentional fuse-blowing. But if so, what was at the back of it? The fuses were those of the landing lights: one on Mitford's landing and another on Barnard's landing, just below. If these had both been put out of action intentionally, there must be some reason for it. I hadn't the full facts then, so I merely docketed the point in my memory for future reference in case of need.

"Now take the revolver. It was Sternhall's. From what we know of Sternhall, he would load all six chambers before he set off for The Grove. In his preparations he was always thorough, you remember. Six cartridges to start with. One shot killed Sternhall. One shot killed Mitford, if he suicided. Remainder: four unused cartridges. But actually we found only three live cartridges in the gun, along with the empty shell of the shot fired in Mitford's room. Queer, eh? That made me sit up and take notice; for if Mitford had simply shot Sternhall and then suicided, where did that extra cartridge come in?

"Then there was that tiny rubber strap hanging on the key shank inside the door. It was a bit of luck that it hadn't been wrenched away, as, I expect, Barbican assumed it would be. When I saw that, it didn't take me long to make up my mind; for I've thought over the theory of these 'locked room' cases a good deal, just as a theoretical problem. And, of course, the dousing of the stair lights fell neatly into place at once."

"I don't see it," Wendover admitted.

"This was what happened," Sir Clinton explained. "Barbican fixed the rubber ring on the key shank. He then slipped through the rubber ring the muzzle of Sternhall's revolver, with his faked blank cartridge ready for firing. Then he threaded a piece of packthread or some such stuff through the trigger guard in front of the trigger. Then he passed the two ends of the thread through the keyhole. With the thread just taut, the revolver would be held with its trigger level with the keyhole and with the muzzle held up by the rubber ring. A good twitch on the two ends of the packthread would pull the trigger and explode the blank cartridge. It needs careful management; but I've no doubt that Barbican had practiced the whole business on one of the inner doors of his flat beforehand, so that he didn't fumble the trick.

"He then closed the door. Now he had to lock it from the outside. He needed both hands free for that job. So he took the ends of the packthread across the landing and pinned them down to the rail with a bit of modelling wax, which would set hard almost at once in contact with the cold metal. That kept the revolver in position while he manoeuvred with the door. I don't profess to know what method he used to turn the key from outside. Perhaps he threaded something through the ring of the key and pulled it round with a thread passed under the door—an old dodge. Or possibly he simply turned the key by gripping the outer end with a pair of fine pliers, inserted in the keyhole. He was a handy man with tools. The exact method is of no great importance.

"The next thing was to take the ends of the packthread downstairs to his own landing, below Barnard's, and fix them there somehow temporarily. Then he probably went up and scraped away the modelling wax. But he'd rubber gloves on, so he left some traces on the rail, which I found later on.

"Now the next difficulty was leaving the double thread hanging down the well of the staircase. Barnard was coming back. He mustn't see that. So Barbican blew the fuses of the two lamps on the landings. Or, more likely, he had a couple of fuse holders ready with blown fuses in them, and he simply inserted them in place of the sound ones in the box in the hall. It's easy enough to blow a fuse by an intentional short in your room circuit."

"You needn't go on," Wendover interrupted. "I see the rest of it. He waited till Barnard came back, because Barnard was to give him his alibi. Then he went out quietly and tugged the double thread to fire the pistol upstairs. Barnard flew out and up the stairs. Then Barbican pulled on one end of his thread and reeled in the lot. He must have been in a hurry, for unless he got it all away, Barnard would come up against it when he ran to Mitford's door. Then, with his thread safe in his pocket, Barbican clattered up the stairs in his turn. That accounts for his being second in the field. And it also meant that Barnard would have to swear that he was between Barbican and Mitford's room all the time until Barbican joined him on the top landing, long after the shot had gone off. That was how it was done, wasn't it?"

"That's more or less how I *think* it was done," Sir Clinton amended. "And that's why we impounded those blown fuses. Fuse wire varies a trifle from sample to sample; and I'm in some hope that our analytical shark may be able to prove that the blown fuses correspond to the reserve fuse wire in Barbican's flat, and differ from the fuse wire of the remainder of the fuses in the box. But that's only a minor point. What do you make of the eucalyptus?"

"The eucalyptus?" echoed Wendover, obviously at sea.

"Yes, the eucalyptus that Barbican had scattered about so freely in his flat in his effort to fight down that nonexistent chill of his. It stares you in the face. That was to cover up any smell of powder that might be left in the place, of course. And the big fire on a summer's night. That was to destroy the blood-spattered news-papers, the remainder of the lycopodium, Mitford's real letter to me, and anything else that might be incriminating. Oh, it was quite a neat little idea.

"But he made a slip or two, as even the best of us do. First of all, he forgot that Mitford's body had been lying about for a good while before the 'fatal' shot went off upstairs. There was some co-agulation round about the wound. And yet some of the blood on the floor was quite fresh, by comparison, when I saw it. We'd al-ready had a two-bloods business in the Sternhall affair; and that put the thing into my head. I mean that the murderer might have had to produce some extra blood to make things look dirty enough. So I took the opportunity of giving both Barnard and Barbican a friendly grip on the arm—which is not my habit with strangers. Barnard yelped like a good 'un, because he really has a sore arm. But when I tried Barbican, he did his best not to wince and to com-plain quite naturally. But I felt the wince, all right. And when I ran my hand down to his skin in letting him go, he was no more fever-ish than I was. Which didn't look much like the chill he made so much fuss about. But the crowning blunder was in posting that letter to me without taking note of the hour of collection. By the time he got it into the letter box, Mitford was 'officially' dead."

"Well, I suppose he was between two fires," Wendover pointed out. "Barnard had seen the envelope in Mitford's hand. It had to be posted, whether Barbican liked it or not."

"Well, that's what's going to hang our friend," Sir Clinton de-clared confidently. "That and the lycopodium traces. Of course, there's a lot of routine work to be done yet. Chesilton will have a busy time of it. Luckily, he rather likes that sort of thing."

"What have you to do?" Wendover asked, rather indifferently, now that the main problem had been expounded.

"Oh, we have to check the details of his career, so as to be sure of all the items he gave us in his autobiographical sketch and which came in so useful to me. That reminds me, Squire, you quoted Macaulay not so long ago.

'Those trees in whose dim shadow
  The ghastly priest doth reign,
The priest who slew the slayer,
  And who shall himself be slain.'

"Well, your 'ghastly priest' has turned up, after all these years. At least, with a little poetical licence, if one calls The Grove avenue 'those trees' and Sternhall 'the slayer.' Don't you remember that Barbican told us he started life as 'a pale young curate'? That's true enough. It was easy to ferret that point out in no time, with an uncommon name like his, and the fact that he was unfrocked as well. So he was a 'ghastly priest' in more senses than one."

"And what else are you hunting up?"

"The accommodation-address affair; the purchase of lyco-podium—he bought some just before the Sternhall murder, so I suppose he used it in writing his letters to Sternhall also—the date of his winnings in the Irish Sweep, which was probably a lie to account for the money he got out of Sternhall; and his career as a pedigree-hunter, investigating Miss Degray's ancestry; besides a few other points. We've gone into Mitford's relations with Mrs. Sternhall of The Grove, which turn out to be rather creditable to both of them, I think. Altogether, Chesilton and Company have enough on their hands."

"But won't he make a break-away while you're busy with all this stuff?" Wendover demanded.

"He's too clever to make Crippen's mistake," the Chief Constable rejoined. "Besides, we've had two men watching him ever since the night of the Mitford murder, though he doesn't know that."

"I don't like that fellow being left on the loose, Clinton," said Wendover soberly. "There's been one life lost already owing to delay—necessary delay, I admit," he added honestly.

"Calm yourself, Squire. In point of fact, we propose to lift him tonight. We've got sufficient evidence now. Chesilton will be here shortly. You shall sign the warrant yourself. Then, I think, we'll all three drop in on Mr. Barbican. A little surprise for him. I confess I'm interested in seeing how he takes it."

18
ARREST

"Well, Inspector," said the Chief Constable, pouring out a whisky and soda for his new guest, "our friend's at home, I take it?"

"He hasn't been out tonight, sir. I've got a uniformed man in the hall all the time. We're supposed to be still ransacking that top flat for evidence, just to give an excuse for posting a man on the premises night and day. And I've two plain-clothes men in The Grove to take up the trail when he goes out. But tonight I left orders that the constable in the hall was to detain him if he tried to go out. Just to make sure."

"Right! Then, when you've had your drink, you can swear information and Mr. Wendover will sign the warrant for you. After that, we'll drop in at Ravenswood Mansions."

"It'll be a surprise packet for him, sir," Chesilton said, with a quickly suppressed smile. "He hasn't a notion we're after him. I met him the other day and he was a shade more impudent than usual about police stupidity and bungling. Very sarcastic, he was. But I kept my face straight, thinking the joke was funnier than he imagined."

"By the way, has that report on the two bullets come to hand?" the Chief Constable demanded.

"Yes, sir. I've got it. The rifling marks on the bullet that killed Sternhall are the same as those on the bullet that killed Mitford; and both correspond to Sternhall's revolver. They tried that out, just to make sure."

"Then probably he hasn't got a pistol of his own," the Chief Constable commented. "Still, you'd better keep a wary eye on him at the critical moment, Inspector. Don't run any risks out of mere politeness. I almost wish we could get up a little horseplay and make his nose bleed. A sample of his blood would be another link in the chain of exhibits."

"That will be all right, sir. I took a leaf out of your book and gripped him friendliwise by the arm, enough to reopen that cut he made with his penknife. We'll get a sample of his blood off the bandage when we pull him in."

"Very neat, Inspector," Sir Clinton commended, with a smile. "If we can get that, and prove it's identical with the second brand of blood in Mitford's flat, it'll take a smart barrister to throw dust in the eyes of a jury on that point. And now, if you've finished, Inspector, you'd better go through the formalities and get your warrant. Then we'll go."

As their car drew up before the door of Number 1, Ravenswood Mansions, Wendover noticed a shabby-looking man on the pavement give it a quick glance and then, at the sight of Chesilton, shuffle off down the street, searching the gutter for cigarette ends.

"One of our fellows," Chesilton explained curtly to Wendover, as they alighted and entered the flats. The uniformed constable in the hall saluted and made a significant gesture; but he did not offer any verbal information and they climbed the stairs to the first floor. Chesilton rang the bell, and in a moment or two Barbican opened the door. At the sight of them, his face broke into a broad smile.

"Here we are again!" he exclaimed, rubbing his hands in pretended glee. "The old familiar faces. Harlequin"—he made a cheeky bow to the Chief Constable—"Pantaloon"—he turned to Wendover—"and of course Joey—I mean, Inspector Chesilton. Like to send round the corner to Number 5 and rake out Columbine to make it complete? Step inside. Don't mind my feelings but be wary of the doormat. It might snap at you. One can't be too suspicious of everything, in these days."

"I'll risk it," said Sir Clinton pleasantly, as they filed into the flat. "Now, Mr. Barbican, perhaps you can help us. You had some notes by Mitford, hadn't you, about what you're pleased to call 'Harry Keary.' I'd like to see what he had to say about it, if you don't mind."

Barbican's smile remained as broad as ever, but he threw a shrewd glance at the Chief Constable.

"Not much to the point, I'm afraid," he retorted. "Still, you're welcome to the late lamented's jottings. I thought of destroying them. They bring up sad thoughts, and all that, you know. Then I thought, 'No, these clever blokes with the thick boots might want them. Cipher message, maybe. Read every seventh word backwards and see what you get. It'll amuse them in the long winter evenings while they're still fumbling about on this case.' So I kept the stuff. Thoughtful of me. Think how I'd have felt if I couldn't produce it."

He went over to a desk, rummaged in a drawer, and produced a sheaf of papers which he handed to Sir Clinton.

"And that reminds me," he went on, "how's the Sternhall case getting on? Police baffled? Another unsolved mystery? Well, I give you the tip. Columbine could tell you something. You go and take a few French lessons from her; get her into an amenable mood, you know; and you might pick up something fresh. But keep off the Bogey Man, the Black Brother-in-law of Bazeilles, or wherever he comes from. He might pop in and blackmail you, you know. Looks just that sort."

"You're not quite so funny as you once were," said Sir Clinton critically. "But no doubt you'll soon find leisure to compose a few fresh quips at our expense, for I'm going to detain you on suspicion of murdering Mitford. Just call up the constable, Inspector, please; and have this man taken into the back room, there."

Wendover, watching Barbican's face, saw it harden swiftly, though the white teeth showed in an amused smile.

"Another Bracknell blunder?" Barbican queried. "What damages does one get for wrongful arrest? I'm always open to make a little money."

Sir Clinton made no reply, but waited until the constable had led the prisoner into the back room and closed the door.

"Now, Inspector, the first thing is to get hold of his bank passbooks, if he's kept the earlier ones. Try that desk."

Chesilton obediently ransacked the desk, drawer by drawer. At last he gave an exclamation of satisfaction.

"We're in luck, sir," he reported. "Here they are, going far enough back for our purpose."

He laid the little volumes out on the desk and consulted the paying-in side of the accounts at several dates.

"He's been too smart to pay in the cash all at once on each occasion, sir," he continued. "But there are fairly large payments in succession just after the dates of each of the Sternhall cheques. It's plain enough."

"Did you come across a packet of rubber bands, while you were rummaging?" Sir Clinton inquired.

Chesilton shook his head.

"No, I expect he put those in the fire immediately. He'd hardly leave them there to be compared with the one on the doorkey, sir."

"Evidently he didn't. Still, you can keep your eye open for any stray one that may be lying about. Now what about his notepaper?"

"Here's a sheet or two, sir. It's the same as the 'confession' sheet. Wonder why he didn't destroy that also."

"Even the best murderers make mistakes," Sir Clinton pointed out. "And our friend had a deuce of a lot to think about, remember."

He reflected for a moment or two.

"No packet of lycopodium?" he inquired. "No? Well, I hardly expected him to leave *that* lying about. It went into the fire straight away, that night. It's no odds, since we've got the druggist's evidence to go upon. And now, I'll leave the rest in your hands."

"Very good, sir. I know what we want. His blue serge suit, in case it got some blood on it on the night of the Sternhall affair; any bits of modelling wax, if it didn't go into the fire; ditto packthread; a pair of his shoes to get his size and see that it agrees with the casts from the footprints; rubber gloves; if they haven't been burned; and the pistol silencer."

"You won't find that," said Sir Clinton positively. "He would dismantle that, first thing, and get rid of the pieces. It would have been the worst bit of evidence against him, if we could have laid hands on it."

Chesilton nodded in regretful agreement.

"I'll comb the place thoroughly, sir; and if anything fresh turns up, I'll let you know at once. And now, shall I formally arrest him?"

"Yes. Bring him in here."

In a moment or two Barbican reappeared, followed by the constable on guard. The smile was gone, now; but he seemed to be striving to put the best face possible on his situation. Sir Clinton looked him up and down before speaking.

"Almost every time we've met, Mr. Barbican," he said coldly, "you've asked, 'Have you anything for me?' Well, this time I have something for you. It's a warrant. Read it to him, Inspector, if you please."

>>> If you've enjoyed this book and would like to discover more great vintage crime and thriller titles, as well as the most exciting crime and thriller authors writing today, visit: >>>

The Murder Room
Where Criminal Minds Meet

themurderroom.com

www.ingramcontent.com/pod-product-compliance
Ingram Content Group UK Ltd.
Pitfield, Milton Keynes, MK11 3LW, UK
UKHW022317280225
455674UK00004B/350